ECHOES THROUGH
DIVINOROS
DAWN OF DARKNESS

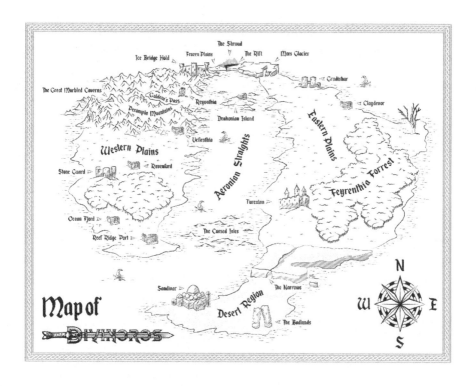

BLAKE SEITZ

Copyright © 2024

All Rights Reserved. Any unauthorized reprint or use of this material is strictly prohibited. No part of this book may be reproduced or transmitted in any form or by any means, electronic or mechanical, including photocopying, recording, or by any information storage and retrieval system without express written permission from the author.

All reasonable attempts have been made to verify the accuracy of the information provided in this publication. Nevertheless, the author assumes no responsibility for any errors and/or omissions.

This book is dedicated to my wife, Kathryn Seitz.
For the initial conversation of "I think I am going to write a book." She has been nothing but supportive, willing to listen to many long read-throughs, revisions and more. I would also like to dedicate this to our little one joining us this year.

Contents

About the Author

Born the middle child of four in Broomfield, Colorado, Blake Seitz has always had a deep fascination with the diverse narratives that define human experience.

A debut author, Blake has long been a fan of fantasy and science fiction, drawing inspiration from the myriad books he devoured. His journey into writing began with a simple wish to craft his own world— a world as vivid and sprawling as the landscapes he explores with his wife. The pair have a spirit for adventure, Blake finds the wilds of nature a wellspring for creativity, from the ancient allure of Florence's Duomo to the stark beauty of Iceland's black sand beaches.

"Echoes Through Divinoros: Dawn of Darkness" marks his first foray into an epic trilogy that promises to blend the mystique of ancient legends with the visceral struggles of its characters. Influenced by the likes of Christopher Paolini, Pierce Brown, and Patrick Rothfuss, Blake's writing thrums with the pulse of battle, the depths of lore, and the constant quest for goodness in a world overshadowed by a dark deity and violent history.

As he continues to write, Blake remains committed to weaving tales of valor and the enduring battle between light and darkness, mortals against the infinite. His narratives are not just about the fate of fantastical realms but the unyielding human spirit that dares to defy the odds.

Preface (Power Unleashed)

Kei-Tel Turenia gazed over the endless icy expanse that stretched out before him. A cold breeze tore at him, cleanly cutting through the gaps in his well-fitted armor, but his anticipation of the day's events kept his mind from focusing on the chill. His army had reached the Frozen Plains. Great pillars of ice jutted from frost-covered earth as if the Gods had skewered the ground with knives of frost. No life persisted here; no sound filled the air. The consistent cold had long ago driven the herds of deer and flocks of birds south to the Perampla Mountains as they sought shelter from frigid temperatures and deadly crevasses that cracked across the frozen surface. The land felt dead, looked dead, and scanning the horizon, Kei thought it was fitting that this was where the world fell into oblivion.

After months of marching, chasing back the monstrous creatures released from the Rift, Kei-Tel and his ten remaining elven battalions had reached the source of the scourge that threatened to doom the world to the tyranny of a power-hungry deity.

"Your Majesty," came a voice behind the elf king, pulling him from his thoughts. Celestra, his highest ranking general to survive the year of campaigning north, strode forward and stood at parade rest to his right. She rested her glaive—a long spear-like weapon with a sword-blade head—against her shoulder. Celestra wore her dark red hair in a tight braid that reached midway down her back. She stood seven feet tall, just below average height among the elvish race, and you could see her lithe muscle rippling beneath the tight-fitting chainmail as her balance shifted from foot to foot. The tall, slender build may appear delicate, though, in truth, it was anything but. It afforded the race supreme agility and strength against their enemies. These gifts had allowed the elves to combat the dark forces being summoned from the Rift.

Kei-Tel sighed, his breath visible in the icy air. "General. We make our final stand. The fate of Divinoros will be determined this day. Is the army ready?" asked Kei-Tel, keeping his gaze focused on the horizon. There was tension in his voice. If the elves fell today, darkness would reclaim the land, consuming all life and collapsing this world into darkness under the rule of a malevolent deity.

"Yes, your Majesty. The army is eager to end this war. We have set up triage tents at the back of each battalion. Those with minor wounds from fighting in the Perampla Mountains have been armed and instructed to remain behind the front lines. They are ready to be used as reserves once the enemy begins to emerge," replied Celestra. She turned to her king, and as Kei-Tel looked toward her, he could see that his young general no longer possessed the hunger for battle she displayed when they first set out from the shores of Turenian. Fear and trepidation had extinguished any excitement.

Before this final push, they had already lost tens of thousands of soldiers, many of whom were dear friends. The terrors they had fought had not only resulted in dead and injured soldiers, but the brutal nature of their enemy had already left scars on the minds of all those who had survived. Kei-Tel rested his hand on Celestra's shoulder and nodded to her. "Then let us end this plight."

Kei-Tel turned to his army. He held his glaive in one hand raised above his head. It was a beautiful weapon crafted from a single block of pure silver material, embroidered with images of great wars fought and won by the previous monarchs to have ruled Turenian over the centuries. The weapon had a glow to it, emanating the power that resided within. "Today," he shouted to his army, his voice amplified by magic, "we rid this plague of evil from our lands. We did not release these monsters of the divine, but we are the few who can stand against such might and prevail. Today, we slay an immortal. We refuse to bow before this higher power. We stand in the face of it and demand retribution for the crimes committed against so many innocents! Today . . . Today, we kill a God."

Turning back to Celestra, he called over the cheers of his army, "Give your orders to the colonels. Form rank. We march on the Rift."

Celestra nodded and strode toward her underlings, who awaited their commands. Once instruction was issued, they ran to the head of their ranks, relaying their generals' bidding. Once set, the army marched directly toward what appeared to be the end of the world.

The Rift was a great scar through the earth, cleaving the land into an endless pit that fell to the very center of the world. While the pit had been a part of these lands for eternity, it now had a new companion. As they approached the giant crevasse, a dark shroud came into focus. The mass of darkness hovered above the Rift like a dense wall of swirling black smoke. It crackled as if a fire was burning, and liquid tendrils continuously snapped out from the central mass, eliciting a loud crack with each instance. Despite knowing the atrocities the ever-changing shadow mass could spit out, Kei could still appreciate its daunting visage.

The wall stretched thirty feet high and at least a quarter mile long. The air around the formation seemed to undulate with an ancient power that weighed on the air surrounding the wall. Though Kei-Tel had lived well over a thousand years, he had never before seen a power quite like what stood before him, and he found that he was awestruck at the sight. He wasn't sure what he expected once he reached the campaign's end. Every creature they had faced had been new to him, and so was this.

How could the humans have summoned a force of this magnitude?

Kei raised a fist into the air, signaling the army to stop marching.

They stood about a hundred paces from the edge of the Rift. Kei thought to form rank here and wait for the enemy to make itself known. He did not wish to walk into a trap. Just as he scanned his front lines to confer with Celestra, a deafening shriek filled the air, causing Kei to drop to a knee and cover his ears, saving them from the brunt of the piercing scream.

The sound seems to rise from behind the smoke wall . . . no, not behind. It was coming from within the darkness.

As the horrible screech cut off, Kei could hear a subtler noise, thousands of legs scratching and pulling forward. And then, beasts began dragging themselves free from the black wall, forming from the dense mist into solidified creatures of death. As they landed on the cold, hard ground, their forms were fully congealed, and their hungry eyes fell on the remnants of the elf king's army.

Thousands of beasts—an army of creatures known as krakenshi—materialized from the floating wall. As soon as their legs hit the ground, they sprinted at incredible speeds toward the ranks of elves. Each krakenshi stood ten feet tall, with triangular heads supported on thick muscular necks. Small red eyes lined each side of their skull in sets of three. Their upper jaws were lined with teeth like daggers, with the bottom jaw separated into two mandibles lined with serrated teeth that allowed the creatures to cut through any unfortunate soul caught in their jowls. They had long, narrow bodies with three powerful legs protruding from each side along their sleek abdomens. Each leg ended in deadly curved claws that edged into talons longer than the dagger Kei carried at his waist. Perhaps most dangerous of all was a thick tail as long as the elf stood tall, that ended with spikes.

These monsters were destruction manifested in solid form, a being designed with one cruel intention: to tear apart life. While there seemed to be many forms the darkness was capable of releasing, the krakenshi sewed terror and chaos unlike any other. Kei had seen what those mandibles would do to a soldier caught within, how their claws cut an unarmored man in two, and how their tails could bludgeon ranks and break lines, creating a mess of his army's formations.

A steady thumping rang in the air as thousands of legs continued to pound over the ice-covered expanse, carrying a wave of death toward the elves. As the mass of darkness closed, the ground shook under the weight of the charging enemy. The frozen plains came undone under the vibrations of the charge, the pillars of ice collapsing and shattering around the soldiers.

Kei scanned his remaining battalion and thanked the Gods that the well-trained survivors did not flinch as the creature bore down upon them. The krakenshi roared as they rapidly covered the space between the Rift and the Army. In seconds, a sickening crunch sounded as the two forces collided.

Kei-Tel spun the head of his glaive in a reverse circle and thrust the weapon head up through the skull of the first beast that rushed him. He pulled his weapon free and charged the next enemy. As it lunged toward him, its front legs outstretched, intending to rake the king's chest and face, Kei-Tel slid along the ice and lifted the blade of his weapon upward. The silver metal head sunk deep into the creature, opening the belly of the beast as its momentum carried the creature over him. The open wound released a cascade of vile black liquid mist. The creature seemed to deflate as the ground became saturated with its innards. Curiously, the liquid that fell from the monster started to stream back toward the dark wall as if returning home.

Very curious. The misty innards of dead variants slain on the campaign north did not act in this way. It must be due to the proximity to the wall.

Kei threw himself back into the fray.

To his left, a monster snapped its jaws around a young soldier's waist. His scream was quickly cut off as the beast oscillated its lower mandibles and shook its head violently. The man was severed in two, his torso and legs falling to either side of the beast, bloody entrails leaving a stain of red on the crisp white snow. Kei-Tel exacted immediate justice, bringing his glaive down in an overhead blow to the base of the creature's neck with a speed and accuracy that was rare even amongst the elves. The beast's head rolled, slowly diminishing into liquid as it clattered over the icy floor. For what seemed like hours, Kei fought, a harbinger of death, killing the enemy in droves. He soon stood ankle-high in a black pool of dead monsters, blended with the deep scarlet blood of his fallen soldiers.

As the fighting progressed, Kei-Tel stepped behind his front lines to evaluate the battlefield. Despite the ferocity of the krakenshi, his army seemed to be faring well, forcing the enemy back toward the Rift. All ten battalions seemed to have minimal losses and still held the front lines in a seamless formation that had yet to be broken.

Then the wall screeched again, louder and deeper than before. While the armies continued to clash, Kei-Tel saw three enormous figures slither out through the dark portal. Each serpentine creature was easily eighty feet long, slithering across the ground in the same manner as the giant serpent's home to the forest regions due north of Turenian. Their serpentine bodies rose into a large human-like torso where two muscled arms protruded. Each carried a massive war hammer that appeared to be forged from obsidian. Topping the bodies were human-shaped faces, home to the same haunting red eyes seen on the krakenshi. Each creature had slits for nostrils where a nose would usually be, and, surprisingly, no mouth. His army had only had to fight one of these creatures in the plains just beyond the Perampla Mountains, but that one beast had struck down an entire battalion before Celestra was able to kill it. They were blunt instruments, capable of crumpling groups of soldiers with each stroke of their mighty hammers.

Kei-Tel barked out orders to his runners with instructions to the battalion commanders. They needed to reorient their large battalion formations into smaller, more mobile groups of soldiers. He hoped this would allow his men to surround the serpent creatures and avoid the deadly war hammers. The runners made their way through swarms of bodies to relay the order.

The wall then pulsed again, a single crack in the air followed, the sound of lightning splitting the sky, and a lone figure stepped from the shadowy mass to the edge of the Rift. He appeared to be similar in height to Kei-Tel, maybe slightly shorter. He donned a full set of obsidian armor plates that seemed to move with some sort of magic, as no creases or gaps were visible at the joints. Along the back of the knight was a cloak unlike anything Kei had ever seen. The material was made up of shadows and dark spirits that twisted and pulled around, giving the appearance of flowing in the wind despite the absence of the slightest breeze. The Knight held his hands out to his side, and two long swords coalesced from swirling wisps of darkness and settled into each hand. The swords were also pure black. Each had the size to be a two-handed weapon for most men. Based on the size of each sword, Kei imagined that these would be too heavy for even the elves to wield one-handed. But the dark knight swung them with ease at a dizzying speed as he looped the blades in extravagant movements to test the balance. Unlike the other monsters, the eyes that shone beneath the hood of his ever-changing cloak shined a bright gold.

Could this be the God? Could this be Omnes himself joining this fight?

The elf king finished his quick battlefield evaluation and rejoined the fray, slashing with a precision and grace that had been earned over centuries of dedicated training. The krakenshi seemed to almost fear the king and opted to attack the weaker soldiers when able. The Knight simply watched Kei with a calm demeanor as he hacked more of the krakenshi into pieces with his glaive, seemingly unconcerned as the elf slayed hordes of his monsters. This dark figure was happy to allow Kei-Tel to drain his energy reserves on the lesser monsters before reaching him.

The army's shielded positioning at the start of the battle allowed them to defend against the krakenshi effectively, and they killed the rabid beasts with minimal losses. However, as the battalions reformed into smaller fighting groups to combat the giant serpents, they were exposed to flanking by the six-legged beasts that still swarmed over the battlefield.

Kei heard screams as men and women were raked by the claws of monsters who could now get around the soldiers' defenses. He saw groups of men flung into the air with sickening crunches as the serpents swung their mighty war hammers through groups of soldiers.

To his right, Celestra had managed to climb onto the back of one serpent. He watched as she lunged up to the backside of the creature, stabbing her glaive in between the shoulders of the beast with such force that half of the long weapon sunk into the monster's body. She hung onto the weapon, suspended twenty feet in the air as the creature thrashed, struggling to throw her off. The general swung on the glaive, kicking upward to fling herself to the head of the massive creature. While soaring in the air, she unsheathed two large daggers strapped to her back and buried the gleaming weapons in the base of the neck of the screeching serpent. Celestra twisted the blades before ripping them through the monster's backside, severing the spine of the beast, allowing its head to roll forward off of the broad shoulders. The serpent flailed about as black liquid pumped in spurts from the wounds. Soon, the body ceased to struggle and collapsed heavily to the ground. With one giant beast slain, Celestra and her group of soldiers ran to the aid of a twenty-man unit struggling against the two serpents who remained upright.

Confident that his support was not needed there, Kei-Tel looked to where the obsidian-clad Knight stood, waiting behind the ongoing clash of elf and beast. The king bounded over to the being, who simply stood still and stared into Kei with discerning golden eyes, his head quirked at a curious tilt. The Knight, though silent, seemed to be amused at the idea of fighting Kei. It seemed the Knight did not think an elf, even the elven king, could be a worthy opponent. He seemed to think that Kei, the greatest warrior the mortal world could offer, would only be a mere inconvenience to him and his plans.

The sight enraged the king and Kei wasted no time thrusting his glaive at his opponent's chest. Sure enough, as Kei stabbed, the Knight lazily parried the blow with a flick of his wrist, moving his obsidian broadsword with speed the elf had not thought possible. Kei moved with the momentum of the parried blow, spinning to his left and bringing the head of his weapon around in a powerful two-handed overhead blow. A strike he had used to break steel-plated armor in past battles and duels. The Obsidian Knight blocked it again with ease.

The lazy movements of the warrior brought forth a nervous energy within Kei, and in response, he let out a fury of offensive strikes. Each blow was parried and dodged. While Kei did not relent in his offensive press, desperation crept into his mind, filling the gap left by his fading rage. He continued to bring his glaive down upon the Knight in furious strikes, though none landed. After a complex offensive attack, Kei changed his fighting style and lashed out with a powerful front kick. This finally connected, earning the first blow against Knight. The deity—at least what Kei believed must be a deity—briefly staggered back but gathered his feet quickly.

He locked eyes with Kei, and an amused, distorted voice reverberated in the air. "Well... I suppose it's my turn now."

The Obsidian Knight jumped forward, crossing a large distance in the blink of an eye despite the heavy appearance of the armor he wore. He raised his weapons in an overhead strike as he jumped. Kei gave ground, parrying the powerful blow. Years of training allowed him to defend against a barrage of furious strikes and stabs. However, each blocked blade came with such force his arms soon trembled from the strain. His fingers loosened their grasp on his weapon, threatening to drop the glaive. Too much longer, and Kei would surely be killed.

In contrast, the Knight seemed to gain strength as the contest wore on. Knowing that time was not an ally, Kei-Tel gave in to desperation. After he parried an overhand blow, he attempted a clever riposte that left him exposed. The gambit appeared to have paid off. Kei had disarmed the deity as he wrenched one broadsword from the knight's grip.

Kei, though astonished by his success, did not waste a second, ready to finish this fight as he swung his mighty glaive toward his foe. A strike used to fell thousands of enemies before, hammered into the Obsidian Knight's shoulder, but rather than cleaving him collar to hip, the strike merely chipped the armor and knocked the Knight down to a kneeling position.

His obsidian gauntleted fist landed near his relinquished weapon. His fingers curled around the hilt of his fallen sword, and in one smooth motion, he twirled the blade into a reverse grip. With vicious force, he stood and slashed its razor-sharp edge across the king's chest. Kei's vision blurred, and his world faded into darkness as the obsidian blade sent him sprawling to the ground.

As Kei lay in the snow, gasping for breath, he could see the Obsidian Knight approach, his footsteps echoing ominously. The deity's golden eyes bore into Kei's, and the voice echoed again, "You are brave, mortal, but your bravery will not save you. You are about to witness the end of your world, and there is nothing you can do here to stop it."

Kei's hands shook as he regained his footing just in time to see the dark blades descending toward his head. As he rolled beneath a two-hand cross swipe of the swords, Kei quickly scanned the battleground. His army had defeated another serpent at a great expense. Only a small pocket of soldiers had survived to battle the final serpent and leftover krakenshi. With his army occupied, no help was going to come his way.

I cannot fall, or all is lost. This campaign will have been an unnecessary forfeiture of life. I will not allow my soldiers' sacrifice to be in vain.

As he turned back to face the Knight, he saw the edge of The Rift in his peripheral. He retreated, inching his way closer to the edge of the world.

The elf king knew he was outmatched; his final gambit had failed. *What mortal creature could hope to defeat this, this . . . thing I'm fighting?*

He suspected his army was on the brink of breaking, but that would be a certainty if he died. None of the other warriors would be able to overcome this entity. If he failed, the elves under his guard would be exterminated and executed. And with the last life leaving his army, so did any chance of this world surviving the onslaught from Omnes and his minions. All life on Divinoros would surely be extinguished if Kei-Tel fell today.

The Knight rushed towards him again, and they danced along the edge of the Rift. After a series of stabs, the obsidian swords were brought down with force. Kei caught the blow on the shaft of his weapon. Straining against the titanic might of the Knight, the elf king tossed the swords to the side and twisted around, bringing the momentum into a sideswipe at the Knight. The Knight responded with incredible speed again, releasing his right-handed sword, which evaporated into dark mist. With the now free hand, he seized the edge of his spirit cloak, pulling the fabric up to intercept the glaive's path.

As the glaive came into contact with the swirling darkness of the cloak, his weapon shimmered and passed through the material and then the Knight as if the fabric had turned the weapon into an intangible force. The glaive continued through the Knight with a slight drag, like the pull against a hot knife cutting through butter, before the momentum of his movement carried the strike well past his intended target. The move left Kei's side exposed as his follow-through was exaggerated with the little resistance the strike was met with. Once the glaive passed through the Knights body, he dropped the cloak from his hand, unsheathed an obsidian dagger belted to his hip, and before Kei could twist the glaive down in defense, the Knight rammed his dagger through his armored plate into the gap of his ribs.

He felt a screaming pain surge into his abdomen as the blade sank into his midsection. The Knight yanked the blade free and sunk it into the stomach of the king twice more in violent succession. Kei-Tel's eyes went wide as a gurgling gasp escaped his lips. The Knight twisted the blade, maximizing damage to the organs within, then pulled the dagger free from Kei, who dropped his glaive as he fell to his knees, his now free hands grasping at his abdomen in a feeble attempt to stop the heavy flow of blood pouring from his ravaged midsection. A guttural laugh poured from the obstructed face of the Obsidian Knight, and his voice reverberated in his head once more. "You thought you could contend with the might of a God, did you?"

He stepped up directly in front of Kei, kicking his glaive beyond reach. Kei struggled to his feet. The Knight struck again, thrusting the sword in his left hand through the chest of the elf king. Kei felt an icy sharpness where the blade plunged through his flesh—time slowed now for the elf king. He saw Celestra shriek as she witnessed her king impaled by the dark blade. She sprinted toward him. He saw the remainder of his army being chewed apart and slashed by krakenshi. He saw a broken, elvish army on the brink of collapse. He saw the inevitable purge that would consume all life on Divinoros. The wall of darkness seemed to roar, relishing in its victory.

As Kei's vision blurred around the edges, Celestra drew nearer, her desperation mirroring what he felt inside. The Knight turned his attention to her, laughter dancing in his eyes. But Kei, driven by an inability to bear witness to more death among his ranks, summoned the last reserves of his strength. He seized the Knight's arm, still gripping the sword skewering his chest, and with a determination fueled by sheer desperation, he slipped out the dagger sheathed on his back.

With every ounce of force he could muster, he plunged the blade into the side of the Knight, breaking through the obsidian plate. The Knight snarled furiously, attempting to pull himself free, but Kei held on with a death grip, refusing to relinquish his hold on this monstrous foe.

Before the Knight could regain any advantage, Kei kicked back, sending both tumbling over the edge of the Rift. One figure was now lifeless, and the other was a swirling form of darkness thrashing as it plummeted into the void.

...

Celestra, her eyes filled with a mix of awe and sorrow, watched as her king sacrificed himself to stop Omnes from winning a crippling blow against her people. She dropped to her knees, exhaustion, pain, and grief threatening to consume her in that moment. When she turned her gaze back toward the battlefield, a surreal transformation was unfolding.

The remaining krakenshi began to dissipate, their powerful bodies fading into dark trails that flowed back to the Rift. Once the last monster had cleared, the Shroud seemed to fade in its voracity. Though it remained in place, the daunting visage that had dominated the sky when the army arrived no longer pulsated with the same malevolent energy . . . They had won. Of the ten thousand men and women who had been alive to start this battle, only a couple hundred remained. The war was over, but the scars ran deep. Celestra wept, her tears a testament to the sacrifices made and the world that would be forever altered.

Ryker - Chapter 1 - Selection Day

Ryker woke as the sunlight filtered through a small square window set into the log wall of his family's home. Fall was fresh upon Stone Guard; the mornings began with a brisk chill the sun would work to burn off throughout the day. Ryker preferred this season as he could leave the tattered shutters open to allow the brisk night air to flow into his room as he slept. He sat upright and gazed out the window to a view of rolling hills covered in emerald pine trees. The landscape slowly became clearer as he got dressed. The hills emerged from a shaded silhouette as the sun finally crested over the surrounding hilltops.

Ryker's thoughts drifted to the day ahead. It was Selection Day, a day that had been on his mind for months. He knew the importance of today, not just for himself but for his family. His older brother, Declan, reminded him of that urgency with a shout from the kitchen below.

"Get a move on Ryk! Big day. Don't want to be late to the selection. Lord Frenir wouldn't be happy if you were. Don't want to make the elves mad, especially the important ones!"

Ryker sighed and muttered, "I'm coming, I'm coming." He stood, stretching his lean frame, and ran his hands through his short ash-blonde hair. He chuckled at the unruly strands that always seemed to defy gravity after a night's sleep. Once tamed, he flattened out the wrinkles on his pair of clean work pants and donned a presentable white cotton shirt, then headed for the stairs that led to the main floor of the farmhouse.

Ryker's parents had built the farm when he was a young boy. His father, at the time, had just retired from his post serving in the military under a high lord in the eastern deserts, and his mother was eager to leave behind the hot, dry landscape in favor of the foothills surrounding Stone Guard City. The pair decided to raise their children on honest labor working the plush fields in the rolling hills. Ryker could not remember the voyage with his family, being an infant at the time. The young man's entire life had been on the outskirts of Stone Guard. He had a nice life, working the fields, playing with his brothers, and training with his father, who felt it was important to teach his boys martial skills. "If I ever die, you four will need to be strong enough to protect your mother." He would tell the brothers. They would laugh with indifference at the seemingly incredulous claims despite their father's serious demeanor and constant lessons.

Ryker did miss his sparring sessions with his father. The man condemned violence, despite his mother often hinting that he was a more than capable warrior in the desert army, but he deemed it a necessary skill. As such, all four Marriock boys were schooled in various weapons techniques and grappling from a young age. That work, combined with the hard labor on the farm, has sculpted Ryker and his brothers into forms that could rival nearly any human soldier, though they still paled in physical comparison to the elves they lived amongst.

Two years ago, Declan had taken over the farm's operations after his parents had been given orders directly from Lord Frenir, High Lord of Stone Guard, requiring them to travel to Turenian. Ryker was never told what the purpose of this out-of-the-blue mission was. He also could never understand why his parents, who had retired years ago, were given that order. Even if his father was a decorated soldier, there must have been someone more suited to the task, and the fact that his mother was sent baffled the family. But no human could say no to their elven rulers.

It had been over two years since his parents left, and Ryker and his three brothers hadn't heard from them since. Declan and Ryker had often sought out Lord Frenir, asking about the status of their mother and father, but the elf had never voiced concern for their safety. The high lord simply assured them that the complexity of the assignment would require more time to complete, and though he had not heard from them, he did expect frequent gaps in communication.

Since they had been gone, Declan had grown the farm into a flourishing operation. They now supplied over seventy-five percent of the produce and meat that fed the city of Stone Guard, and Ryker knew his older brother had plans to expand into premade foods and ship goods across the continent to other regions of Divinoros. He thought his parents would have been proud of their second child, and today, he hoped to do something of equal note.

Declan was the oldest member of their family left in Stone Guard since Jebediah, the oldest brother, had left for the North to serve along Ice Bridge Hold five years back. Ryker enjoyed working on the farm. Years of sowing land, turning dirt, and harvesting plants had gifted him with a well-defined physique, and he enjoyed the simple nature of watching crops grow, but he never developed a passion for it as Declan did. His mind regularly wandered to adventure, grandeur, and excitement. And this line of thought led him back to the day at hand, the Selection. At eighteen, he had the chance to enter it and pursue the path of a warrior, a soldier, just as Jebediah had. The idea excited him, but it also carried the weight of expectation. He wanted to make his family proud and, if possible, discover more about his parents' whereabouts. As a soldier, he would have access to information that was simply not shared with common farmhands.

The Selection was a cherished tradition that had been celebrated in Stone Guard for centuries. After the elven army had pushed back the dark forces of Omnes, Queen Celestra seized control over all major human capitals. Her next act was appointing high lords who had sworn fealty to the Turenian monarchy, as rulers over these cities. Once elven rule was established, all humans registered with their local authority at birth so elven leadership could track the activity of their human population.

The first men and women subjected to elven rule a thousand years ago were originally forced into hard labor, treated as indentured servants, or worse, as punishment to the race for releasing a malevolent God of old onto the land in a poor attempt to harness that power and balance the scales of strength between them and the dwarves and elves. Most of the elf population felt this action by the Queen was appropriate punishment. After all, the humans' ambition led them to release a power they did not understand, which effectively killed most of the life on Divinoros.

There were originally only three professions all humans were forced into under elven authority: cooks, farmhands, or house servants. One hundred years into the elven occupation, relations between the races deteriorated and became violent. Riots and uprisings were happening more and more frequently. Many lives were lost to these brutal skirmishes, though far more who died were human than elf. The juxtaposition between the races was evident. Elves were nearly immortal and lived for thousands of years, and, as such, many remembered the assault on their world and felt they had yet to receive repayment for the damage caused such a short time ago in their lifetimes. But to humans, that hundred years covered generations of family lines, and those being punished were no longer linked to the atrocities of their ancestors. As such, they sought freedom and control within their own lives.

A compromise needed to be made, which was when the tradition of the Selection was born. All men and women at the age of eighteen were put through the Selection. Each individual was able to choose the line of work they desired. However, to be granted apprenticeship in their desired field, they would need to prove their merit and aptitude for it.

While the initial options in the selection were slim, the control humans felt making this decision on their own accord satiated a majority of the population for another hundred years or so. Elves were happy with the arrangement, but humans once again changed more rapidly in their opinions and desires than their pointy-eared counterparts. Another hundred years passed, and while the Selection was honored, it continued to evolve into what it is today. Humankind slowly gained more and more freedoms over the next two hundred and fifty years of servitude. While still under elven occupation, this allowed families to build meager wealth and businesses to create something during the shorter life spans. Now, the Selection was a festival in Stone Guard. Each man or woman could pick from any profession they desired. However, in order to gain an apprenticeship, just as in times of old, the human would need to

3

impress, in a public showing to any common attendants and various master tradesmen, their worthiness to pursue a certain field. Each who failed to pass their test would be forced to return to their family's occupation. In Ryker's case, as he wished to train as a warrior, he would be forced to spar against one of the soldiers stationed at Stone Guard City. If he failed to impress any Elites or weapons masters in the city, he would return to live out his life on the farm.

Growing up in a house of four sons, the boys were raised tough. Outside of daily training with their father, the brothers would regularly sneak away in the woods to avoid chores where they could spar and beat on one another with wooden practice swords their father gifted them as soon as they were old enough to hold one. Since the day that wooden blade was placed in his hands, a young Ryker dreamed of fame and glory earned with cold steel. Of a life traveling the world, living off his skill with a blade, defending villages from monsters, a life of *adventure*!

Playing soldiers in the woods evolved over the years as they aged. Soon, the boys were all skilled in swordplay, and they practiced at levels that not many of the enlisted human soldiers could match. Ryker liked to think he had surpassed each of his brothers in the art of the blade as he dedicated himself to the craft beyond what his siblings had felt necessary.

Ryker climbed down the wooden stairs, long faded and cracked with age, and he heard Declan's voice echoing through the house, urging him to reconsider his decision.

"Have you given any thought to what I've said? As your older brother, I can speak with confidence that I know what's best for you."

Ryker could see the annoying smirk that Declan often wore when acting the all-knowing twit.

Ryker couldn't help but roll his eyes as he reached the bottom of the stairs. "We've gone over this already, Dec," he replied. "I enjoy the work here, but I'm eighteen, and I've never been beyond the outer towns of Stone Guard. At least if I am able to win a place in the army, I can travel or request a new station every couple of years. I want to see the world."

Declan responded with a knowing smirk, which Ryker had seen far too often. "See the world! Hard to see the world if someone kills you first. Plus, no say as to where you will be sent, who you'll be told to kill…" Ryker shot Declan a glowering look, and he held his hands up in a placating gesture before continuing, "I know I can't convince you otherwise, but promise me that you will think about it when you head into town. You have the mind to get into engineering or to be a scholar, plus you're the best worker I have here on the farm. I like to think that's because of my expert tutelage, but you are naturally talented and could have success in whatever you set your mind to. Just because you can fight doesn't mean you should." He motioned for Ayden—the youngest

Marriock who was finally woken by his brothers' conversation—to sit by Ryker at the table. "I mean, Jebediah is already serving at the Rift, and Ayden and I wouldn't mind if you hung around a little longer."

"Alright, I'll think about it," Ryker responded as he fondly punched Ayden in the shoulder while he settled into the chair beside him, still rubbing the sleep from his eyes. "But don't think that means I'll change my mind."

Since his parents, Noah and Ava Marriock, had left town, Ryker had only picked up on his training in anticipation of his Selection Day.

The three brothers ate the fried eggs and potatoes that Declan had prepared over a large flat cast iron pan, heated on the open flame cook pit that was set into a wall in the kitchen area. The cooking pit was a worn stone circle built into the side of the house where a large ventilation shaft could be opened, allowing the smoke produced while cooking to flow from the cozy kitchen to the open air outside. As the three ate breakfast, Ayden was given instructions for the extra work that would need to be completed while Ryker was at the Selection.

"You sure you don't want us there? The others wouldn't mind covering for us." Ayden said, pushing back an empty plate.

"Don't worry about it. Of course I want you there, but I understand things need to get done around here. Plus, you and Dec are going to be the first people I talk to after the ceremony once I'm back this evening." Ryker got to his feet and clapped the younger brother on his shoulder. "One more favor to ask, though: can you clean up my dishes? I want to have one more quick training session before heading down to the city square."

He strode toward the door, pushing it open, and laughed, hearing Ayden shouting from behind, "I'll do it this time, but you owe me two favors back! Starting with all my dishes tonight. The other I'm saving, redeemable at any time!"

The sound of his brothers faded to a muffled murmur as the door swung shut. The brothers had always been close, but their bond had grown stronger once their parents had been sent away. Exiting the farmhouse, Ryker felt the weight of his decision. He knew it would be hard to leave his family behind, especially in the absence of their parents. But he also held out hope that if he were selected as a trainee, he might uncover more information about their whereabouts.

Ryker - Chapter 2 - Stone Guard City

The Marriock boys lived atop a large hill about a mile north of Stone Guard—the elves' capital city in the western continent. The small three-room farmhouse was built facing east to allow the sun to warm the homestead each morning as it rose and wake them to start work early on the farm. The two thousand acres surrounding the home had been cleared away of the Giant Pines that were native and prevalent in this area to make fields where the Marriock family and their various employees had worked to rotate crops and raise the cattle, goats, and hogs.

As Ryker walked through the front door, he turned left and set off north toward Stone Guard City, along a well-traveled dirt road built wide enough for a horse and carriage to pull past one another if traveling in opposite directions. It was designed to transport goods to those living within the city walls, making the journey an easy trip for the freight carts employed by the family to take packed grains, produce, and meat to various distribution points within the enormous human and elf city.

Declan planned to widen and pave the road to expedite the travel between the farm and the city. "We'll call it a speedway" he would tell Ryker with enthusiasm. He thought faster travel would mean more income and faster expansion. Declan lectured them constantly about improving the family's business, the importance of lessening their reliance on selling through distributor centers and diversifying their selling directly to consumers and independent merchants.

"If we can cut out the middleman, even just a little, we can boost profits enough to grow the farm. I can see in the future already, full cargo fleets with the Marriock logo plastered on the hull taking our goods to ports all over Divinoros. And that could all start with growing our margins here. Plus, we already lose some of our crops to spoil when we can't move them fast enough on this dust trail. This paved road will open doors, Ryk! Open endless opportunities! Just wait and see!" Ryker would nod along during these tirades. He had complete faith his brother would accomplish the feat. He just had little interest in the business himself. His mindset of disinterest would need to change if he failed in his efforts today.

Along the road, plumes of smoke were beginning to rise from the smaller houses that lined its sides. Buildings sprouted in disorganized clusters just outside the fence-line of his family's home. Scents of fresh bread and fried bacon traveled along the wispy plumes, signaling that the other families who resided near, and worked on, Marriock Farm were beginning to stir for their morning routines.

Ryker took a deep breath, enjoying the crisp morning air as his body warmed with each step. He loved the walk toward Stone Guard and reveled in the sweeping panoramas of lush green forest unfolding before him, the dense green rushing ahead to meet the formidable city walls. As the sun continued to rise over the rolling hills, the Great Pine Forests continued to emerge from the shadows of night still clinging to their branches. What shone through, in slowly increasing brilliance, was an expansive landscape of shining emerald on the horizon. The forest stretched to the very edges of his vision in all directions, but a couple of miles straight ahead, Stone Guard's outer walls rose in sharp contrast to the surrounding sea of trees.

Four great white stone towers stood in the corners of the city, making a perfect square. Each tower stood over a hundred feet tall, making them a little over twice the height of the Great Pines encompassing the city. Each tower was connected by dark red stone walls that glowed blood red in the early morning sun. The walls seemed to be standing defiantly amongst the onslaught of green pressing on the city from every side, the battle between man's creation and the creations of the divine. Each interconnecting wall rose three-quarters of the tower's height, and from this distance, Ryker could just make out small dark dots scattered atop the wall bobbing as the elven guards strolled along the battlements, keeping lookout. The city's walls were rebuilt by Queen Celestra nine hundred years ago after Omnes' forces had reduced the previous human-run city to rubble. According to historical teachings, the reconstruction was a fast process as a result of elvish engineering and an abundance of human slaves. The newer city was constructed upon the same foundations of stone where the human city once stood. It was said to be the only thing of the old Stone Guard to have survived the destruction wrought by the Dark God.

Despite the quickness of the rebuild, the city was said to be one of the most formidable fortresses in all western Divinoros. Many who traveled here regarded the Stone Guard as a symbol of the power and the protection the elves gave humans after they so nearly brought about the end of the world so many years ago. Others thought it a slap in the face to humans, a permanent monument to human slavery. Ryker harbored no strong feelings as he gazed upon the fortress. He hadn't built it, and any of his ancestors that had were now long dead. To him, this city and these hills had only ever served as his home and symbolized family, so nothing but awe filled him when he gazed upon Her walls. While it would always be home, he now had a chance to leave it behind and explore the other wonders that Divinoros held.

The day's first bells began to sound within the tower walls, pulling Ryker from his cogitation. He still had time before he was expected to present himself in the city's central square for the Selection. The

7

celebration was set to begin precisely at the ringing of the mid-morning bells. This gave him nearly an hour to train and warm up for the combat trial he would be subjected to. He knew his skills with a sword were formidable, but the tests to be a warrior were, historically, violent. Not to mention performed in front of thousands of spectators who would gather for the festival. His nerves were already rising, and the thought of all those eyes on him brought on an unexpected wave of nausea, threatening to bring his breakfast back up.

So, to settle his nerves and prepare his body, Ryker turned off the main road and trudged deep into the forest, where he knew he would not be bothered by any fellow early morning travelers. The forest surrounding the capital city was said to be haunted by the souls of brutalized civilians slain in the scourge a thousand years ago, so few ever wandered in. While Ryker had never seen anything of note in the woods, many swore to have heard voices whenever they ventured into the wilderness. Not only that but in recent months, it was becoming common for people who ventured into the woods never to return. Rumors in the city speculated souls from the past claimed their bodies and took them to do their bidding elsewhere, but Ryker discarded these tales as inflated stories designed to scare children and make sure they didn't wander into the wilds. As such, Ryker welcomed the opportunity to train in silence with little risk of interruption.

He strode deeper into the woods, looking for a clearing and a branch to use as a makeshift training blade. Without much difficulty, he found both, pleased to stumble over a relatively straight branch and the length of the single-handed sword. It was far from an ideal training weapon, but this was of little consequence. His main goal was to work out his nerves and loosen the tightness that gripped his stomach and churned his insides.

Finding a suitably large and flat clearing, the young farmer swung the branch in a few fluid, circular movements to get the blood flowing to the muscles, joints, and ligaments in his wrist and shoulder. He rolled his shoulders then fell into a fighting stance his father had taught him and worked through a simple series of sword forms, focusing on the precision of his movements and timing that were integral to the fighting. While his movements seemed slow, each was deliberate, and soon, heavy beads of sweat rolled down the nape of his neck.

Ryker could feel the cool tingling trail each bead carved down his chest and back as he focused on perfect form. Ryker often found he was unable to maintain his balance and precision when moving through the more difficult positions and complex movements, a fact he attributed to not having formalized tutoring in the blade since his father had left over two years ago. Despite the occasional errors, his body felt good. He completed the sequence nearly flawlessly, and doing so bolstered his confidence. He hoped he was ready to earn the attention of a teacher who could build upon the solid foundation he knew he had possessed with the sword.

Upon repeating the sequence, he increased the intensity, and Ryker let his mind wander as his body worked. Knowing he couldn't match the disciplined fighting of a trained soldier, especially if he were set to duel one of elvish descent, he resolved to make up for the gap in skill with ferocity, strength, and pure will that he gained from years of working on the Marriock farm. He assumed even this would prove futile against an elf, but it was all he felt he could lean on.

He thought back on the previous celebrations he had attended and recalled that contestants in the Selection would typically be battling human soldiers. Ryker felt confident he could put on a good showing against any man that he might cross swords with. Ryker completed a series of three additional fighting forms he had committed to memory. Once complete, he dried his neck with his sleeve and began back toward the main path to head into the city as the bells signaled the markets had opened.

Ryker - Chapter 3 - Anticipation

The massive northern gate stood open in front of Ryker. Two pairs of guards were standing on opposite sides of the expansive entrance, inattentive eyes siding over passersby entering and leaving the city on various business. Many years had passed since there had been conflict in the area, and their disinterest and lack of care in evaluating threats hinted that the peaceful years had eroded the guards' diligence, worn away their wariness of others, and eliminated the belief that Stone Guard could truly be threatened. But the city guard liked to maintain appearances, and another group of soldiers stood atop the wall over the gate, looking down as people flowed in and out through the doors.

The gate rose four times as high as Ryker stood, the entrance revealed through the perfect split down two large, silver-plated doors that currently were swung inward on large iron hinges and held open by chains with links the size of a child. Passing under the gate, Ryker gazed up at the ornate doors, taking in the craftsmanship and artistry they beheld.

Each door was inlaid with eight square sections of plate, each brilliantly detailed, molded into scenes that depicted the history of the city from the time it was raised by humans, crushed by a God, and rebuilt by the elves. The top section of the right wall, in particular, captured his eye. A black stone square was carved and set into the silver wall, depicting a distorted beast. The beast was shown with long claws that raked through groups of silver human figures, sprouting floods of ruby blood. The next image showed the aftermath of cleaved-apart human bodies scattered across the elegant background of a city alight with golden flames. The creature in this scene appeared to be basking in his triumph, the dark form twisted and roaring into the air, his lower jaw splitting into two mandibles lined with razor-sharp stone teeth. Amongst the dead lay a silver figure wearing a golden crown. Ryker assumed this man must have been King Humfrey, the human king of Stone Guard, before the fall of the city so many years ago.

How horrible it must have been for these innocent people after the darkness was released from the Rift. Few human survivors from northern tribes were able to make their way to the city. They had fled the northern lands as creatures swarmed their villages, decimating their little worlds, killing not just people but livestock and wildlife as well. The few men and women who were able to flee headed to Stone Guard, their last hope to find sanctuary from the merciless onslaught.

The ones that did make it only delayed an inevitable demise. Death soon found them all trapped inside their walls as krakenshi climbed over, tearing apart men, women, and children alike. The city fell before King

Kei-Tel reached Western Divinoros on his campaign against the Dark God.

Passing through the gates, Ryker was greeted with a bustling scene that quickly drew him from his reverie. The inner city had brick and stone structures built with a structured grid lock layout, as was planned by the elves who designed the reconstruction.

Shops were built on the outermost portions of the city where Ryker now stood. Merchants set up wooden shops and stood along every street side where there was no opening for a brick storefront. Owners of each shop lounged leisurely in their entryways, pleasantly calling to passersby to encourage them to look through their wares. Shouts of, "One a kind cloak procured from the finest linen producer in Sandivar," "New dwarfish chain mail, can take an arrow from point blank range!" and "Finest bread in Stone Guard, just pulled from the oven, just five bronze rounds" filled the air as he walked toward the Selection check-in at the city's central square.

After the first block, Ryker caught the eye of a pretty girl his age who lived on a hill just southwest of Marriock farm.

"Alaia!" shouted Ryker.

The girl spun, waved, and walked toward him. She had turned eighteen in time for the upcoming Selection festival, just a handful of months older than Ryker himself. He had known her since he was a young boy, and in the past few years, he had begun to see her as more than just a friend.

She was beautiful, although he had never dared express this to her. He smiled to himself, thinking he was more nervous to share his feelings toward this young woman he had known for so many years than duel a trained soldier in front of combat masters. On top of her natural beauty, the fact that her family raised and sold cattle and other farm animals directly competing with the Marriock farm resulted in Declan putting pressure on Ryker to court the woman more seriously. Declan hoped to unite the families through marriage.

He knew if he remained in Stone Guard, Declan would pressure him even harder. He was of marrying age now that he had turned eighteen, and Declan's arguments of, "Imagine uniting our two houses! We'd have the largest farming and agriculture footprint in all of Divinoros! Plus, she's easy on the eyes, Ryk. It's a no-brainer if you think about it," would only increase. And Declan wasn't wrong. Ryker did think about the prospects of pursuing her, but right now, he was focused on passing the Selection, and if he had his way, he would soon be dispatched far from his hometown.

Still, knowing there was no future did little to quell the nerves Ryker had worked so hard to dispel just minutes ago. Ryker's eyes wandered over her as she approached, appreciating her dark hair that was tied up, with two strands left flowing down either side of her face, framing her dark violet eyes. The young woman's lips were painted a dulled red for the occasion, contrasting with her light, fair skin. She wore a stunning violet dress that complemented her eyes, and fit her well, forming tightly around her breast and torso in a tasteful manner. Her dress was held up by thin straps over each shoulder, then loosened into a flowing gown around her hips. A patterned shawl lay across her shoulders to cover what the dress did not, as this was the expectation of modesty for a young woman in these parts.

"You look fantastic," Ryker blurted out, feeling a warmth rise in his neck with the ungraceful words.

Alaia smiled. "Thank you. You don't look too bad yourself, although it looks like you've already tested today," she said playfully, tugging the side of his sweaty shirt and making a face of mock disgust.

Ryker chuckled, and they walked together in the direction of the city's center square for the ceremony. "Yeah, I thought I might be able to work out some of the nerves. Doesn't seem to have worked, though . . . How are you feeling about today? Looking to go into engineering, right? No, was it carpentry?"

Alaia smiled at the young man, "Yes, I think I am going for carpentry, engineering, and architecture. My brother already takes me out on all his building jobs within the city. I know my way around chisels, saws, augurs, well, the whole toolkit, really. Plus, I like the idea of lending thoughts to the design of what I am building and innovating structural design. I've been studying both dwarven and elvish engineering trends over the past century. And I, well, I won't bore you with the details."

Ryker nodded. "Makes sense. Sounds like you'll have no trouble then. Nice to know one of us is a shoo-in today. The master's would be lucky to have you as an apprentice." He leaned in and bumped her shoulder with his own, smiling at his childhood crush as they continued to walk. "Wish I felt as prepared to duel . . . Hate that we will be in front of the crowds."

"So, Dec couldn't talk you out of it, huh?"

Ryker thought he noted a twinge of disappointment in her voice before she continued. "You realize that in the past ten years, only four humans have earned the honor to apprentice amongst the elves' military forces."

Ryker shrugged his shoulders with feigned confidence. "Yeah . . . but one of those was Jeb, so who knows? It might just run in the family. There is only one way we can really find out, though, I suppose."

Alaia looked up toward Ryker, and he was surprised to see genuine concern in her eyes. "Just be careful. You know it doesn't go as well for everyone as it did for Jeb. If things go too far, promise me you'll bow out. We've seen people die during the trials, Ryker. I don't want to be forced to watch something happen to you." Silence trailed between them. "But I really hope you do succeed." The last portion sounded a bit forced to Ryker's ears, but he still appreciated the words.

Ryker smiled at her concern, which stirred up conflicting thoughts. Part of him wouldn't mind failing the impending assessment simply to ensure he would not be leaving her behind in Stone Guard. Maybe he should just return to the farm. It would be easy to settle down with her.

If she'd have me, of course.

Alaia had never expressed interest in him openly, and who knows where the master engineers or architects would have her apprentice.

She could be shipping out to Turenian or Gods knows where on projects, then I would be the one left behind here.

The pair rounded the final corner to the open space at the center of the city. The square was, simply put, massive. The floor around the perimeter of the grass space was paved with large gray stone squares, and trampled tufts of grass peaked through cracks in the worn stone surface. Most days, all four sides were lined with various shop carts, but today, three sides remained empty; only one was reserved for the men and women to line up as they waited to be announced and tested in their Selection in front of all the spectators.

Ryker thought he recognized a few people who already stood within the waiting area, including two boys he had grown up with. The two adjacent sides were void of shops, reserved for the spectators of Stone Guard City who would fill in to view the event. A small portion of one of these sections had been roped off, signaling where the evaluators would gather. A mass of older people, varied in race and gender, had already gathered. Some wore robes signifying the order to which they belonged, but Ryker's eyes were drawn to a group consisting entirely of hard-looking elvish and human warriors donning fitted silver plate armor. This group was comprised of the masters of trade, engineering, and war and weapons, who had come as representatives of their orders and guilds to evaluate this year's talent. Ryker saw a stoutly built man wearing a dark gray robe with a silver hammer sewn in the front, likely the forge master, talking to a female elf who towered above him with a beautiful green robe with a golden sash marked with the symbols of the architect's guild. They stood amongst a group of four, but Ryker could make out no other symbols.

Only warriors would send more than one representative. If any should qualify, they would determine who would train the apprentice according to the skill set displayed. The group of warriors did not converse with the others assembled. Instead, they looked over those checking in for the Selection, evaluating builds as if examining cattle at auction, seeing if any may be worth their time and tutelage.

13

They want to know if there is any clay here worth molding.

The final side of the square was laid out with tables of fine food and drink for sale. Now that the time had passed mid-morning, spectators were slowly beginning to file into the square, partaking in the drink and food brought in abundance in anticipation of the large crowds that would be drawn to the day's event. The merchants working the stands licked their lips in anticipation of the events knowing full well the guests' purse strings would loosen as the libations flowed.

The middle portion of the square was a large open area of well-kept blue-green grass. This is where Jeb had won his contest to join the elvish military, being selected by the master who ran multiple battalions stationed at Ice Bridge Hold. This is also the site where Ryker had seen countless young men brutally maimed and disfigured in intense combat with a chosen "examiner." He'd even seen one man killed after refusing to accept defeat and attacking his examiner after the test was halted. That act resulted in a bashed-in skull that the healing mages present were unable to repair before the cold grip of death swept away the man's soul. This was the test Ryker was required to pass if he wanted to become a soldier's apprentice.

At the center of the square, Lord Frenir stood surrounded by six members of what Ryker assumed was his honor guard and one spindly human woman who might have been as old as some of the elves based on her aged appearance. She sat slightly behind the high lord, supported by a simple wooden stool, with a scroll and quill recording names and desired apprenticeships for the candidates who checked in for the Selection. The six honor guards stood nearly a head taller than Ryker and were brandished with gleaming gold-trimmed armor and polished silver helmets with the crest of the honor guards melded to the front. Their armor was form-fitting, and Ryker imagined they could move just as quickly armored as they could unburdened. Each carried a glaive in their right hand with a long dagger belted around their waists. They were imposing, but Ryker refused to shrink from their gaze as he and Alaia approached the city's high lord. Alaia strode slightly ahead of Ryker.

Once within earshot of Lord Frenir, he instructed in a formal, commanding voice, "Speak your Selection and your name for records. Then, proceed to the waiting area to be announced. We will begin upon the noon bell."

Alaia stepped up. "Alaia Blackmoor, carpentry and architectural engineering."

The high lord gave her a curt nod, and scratching sounded when the quill contacted the scroll to record her decision. She curtsied in return, then immediately strode toward the waiting area but glanced back at Ryker to give him an encouraging smile.

"Ryker Marriock, warrior."

Lord Frenir raised an eye as he looked over Ryker. "Good luck, Ryker. I hope you succeed as Jebediah had," Lord Frenir stated flatly, his silver eyes staring directly into Ryker's own.

"Thank you, Lord Frenir," he responded, bowing slightly, but before Ryker strode after Alaia, he hesitated. "Lord Frenir, do you think you may have time to speak with me after the demonstration? Declan and I were hoping you had heard from my parents. I thought they might have sent word since we last spoke, well, with it being the Selecti–"

He was cut off as one member of the honor guard stepped around Frenir, grabbed Ryker's upper arm, and flung him in the direction Alaia walked. "Move. You're holding the line," he spoke forcefully as he threw Ryker. Lord Frenir looked to him with no display of emotion and nodded to the area where Alaia now stood, indicating Ryker to continue toward the waiting stage.

Apparently, now was not the time for questions.

Ryker glared over his shoulder at the guard, frustrated with the gaping discrepancy in strength between the pair. He hated the humiliation he felt at being so easily tossed about by another man.

I will become more than him. One day, no one will dare handle me with such disregard.

He strode to the space Alaia had held for him. She said nothing, though he could see the sympathy in her eyes, having witnessed the exchange. Nodding his thanks, Ryker settled into line, waiting with the other humans who were of age, and opted to participate in this year's trial.

Now that he was checked in and waiting, his mind raced, lost in thought of how he could possibly hope to impress the masters enough to want to take on a human apprentice. His gaze continued to fall on the member of the guard who had thrown him.

Maybe I can fight him... I wouldn't mind beating him around a bit... Though if I were being honest, I would be hopelessly outclassed against one of the best fighters in the city.

Over the next hour, waves of citizens filed into the ale tents and wine bars set up on the opposite end of the square, flowing to fill the spaces reserved for spectators until thousands crowded the area. Knots formed in Ryker's stomach, his heart was beating through his throat, and his palms began to sweat. Anticipation was building, and then, the midday bells sounded, signifying the Selection would begin. Lord Frenir turned to the group. "Let us begin."

Baelin - Chapter 4 - Ancient Discovery

Only one God was ever truly feared by his followers. Only one expected subservience from all lesser creatures. Only one killed those who denied him. - Gods of Divinoros, Historical Accounts of the Divine

Frustrated, Baelin closed the thick book, "Gods of Divinoros, Historical Accounts of the Divine", setting the thick text on the wooden table before him. The heavy pages kicked up a cloud of dust, seen drifting within the small beam of light directed at his seating place through the sorcerer's lamp hanging on the wall behind him. The aged dwarf ran his thick, stocky fingers through his aged white beard, re-adjusting how it fell and laid in his lap as he thought about the pages he had just read. The man was a scholar and had studied one topic for the past two and a half centuries: the Year of Darkness. Omnes's scourge.

After so many years, he had finally concluded that there was nothing more he could study on the subject. Baelin had set out to discover all he could about the Year of Darkness. How had humans summoned a God upon the lands, how did these powers escape detection from the more ancient races before their release, and most importantly, how could the Shroud that still hung above the Rift, the same Shroud responsible for unleashing unprecedented destruction, be dissipated? Finally, how to go about removing the divine threat from the world permanently.

While it was true that there had not been any confirmed sightings of Omnes's minions since Celestra had witnessed the great elf, King Kei-Tel, pull the Obsidian Knight into the abyss of this world, Baelin still suspected that granting an immortal deity a foothold to the mortal world was akin to ignoring a sleeping archdragon in the center of a city.

If those floodgates opened once again... Baelin shook his head, not wanting to consider the implications. *Could Divinoros truly have a chance of facing a God set on returning?*

He had set out in his studies to resolve the potential threat. However, all he was able to discover was religious theory on the nature of the Gods who had long ago come to this world and long ago left it. While he confirmed countless times that Omnes was the malevolent, brutal deity prone to violence, he was never able to ascertain how he was summoned back to these lands after the four Gods left it, nor had he succeeded in understanding how he may be able to dispel any lingering connection between this world and the tethered God. After long years dedicated to the topic, he feared he had exhausted nearly every avenue available to him to further his research.

But what can I do, thought Baelin, as the dwarf rose from the padded wooden stool he had sat upon the past twelve hours scouring over yet another iteration of Divinoros's history.

After all these years uncovering the secrets behind Omnes's scourge... am I ready to admit to myself that there is nothing more to finally lay this topic to rest?

The old dwarf picked up his book and looked down the hall that stretched for nearly a mile through the Archives. The dwarven library was massive, and while he had yet to read every novel, journal, or fable about the Dark God, his lack of findings over the years and repeated dead ends had been rather disheartening. And while his eyes hadn't graced every page available, they had rabidly devoured plenty to no avail.

More than a few have told me to leave this be. Maybe it's time I listen? Finally, enjoy the world before age consumes me and the Reaper greets me with open arms.

He scurried from the cove he had nestled in for the day carrying a stack of texts he intended to return to their places and turned down one of the main corridors in the Archives. Every few paces, a lavishly embroidered metal bookcase rose high into the air, reaching heights greater than most towers seen in the various elven capitals he had long ago visited.

Nobody can build like the dwarves.

Crystal stalactites of ruby red, deep blue, and emerald green gleamed above the bookcases, diffracting the soft glow emanating from the mounted perpetual torches below, a curious invention where dwarven mages entombed a flame in clear stone, freezing the flame in place. They only existed in places where delicate wares were kept on account of expensive and time-consuming production.

The torches clung to the sides of the bookshelves and areas of the ceiling far above, twinkling like stars in a night sky. Once out from the secluded cove, Baelin had to navigate through throngs of dwarven scholars that bustled between bookshelves. Most he passed had eyes cast down, entrenched in their self-appointed fields of study. Hanging from the top of each bookcase was a single lift made of solid steel. Each personal lift platform and structure was set on rollers to make retrieving books from the upper shelves possible. Because the lifts were enchanted by the dwarf mage sect, they were able to move up and down the shelves without a complex series of pulleys and cranks cluttering the space.

Baelin, despite spending the better part of the past two hundred and fifty years pouring over books housed in the Archives of the dwarf city, remained impressed with the elegant yet functional designs found in the Marbled Caverns. The Archive itself was the greatest collection of writings in all of Divinoros, housed on the outskirts of the dwarf capital.

Not only did these halls contain the majority of all historical text, but they also housed some of the rarest books in the world. This made the Archives a frequented destination, not just for dwarven scholars but for humans and elves who would often travel hundreds of miles hoping to gain access to the greatest source of knowledge available in Divinoros.

After nearly half an hour of walking and cursing the aches in his knees and back, he arrived at the historical section of the Archives. Groaning through the stiffness plaguing his joints, he set down the stack of books he carried on a table running between two rows of shelves.

Yes, maybe it's time to give this wild hunt up. I would like to see the southern cities. And it's been a lifetime since I visited Turenian. Perhaps a trip would soothe my mind.

It had been years since he came across any new discoveries on how Omnes's scourge was released on Divinoros. There were many texts he had yet to ponder over, but new discoveries of that time were becoming far more infrequent. His last big discovery was over fifty years back, and since then, he had merely read regurgitated information that provided no valuable insight other than the stark differences in the author's biases and writing styles.

He imagined that, along with most of life being eradicated during the time termed the Year of Darkness, texts documenting the period were also likely lost or destroyed. Baelin hypothesized that most histories of the period had to have been based on a limited set of original texts, leading to redundancies in the information he delved into. The only city that was left untouched by the scourge was Turenian and some other inconsequential cities in the deserts to the south of the elf's capital. He thought there might be something he could uncover there, but at his age, a hard trip on horse, ship, and foot to Turenian or beyond held little appeal for the dwarf. To his swollen joints, it would likely feel much like a death sentence.

If I were to travel at this age, I would do so in luxury with no consequences for taking my time.

So, Baelin conceded, it was now time to move on, to find another area of study to devote his final years before rejoining the stone, or to find a nearby village to experience something new once again. As he placed the leather-bound books back into place, he thought back to his one great discovery, finding a document outlining human religion from before the Dark God's scourge.

He knew that humans, just as dwarves, had worshiped four deities that were said to have stabilized their world after the war of dragons and demons had nearly wrecked the land. There were three Gods of light: balance, creation, and wisdom, and one God who was power-hungry and driven to gain more wherever he might. It was this Dark God, an extremist religious sect held in the highest regard, Omnes, he was called.

18

The other three were known as Vitala, the Goddess of life and beauty; Sapiena, the Goddess of wisdom; and Comporian, the God of balance and virtue. Baelin had thought it odd these people had chosen Omnes to be the God they wished to dedicate their lives to, for in these texts, the people who described Omnes did so not with love but with fear and trepidation.

After reading through their holy manuscripts and applying them against his knowledge of the time, Baelin reached three conclusions. Firstly, he believed that the humans at the time had meant to gain respect from the more powerful races of the dwarves and elves by increasing the innate power of their race. A common enough theory explaining the motivation behind the action of this sect. Secondly, in their plan to do so, they attempted to tap into the power of a God and harness it for their own use. This attempt invariably summoned the mist, which quickly ascended out of their control and allowed Omnes to release minions of death into the world. And thirdly, Baelin did not believe Kei-Tel succeeded in killing Omnes as the God was tackled into the Rift. For if he had, the mist would have retracted to where it had first emerged since the Shroud was a force of the God. But even more so, Baelin believed that the Shroud *was* Omnes, at least in part. Over the past few days, he reached his fourth and final conclusion: the methods used to release the God were either destroyed or lost to time, likely never to be recovered.

After Baelin had finished placing the books back into their snugly fit homes side by side with their leather-bound siblings, the graying dwarf sat down heavily on a stool, rubbing at his sore knees to alleviate the pain and swelling that resulted from his brief walk.

Damned joints.

He leaned back and arched his spine, setting off a series of pops and cracks. He groaned from the stretch.

Something caught his eye as he looked up at the wall of books. He noticed a small, seemingly inconspicuous journal tucked between two gilded leather-bound texts. It seemed as though the black journal, aged and worn at the edges, was attempting to shy away from any notice, comfortable within the shadows of its much larger brethren.

Curious, I've looked at this wall of pages hundreds of times but had yet to notice this one. It does seem rather unremarkable but old... Yes, it seems very old.

The booklet sat at a middling height and, unless seated where he was now, would be covered from sight by the domineering texts and shelves surrounding it.

Baelin grumbled as he ceased rubbing at his left knee, now annoyed that the ache in his legs was replaced with an insatiable throbbing in his knobby knuckles. He pushed himself upward, muttering all the while, "I dedicated a couple centuries to this cause. What's one more book?" He stood, grabbing a rail on the ladder lift before him, and urged the device upward.

Nienna - Chapter 5 - Endless Dunes

Nienna rolled to her stomach to position her face over the edge of the dune, exposing it to the whipping winds that sent her long blonde hair swirling about her. The wind seemed to be picking up, kicking up sand, and obscuring her visibility of the massive dune sea frozen in rolling motion before her.

She strained her blue eyes to focus on the horizon but ended up pulling down her wooden goggles with two vertical slits to help minimize the light and block the sand that was blowing into her eyes. The goggles were of her own design, admittedly ugly, but they offered protection from blowing particles that could otherwise render her eyes useless in the desert, and since she needed them, she wore them.

A sandstorm was forming, appearing as a large dark-brown cloud swelling up from the surface of the earth in the distance.

"Hmmm, well, that will at least help to cover our approach if it holds, Zarou," she muttered, turning back to her companion, a towering Sand Lion. Zarou purred affectionately, his response indicating his understanding. "Guess we better get you all set up," Nienna said, scratching at the hard-plated scales behind Zarou's ear.

He stood, shook his body, and stretched out his front legs, pressing his chest low to the ground while flexing and stretching his scale-covered paws. From each toe, a six-inch dagger-like claw elongated, raking the sand as he pulled his paws back toward his body. Finally, he shook his massive body and held a still-standing position, nodding his head toward Nienna, indicating he was ready for her to outfit him.

Nienna pulled the harnesses out from her travel sack, securing the leather straps around Zarou's front legs. She attached each leg loop across the animal's chest and back with two straight leather straps, forming a lightweight harness. Once secured, Nienna pulled the strap to test its strength and swung up onto the giant cat's back. They had tested out full saddles commonly used on horses, but they had been too bulky for the feline to move as quickly as he pleased.

Despite the beast's size, he stood two feet taller than the elf woman at his shoulder. Zarou seemed to prefer the lightweight harness and outright refused to run when strapped to the bulkier equipment horses and other beasts of burden wore. Nienna smiled at the memory of the ferocious killing machine flopping on his side and itching his back into the ground as he refused to take even one step with the custom-made horse saddle.

Was a waste of good coin.

Once the lightweight harness was in place, Nienna could hang to the top of each arm loop positioned near the cat's shoulders, allowing her to secure her upper body low against the feline's back. She would then hook her legs around the creature's midsection with her long, powerful legs. Because the cat was armored with gritty sand-colored scales, Nienna wore thin linen clothing to allow the desert breeze to flow through but had stitched-in light leather padding along the thighs of her pants and chest of the flowing linen cloak. This offered her protection from the living armor as the cat carried her.

She recalled back to when she first rode Zarou with the light harness and how her thighs and body were ruined by his scales in a matter of seconds, making every movement for weeks an unpleasant experience as the resulting dark red scabs continually cracked and bled. Since then, however, she loved the exhilaration of moving at coordinated breakneck speed when on the great animal. It wasn't often that she was required to ride Zarou, for elves were fast and capable of covering great distances in a short time, but still, Zarou was faster, and in the desert, his wide paws, larger than Nienna's torso, were better suited than feet to run across unstable sands.

Two days back, Nienna's talents had been procured by the high lord of Sandivar City, Lord Sennin. She was tasked with taking payment to a human crime family, the Bankhofts, in exchange for some undisclosed artifact that was lost to the elves after the sacking of their city known as the Oasis.

The Bankhoft family had long ago killed the elven leadership in the Oasis, located in the easternmost region of the Sandivar Desert. Despite Queen Celestra's best efforts, she had been unable to take back the city by negotiation or by force. After it fell three hundred years ago, just before Nienna was born into this world, several campaigns were levied on the residing population, but every military unit sent into the area would disappear. Oftentimes, armies would be met and consumed by monstrous sandstorms appearing in what was thought to be a peaceful day. Nothing but death seemed to reside within the blowing gales that engulfed the soldiers, and while none had been able to figure out what happened to those within the blowing storms, scouts sent to find evidence and intel always returned with haunted eyes, mumbling about the gore and dismantled remains they would come across.

The most recent attempt to reclaim what was now known as the Badlands was around one hundred years and some months prior. Queen Celestra had sent in three elven battalions, assuming three thousand elves and a few well-trained men of the Royal Turenian Army could surely overwhelm a human resistance that hid deep in the desert headed by a crime lord.

One scout sent in the aftermath of the battle returned with what many described as a semblance of sanity. He explained through whispered, shaky words that all that remained of the elven army were pools of scarlet blood held in troughs of sand that had become too saturated to absorb any more of the viscous scarlet fluid. Limbs, innards, and armor had been ripped from the bodies that once held them. These were strewn about in a half-mile radius from what appeared to be the center of the carnage. The scene described seemed to have been more of a bloody execution than a battle.

To make matters worse, no human remains of the enemy were found, nor were any survivors of the Queen's forces found. The mere savagery of the scene left the scout unable to guess what could have caused the destruction of such a mighty force. He had never seen anything like the devastating butchery he witnessed in the desert. The only thing that held any resemblance, he told his superiors, was the kill sight of a moose carcass ripped apart by packs of Feyvawolves. Since that day, this portion of the desert remained in the hold of the Bankhofts and was primarily left undisturbed outside a few unsuccessful attempts at communication with the crime lord.

According to High Lord Sennin, the artifact this Bankhoft family was said to be in possession of was an old text that contained something important enough for Sennin to pay handsomely for. Nienna assumed it was likely something of value stored in the city long ago, likely after Omnes's scourge, as the Oasis had once been the shining gem of elven occupation in the desert. It remained the pearl of the sands until the city eventually crumbled after many years of corruption within its walls.

Hedonism disguised as liberation, lifting of restrictions on illicit drugs, sex houses, and other debauchery had many humans and elves alike praising the city's officials for *freedom*, only a few realizing these actions would spur a decay in morality within its inhabitants. And as evil spread within the Oasis's walls, seeded by the Bankhoft family, it was eventually easy for them to put a stranglehold around the necks of the politicians in control of the city.

Blackmail, solicitation, and bribery became commonplace before long, making the city's high-ranking officers little more than puppets. The crime family found a weak point in the city's leaders, and once a small crack was found, they dedicated resources to rotting away any semblance of decorum that the high lords and ladies of a city like the Oasis were believed and expected to have.

As the strength of leadership and influence of the Turenian empire eroded further, riots, terrorism, and destruction forced its population elsewhere. It got to the point that Celestra was forced to build a new stronghold in the Sandivarian deserts along the western edge of the region, Sandivar City. So, given the history of the Badlands and Bankhofts that still controlled the area, Lord Sennin wanted to hire someone he believed had a chance of success, so he sent for one of the most infamous figures in Divinoros, one known to nearly all but herself

22

as the Ghost. A figure many thought to be fiction, fantasy, a legend built off the unclaimed accomplishments of many others.

Nienna smiled.

It does not matter what others think. I have done the impossible many times over. Of course, it is easier to discard my accomplishments as fantasy.

While Nienna masterfully crafted her reputation as one of the continent's most dangerous and skilled freelance assassins, she had been nervous about taking this job. And rightfully so, given who she would be in contact with. Lord Sennin had told her he had communicated back and forth with the head of the Bankhoft family, arranging the exchange of the manuscript he sought for twenty gold rounds and a medium-sized diamond brick, a fortune to anyone not born of royal descent. But these people had a history of secrecy and savagery. No one knew the name of the man running the family, only the title.

When Nienna took the job, she was sure to do her research, so she knew that, just like those who ruled the family before him, their current head of household was called "The Knife." The culture of the Bankhofts was to ascend in power by capitalizing on the weakness of those in a higher position, a culture that ensured those who remained in power were worthy of their rank. The current Knife was no different, and he had earned his namesake by driving his own blade through the skull of his father, who finally grew too weak to hold his claim as the head of the family. This behavior was not frowned upon but was expected and celebrated in their organization. Nienna had killed plenty, but the thought of so casually killing your own family was distasteful and wrong in her eyes, and she struggled to grasp the savagery these people must live with.

After being contracted by the Sandivar's high lord, and only once her independent research had been completed, Nienna and Zarou had agreed to his terms and set off toward the Badlands across the expansive Sandivar Desert. All she had packed was some dried provisions, three large pouches containing the treasure to be offered in payment, her two favorite daggers nearly the length of a human short sword, though far thinner to allow for a faster style of fighting, along with an assortment of ranged weaponry secured to her person. The trip was easy on a Sand Lion, so she expected a quick excursion. Each stride from Zarou covered nearly fifty feet of the desert sea, and he could move at great speeds for long periods of time, pulling energy from the baking sun so common in the desert climate he was so well suited to.

On the morning of the second day, she had begun to glimpse evidence of a city in the near distance. Two large towers were leaning heavily toward each other. The eroded base of each structure had long ago given way to the stony bulk above it. The towers appeared to have collided as they were toppling over. They now remained partially upright, rested against one another at a steep angle, each tower supporting the other's weight.

It was a strange sight to see the collapsing elven architecture, now appearing to form an unnatural triangular stone gateway in the distant horizon. Nienna continued to scan the distant city, finding there was also evidence of two walls, likely an inner and outer wall that at one time would have circled the ancient city. These were largely deteriorated and covered in dunes of sand, but occasionally, the wall jutted through the grainy surface, making certain areas difficult to pass over. Nienna dismounted Zarou.

"So, what do you think, Z? Do you smell anything out here?"

Zarou grumbled his acknowledgment of the comment, gently parting his mouth to taste the breeze while he inhaled air through his large nostrils. He didn't seem to smell or sense any danger, so they continued on foot.

The companions soon passed what once must have been the inner wall of the fallen Oasis and still had seen no signs of life, birds, rodents, reptiles, or scorpions. As they crossed the threshold of the inner wall, Zarou froze, his ears flicking back and to the sides as if listening intently to some sound that had yet to reach the elves' own ears. Nienna followed her lion's lead stopping, tilting her head toward him, and cocking an eyebrow in a questioning gaze.

A moment passed before she heard a low warning grumble emanate from Zarou as the great cat shifted his weight to his back legs as if he were ready to pounce or spring into action. Then she heard it. A subtle buzzing. The sound of dry cloth rubbing together filled the air, subtle but growing louder fast. She was unable to pinpoint the source.

Could it be coming from beneath us?

Just as the thought crossed her mind, the sand began to bubble around where they stood.

Nienna sprung onto Zarou's shoulders, screaming, "Run, Zarou, we need to get off of the sand!"

Zarou moved before she had finished calling the orders. The great cat bounded toward a section of the wall that still protruded about twenty feet above the sand and easily jumped the height, landing silently.

Nienna jumped onto the solid dark stone that now lay below her feet and looked back to see what had caused the sand to roil. But when she looked back, the sand seemed to have settled, and the eerie sound started to fade. She felt an uncomfortable prickle on the back of her neck. Something had known they entered the Badlands, and she couldn't shake the feeling they were being watched.

Nienna - Chapter 6 - Broken Lands, Haunting Men

Nienna stayed atop Zarou's shoulders as he bounded across the brief sandy expanse toward the leaning towers. Zarou was careful to avoid the desert sands, opting instead to bound between the sections of the exposed wall and various rubble that peaked through the sand as the pair edged closer to their destination. Nienna did not want to encounter whatever toiled beneath the surface.

The short zigzagging trip to the center of the city took what seemed like ages after multiple days of freely sprinting without obstacles, other than the small storm, of course. After reaching the collapsed towers, solid ground and remnants of streets allowed them to move without concern for what lurked beneath the sands. The pair had arrived at the long-abandoned Oasis and began their search for the Knife.

Lord Sennin had sent his communications via messenger bird to the Badlands, so he did not know where the main stronghold of the Bankhoft family was located. It could be hidden somewhere in the ruins or somewhere further on, in the distant dunes beyond the city. Despite the lack of information, the message Sennin relayed was clear: she was to meet the Knife at the center of the Oasis.

"Smell anything here, Z?" Nienna asked as they strode past an abandoned storefront with the walls collapsing inward. The cat raised his large, scaled head and tasted the air, looking for unfamiliar or threatening scents. Zarou lowered his head, nodding toward a road that passed near one of the ancient towers. The road that Zarou indicated led through the heart of the Badlands.

As they walked in that direction, she reached up, scratching underneath the massive cat's jawbone. "That's a good boy."

The air around them reverberated as a low purr rumbled in Zarou's chest, and Nienna's tension eased. Knowing she had the loyalty and companionship of one of the fiercest animals on the continent had a way of solidifying your confidence in most situations.

As they rounded the street Zarou had pointed toward, his purring cut off. At the end of this road, three figures stood in dark cloaks, with hoods pulled up, obscuring their faces. Nienna didn't break stride. She had worked in the grime of human and elven society for over a hundred years. The first thing she learned when dealing with dangerous people was to show confidence in abundance; any hint of weakness would be pressed upon, and she intended to show no sign of any. She had learned to carry herself in such a way that people believed they could not threaten her. This was easier now as she had killed people believed to be untouchable, smuggled goods along impossible passes, and cemented her status as a ghost amongst the living, the huntress of the elite. Few had not heard whispers of her deeds throughout the lands and her reputation often satisfied her demand for cautious respect from those she dealt with. The Knife certainly had a reputation of his own, but it was no more impressive than her own, albeit more brutal with less nuance and subtlety present in the tales of his reign.

As she continued toward the three hunched figures, the form in the middle moved toward her, pulling back the hood covering his face. The man's head barely rose to the height of Nienna's breast, but he walked as if the world would obey his command.

They both stopped once they stood arm's length apart. Zarou stood slightly behind Nienna's left shoulder, his lip curling dangerously. The man standing before her had a hardened expression that remained unfazed by the giant Sand Lion.

Impressive, no reaction to Zarou.

His nose was flat, swollen, and contorted at multiple hard angles, showing signs of repeated breaks, too many to properly set the nose back into place. His left ear hung limply to the side, having been partially cleaved from his head. Rather than removing the ear, he allowed it to flop against his face, held in place by a thin sinew of flesh just above the lobe. And his face . . . his face was covered in long, thin scars along the left side. The thin white lines eventually faded into the mottled keloid covering the right side.

It was strange to see a man's face melted into smooth burn scars of shiny silvery flesh. Whether from battle or attempts on his life, it was clear this man was a survivor, if nothing else. Set sunken in his mangled face were two beady black eyes that stared unblinking into her own, like those of a raven.

There is evil in his eyes. I can feel it even as Zarou senses it.

As if to reaffirm her speculation, Zarou maintained a low, rumbling growl. The presence of the man before her left no doubt in her mind that this was none other than the Knife.

Nienna was surprised to hear a friendly, high-pitched tone emanate from him as he spoke. A sound in stark contrast to his grueling appearance. "So, you are who Sennin sent to do his bidding . . . I've heard stories of you, Ghost. I must say I was not expecting to see someone so... young. So... pretty." He traced his fingers over the thin scars on the left side of his face as he spoke. The Knife didn't even glance toward Zarou, which surprised Nienna. Most people were terrified to be in the presence of her giant-scaled lion, but this man clearly felt as though neither elf nor beast posed any threat to him.

Curious, he shows no fear for someone born to such a weak race.

"Some may find my appearance young, though I assure you I am anything but. As for looks... well, I would say that in the present company, it is yours that stand apart, though I wouldn't use the term pretty to describe them." Nienna's words drew a quick scowl that flashed across the man's face so quickly she thought her eyes may have deceived her.

"Where is the artifact Lord Sennin brokered for," asked Nienna flatly. This Knife, despite his pleasant tone and small stature, was off-putting. She wanted to make this transaction and leave the Badlands behind her. She was uneasy in the presence of the Knife and the two cloaked figures looming in the background. The boiling pools of sand that threatened to surround her earlier had left her on edge, and this meeting did nothing to abate the tension in her chest.

"No need for rudeness, lass. I hoped to be able to converse for a while, given your... eh, shall we call it, fame. Though I see you have no time for pleasantries," said the Knife as the grin vanished from his face and a cold edge now entered his tone. "I don't like doing business before I get to know someone. What my family has built over the years has stood the test of time, the test of elves, and our reason for success hinges upon one thing." His fingers now caressed his mottled burn scar as he spoke. "We all have an intimate understanding of each person's desires and how those desires may benefit our own. So, I ask you, Ghost of Divinoros, why are you here? Why should I trust that you will hold to the terms agreed with Sennin?"

"Frankly, I don't care how you typically do business," Nienna said. "I was paid for a job many others would refuse, and so I earned a premium on completing this transaction. That is why I am here. So, I ask again, did you bring Lord Sennin's artifact, or do you plan on wasting more of my time?"

The Knife pulled back the side of his cloak, revealing a long twelve-inch dagger with a beautifully embroidered obsidian blade tucked into a sheath on his belt. The blade was slightly curved and sharpened on only one side. The backside of the weapon was wider than a typical dagger, giving the piece a weighted look. The hilt and handle appeared to be plated with smooth ivory so white it held the color of a bleached bone. The same color a carcass took after spending years drying in the desert sun, all remnants of its former life siphoned out. This blade was made for graceful combat precision, and though it seemed nearly ornamental, it looked to have the weight necessary to cleave through flesh in a violent fashion when needed.

If death took a form, that blade would be it.

He grasped the hilt of the weapon. As his fingers curled around the hilt, Nienna saw the borders of the man's eyes fill with swirling darkness, blocking out any of the little white that surrounded his black irises. The

27

darkness pooled into them until they were nothing more than two dark orbs set into his mangled face. As he unsheathed the knife, Zarou increased the volume of his low growl. At the same time, Nienna unconsciously slid her right foot back into a balanced dueling stance, resting her palm on the hilt of her dagger. What she saw was unnatural. Zarou could sense it as well. Some force was emanating from the blade, and the Knife appeared all the more threatening with the dagger in hand.

The cloaked figure chuckled at her response, but his only move was to cut a leather-wrapped case, secured by a leather cord, from the other side of his waist before he sheathed his blade. Nienna blinked and the dark pools had faded back into normal eyes.

Did I imagine that?

"Little antsy, are we?" the Knife commented with a cocked eyebrow or what would have been an eyebrow on the scorched side of his face. "Let me see the payment," he said coolly as he extended his free hand palm up.

Nienna untied the pouches from within her cloak containing the payment Sennin had sent her with. She set them on the weathered cobblestone street at her feet while maintaining eye contact with the man standing before her. She dared not break eye contact, fearing that something dangerous was residing within this man.

"Throw me the case, and Zarou and I will leave. Then you can retrieve your treasures," Nienna said firmly.

To her surprise, the Knife obeyed her request. Grinning, he tossed the container toward Nienna with no complaint. She caught the parcel in her left hand. The package had surprising weight for a book of that size. She secured the package within her linen cloak as the crime lord spoke.

"I'm surprised Sennin is interested in this incomprehensible scripture. The pages contain many ancient depictions and scripture revered by my ancestors, but trying to translate them is useless. I've kidnapped a couple of the best philologists and historians in Turenian to translate it. Had to kill them all, though . . . not one was worth a damn trying to interpret that jargon. Better money than worthless words, I suppose."

"Pleasure doing business with you," said Nienna, who backed away a few feet from the Knife and then spun back the way they came. She stopped cold. The retreating path was now blocked by five hooded figures that had somehow managed to position themselves without triggering her or Zarou's acute senses. Nienna scolded herself for the slip. She should have been more aware of her surroundings rather than fixating her full attention on the single man before her.

How did Zarou not hear them?

28

Each of the five figures held glimmering swords angled down as they paced slowly toward her.

"What is this," hissed Nienna, turning to face the Knife, unsheathing her own blade as she spun. Within a second, she stood with her long dagger point pressed against the smiling, scarred man's neck, but not before he retrieved his own shorter blade, cascading his eyes back into darkness.

"I suppose I would rather have both the money and the book," the Knife shrugged. "Plus, I've always despised you pompous elves. Think you own us humans, you do. You have for a thousand years, I suppose." He waved the point of his dagger at Nienna to emphasize his point.

"For years, my family has destroyed any attempt by your old hag of a queen to take back our lands. Gah, how I love to spill the blood of your kind." He shuttered, though from excitement at the thought of the elven legions he had slain, or at a tickle from the beads of blood that sprouted from his neck where Nienna's blade pressed, she could not tell.

"Killing your kind is rather therapeutic for my rage. But be thankful, Ghost! Soon, your blood will join your kin, which I have spilled to soak these very sands. Know my reputation, you thought? You know nothing."

Power emanated from the man, a dark energy contorting the air around the two.

"Had Sennin sent a human to complete this exchange, well, I may have stood by the terms of our agreement. But you? The Ghost of Divinoros, who is known through legend for her skill of working within the shadows. Unfortunately for you, I am darkness embodied. Shadows will not be kind to you here."

Nienna began to get nervous, thinking through how she might escape.

The Knife continued, "You, I will kill. And I will mount your head in a reminder to your kind to keep away from the Badlands."

The Knife squeezed his fingers around the hilt of his blade and fixed his dead eyes on the Ghost. His skin faded to an ashen white, revealing crawling black veins beneath the scarred tissue, a web of dark tendrils climbing up his neck. The Ghost knew time was of the essence. She needed to take control of the situation.

"Drop your blade, or I will plunge my dagger through...," but she was cut off as the sounds of rubbing fabric came to life beneath her feet. Zarou hissed and backed away from where the Knife stood. The cobblestone road beneath them trembled and cracked. Wisps of black smoke now rose from the fissures between the cobblestones, forcing the stone to crack and open wider. Sand spilled onto the surface of the road.

Nienna had no more time, so she acted. With sudden force, she drove her blade through the neck of the man before her. The Knife collapsed to his knees, grasping his one free hand to his throat in a feeble attempt to quench the flow of black blood now pouring from his neck and grinning mouth. She spun to leap on Zarou's back and saw a thick cloud of smoke that rose from the ground, swirling to encompass the kneeling Knife.

She had no interest in waiting to see what happened. She leaped to Zarou's back. "Go," she shouted, and the sand cat ran at the group of cloaked humans. The figures did not cower. The ground continued to tremble around them as they fled. She didn't have time for this fight, so she told Zarou to avoid them.

The cat sprung onto the wall of the surrounding building, far above the figures' heads. Using his claws to grip the wall, Zarou sprang beyond cloaked humans, rendering their blockade useless. As they soared overhead, Nienna, out of rage at these men thinking to trap her, sheathed her dagger in favor of grabbing three throwing knives tucked on the bottom side of her leather chest sheath.

With practiced fluidity, she threw them in one smooth motion. Her aim was true, and she heard a succession of satisfying thuds as the small blades sunk into the Bankhoft thugs, severing the jugular of one man and severely injuring the others. Zarou did not stop his sprint back toward Sandivar City until the pair was far beyond the wall.

Ryker - Chapter 7 - Trials

Ryker was soon standing alone in the waiting area, the last bull in a stable waiting to be led to the auction floor. He was the last to turn eighteen from the group of participants in this year's Selection cycle and, as such, would be last to demonstrate his worthiness for his desired profession. In this year's group, no others were seeking to fight their way into an apprenticeship with one of the soldiers. So naturally, the crowd had grown increasingly unruly as they awaited the often-gory spectacle.

Though many participants had failed their tests, one young man and woman were awarded apprenticeships as a scholar and one as an engineer. While these tests could be entertaining, one year, an engineering apprentice had thirty minutes to construct a glider that would stay afloat indefinitely. It was to be constructed to include the one magical component provided by the evaluators, but as always, it was the promise of violence the crowd awaited eagerly. The test of a warrior.

Because Ryker was to be tried last, the crowd gradually continued to swell into a dense mass of citizens that formed a human and elvish wall surrounding the central square. As the number of bodies increased, so did the boisterous behavior of the crowd. Before long, thousands of unfamiliar faces formed a sea of bobbing heads. As the wine continued to flow, the volume and cheers emanating from the crowd continued to rise as if in response to the increase of Ryker's heartbeat as his examination neared. As his nerves built, Ryker regretted telling his brothers not to come. Their faces amongst the rambunctious crowd would have helped put his nerves at ease.

Ryker's eyes were fixated on the middle of the square, where Alaia now stood. She was completing her brief proclamation of carpentry tools and understanding how to build various structures, from fences to bed frames, to support beam placement on a catapult, and to find the best wood and metal to use in the construction of ballistae. Her knowledge was clearly profound in the subjects of engineering and architecture know-how, as well as the practical application of that knowledge.

Upon completing her final trial, designing a miniature building with a complex helix component that could withstand simulated tectonic vibrations, four masters stepped forward to offer apprenticeships. Alaia gracefully curtsied to each.

Two were portly men who had traveled from the Ice Bridge Hold, promising the development and study of leading-edge fortifications and magical defense systems. One male elf traveled from Sandivar City in the deserts of Eastern Divinoros and attempted to sway Alaia's decision with details around his most recent projects of building various vehicles to assist trade transport over the expansive desert region. The final

31

master was a stoic, raven-haired female elf. She was short for her species, not much taller than Ryker was, but an air of confidence emanated from her. A confidence that can only be gained from repeatedly earning the respect of her peers through accomplishments. The other three seemed to regard her with deference.

As she spoke, Ryker could tell Alaia had made up her mind about who she would apprentice under. The woman was an engineer of the highest class in the order of builders, a guild created by the Queen herself nearly a thousand years ago to rebuild the fallen world. From what Ryker could pick up from their brief conversation, she planned to start Alaia's training in Stone Guard as she was consulting on a defense project for Frenir but would then be traveling all over Divinoros to support a broad range of projects from restoration, defense fortification, and weapons defense machinery.

Alaia curtseyed deeply to the raven-haired elf, and her excitement could not be contained. A wide smile graced her elegant face as her eyes locked on Ryker's. For a moment, Ryker forgot all about his impending contest as her smile seemed to have a gravitational pull on his attention. He mouthed the word "Congratulations!" but knew he would seek her out following the festival to offer her his genuine happiness for her accomplishments.

"Clearly," the sharp voice of High Lord Frenir cut through the crowd noise, recapturing the audience's attention and bringing the ancillary volume down to a whisper. Alaia has demonstrated her tremendous aptitude in this field. As you have many masters offering you opportunities to study, I would implore you to make this decision carefully, though it seems you have already made up your mind, if I am not mistaken."

The group of masters stepped back to give Frenir a clear line of sight to the young woman. Alaia nodded to Frenir. She bowed her head toward the raven-haired elf, "Yes, Lord Frenir, I intend to serve under Lady Lefaye."

A burst of applause filled the air as the spectators in the wine house clapped in response to the accomplishment of the young woman. All who gathered knew of Lady Lefaye and, if not her, surely knew of her works. Alaia curtseyed once again to Lord Frenir and started walking to the crowd of observers side by side with Lady Lefaye, her excitement clear by the bounce in her every step. Before traveling too far, she turned to look where Ryker still stood. She winked and mouthed "good luck" in his direction. Lady Lefaye gave her charge instructions as to where to meet and dismissed her young apprentice to seek out her family at the wine house where she could celebrate properly.

Once she disappeared into the crowd, Ryker could feel his palms begin to sweat, his stomach clenched tightly, and his heart beating heavily in his chest, hammering at his ribs with such force he felt the vibrations through his entire body. "Well, my turn," he mumbled to himself as he looked down, closed his eyes, and took a long deep breath. *A moment of excellence is all I need, just a moment of excellence.*

When he lifted his gaze, he saw Lord Frenir standing in the center of the grassy area. To his left stood an older man known as Berk, the well-known weapons master and proud owner of the city's largest forge. The weapon's master was busy arranging an assortment of his wears. Once finished, he faced Ryker holding a beautifully crafted, yet simple, glaive in his right hand. A broadsword, the blade a handsbreadth thick, was clasped in his left hand, the point digging into the soft ground near his feet. Laid out before him was a long hand and a half sword, a short sword, a curved two-handed blade, one large iron mace, one round and one rectangular shield, along with an assortment of smaller daggers, knives, and hatchets.

To his right stood a tall elf that Ryker hadn't noticed before. The elf stood amongst the group of soldiers when he had first entered the square. His silver-gray hair was tied into a neat bun that rested behind his head. He donned a black metal armor chest plate held to his body with black leather straps over a dark charcoal-colored tunic. Hanging around his shoulders was a slightly darker cloak that flowed out behind him. He looked like a wraith from the tales of the Year of Darkness. His cold silver eyes bore into Ryker as he looked the young man up and down. Despite never seeing this elf before, Ryker felt that he knew this man.

"Next, we have Ryker. The only person from today's Selection who wishes to be trained as a soldier worthy to serve amongst the queen's Elites. To prove his worth today, he will be fighting one of Divinoros's most distinguished and accomplished figures, a man whose deeds are known throughout our history. His feats through the past centuries have been told and fabled to humans and elves alike. Even the dwarves know his name. Many of them fear it. He is a silent reaper in the night, an unstoppable force in open combat. He has no equal in battle. Not with the glaive nor the sword. He's a descendant of our greatest King, Kei-Tel. Today, Ryker must prove his worth in a duel with Aegnor from the distinguished house of Turena."

At the mention of Aegnor's name, a roar like none Ryker had ever heard before erupted from the crowd as delighted cheering and applause filled the square. The noise grew until it reached a crescendo that nearly forced Ryker to cover his ears. No one had expected to watch such an accomplished warrior test a lowly, hopeful apprentice. Ryker's memory flooded at the mention of Aegnor's name, reaching back through the recesses of his brain to scrounge up any detail he could remember of the man through legends he heard long ago.

33

He would often pretend to be the elf in duels against his brothers when they were younger. This was an elf Ryker's father had told him and his brothers' stories of as they grew up. A man who had performed fantastical feats in the elves' war against the dwarves, slain hordes of lesser demons that slipped from the Cursed Isles, and survived countless encounters with boggarts, changelings, and other harmful beings of power that stalked the corners of Divinoros.

Aegnor took a step toward Ryker and bowed ever so slightly. As he straightened back to his full height, Ryker realized the elf stood at least a full head and half taller than him. "I look forward to your challenge, young Ryker. Please do not hold back. This is not a test for sport, despite what this..." he gave a wave of a hand toward the drunken audience, "raucous crowd thinks. I have come here to evaluate your ability to kill and avoid being killed. Combat is the art of lethal force, and she is rarely forgiving. I wish to see your proficiency in the matter. Hold nothing back. I will be fighting with my glaive. Choose your weapon carefully," ordered the dark-clad elf. He turned on his heel and strode to the far side of the dueling square marked with paint in the grassed field at the center of the square.

Ryker opted to say nothing in response to the serious nature of the man and instead simply nodded toward his opponent in acknowledgment, doing his best to hide his trepidation at the impeding task before turning his attention to the weapons laid out on display.

Ryker had always been drawn to the sword. It was his father's weapon of choice, and while the family's patriarch encouraged his boys to train with other instruments, particularly the glaive that most elves wielded for longer attack reach, Ryker would always come back to a sword. He knew that he would be at a disadvantage with the length the elf would possess from stature and weapon, but he did not care. He would simply need to find a way to get inside the elves' guard.

With this in mind, Ryker quickly moved on from the selection of glaives, spears, and halberds the weapons master had laid out. Ryker continued perusing the inventory but quickly moved on from the various mace, clubs, and axes laid out in the grass. While he possessed the strength to wield the weapons properly, he thought that the elf would be able to take advantage of the slower movements that would accompany wielding the heavy, armor-smashing tools. Next to the axes were the swords. A wide array of beautiful gleaming steel. Each blade was a masterpiece.

The quality far exceeds any blade I have ever wielded... ever seen really, with the exception of father's.

He saw a two-handed broadsword, but the blade possessed the same issue as the mace and clubs. Its bulk would mean slow movements and require him to use both hands, and Ryker knew he would need a shield to have any hope of surviving even a minute against a far superior opponent. "If you must choose between a weapon and a shield, always, always take the shield," his father's lesson rang in his head.

There was a beautiful falchion with an ornate golden guard, but Ryker was not trained in the intricacies of fighting with a single-sided blade. The short swords had too little reach, but finally, Ryker picked up a hand-and-a-half longsword that was displayed in the last row of weapons. He grabbed the blade in his right hand. This would afford more reach than the short, lighter weapons lying nearby without being overly heavy. Any length would be valuable against his longer, faster enemy, and the extra-sized hilt could be used to increase his striking distance in a pinch.

He swung the blade in a few practiced circular rotations to feel the weight. To his surprise, the weapon felt perfectly natural in his hand. It was exceptionally balanced, feeling like an extension of his limb. Up until this point, Ryker had only ever dueled with wooden practice swords or swords that were severely damaged, riddled with rust, or cheaply produced with poor weight distribution. A delighted grin fell in place on his face as he marveled at the weapon master's creation. Although there were no elaborate decorations along the silver blade, Ryker believed this sword would match, if not exceed, the quality of any weapon in Stone Guard. The blade was shined, gleaming silver steel down its entire length until the bottom of the blade became buried into the hilt. The hilt was composed of a much darker metal. It was formed as a simple cross guard with the sides curving slightly upward to enable effective blocking and catching of opponents' weapons. The handhold was wrapped in a dark blue dyed leather cord, the deep color contrasting with the gleaming steel blade and darkened hilt. It was beautiful, simple, and crafted with one intention in mind: discarding any need for foolish intricacies and embroideries that would merely cheapen and hinder its purpose.

"Ahhh, that is an excellent choice of blade," Berk, the weapons master, commented, the corners of his lips pulling into an approving smile. "That is one of the finest swords I have had the privilege of crafting. A perfectly balanced blade. I made the hilt with a unique material mined near the ice bridge. Incredibly strong but better for a hilt than a sharp edge. Otherwise, I would have used it for the whole blade. However, I did fold some in with the remainder of the steel used for the blade. The material was incredibly lightweight but had a surprising durability... stronger even than the dwarfs forged steel! Truly, no other weapon like this exists. I wonder, though, if you will prove worthy of it in this contest. I doubt you have much of a chance, but maybe you shall prove us all wrong or at least put on a good show." Berk smiled encouragingly, despite the words.

The man seemed genuinely curious to see how the blade would perform in his hands, thought Ryker. He could feel the weapon master's gaze looking over and evaluating him as he continued to peruse the armament. "I am honored to carry it, even if it is just for this bout," Ryker said as he nodded his respects to Berk.

Carrying a single-handed weapon meant he had room to wield more. He picked up a circular wooden shield that could be strapped to his left forearm. He was certain he would quickly take blows and needed a way to block any attacks he was too slow to dodge or parry. There would likely be many.

As he was about to turn to face the elf, he saw a vengeful-looking twelve-inch dagger with one serrated side. He shrugged and murmured to himself, "Can't hurt to have more weapons, and every man ought to have a good knife." Ryker picked up the blade, sheathed it, and belted it around his left leg, hilt near hip height, so he could quickly grab the knife with his left hand in the event his shield was battered beyond use.

He then turned to face the daunting statue that was Aegnor, standing unmoving in his starting place, one arm hanging by his side and the other holding the mid-section of his glaive. The weapon was planted in the ground next to him. As Ryker strode toward the painted dueling area, the elf shifted his feet to a dueling stance as he swirled his glaive in a tight reverse circle until it was level and pointed directly at Ryker's chest.

The elf unnerved Ryker. He was tall but didn't feel as physically imposing as some of the other elven guards Ryker had come across. There was just *something* in the way he stood and the fluidity with which he moved. On top of that, he made each movement so silently. It was as if the very wind passed through him to avoid making so much as a whisper that may arise if the air passed around him.

Ryker could feel the weight of Aegnor's silver eyes as they bore down upon him, dissecting even the most minute detail of the young challenger, from his body language and movements to where Ryker directed his gaze as the man observed him. Ryker knew that Aegnor was breaking down any hints given as to the capability Ryker had with the sword. He was beginning to draw conclusions, to anticipate if there were any threats he could pose as the challenger.

By the time he reached the corner opposite the elf, Ryker was sure Aegnor had already ascertained the most efficient means to end the duel quickly. He only hoped the elf meant to evaluate his talent rather than demonstrate his own. If Aegnor planned for the latter, the duel, Ryker feared, would be short-lived.

When he found his starting position, Ryker fell into his own practiced stance and locked his dark green eyes on the silver of Aegnor's, issuing an unspoken challenge.

I will not let him know I am intimidated. I cannot show fear. Just a few moments of excellence to achieve my goals.

A hush fell over the crowd now, their anticipation as palpable a taught cord the warrior and challenger would cut with their first movements.

"It is an honor to test myself against you, Master Aegnor," Ryker said with a nod.

Aegnor dipped his head in response. "I admire your courage. Most, even my own race, would have forfeited the competition, seeing I was their opponent. I remind you, you will attempt to kill me, and I will respond and act in kind. There have been few who I have allowed to walk from a battle against me. If you do not prove your worth, you will not either."

Ryker was surprised to feel his nerves settle at the statement.

I know how to fight. I've worked for this. Other than farming, the sword is my life.

Aegnor did look as though he meant his statement as a threat, but Ryker thought the comments were a promise of mutilation, if not death.

That is hardly a comforting idea.

He was past the point of no return, however, and the simplicity of a single path forward focused him. He rolled his shoulders, feeling the weight of the shield and blade he now donned. "Yes, sir," was Ryker's simple response.

On Lord Frenir's count, the battle began, and the two contestants circled one another. The crowd instantly came alive. The sudden noise from the audience startled the young contestant. He briefly let his gaze flash off his enemy to the blurred crowd hanging in his peripherals before returning his attention back to the elf. In that split second, Aegnor burst into action, thrusting his glaive with supernatural speed at Ryker's neck. Ryker was barely able to bring his shield up in time to catch the blow, but the force of it sent him stumbling backward. His backside slammed into the grass, but he rolled with the momentum, allowing it to carry him back to his feet.

Aegnor gave no reprieve, pressing his attack with a series of slashes and swipes from the glaive as he spun the long weapon in fluid movements faster than Ryker thought possible, even for an elf. The crowd quieted, staring in amazement at the display from Aegnor, shocked that the young man had yet to be impaled. The sight of a glaive master in a full attack was something to behold, and Aegnor certainly would be considered a master, for no word existed that could be applied to one who had moved beyond mastery to something far closer to perfection. The silver staff moved with such speed and ferocity that Ryker was doing all he could to simply avoid being mortally injured in the early moments of the bout. He parried and blocked the blows coming his way but never seemed to catch a window to press an attack of his own as he continued in his retreating circle.

Aegnor's face had not shown any hint of emotion during the battle so far. He almost seemed almost bored as he forced Ryker to continually cede his ground. After minutes of the frantic onslaught, Ryker's left shoulder burned from the strain of deflecting strike after strike from the enemy's glaive on his shield. The shield was in worse shape than his shoulder, already split and cracked to the point that Ryker was unsure how much more of a beating it could take. He was clearly outmatched, but he needed to find a way to press some sort of offensive. He knew, despite the overwhelming onslaught, that Aegnor could have ended his life immediately had he chosen to do so.

He wants to see what I can do.

He took a powerful overhead swing to the shield, forcing Ryker to his knee, and two more overhead blows followed in a flurry of movement. The impact from the second strike splintered the shield, and on the third impact, the shield broke away from his arm. A grunt escaped the young man as Ryker felt both bones in his forearm fracture with a surprisingly loud *CRACK!* The pain didn't come instantly. A slow warmth built in the area where the bones had fractured. Once the body finally caught up to the shock of the violence, Ryker resisted the urge to cry out as he struggled to blink away the mist rising in his eyes. Tears that now obscured his vision. There was no time to live in the moment of the pain. He did his best to block out the sharp spikes of agony stabbing in the location of the break, and soon, the adrenaline overwhelmed his brain's receptors until he only registered a dull throbbing that indicated his forearm was swelling.

He tried to plan his next move. Ryker was growing desperate and soon would need to yield to the elf if he wished to keep his life.

Just a moment of excellence.

The young man couldn't hope to tire the elf out. Aegnor hadn't even shown signs of respiratory discomfort, each breath still coming even and measured.

Ryker needed to press an attack of his own. After all, Aegnor wanted Ryker to come at him with his entire arsenal. To come at him with vigor as if he was truly attempting to kill the elf. That wasn't even a remote possibility if he stayed on the defensive. He paired another lazy thrust from the elf with an upward flick on his sword arm, causing Aegnor to quickly spin with his glaive, whipping the weapon around his body in a powerful sideways swipe. Ryker jumped just out of reach as the tip of the bladed head kissed his chest. It sliced its way through his sweat-drenched shirt, leaving a shallow red line beneath. Thankfully, it was little more than a scratch, his shirt taking the brunt of the damage. He had seen this same move earlier in the fight. Noticing the pattern in the elf's attack gave Ryker a spark of hope, and a plan came to him.

Ryker continued to back away from the experienced veteran. He began slashing long gouges through the grass, lifting the turf into uneven patterns with swipes from his longsword. The young challenger was now retreating over a smooth grass surface, but Aegnor would have to advance over an uneven landscape. It wasn't much, and while the effect would likely be minimal, Ryker hoped this would marginally slow the elf. Hopefully, requiring him to focus a portion of his attention on avoiding rolling an ankle in one of the ruts. While Aegnor was only slightly inconvenienced, the reprieve from the added fraction of a second between each attack seemed to make a world of difference to Ryker, who was in much worse condition than when the fight had begun.

He also hoped Aegnor would grow bored of the seemingly panicked retreat. The noise of the crowd changed from excitement to harsh criticism and booing. Many jeered at the challenger, "Coward!", "Where's your balls, boy!", "You're pathetic! Worms have more spine!" Ryker ignored the spectators, focusing on the task at hand.

Ryker was used to hard work and long hours, so despite the exhaustion, he willed his body to move with the same speed he had at the start of the fight. He could hear his father's voice, *"Pain is merely a bodily sensation. Control your mind, control your thoughts; do not allow the physical to dictate your limits. Mind is greater than the matter in front of you."* And so, as another thrust came at Ryker, he willed his sword arm to deflect the blow upward with a quick movement. Recognizing this as the beginning of the glaive attack sequence he saw earlier, Ryker immediately changed course, reversing his retreat, and jumped forward in a rolling dive.

Just as Ryker had guessed, Aegnor brought the glaive around in a sideways swipe where the challenger had previously stood. But with the dive, Ryker passed under the attack and was now standing within feet of the elf. Ryker had an opening for an offensive and brought his blade around in a close-bodied swipe toward the elf's midsection, attempting to cleave him hip to collar. At the same time, he unsheathed the serrated dagger with his left hand in a downward grip. His broken forearm screamed in pain as he grasped the smaller weapon, but he was able to maintain his grip despite the fire he felt as he squeezed the hilt.

Aegnor stepped back, bringing the back of the glaive up to deflect the slash from the sword. But Ryker had managed to force Aegnor, the mighty Aegnor of house Turena, to take a step back.

The crowd gasped, their jeers giving way to a brief silence before the suddenly muted crowd swelled into a roaring chorus of cheers. The collective energy vibrated through the air, turning the atmosphere of stunned silence to one of electrified exuberance.

Ryker let the noise fuel him, and he continued to press his advantage, bringing the dagger across his body and attempting to slash across the stomach of the elf. But Aegnor was fast, and he dodged away from the blow with a small half-step away from the strike.

I'm counting that pivot as a second step of retreat, Ryker thought to himself, relishing in the minor success. He could feel a new energy pour into his exhausted muscles with the momentum of his offensive press. He continued with the rotation of his missed slash, whipping the longsword in a powerful backhand cut aimed at the elf's knees. Aegnor dropped his glaive into place, perfectly blocking the blow. Ryker thought he saw a small grin beginning to appear on his opponent's face.

The tall, practiced elf seemed to barely move from his now-rooted location in the dueling square, refusing to give Ryker any additional ground. Despite his refusal to retreat, the elf was still able to expertly dodge and parry the stabs and slashes coming in rageful force from the human challenger. But, just as before, Aegnor avoided these sequences of attack with ease.

Despite the energy from the crowd, Ryker again started to fade, and the vigor of his offensive press waned. On the next move, Aegnor elegantly swayed around a thrust from Ryker's sword, grabbed the young man's sword-wielding wrist, and yanked him closer into the elf's grasp. Dropping his glaive and still holding Ryker's sword wrist, Aegnor violently brought his knee up into the wrist joint. Ryker screamed out in pain and dropped the blade as another loud crack accompanied the snapped wrist bones in his right arm. Ryker dropped to his knees, groaning in pain. He heard the crowd gasp in sympathy for the young man's harsh injury just before a heavy fist slammed into his face.

Ryker fell with the blow but quickly got to a kneeling position despite the agony he was now feeling. His vision was hazy, but in front of him, Aegnor had already turned to the crowd, bowing his victory. Ryker's vision ran red, and no thought sat in his mind other than kill or be killed.

Never accept defeat. Never accept a loss.

After all, this elf had asked for death at the start of the fight.

So, while the elf was distracted, convinced of a victory, Ryker reversed his left-handed grip on the dagger he held so the blade now pointed up in his grasp. With a yell, he brought the dagger up in a swift motion toward his opponent's thigh. Aegnor shouted in surprise as he looked down and saw a large dagger protruding from the outside of his leg, grasped by a bloodied, broken, grinning human. A boy just barely turned man.

Ryker then grasped Aegnor around his knees and, with a final showing of strength, lifted and slammed the warrior into the ground with all the force his hardened farmer's frame could manage. He landed atop the elf and drove his shoulder hard into Aegnor's stomach, with all his weight behind the impact. He had hoped to crack the elf's sternum, but the elf's armor prevented that, and Aegnor was able to exact quick retribution.

The silver-haired elf rolled to his side so the pair were lying on the ground facing one another, and he kicked Ryker in the chest with enough force to crack a number of the young man's ribs. Ryker rolled to his back, gasping and tasting blood, but again refused to stay down despite the snot and tears that flooded from his face as he convulsed in pain.

He started to rise shakily to his feet, but the elf was once again faster. Before he could get his balance, he saw Aegnor close in on him with blinding speed. The last thing he remembered before his world went dark was a leather boot streaking to his temple.

His eyes opened to blue skies surrounding the faces of four healers crowded around him, muttering about "How cruel this event was" and the fact that "Healers were meant to save those who needed it, not to patch up people who thought it a good idea to beat one another for sport." They soon noticed Ryker had opened his eyes. Over the ringing that was reverberating in his ears, Ryker heard one of the healers ask, "How do you feel, sweetheart?" He thought the question was coming from an older woman, a mage who had been tending to his wounds. Humans and elves could both access magical powers if born with the gift, and Ryker had never been more thankful for medicinal magic that had been used to heal him from the worst of his injuries.

"Ugh… well, I feel like I was just kicked in the head," groaned Ryker. "But other than that, I actually feel pretty good."

The older woman cocked an eyebrow. "Well, the best way to avoid that would be to make sure your head stays out of places it's likely to be kicked."

Ryker chuckled, appreciating the dry humor as he pushed himself onto his feet. "Gods, I love magic," he said, rolling his wrist with no pain. The cracks must have been healed before they brought him back to consciousness. He also felt no pain in his chest as he breathed. As the ringing in his ears subsided, he could hear the crowd chanting his name and clapping.

Funny to hear your name chanted after being thoroughly manhandled and embarrassed by a master elf who was clearly holding back.

"Thank you all. My recovery would be far more grueling without your services."

The healers nodded their appreciation at the words as they retreated from the center of the arena where he had been tended to.

Aegnor still stood on the opposite end of the dueling square. Ryker faced the elf. The crowd once again grew silent, attempting to hear any

41

exchange of words between the competitors. Lord Frenir strode toward the two contestants.

"You were holding back," accused Ryker as he retrieved his sword and sheathed the blade from the ground where Aegnor stood.

"Well, of course," stated Aegnor. "There wouldn't have been much to gain from me killing or incapacitating you immediately. I am here to evaluate your talent."

Lord Frenir stopped at the side of the painted dueling square and motioned for Aegnor to come forward. He strode to Frenir and bowed ever so slightly in respect, a gesture Frenir returned.

"How would you grade this latest challenger, Aegnor?" questioned the high lord.

The mysterious warrior spoke loud enough for only Lord Frenir and Ryker to hear.

"His technique is clearly unrefined, as to be expected with someone who has yet to have an apprenticeship. He moves inefficiently, wasting time and energy on imprecise thrusts and slashes. He is careless with his footwork, leading to many of the errors in his fighting style. His strength is far above average for his race. While he is not nearly as fast as many of the Elites in the Queen's army, he is still young and can improve with intense physical conditioning. And as you saw, he has will. Will cannot be taught. With diligence, he could come to be equal in fighting with higher beings and magical warriors our kind often contend with. Overall, the shortcomings are all things that can be corrected. And he has more heart than I have seen in decades."

Raising his voice so the crowd could hear, he stated, "There are positive attributes. He thinks quickly on his feet and has a will to fight on even in the face of defeat. The fact he was able to land a score on me is impressive in itself, despite what some may consider backhanded tactics. Not many in the kingdom have been able to do so. I would request that he receive formal training in the sword."

The crowd burst into a jubilant roar, chanting, "Ryker! Ryker! Ryker!"

The noise covered up whatever Aegnor said next to Lord Frenir, but the young warrior saw Aegnor lean in toward the high lord. As he spoke, Lord Frenir furrowed his eyebrows into a puzzled expression as he let his gaze rest on Ryker for a long moment, as if he were looking for something *in* him. The young apprentice noticed that the other masters who had observed the event were approaching, hoping to offer him various positions in their ranks. However, as they approached, Lord Frenir motioned for Ryker to join him and Aegnor, waving off the approaching soldiers.

Ryker bowed deeply. "My Lord." As he stood, the cheering from the crowd fell once again, hoping to hear what Lord Frenir would rule on Ryker's future station.

"Aegnor has requested to train you personally." Lord Frenir paused as the crowd exploded into boisterous cheering once again. It seemed much louder than it had in the earlier parts of the day, likely due to the hours the guest had spent drinking leading up to the gladiatorial tests. As the outburst continued, Lord Frenir looked to Ryker and said, "This is a great honor, human. Learn well."

Ryker bowed to the city's highest-ranking official, "Yes, my lord." He then turned to face his new mentor and bowed deeply once again. "Master, I am truly honored to be given this opportunity. I am yours to command."

Aegnor nodded his head, and a soft smile appeared on his face. "No man or elf has landed a blow against me in over three decades, boy. Despite your significant disadvantage in speed, strength, and experience, you accomplished this feat. Yes, I did hold back, but you are tenacious and smart, willing to adapt new tactics once you realize you are failing. Above all, your cunning and determination will serve you well. This is a foundation I can build upon as we begin to unlock your potential. Go and celebrate. Tomorrow, I will send for you at first light. There are rumblings in the north I must see to. You will accompany me."

Ryker's mind raced with excitement, though he tried his best to hide the child-like giddiness at the prospect of traveling with Aegnor. Just two days ago, he was working for his older brother on the farm. Plowing, sowing, and harvesting had been his life for so long. Now, in one day's time, he was to leave, he assumed on orders of the Queen, with the most accomplished and revered warrior known in Divinoros. Ryker snapped back to the present moment, realizing he had been staring up at the elf with his mouth agape for longer than was appropriate. Aegnor dismissed the apprentice with a curt nod, and then Ryker bowed once more. "Until tomorrow, Master," he said before turning to return his borrowed weapons.

Berk was bent over his equipment cart, ensuring his stock was loaded and secured for transit. He heard Ryker approaching and turned to face him.

"Thank you for allowing me to borrow such capable weapons, Master Berk. I doubt I would have been able to impress Aegnor with anything of lesser quality."

Ryker's kind words set the man beaming, and his smile stretched to both ears. This did not fade as Ryker began his apology: "Sorry about the shield, though I must say I was glad to have had it. I don't think I'd have lasted more than a couple of seconds without it. I can work to pay you back once I begin earning a wage."

The cheery old man chuckled at the comment. "Oh, it is no problem, boy! I figured it was good as spent once you strapped it to your arm. After that spectacle... I dare say I haven't seen anyone so competent in the Selection challenge in the many years I have served as weapons master of Stone Guard. You looked to be more comfortable with a blade than any human I have seen in the past. More than some of the men already apprenticed. Even more so than Jebediah! I suppose the weight of a blade is probably light to a man who spends time tilling fields and turning soil, but it was astounding the speed you already move at."

Ryker unstrapped the blade and serrated dagger from his person. "One of the many benefits of growing up on a farm, I suppose. I'll have to thank Declan for delegating most of the heavy work onto my shoulders."

Before Ryker could unstrap the blade, Berk cut in. "Keep the sword, boy." And for the second time in less than a couple minutes, Ryker stood there dumbfounded. This was a master blade. Perfectly balanced and crafted by one of the most respected elven forgers in Western Divinoros. This blade rivaled the weapons produced in the forges of the Great Marbled Cavern. "And, take the dagger too, seeing as it is the weapon you successfully landed a blow on Aegnor with. It only seems right you should carry it."

"But Master Berk, I cannot take this. I cannot pay for this," gapped Ryker, astounded by the aged elf's generosity. A blade of this quality may be worth more than the entire Marriock farm.

Berk shrugged. "It is of no concern to me; I can make more. I wish only that you return here and tell me of the great adventures these weapons served you on. Knowing Aegnor and seeing this duel of yours, I imagine there will be many for you to tell. Life gets dull in the forges, you know. Tales keep me and my staff company from monotonous hours that stretch out each and every day."

Ryker nodded his head, astounded and appreciative. "That I can promise Master Berk, thank you."

The young apprentice retightened the leather straps holding the blade and dagger to his body, then turned and strode toward the crowd assembled at the wine house, cheering and whooping his name.

Ryker - Chapter 8 - Celebrations

As Ryker drew nearer the crowd of drunk patrons filling the wine house, he noticed an oddity. A trail formed as the observers were parted. It was as if something was forcing its way through the crowd but was not tall enough to be seen above the heads of the men and women. With happy surprise, the trail reached the edge of the crowd nearest where Ryker approached, and his youngest brother Ayden burst through the final layer of the audience out into the open expanse of the square. He ran toward Ryker, coming to a sudden stop just before his older brother by excitedly ramming into Ryker, both hands extended, shoving him in excitement.

"That was incredible!" Ayden shouted with a wide grin on his face. "You fought Aegnor, Ryker. THE AEGNOR. Never in a million years would I have thought I would see him, much less see him spar with you! And you stabbed him in the leg!" Ayden broke down in a fit of laughter, "I can't believe you stabbed Aegnor in the leg! I know we all used to practice and play, and you took training more seriously than Dec and Jeb... But still. Can't believe it! Thought he killed you for a minute there, if I'm being honest. And, well, I'm glad he didn't kill you. I was worried. Not quite as bad as Dec was, though." The boy stopped briefly in his tirade of excitement to gasp air.

Ryker laughed, amused at his brother's enthusiasm. He rested his hand on his brother's shoulder. "Well, he was holding back, Ayden. I think he could have gutted me more than once throughout that duel. I'm lucky to have evaded him for as long as I did. Speaking of being killed... Where is Declan? He'll be furious you ran off! I'm surprised you convinced him to come watch."

"I didn't even need to talk him into it!" Said Ayden, a stupid grin still plain on his face. "It was his idea to come! After we got the workers going, he left old man Wink to watch over things for the rest of the day. He didn't want to say anything to you this morning. Thought you might be nervous if you knew we were going to be here." The younger boy peered back over his shoulder and waved. "There he is."

Ryker could now see his older brother working through the crowd in his direction. He moved slower than Ayden as he was less willing to shove through the drunks that quickly filled in the seam formed by the charging youngest brother.

Once through, Declan clasped Ryker's forearm in a warm embrace and wide smile. "Well, that was something. Where in the hell did you learn to do that, Ryk? And to train as Aegnor's apprentice... Guess I have no hope of persuading you to stay at the farm now, do I?" the older brother chuckled.

With that comment, Ryker felt a sudden pang of ambivalence. A smile fell from his face. He was elated to have performed so well in front of his family, but he knew that soon, sooner than he'd have guessed, he would have to leave the place he had called home for his entire life. "What's wrong?" asked Declan, noticing the change.

"Nothing's wrong. I am just as shocked as both of you to have performed so well, and I don't think the queen herself could pay for a better tutor. But I leave at first light in the morning. Not much time for getting my affairs here in order. Not that I have much to get in order, but despite wanting adventure... I'm going to miss the both of you."

Declan and Ayden looked at one another, slightly downtrodden by the news another Marriock would be leaving the city in which the boys were raised. The trio had grown even closer after the departure of their parents and Jeb. The transition to another family member leaving would be hard on all of them. No one needed to say it. It was clear in the facial expression each wore. But being the endlessly optimistic little brother, Ayden refused to allow the mood to dampen during such a momentous occasion. He looked sideways at the grime-covered Ryker. "Well, at least I get the big room now! Since you're leaving so soon, I guess you won't mind me moving my things into it tonight."

The three laughed, and Declan chimed in, "I suppose if it's one last celebration, we will do it right. Come on, Ryk, let's get you a pint. The first round is on me; the rest are on you since Ayden and I are going to be picking up your slack."

The brothers celebrated late into the evening with various townsfolk and neighbors that the Marriock's were acquainted with. Many who witnessed the legendary duel wanted to give Ryker their congratulations. When Alaia finally approached to offer her congratulations, Declan pulled Ayden aside to help carry empty mugs to the bar for refills, giving the pair a brief moment of privacy.

"Well, well, Ryker had to show off for everyone, did you?" she mused, a playful gleam in her eye.

"I got stuck trying to follow up on your performance. That's no small task, mind you. I needed to do something to stand out. Honestly, I just lucked out that Aegnor didn't want to turn me into a skewered roast on that glaive of his. It could have been brief, had that been the intention."

Alaia reached out lightly, touching Ryker's arm as she chuckled, sending a nervous exhilaration through his body. "Always attempting to stay humble. So, what is next for the now famous apprentice?"

Ryker shrugged, "I don't really know, to be honest. Aegnor is taking me with him on some journey north. I don't know where to or what for, only that we will be leaving at first light."

Her expression softened, shoulders slumping in disappointment. "I'm going to miss you here. Lady Lefaye thinks we will spend most of my first year, maybe longer, working on a project here in Stone Guard. Sounds as though she was asked by Lord Frenir to consult on some new defense work." She looked up at him and nudged him with her elbow. "Was hoping you might be around a little longer."

Ryker's face flushed. "You're going to be great here. I wish I could stay to see the grand upgrades that Mistress Alaia will think up to make the city impregnable! It's going to be hard leaving this place after eighteen years. It's all I've ever known. Ever loved." Ryker's gaze lingered on Alaia's face. He was very aware of the way she rocked back and forth on her feet as she twirled her dark hair between her fingers.

It's like she's waiting on something.

The boy had never stated his feelings toward Alaia, but the way she bit her bottom lip as he gazed at her compelled him into action. She was beautiful and captivating, and building on the confidence he earned from his duel, he grabbed Alaia around her waist and kissed her. He could feel the warmth of her body press against him as soft lips brushed against his own.

After a moment of elation, the pair broke apart. Ryker immediately broke into a massive grin. Alaia looked at him with rosy cheeks and a sheepish smile to match his own. "Guess it only took you leaving for an untold amount of time and into unknown danger to push you to make a move on me. I've been running out of hints to throw your way," Alaia teased.

Ryker laughed and was about to respond, but at that moment, Declan and Ayden returned carrying four mugs, three of fine mead and one of grape juice for Ayden. Ryker raised an eyebrow at Declan, who quickly responded. "Alaia, join us in our send-off, will you? I got three pints of the good stuff, and", scrunching his face in distaste, "that nasty sugar water Ayden likes drinking."

"Hey, that sugar water just happens to be delicious. Now, hand it over, please," protested Ayden.

"I would love to," Alaia said through a chuckle, reaching for the mug. The three raised their drinks in toast, beginning the celebration in earnest.

As the evening slipped later into the night, Ryker broke away from his brothers with Alaia. The new apprentices settled down on a stone stair away from the drunken crowd still partaking in the wine house casks and barrels of mead. Alaia leaned into Ryker, resting her head on his shoulder. A pleasant feeling. He looked down at her just as she looked up toward him, her violet-colored eyes deep and captivating, holding his hungry gaze.

He searched for words to explain how he felt. How, in this moment, he wished he had pursued her earlier. How he wanted to stay but couldn't. He was surprised, exalted even, to see those feelings mirrored back in her breathtaking eyes. He couldn't seem to wrestle the right phrase together, for he didn't know for how long he'd be gone; he didn't know where he was going. In fact, he didn't even know that he would ever return to Stone Guard.... Return to her.

Alaia read the emotions plain on his face. "It's okay, Ryk. I'm going to miss you too." The two sat there enjoying each other's embrace until Declan's voice broke up the tender moment. "Ryker, it's getting late. I'm going to take Ayden back for the night. You coming?"

He nodded and said farewell to Alaia. It was awkward and far less intimate than he would have wished, being that they were in the company of his brothers. But, once they said farewell, Ryker looped his arms over his brother's shoulders, and the three boys stumbled through the city toward the impressive gates and started walking back toward the farmstead.

Ayden scrunched his nose as they walked. "You didn't, well, you didn't kiss her, did you Ryk?"

Aegnor's apprentice furrowed his brow, "What do you mean?" Ayden slowly moved Ryker's arms from his shoulders, "You smell like a pig that rolled in his own filth."

Declan laughed mid-drink, wine erupting from his nose before nodding and then following suit by relieving himself of his brother's arm as they continued walking homeward.

They arrived home under a blanket of stars gleaming in the sky above. Ryker wondered where his adventures would take him. Would he ever return home again? Once inside, through the battered door, Ryker took a moment to relive the memories made in the house with his loving family, packed a light travel sack, and laid back on the straw-padded bench in the living room to rest his eyes. Before he knew it, he was woken by a sharp rapping on the door.

Aegnor had summoned his apprentice.

Nienna - Chapter 9 - Requests of a Dignitary

Nienna pushed Zarou to his limits on their frantic retreat from The Badlands. The mysterious power the Knife seemed to wield unnerved Nienna, and she wanted to put leagues of distance between herself and that evil place, those evil people.

If they were even people.

In all her travels across Divinoros, she had never seen something as haunting as the Knife. The image of a shaking city and those swirling black eyes sunken within a scarred, mutilated face continued to haunt her each time she closed her own.

Taking no time to stop, Zarou was able to cover the distance back to Sandivar in half the time spent to get there. In doing so, they would have handily outpaced the demented humans, should they have tried to follow her. But, knowing they wouldn't feel safe till the walls of Sandivar stood between her and the crime lord, Nienna had never been more grateful for the Sand lion's endurance.

Over the desert traversal, Zarou fared far better than she did. They had run through the night, and as the morning sun crested over the dunes, turning the sky into a brilliant array of purple and orange, she saw the circular stone walls of Sandivar City cut through the blanket of sand that stretched infinitely in every direction. Nienna dismounted Zarou and nearly toppled over, her body screaming at her in agony. Her joints throbbed and ached. Bloody sores covered her forearms and legs where the leather-padded clothing had not been sufficient to protect her against the scales on Zarou's back from chafing and ripping her skin over such a long sustained ride. She cursed silently to herself, knowing she would need to find suitable replacements before she left Sandivar.

She took a sip from her water skin taking a break to allow her locked-up joints to grow reaccustomed to carrying her own weight as she stood upright. She started walking toward the elves' desert capital; ignoring the trails of blood the simple movement sent cascading from her blotted sores. As she approached, she could see several guards walking along the upper battlements of the enormous wall that stood proud, seeming to touch the sky.

Amazing, the Oasis once stood as formidable. Perhaps we elves are not unconquerable forces despite building monuments that nearly touch the heavens.

Along the walkway, different sentry outposts, with giant mounted ballistae, were manned by teams of four every ten paces or so. These were said to be for protection against the desert dragons and sand buffalo, but Nienna thought it just as likely they would be needed to protect against the Bankhoft family should the Knife ever wish to expand his influence beyond the Oasis.

He certainly doesn't seem to be the type to be content with what he has. It's only a matter of time till he weasels his influence behind these mighty walls. Sennin should be concerned.

Nienna was the only person entering the city at this early morning hour. Before she could get through the gates, a human soldier stepped in front of the open passageway, blocking her path. He shouted in a thick Sadivarian accent, "Oi, who goes there? State your name, 'long with your business in the city."

Nienna glanced down at the human soldier, raising her eyebrow, far from in the mood to be inconvenienced. While she didn't like annoyances, she recognized this man was simply doing his job. "My business concerns only myself and High Lord Sennin. I'm returning from a job he hired me for."

The guard glanced nervously at the imposing woman and the monstrous beast looming behind her. He clearly wasn't satisfied with the response, but it was equally clear he did not wish to argue with an elven warrior covered in blood-smattered garb. In a shaky voice, he asked, "W… well I'm just relaying proper protocol here ma'am, not suppose' to let no one in before the sun come up fully… and I wasn't informed of any guests showing up today for Lord Sennin, ma'am."

Nienna was tolerant, most days at least, but today was not one of those days and this man… Well, this man was testing her resolve and was close to breaking her calm demeanor with the unnecessary delay. "I was hired for a job by Sennin, and he is very interested in the item I was sent to procure for him. Would you like to be the reason he is delayed in obtaining an artifact so important he hired the Ghost to retrieve it?"

The man paled at the name. All of his questions about the bloody mess before him were answered with that one title: *the Ghost*. "Sorry, ma'am, I sure didn't recognize you. Don't think anyone would rec'nize the likes of you though. Ahhh, why don' you just go right on through, jus… just please don' cause no trouble, or that'd fall back on me." He nodded his head toward the entryway and stepped to the side for the elf to pass.

She strode through the city in the direction of the capitol building. Her tired legs sang with delight as she stepped up from the sand to stride on the cobblestone roads, pleased to be on the ground that no longer gave way beneath her feet with every step. The streets were wide enough for Zarou to tread next to the elf, and Nienna rested a hand on his shoulder as they walked together unmolested on the quiet morning streets. Nienna had always enjoyed this hour of the day; a calmness would hug civilization in the early hours of the morning. It was as if the worries of the world had yet to awaken. Waiting to arise with the citizens of the city, who had retreated to the safe haven of unconsciousness during the night and had yet to emerge. Not to mention, mornings meant no crowds. Zarou could cause such a stir in a crowd, and Nienna didn't wish to entertain folks at the moment.

Despite the fact that all the city's inhabitants had yet to crowd the streets, there were still signs of life, unlike the abandoned Oasis. Smoke was beginning to rise from chimneys throughout the many elegantly erected white and black stone houses. The scent of burning wood ovens wafted through the air, carried on slight breezes that swept past Nienna, cooling the exposed flesh of her sores that still burned with each step. Sounds of mothers waking husbands and shouting children, still too naïve to dread the day, flowed from open windows through billowing curtains.

The seed of uneasiness in the back of her mind faded amongst the mundane sounds and scents ever-present in established civilization as she walked toward the High Lord's estate. The impressive home of the High Lord was nestled amongst the city's largest buildings at the center of the city. The entire area grounds sat surrounded by a four-foot stone retaining wall. The low structure was not meant to keep the inhabitants of Sandivar from the area within but simply marked the perimeter of the palace and other government buildings built in the estate. The central portion of the city didn't have much in the way of extensive security measures as most everyone in Sandivar knew Lord Sennin had possessed two trained sun dragons. Though they were small by the scale of dragons, they were more than enough of a deterrent to any would-be trespassers from entering unwanted. Be it elf or human, a lone sun dragon, even younglings as Sennin possessed, could tear apart legions with ease.

Within the walled square, two prominent structures were built with an elegance beyond the others. The more domineering of the two sat in the center of the square. A large building with eight spiraling columns of white and black stone common to the region. The base of the building was easily a quarter acre in diameter, and as the building rose, it slowly tapered in until reaching a point easily eclipsing the height of the outer city wall. Ornate stained-glass windows contrasted against the black and white building material that framed precisely sculpted scenes within. Many portrayed detailed images of ancient sand elves and humans who worked together to colonize and settle the desert. There were images of great greenhouses built by human carpenters, elves channeling life magic to help plants root in the loose sandy soil, great sun dragons, and monstrous desert buffalo slain by skilled human and elf hunters.

The sight was truly breathtaking. Nienna had seen the tower many times, but each time, she walked away with more appreciation for the ingenuity and creative thought that went into the construction of the spiraling tower. It was dedicated to the worship of the Gods, specifically to Vitala, who was captured in many images creating and placing various creatures within the desert lands.

Maybe one day I'll retire from death and spend my days studying the arts. Create something beautiful. Zarou wouldn't mind, so long as he could find prey to hunt and sun to rest in.

Behind the tower in the left corner of the square rose a towering four-story palace of solid marble with a black stone tiled roof. The stone was shined and polished to give the home of Lord Sennin a dramatic appeal that matched his boisterous and bold personality. Unlike the cathedral spire, the palace had no stained-glass decoration but rather had intricate ironwork inlaid into clear glass windows. The images here showed the horrors of the Year of Darkness. As you looked from left to right, you could see the progression of the great King Kei-Tel and his conquest over the Dark God Omnes. Kei-Tel was depicted in wonderfully intricate bronze work, looking bold and brilliant against the surrounding scenes of twisted, melded dark iron.

The grounds surrounding the area mirrored the buildings, paved with rough, unfinished white and black stone, creating paths through a sandy floor to connect the various entries between the many buildings that were constructed within the estate's walls. As Nienna strode along the path winding toward the palace, she saw the two sun dragons Sennin possessed lying in the warm sand, soaking in the morning rays. The dragon's shoulders reached the height of Nienna's chest while they lay slumbering. *So massive when so young. Beautiful creatures.*

They were covered in fine white scales, with tan leathery wings folded along their backs resting alongside foot-long spikes running down each beast's spine from the base of their horned skulls all the way to the end of their long tail. Each had four muscular legs as thick as the Mystwood Pine found in the outskirts of the Feyian Forest. Their powerful legs tapered down into oversized feet, evidence they were far from fully grown, perhaps a little over a quarter of their full-grown size, with wide razor-sharp black claws designed to help the beasts move quickly on sand or dig into the sand to lay in waiting underneath. Both dragons were resting their massive heads on the ground, eyes closed, though they seemed to sense her presence, indicated by the tilt of their heads in her direction. Their skulls were thinner and more prolonged than Zarou's, each lined with shorter serrated teeth designed to tear flesh rather than pierce it. Each dragon had different colored eyes; one was a dazzling golden yellow, and the other was a light blue of a clear sky. Nienna could see the jewel-colored eyes open and track her movement as she strode along the path toward the palace. Each dragon tasted the air and, recognizing her scent, continued to lounge while still tracking her movements.

She looked over her shoulder and, to her surprise, did not see Zarou. Looking back toward the dragons, she noticed him stealthily creeping up on the dragons opposite where she stood, ready to pounce. He was out of vision of the dragons, who were solely focused on the passing elf. Once Zarou was within thirty feet of the dragons, he froze, wiggled his hindquarters, tail whipping in anticipation, and then sprang through the air toward the blue-eyed dragon with outstretched arms. He landed on the dragon with a heavy thud, grabbing onto the beast with sheathed claws. Rolling with the momentum of his pounce, Zarou pulled the dragon with him into a savage tangle as he kicked his hind legs at the beast in repetitive strikes. Sand burst up all around them, masking the fight within the torrent of stirred-up dust. The golden-eyed dragon gave Nienna one last look as it stood and stretched, then dove into the tangle of limbs and scales, joining the fray.

Nienna smiled. Not many creatures could rough house with a Sand Lion. "Be careful with them, Zarou! They aren't your match just yet!" As the kicked-up dust cloud settled, Nienna could see Zarou with a dragon pinned beneath each front paw. The great feline laid down purring and began licking the heads of the dragons, who flicked their tails, happy and content beneath her lion's heavy legs. *At the rate they are growing, it won't be much longer before Zarou will be overwhelmed by their power.*

As she continued forward, she saw a group of soldiers in golden and silver-plated armor appear from the front doors of the palace with a frazzled, tall elf dressed in elegant silk robes trailing just behind the armed men. Once Lord Sennin saw the lion purring in the courtyard, snuggled up to his ferocious dragons, the look of anxiety seemed to leave the man. His shoulder relaxed, and he fixed his gaze on the approaching female elf.

"Good day, Lady…" Sennin tapered off, his courtly mannerisms getting ahead of him as he realized he still did not know the name of the elf standing before him. He only knew Nienna as the Ghost and so couldn't complete the title. "I see your cat and the dragons are getting along."

"Yes, it is nice to see Zarou play. I may need to get a dragon of my own to keep him company on our adventures, though I am not sure where I would keep one once it was fully grown," said Nienna as she looked fondly over in the direction of the playing creatures.

"I wasn't expecting you back so soon." He looked over Nienna's disheveled state. "I am glad you're alive. I trust the mission was a success."

"It was," Nienna responded.

"It looks as though you may have a tale to tell... So, you do have the text?" asked Lord Sennin. The skipping of small talk showed that he was very interested in obtaining the ancient scripture.

"It did not go according to plan," Nienna scowled at the lord. "In fact, the Knife was intent on killing me after getting his payment. Seeing as you're the only one to have contacted him before I arrived, I am tempted to think the worst of the situation. It appears you may have paid handsomely for my execution."

The guards exchanged wary glances, hoping they wouldn't have to defend their high lord against the Ghost of Divinoros.

Lord Sennin sighed in exasperation, his face falling from a cordial grin to a deep scowl. "Pray tell, Ghost, why would I do that... and how dare you accuse me of such dishonorable action. You knew the type of man you were dealing with and the dangers associated. You should have thought a man leading the Bankhoft family would try something like this! Any amount of unpreparedness would not fall onto me, Ghost." Sennin said defensively, slightly perturbed that someone would question his unflappable honor. A man of his station was not used to open accusations on his character, but the words appeared genuine, so Nienna decided to let it go. She had survived, and despite the ill-fated turn of the exchange, she didn't honestly believe Sennin had set her up; lack of sleep had worked to shorten her temper.

"Fair enough, Sennin. It was a trying journey. I imagine the tale will shed some light on why your queen has failed to reclaim the ruined lands. Zarou and I succeeded, yes, but we were very nearly killed for our efforts. "She intentionally omitted the man's title to remind him she did not fall under his rule or submit to his authority. She gestured back toward the palace, "Let us walk. I have retrieved what you want, but I doubt you wish to discuss it in the open despite the city being largely asleep."

The agitated expression faded from the lord's face, and he turned in the direction of the palace. "Yes, let us move to my study. Will Zarou be okay in the yard?"

"Yes, it will be good for him to play with others who can bear that beating. It is not every day that we run into a friendly beast like these two. Your dragons are truly magnificent creatures," Nienna said fondly, looking in the direction of the wrestling monsters.

Smiling at the kind remark, Sennin steered Nienna into the palace.

Once inside, Lord Sennin twisted his fingers, creating an open palm as if holding a bowl by his fingertips, and multiple ember orbs sprang from his hand, soaring down a dark hallway to ignite the lamps laid out along the palace's walls. Nienna had heard that Sennin was a capable power mage, a direct descendant of the Deuseleya house, the first of the elves gifted power magic. It amused Nienna that he lacked the seriousness that most wielders of the strange art seemed to possess.

He was known to be a light-hearted man, but tales of his skill with the power placed him as one of the most formidable combat mages in the modern era, and she knew his focus was on fire control. This was on display by his mastery over multiple small orbs—each bulb a mass of potential energy ready to burst at the slightest loss in mental focus. He wielded it with expert precision while carrying on their conversation.

Nienna recalled the other magi she had come across. Power mages were often flagrant and destructive with their control over fire and lightning. Life mages were the most valued by people in her line of work, and she knew one in every major city to heal various ailments and wounds she often accrued. The other branch of life, magi, an exceedingly rare breed, could also gain dominion over water, making them valuable in a variety of industries, especially in desert regions like Sandivar. Then there were the mind magi, the thought weavers, who Nienna feared most as they could break into your mind and steal information, even leave behind fictitious memories if you were not trained to defend against them. They were known to force people into insanity with a whisper.

The palace's opulent interior soon pulled Nienna from her thoughts, its meticulously crafted details demanding her full attention. Masterfully painted frescos covered entire walls framed by elegant molding. The walls of the hall were lined with pedestals housing treasures of war passed down through the ages: display swords, spears, sculptures, along with countless other priceless artifacts procured from all over Divinoros. While Nienna knew the lord's reputation as a skilled mage, she had no idea he was a passionate collector of priceless artifacts.

"You have a beautiful collection here, Sennin. I am surprised you would want some old parchment from a known elf killer to display in the same halls that hold such fine art and weaponry," Nienna commented, still taking in the surrounding scenery.

The corner of Lord Sennin's lips curled to smile, and he bowed his head, genuinely proud of his collection. "You are kind," he said, stopping in front of a silver glaive with images embroidering the staff leading up to a dulled, bent blade. "This was the weapon wielded by Queen Celestra, an old childhood friend of mine, before she was bestowed the glaive wielded by Kei-Tel when she took the throne in his place. This weapon was used to slay countless creatures released by Omnes—krakenshi, serpents, and hosts of others our armies encountered as the elves' marched on the Rift." He ran a finger down the shaft of the weapon, admiring its beauty.

"I find the stories an old piece of metal, or piece of cloth, can tell fascinating. Objects are imbued with history should we choose to listen.

This weapon helped free all life on earth from an inevitable fate of annihilation. Many of the items you see in this hall have helped to build a foundation for elvish rule throughout Divinoros. In establishing rule over humans and leaving dwarves to their hideouts in the north, the queen established the longest period of peace we have seen in this world. Well, the longest period of peace since the years after the First War, at least. You see, this weapon, as well as all the other items in my collection, has a story that played some integral part in shaping our world, our society, and our culture. The importance of them now rests with me, and I am always ready to tell their stories for them." Lord Sennin spoke proudly as he gestured openly around the displayed items.

He continued forward and turned into an open door leading to a grand study, all the while lighting more torches with brilliantly colored orbs of flame sent from his palm. Lord Sennin gestured to a seat, and Nienna obliged, happy to relax in a comfortable chair after nearly a week in the desert. She collapsed into the luxurious chair, disregarding the blood and dirt caked to her clothes, unconcerned with the crime both would commit against the royal fabric.

Sennin seemed not to notice as he continued in his self-important monologue. "But what I find most interesting of all, as it pertains to the Year of Darkness, is that even after our victory, we have no insight into *how* humans tapped into the power of a God. None of my trinkets out there have clued me into this. *How* did humans release the force of a deity onto our land? We may have won a battle, but Gods are infinite. To Omnes, this may just be the start of his war on us. The Shroud still clings above the Rift, and it seems to me we are just waiting for the second coming. With our lack of knowledge of how Omnes was released or how to disband it, it seems like that power is still just hanging out there for someone to seize. The knowledge of how a God could be released was discovered in ancient times, but it is somehow lost to us now! And it was found by humans, no less! This knowledge, I believe, must be stored *somewhere*. And we… elves, that is, the superior species holding peace and order together in this world, have been okay with being left in the dark on this matter. Have been okay with a dormant power festering in the dark reaches of Divinoros. Like all wounds, festering will eventually spread. The scripture you obtained may change *everything*. It may be the key to our understanding."

"So, you are hoping to learn about how humans have tapped into Omnes's power. Why?" Nienna asked, raising an eyebrow and stiffening in her chair. "Do you really wish to repeat mistakes of the past? This is nothing we should be tampering with."

Sennin raised a finger in protest."Just the opposite. I want to ensure that never happens again and to avoid the mistakes of one's past, you must begin with an understanding of the events that caused it. And Lady, ummm..." He again paused awkwardly, waiting for Nienna to provide him with a name to call her by. She gave none. Forging ahead, the high lord continued, "I have received this." Sennin grasped a rolled parchment from the large, shined rosewood desk supported by delicate Ivory leg posts. He thrust the sheet before her. "A letter from Queen Celestra herself. I have known her since we were children, I believe I mentioned, and as such, she is more, shall we say, liberal with sharing her concerns with me than some of the other nobles. Take it. Read it. I don't share this lightly." He shook the parchment again until Nienna sighed and took the paper.

Sennin,

Reports have begun trickling in from Gradishar. The most recent news is that there have been brutal killings north of the city's outer walls. While the initial killings were restricted to children, more adult deaths have been reported since. There have been no sightings of any creature or man, elf or otherwise, near the killing sights. As such, I have few leads in tracking the cause of these murders. To date, a total of ten, half of which had been elves, were found dead in various areas on the border of the Ice Cap and Grassland regions. A large group was sent to search for the children the night after the initial disappearances, only to be found dead as well.

Initial scouts sent to report on the findings have only found remains and brutal kill sites. It was described as walking into a dragon den, just that, in this case, the meat was left on the bones to rot. The deaths were not for food but sport, it would appear. There are predators in the area that could have easily killed a large group of humans and elves; the ice-backs in this region do not typically seek contact with human or elfkind, preferring the frozen peaks to the lower altitudes we've settled, and we haven't seen any ice dragons in the area for over a century. Other predators like pantera's could not have been responsible. They would have eaten their kill.

I tell you this detail to raise the importance of my next statement. I believe I know what is responsible for these killings. Everything related to the wounds found and the savagery of the kill site... I cannot help but think of the beings of power we fought so long ago. Omnes must have returned, perhaps only in part. Despite my suspicions, Lord Niall has not sent word of any disturbances at the Shroud, so I do not know how this could be or where the creatures are coming from.

Even if I believe Omnes may have returned, my knowledge sorely lacks in regard to how such a power could have ever been released and if it is possible to seal him away for good. If the Dark God returns... If he returns... I fear the dominion of the elves will collapse under his might.

What I am about to say, I tell in confidence, I expect this to be burnt after you read it.

Two things remained in our world when Kei-Tel tackled the Obsidian Knight into the Rift. I will not divulge what, but I believe those items must be tying Omne's power to Divinoros, though, of course, this is all just theory.

After Kei-Tel fell, I sent scouts to all human cities for one purpose: gathering up all scripture used by the ancient humans. I burned a vast majority of the scrollwork and books collected out of fear of a second coming. Out of fear that a fool hearty human would seek to again attempt to balance the power discrepancy between our races. Living as long as I have, I think this may have been my first failing as queen of our people... No one person should be individually responsible for the destruction of knowledge. I did keep the original holy text found in the Dark Hall of ancient Stone Guard, thinking it may one day be needed.

Before our armies forced back the Dark God's army, the scourge had reached all corners of Divinoros, all except the deserts of the Sandivar region. The Oasis was flourishing at the time before their fall, and being in the deepest regions of the desert, I sent the book there for safekeeping. Perhaps my second greatest failing.

Old friend, I know I ask much, but I need you to broker a deal with the Bankhoft family, who is now holding the ancient ruins of our desert gem. Reclaim the book and have the text transported to me in Turenian. Your service will be rewarded.

Dearest friend - Queen Celestra

"Why would you let me read this? This is clearly intended only for your eyes alone," said Nienna. She looked up from the letter, handing the page back to the High Lord, who immediately, without a word, set the page aflame in his fingers.

"Because I have another request to ask of you. The attacks in the North are not secrets. I have also received reports of attacks and raids sparking up north of Stone Guard City in surrounding villages between there and the Marbled Caverns. Not all monsters of mystery; many of these violent acts are simply people preying on the weak. But this is a signal of discord in our world, a signal of *something* stirring beneath the surface wishing to cause dissent and disorder. People are beginning to question the Queen's hold on Divinoros. The land can seem to sense impending change. What that change will be, we do not yet know, but the roads have grown dangerous. It has been some time since we have received transit through the Narrows, so I seek the help, the services, of someone highly capable of completing the remainder of my transaction with Her Majesty."

Nienna held the lord's eye. She knew where this was going and sighed loudly. "I am no delivery girl, and I am not yours to order about, *High Lord* Sennin," she said, dragging out his title in a slightly mocking tone.

Sennin held up his hands in a placating gesture. "I know you are not in my command, which is why I gave you the context of the queen's letter. But I do ask you to escort a team of my soldiers, Elites, to Turenian. I fear the roads between have become unruly, and while my Elites are more than capable, they lack your subtlety, and I must ensure the success of this delivery."

While she did plan to leave the desert, she did not like the idea of being slowed by a team of Sennin's soldiers. "Why would I need your team? Even if I were inclined to agree, they would only slow me down."

"They will not slow you. I have a team of three of my Elites selected for the mission—each gifted a pure-blood Sandshari. Even the lion could not outpace those horses."

Nienna was impressed. Sandshari were uncommon. The wild desert horses were known for their speed, stamina, and famously wild temperament. Breaking a Sandshari was no small feat. Typically, only the political elite possessed the cash to be able to employ the teams needed to even attempt to break a Sandshari into riding temperament. Those influential people who succeeded in the daunting feat, not to mention the costly feat, would keep the horse for their own. Not many animals could keep up, much less outpace a fully grown Sand Lion, but she knew these horses to be a rare exception to that general rule. Each is worth a small fiefdom. Nienna was interested.

"What would be in it for me?"

Sennin smiled, knowing he had captured her full attention and nearly her service. He scratched gently at his chin as if contemplating, "Well, you would be in favor of the high lord of Sandivar City. Behind the queen, few possess the influence I do throughout Turenian. In addition to that, I will offer you this writ of protection stamped with my seal. No lord nor lady will be able to deny you access to their city or township. I know you possess the skill to sneak in wherever you would like, but this could save you time and headaches. Not to mention, if you were ever to be in any trouble, you can present this to any Turenian soldier, and they will not refuse your request." A corner of his mouth raised to a knowing smile, "I imagine one in your profession could find great use of a gift intended to open doors and turn away questions."

Nienna blinked in thought. This was a good deal... The trip to Turenian would likely only be four weeks, given the speed and endurance possessed by Sandshari mounts and Zarou. Still, there would be a high likelihood of encountering bandits along the path, not to mention this whole business of discord in the Narrows. In theory, all but the most extreme threats would prove no more than a minor nuisance to her and three Elites. The main thing that unnerved her was being in the company of the three elves. She was uncomfortable being in the presence of others, much preferring solidarity on her travels. Few knew who she really was, and a month of travel without the willingness to open up could prove uncomfortable.

Not to mention, these warriors were regarded as some of the fiercest in the kingdom. She was unsure if even she possessed the ability to defeat them at once should they all choose to, or be ordered to, turn on her. She thought that would be unlikely, however, as Sennin likely would have paid the Knife to kill her rather than the soldiers of his armies if he intended to see her dead. And that opportunity had come and gone. "I accept. But before I go, I would like to bathe. And I need you to send me a tailor. These are rather," she gestured to her worn and red-stained garb. "Well, rather bloody."

Lord Sennin smiled and handed Nienna back the book she had just fled the Badlands with. "You have a deal, Ghost."

Baelin - Chapter 10 - Hopeful Beginnings

Baelin set the small, worn book on the table before him. Based on the inscriptions on the inner cover, he believed this text to be a journal kept by foot soldier Durenthi Bari in the elvish army in the period Kei-Tel warred with Omnes. His curiosity was instantly piqued, and he dove into the pages.

Today, we will depart from the eastern shores of Turenian. I have never seen such a mighty elven force. Ahh, the magnificence of it is something to behold. Nearly seventy thousand men and women departed from Turenian to Reef Ridge Port. The port in Turenian was filled with several grandiose three-mast battleships alongside a full armada of smaller, faster skiffs. All nodded slowly up and down within the tempered harbor. The rolling water sent the vessels into a symphony of gentle bumping and sloshing. The docks were full of boats, men, beasts, and gear awaiting our glorious victory, our swift defeat over an imperial might. We sat awaiting our quickly approaching destiny.

The scene must have looked like an ant colony to the sea birds that began to congregate above the commotion. Men and women formed ranks, boarding their assigned vessels for the three-week-long sail across the Aeronian Straight and down the coast of Western Divinoros with machine-like efficiency—a testament to our great King's insistence on drilling during times of peace. "Peace is the great enemy of any people. The masses become placated, pacified by stillness, and when that stillness is shattered, only our never-ending diligence will save them," Kei would voice to his army during their long training hours, long before any threat was levied upon our world.

Three weeks at sea... How much time we'd save if we could simply sail through the cursed isles? We'd be able to cut our trip by a week! But, it is not to be, and I rather look forward to the tranquil sea air before we descend into battle. This will be the first war waged in thousands of years!

I was slated to be in the final group to board, so I watched as horses and Northern Grassland bulls were loaded into livestock vessels. The campaign north would not be an easy trip, we were told. The animals would be needed to carry supplies, and based on reports describing the monster's sizes, King Kei-Tel determined we would need as many cavalry horses as we could muster.

From what I have seen gathered here, I can imagine no force conjured in Divinoros that could bear the full might of Turenian, the full might of Kei-Tel. I have heard tales of the time before elves when

dragons and demons battled for control of this world. But in the face of
a force such as this? I doubt even those titans of old could withstand our
might amassed as it is today!

Given the well-trained military, loading boats took most of the
morning, and we set sail behind the King's vessel just after the mid-day
hour.

Sitting aboard the deck to enjoy the last few moments of peace
before war has given me time to reflect....

Baelin flipped forward in the journal. He was looking for more
information and didn't care to read the many poems and sonnets
describing the fleet, ocean, and everything else that Durenthi had laid
his eyes on as they sailed. The old dwarf grumbled about the "soft,
dainty fairy folk" as he flipped forward by a few pages.

Day 19. We arrived ahead of schedule and deboarded our ships
early in the morning. The trip was long, and it was good to see land once
again, a distant visage promising a solid surface beneath my feet. After
deboarding, though... The unearned arrogance of our mighty force was
deflated before a blade sank into flesh. My excitement for the coming
war blinked out. I wished and longed to be back aboard the confines of
my vessel, heading home to my dearest Clariana. The entire port of the
once grand human city, Reef Ridge Port, had been deserted, or so we
thought from afar. The first sign something was wrong was the smell. A
smell that grew as we approached, but none of us could have guessed
the horrors that awaited us ashore.

Pulling into the port, we could see broken masts and shattered hulls
of human warships that had once been the pride of these seafaring
peoples. Rotting, brutalized corpses were scattered across the docks
amongst shredded banners hung from cracked flag poles. Pale bodies,
bloated with sea water, bobbed lifelessly in port. The beach we initially
thought to be mounds of pebbles, but as we neared, those pebbles moved,
and the pebbles became crabs swarming about a field of bodies picking
at the unmoving flesh, with little care if it once belonged to a soldier,
fleeing woman, or a newborn babe disassembled limb from limb...

Despite myself, I heaved violently. I wasn't the only one amongst us
to do so. Based on the smell, this massacre must have been a few days,
if not a week, before we docked. As the realization of the scene
broadened amongst our ranks, an eerie silence settled over all. The port
felt haunted. Haunted by the atrocities that could leave such wreckage
behind. Life was mercilessly slaughtered as it fled an unknown horror.

I have seen death before. I have been a part of small battles and
seen people skewered, bleeding, and dying on the battlefield. This was
different. There was no fight, and these people were not soldiers. As we
approached, the blanket of crustaceans scurried back beneath the
surface of the sand, revealing the full horror of what we sailed into.

Tears streamed down my face and my hands trembled. What I saw...
was genocide, indiscriminatory murder. Heartbreaking scenes of
mothers with their backs clawed through to their fronts, only to reveal
the lifeless children they had tried to shield with futility from the
monsters that attacked them. Monsters that ripped their way through
their bodies to ensure nothing was left alive. Whatever we faced, all
dreams of swift victory faded into night terrors of violent, thorough
defeat.

My thoughts drifted once again to my dear Clariana, to our newborn
babe. My confidence, so brazen just weeks before, now wavered. And, it
was not just me who wavered. Fear rippled through seventy thousand as
if the sea winds were promising us certain death. As the ships docked
and the carnage was witnessed by all, a foreboding silence gripped us.
But it was more than a simple absence of talking. No gulls or carrion
birds cawed or picked at the dead. It was as if they, too, were afraid of
whatever killed these people. That they would rather stay away from a
large meal than allow their cawing to draw those beasts' ire unto
themselves.

Unsurprisingly, the deboarding process took much longer than the
loading. The horses, while well trained, sensed evil onshore and refused
to leave the livestock ships. Our mind mages were forced to assist the
handlers, soothing the beasts by speaking directly into their minds. The
remainder of us, without assigned tasks, worked to clean up the carnage.
We were not ordered so, but what else can one do when encountering
such an atrocity. Our only intent was to offer what little peace we could
to the poor souls who had died trying to flee whatever descended upon
them.

It felt wrong to leave hundreds, maybe thousands, of corpses out in
the open, so ten large pyres were built along the shore due west of the
harbor. We piled the bodies on the pyres and burned them, sending their
ashes skyward, back to the Gods. I can only hope their spirits were
released with the smoke and ash that drifted in the ocean breeze.

Once we had the beach cleared, our battalions put in formation, and
the bulls burdened with the campaign supplies, scouts were sent from
the harbor to the main city. Upon their return, they reported no activity.
There was only more of the same. Scattered remains of humans with
bloody entrails spewing from open bellies now swollen with rot.
Hundreds more lay dead in the streets, faces frozen in their final pained
expression before death finally allowed their escape. With the scout's
report, King Kei-Tel ordered his army to march into the city to make
camp for the night. He should have known not to camp amongst the dead.

The going was slow, slower than the King would have pleased, but
it couldn't be helped. Bodies littered the paved streets, clogging
passageways. We needed to clear the way ahead of our heavy carts so

they and the beasts of burden could pass through. Despite the slow pace, we continued toward the city's center, looking for a defensible position.

No one would mistake Reef Ridge for any of the great elven cities, but it was expansive. Small mud brick homes with thatch roofs were built in what appeared to be an organized gridlock pattern. Streets generally seemed to lead directly from the port to the city's capitol building and central square. Smaller side streets and alleys broke off the main road, cutting through rows of houses and shops just wide enough for two elves to pass by in opposite directions.

Many of the houses we passed were partially collapsed, broken, contorted bodies of people who once inhabited them crushed underneath. The sight of limbs bent at unnatural angles and torn flesh did a number on many of our ranks. I can't honestly say I fared better. My stomach was soon lighter after the contents of the morning's meal were forced up, but even with my stomach empty, still my nausea refused to abate.

Despite the abhorrence of the environment, I took in as much detail as I could. The ground was littered with large claw marks grated deep into the cobblestone streets and walls of the buildings. I did not know what these could belong to. No animals in the area possessed such size. I'd spent my youth hunting, and the impressions that the creatures left behind seemed to indicate a monster as large as our biggest cavalry horses. Dragons were nearly extinct, Sand Lions not far behind them, and neither of the species had a presence in the area...

I wish we would have camped outside the city. I could feel the place whispering our doom. The men felt the same. I understand the king sought fortification, but if he had only allowed us to camp in the grasslands north of the city... Well, then maybe more of his army would have lived through the first night... No one needs to be taught that lesson, I thought. We just know. One should never sleep amongst the dead lest you welcome your doom.

The king and his generals set up a command center in the capitol building after my troop leader took our contingent in to clear the building and surrounding homes. I do not wish to describe how we found the human ruler and his family, but nothing living waited in surprise within the once beautiful home.

The other high-ranking officers and commanders set up tents within the central square and began planning out the camp stations and scouting shifts. The remainder of the soldiers scouted buildings closest to the city square while others worked to drag broken wagons and merchant stands to form barricades along the outermost perimeter of the encampment. This effectively walled the capitol buildings, city square, and maybe a hundred or so smaller buildings in the immediate surrounding area. A sense of security fell over the army, and soon

64

chatter and conversation buzzed in the air, even the occasional laughter, though that still felt misplaced when it landed on my ears.

Then the night came, enveloping the army in darkness, the deep black of a starless night. I remember glancing at the sky, hoping for the silver shine of the moon, but clouds hid any possibility of light sneaking through. The atmosphere within the army was filled with tension that night.

I was on first-guard duty in the northwest quadrant. Since I had not been asleep, I heard the screams as soon as they started. They seemed distant, coming from the opposite end of the camp. I was atop a thatched roof mud home, thinking the height would afford a better vantage point. But as I said, the night was cloudy, and I was unable to make out any movement as I stared in the direction of the sound.

With my attention no longer on the perimeter, something that must have been lurking in the darkness just beyond our barricade struck. I felt a rush of air and heard an ear-splitting screech as something seemed to materialize from the cover of darkness.

As I turned, I saw six burning orbs, but before I could make out the monster the eyes belonged to, I was hit in the center of my chest with such force that I was lifted off my feet and propelled over two houses before impacting the wall of the third. The blow knocked the wind out of my chest, and when I opened my mouth to scream in warning to my sleeping companions, no sound came out. I began to panic as I heard the crawling legs of something large climbing over the mud thatch homes...

My heart raced, and tears welled up in my eyes as I wailed silently, trying, despite the pain in my chest, to warm my brothers and sisters in my arms. But before I was able to shout in warning, screams that were not my own, the screams of sudden and pain-filled death erupted all around me. These crawling monsters with glowing red eyes kept their forms hidden in the dark night, rendering them nearly invisible, nearly unstoppable. Hundreds poured over our quadrant, slaughtering elves before they could even wake to defend themselves. Slaughtering the people sleeping silently or stirring from their pleasant dreams, knowing I sat guard to keep them safe...

I joined the fray as quickly as I could. I found stragglers and formed up a unit, and we limped through the streets, slaying monsters if we could and helping any wounded who were mobile. I... We... We left so many behind to die as we retreated toward our king's central location. The whites of the eyes of the dying, wide with fear, the murmurs for mercy, the pleas for help... They haunt me when I close my eyes.

The attack lasted less than a quarter-hour, but so much damage was wrought in that short time... I thought writing out the details may help, but I am not ready to describe these events... Maybe another day... What

I will say is we lost over five thousand of our numbers that night, and at least another five thousand were injured only to die within the week. My confidence has been shaken. Where I thought our forces invincible, I now do not know if we can survive the week.

Baelin sighed and leaned back as he pushed the book away from himself. He had read historical accounts of the great war waged on the Dark God by the great elf King Kei-Tel. He had read recorded accounts from survivors of the great war. Queen Celestra herself was there. But something about this detailed first-hand account had shaken the aged dwarf. He had a sudden urge to gather a few more mage lamps to line the dimly lit corridor of the Archives he had settled in. "Ahhhh, quit being so jumpy. It's just an old story," Baelin muttered under his white beard. He pulled the book back toward himself and continued to read.

Ryker - Chapter 11 - The Path Forward

Aegnor had, as promised, shown up to the Marriock farm with the rising sun. A fact more than a little disappointing for the young apprentice given the fact he failed to avoid imbibing a plethora of sweet ale at Declan's insistence the night before. At a sharp rapping at the door, Ryker jolted from his rather unrestful night of sleep in the living room. Quickly standing, Ryker attempted to rub the sleep out of his eyes as he stumbled toward the worn front door.

Ayden couldn't have waited just one more night to take my bed.... could have used a nice mattress last night, Ryker thought to himself.

The aged wooden door groaned on its rusty hinges as it swung open, revealing Aegnor dressed in his travel attire. His clothes were not overly flashy, as one might expect from someone so revered, but it was clearly constructed of fine material and free of even the slightest stain or wrinkle. Over his dark tunic, just visible underneath the charcoal cloak, Ryker could make out a thin, dark-stained leather chest plate along with at least four weapons on his mentor's person. The elf had a hand-and-a-half sword strapped to his hip and a long dagger secured to his upper leg. Across his back, Ryker could make out the hilt of a large two-handed sword exposing its hilt behind the man's left pointed ear, and finally, the beautifully ornate glaive that had bested Ryker the previous day was also secured to the dark warrior's back angled behind his right ear.

The sun's barely crested the hills, and this man looks ready to attack an army.

The apprentice bowed, struggling to keep down the bile in his stomach as the movement set off waves of nausea, sending the world spinning with the slight down and up motion. Gathering his breath, Ryker barely choked out, "Master, I have a travel sack prepared. I will say farewell to my brothers, and then we can be off."

Aegnor stared at the apprentice, unamused with the state of his evidently hungover mentee. "Very well. But speak with them quickly. We must arrive in Ravenford by the week's end."

Ryker furrowed his brows, puzzled by the comment. Ravenford was only a three, maybe four, day ride due north. The two should make it with time to still spare, but he did not wish to question Aegnor, at least not before his training even began, especially with his head feeling like it was being chiseled from the inside.

Turning back to the interior of the house, he saw that Declan and Ayden had already begun to descend the stairs, woken by the noise on the main floor of their home.

Declan smiled ear to ear and grasped Ryker's forearm. "Thought I heard you stirring, little brother! You look fit for travel..." he chuckled, looking at the pained expression on the face of his younger brother. Declan's expression sobered. "We will miss you, Ryker. Travel well, travel safe. You will always have a home here with us. If you ever wish to return, you know that you are always welcome. Even Father eventually got tired of fighting."

Tears rimmed the older brother's eyes, knowing all too well it may be years before they were reunited once again. Knowing that Aegnor would undoubtedly be leading the young man into unknown dangers.

The young apprentice pulled his older brother into a hug. "This will always be home Dec. Even after Mother and Father left, you ensured it was. I will return here as often as I can."

As soon as the two separated, Ayden rushed in to hug his older brother around the waist, tears streaming down his tired face.

Ryker gripped his younger brother by both shoulders and knelt to look at the boy's face. "Dec is going to take care of you while I am gone. But remember," the young apprentice said with a wink. "You're the best swordsman in the house with me leaving… make sure you keep practicing for me. I will test you when I am home. Maybe even force Dec into a few sparring matches if you can. You're going to have to protect the house with me gone."

Ryker stood as his youngest brother nodded at his words but stayed silent, worried that speaking might bring a fresh bout of tears. "And remember this, Ayden: I am traveling the world with the most skilled warrior on Divinoros. When I return, I will have many grand adventures to tell you of."

The young boy's sadness was immediately revered at the comment. Ayden smiled broadly, and with his eyes still puffy, Ayden said, "You better bring me a dragon scale or something for all the extra work I'll be doing now that you're gone… You at least owe me that!"

Ryker laughed and ruffled the boy's hair. "I will write to both of you if I am able. And until I see you again, may the Gods smile upon you."

With that, the apprentice turned and grabbed his travel sack and sword. After eighteen years, he found himself without a concrete plan to return to his family's farm, and that thought brought a touch of sorrow that weighed on his heart as he strode out the door. But as the warm rays of the sun cut through the cool air outside, it brought a fresh rush of excitement at what was to come. Such pure energy that even the lingering traces of the hangover from the previous night's festivities slowly faded away.

Aegnor stood a couple of paces from the door frame, gazing over the forests stretching north. He stood there like a vigilant guardian, an unwavering sentinel, surveying the vast, sprawling forest from the Marriock farm to Stone Guard and beyond. His very presence seemed to offer solace to the great forest's inhabitants that no looming threat could break the tranquility of this place.

"You have a beautiful home," said the elf, sensing the apprentice approach.

"I do," Ryker affirmed, looking out over the cleared farmland to the rolling forest beyond. A tightness continued to grip his chest. He would miss this place, but one day, he intended to return. He took a deep breath and exhaled forcefully to loosen the tension he felt before turning to his master and saying, "Well... Let us be off then."

Without a word, the silver-eyed elf hefted his pack and started walking at a brisk pace North toward Ravenford on a path that traveled around the city. Ryker found this unexpected, and his emotions swiftly shifted from sadness and excitement to a sudden sense of dread. "Master, do you have horses tethered nearby? I assumed we would need to head into Stone Guard to retrieve mounts from the stables," questioned Ryker as he quickened to keep pace with the elves' long stride.

"We will be traveling by foot. Do not fall too far behind," he stated flatly, and he started to run.

Ryker's jaw went slack. "We're going to run?" he shouted after the bounding elf. The elf was quickly separating from the apprentice, so with a groan of frustration, Ryker bound after the flowing silver hair that was rapidly gaining distance on him. The only thing that crossed his mind was a string of curses so foul his mother would feint if she heard them.

Stone Guard and Ravenford often traded, so the path between the city and town was well maintained. Despite the quality road conditions, after an hour, Ryker's knees began to ache, his head began to throb, and a sharp pain stabbed at his side. He had run before, but never more than a couple miles at a time. Not one of those instances required him to carry a travel sack or a sword. It was clear his conditioning would need improvement, a realization that Ryker was reluctant to admit in just the first moments of his journey.

As the sun rose, so did the number of travelers carrying freight between the two centers of civilization. Many were simple merchants walking alongside mule-pulled carts. Some had fresh harvests of various fruits and vegetables piled high, but most impressive was the livestock carriage of a single-spirited Ravanian steed in transport to the capital of Western Divinoros. Each group he passed looked toward the young man quizzically. Some openly called out taunts, "Should've brought your horse, eh boy!" or some other comment as they laughed at the sweaty, loping man.

Ryker ignored all glances from the more comfortable travelers, only able to focus on his next step. *Left. Right. Left. Right.* Another hour passed by in a pain-filled blur of steady movement, his only stops to vomit bile, and once his stomach was empty to heave without any seeming purpose. *Damn hangovers*. Thankfully, as he rounded a bend in the road, he saw Aegnor sitting on a large rock, two plates set out before him.

Ryker stumbled up to the spot Aegnor found in the shade. "I'm impressed. I would have thought you were further behind. Sit. Eat. We have made good progress this morning," the warrior said, motioning to the plate to his right.

Ryker collapsed ungracefully into a heap on the dirt, allowing the weight of his travel sack to pull him heavily into the solid ground. Breathing heavily, he rolled over to pull off his travel sack, allowing the slight breeze to cool his sweat-soaked back. Before he could even think to say a word, he retrieved his waterskin and took a long pull to soothe his dry, bleeding throat. He could taste the iron in his mouth as he coughed before washing away the taste of blood with more water.

The apprentice pushed himself back to his feet and walked over to grab the plate of salted meat, butter, and bread Aegnor had prepared before sitting back down to catch his breath. The apprentice looked to where his master sat, seemingly unphased by the two-hour run they had just completed. "Why," gasp, "did we," gasp, "not just get some," gasp, "some damn horses," gasp "from the stables in Stone Guard?" he finally got out.

Aegnor looked at him with discerning liquid silver eyes. "Because where we are going, what we will be doing, I think it's likely we will need more than *just* a horse. We will need Ravanian steeds bred by Cyrus. And these are only available in one place, Ravenford. I did not wish to buy horses twice. Plus," Aegnor lifted his nose toward the slouched man still panting between breaths, "You need the exercise, it would seem."

Ryker huffed at the comment, in disbelief that Aegnor would have the pair run nearly a hundred miles in just a few days' time carrying full travel gear because the elf thought he needed exercise.

"You disagree?" asked Aegnor, raising his brow.

"Well…" Ryker hesitated, not wanting to contradict the tutelage of Aegnor the Great on his first day of apprenticeship, "Maybe a bit… I mean, no offense, but why would a soldier need to run a marathon? Ever? I have worked on a farm for eighteen years… you would be hard-pressed to find a man in Stone Guard with more physical ability than me. I think we could have found… more efficient means of transportation is all. Plus, well, Gods I hate running," shrugged Ryker.

Aegnor tilted his head, acknowledging the point. "Then consider this your first lesson. Where we go and what I train you for is not the life of a common soldier, not to fight against humans. You will be opposing superior beings, beings of immense power that currently best

70

you in nearly every way imaginable: they will have better strength, speed, stamina, and discipline. Some, most even, will be far smarter than you, not to mention more experienced in killing, by decades if not centuries. I picked you as my apprentice because you showed ingenuity and creativity. A willingness to absorb the details of your situation and adapt strategy when fighting an opponent far beyond your current skill level. This will forever be your greatest advantage over the powers we face, but it's a far cry from being sufficient to cover the gaps I just mentioned. So, I intend to help you close the vast chasm in talent that currently exists in the areas of physical and mental ability." He paused to ensure Ryker understood the gravity of the situation he was now in before continuing.

"Hence the run. Not only are you gaining much-needed conditioning, and believe me, boy, you need much of it, but just as importantly, the upcoming days will push your mind to the point of breaking. Of wanting to quit and crawl your way back to your safe little farm. I am curious to see if you give in before we even truly begin. I will require you to push yourself well beyond what you believe to be within your current capabilities. I can see the potential, but potential means nothing if you do not possess the mental fortitude to harness it and bring it to fruition."

Ryker furrowed his brow, shocked by the thoroughness and thoughtfulness in Aegnor's response to his simple complaint. "Yeah, I get all that, and you are right." Ryker paused and eyed Aegnor before muttering, "But no matter how good my conditioning gets, I will always hate running. It's a sport for the long-legged elves, not humans."

He ultimately agreed with the elf's disposition. Still, Ryker had always appreciated a healthy dose of innocent complaining as an outlet to the strains of manual labor. It was commonplace on the farm among the brothers and other laborers. He would need to be more careful about commenting without enough thought in the future, especially if he meant to question Aegnor's decisions. But luckily, the elf seemed to show some amusement at the young man's outlook.

Aegnor's gaze softened slightly, and as if reading Ryker's thoughts, "You are not wrong to question, and I will never admonish you for expressing doubts or questioning a lack of reason in anything we do. I have lived many of your lifetimes. Critical thinking and questioning authority are important. Every great kingdom and empire has fallen once its individuals lose the ability or desire to think for themselves. Once that happens, atrocities can be waged, genocides committed, and civilization stripped down until an entire culture collapses. I have seen it. That said, at this point in time I am your better. So, question me regularly, but ensure you learn from my responses."

71

Ryker nodded, and the pair continued to eat in silence. "Where are we going?" asked Ryker, changing the subject. He ate now that his breath returned to a normal cadence.

"To see an old friend in the Marbled Caverns. I seek information on the great war waged by Omnes a millennium ago. He has been investigating the matter over the last two hundred or so years."

Excitement welled within the young man at the mention of the Marbled Caverns. He had heard stories detailing the grandeur of the dwarven stronghold but never imagined in his wildest dreams he would set foot within their hollowed mountain fortress. "We are on a mission from Queen Celestra, then?"

The corner of the elf's mouth twitched at this. "No, not quite. The queen and I have a, shall we call it, an understanding... She is allowed to portray to the world that I am her most valued secret agent doing her bidding across Divinoros. The reality is quite different. I am more of a freelancer, a mercenary with a conscience, or perhaps I could be considered an independent influence across these lands. In return for my imaginary servitude, and as my initiatives and interests generally align with Her Majesty's, she allows me to continue to operate without oversight or hindrance. As long as I continue to feed her pertinent information on her enemies and help to ensure the safety of her people, she will leave me be. It's a mutually beneficial relationship. As you might have guessed, I do not like to have any authority dictating my actions. I choose to do what I do because I believe it is the right thing to do and because oftentimes, I find it easy to profit from the skillset I possess."

"You are not worried about me letting this slip to unwanted ears," questioned Ryker, surprised that the elf would reveal so much about himself to a pupil just recently placed under his guard.

"It would not matter if you told every man and elf in Divinoros. None would believe you. After all, the perception of my actions is far more influential than the words of a man just barely aged into manhood," Aegnor said as he shrugged and packed up the small plates.

"Fair enough. But then, if I don't matter, why train me?" Ryker asked.

Aegnor acted like he did not hear the question as he looked to Ryker and said, "Load up your pack. We will walk the next couple of hours before resuming our run."

Praise the Gods, thought Ryker as he stood on shaky legs and went to re-tie his sword to the top of his travel sack.

Noticing this, Aegnor shook his head. "We head into the dangerous territory after Ravenford. You must carry your weapons in a way that they can be drawn and ready at a moment's notice," he said, pointing to the long sword strapped to his back. "Strap your blade on as such; it's your most valued tool in your new profession. The weight of your sack will hold the sheath in place, but if needed, you can access your sword quickly. You must get used to this despite it being rather uncomfortable."

After the appropriate adjustments were made, the two stood and continued their travels north to Ravenford.

Ryker soon came to learn that with Aegnor, no time would be wasted. A walk turned out to be little more relaxing than the morning run. Aegnor grilled the young man on his knowledge of the major capitals through Divinoros, the landscapes surrounding them, and the natural dangers that persisted within them, along with the political happenings in the Kingdom.

Ryker was surprised to learn that there was political turmoil in many regions of the empire. Prolonged peace had allowed a growing tension to form between prominent house leaders and the Queen. There were also dangerous factions of humans, causing trouble in many major cities. Lord Sennin of Sandivar remained steadfastly loyal to the Queen, but he fought an ever-present uprising from a human crime lord running the Badlands.

Lord Frenir, to Ryker's great surprise, had his sights set on grasping more power in Western Divinoros. Apparently, the High Lord wished to free himself from Queen Celestra's oversight entirely, establishing Stone Guard as a separate monarchy to the west, but Celestra still portrayed too much strength for the wealthier families to back his movement.

"Is that why you were in Stone Guard then, to threaten Frenir?" asked Ryker, astounded at the turbulence within the elite class of elves he had not been privy to.

"Not entirely. I tend to stay out of any government affairs, but it is prudent to remain knowledgeable about the latest happenings throughout the monarchy and the reasons behind any potential treasonous action that may arise in the future. I was there for two reasons. The first reason relates to you. I needed an apprentice. Secondly, as I mentioned, because I am… independent in my loyalties, I like to remind the powerful leaders in this world that no matter how high they rise in affluent communities and in public perception, I can always reach them. Regardless of who is in power in any given region, I remain free from any one man's, or woman's, grasp. The night before your trial, I surprised the High Lord with my presence in his chambers. Despite the fact he has been positioning an elevated guard for fear of Celestra reacting to some of his power-grabbing plans with force or assassination."

Ryker looked at the silver-haired man in awe. He had seen the fortifications Lord Frenir kept in place. He was genuinely impressed with his master's skill. He had heard of the grand combat feats of Aegnor

73

the Great, the monsters he had slain. How he had been able to kill hundreds of combatants single-handedly ending various uprisings over the past eight hundred years, picking apart frenzied dragons that fled the Drakkonian Isles with a death of a thousand cuts, even killing Kedri the Dark Elf after his brief reign of terror stemming from the outskirt Cursed Islands in the Aeronian Straight. But he had no idea Aegnor possessed such subtle skill that would be required of one breaking into a high lord's quarters unnoticed.

The hours passed, and soon, just after midday, the two began to run at the same pace as in the morning to cover another chunk of miles before setting camp. The sun was warm, and Ryker was grateful to have the large pine trees spilling down cool pools of shade on the road they were traveling.

A few hours before nightfall, the two found a clearing to set up camp. They ventured into the woods a quarter-mile off the beaten path to ensure no other travelers stumbled upon them that night. They dropped their packs, quickly made camp, and settled in for another ration of salted dried meat, cheese, and hardened bread.

Shortly after the meal had been completed, Aegnor stood and motioned Ryker to do the same. "Get your sword."

The apprentice groaned.

I think he's going to kill me. Not intentionally, perhaps, but by over-exertion. I don't think my body can take any more of, well, anything today. Frankly, I don't know if I can even stand.

He didn't voice his concern this time. He didn't need another tirade from the elf on how weak he was mentally or physically. So, ignoring his brain screaming at him in agony, he stood, unsheathed his blade, and faced his master.

"You know a handful of fighting styles and forms, do you not?" asked Aegnor. Ryker nodded. "Good, then I will teach you another."

"Follow my movements and copy my stances. I will teach you a balanced routine with both attacking and defensive movements. The entire flow will be done in a storm stance, which should suit you well. The entire routine is designed for a fighter who is strong but gives you the flexibility to incorporate quick movements and counterattacks within the natural flow of a fight. And most importantly, it allows for the addition of a second blade as you progress in talent."

They fell into form, and immediately, the elf corrected Ryker's foot placement down to the centimeter and minute angle of each foot. Then, they flowed through the movements with more speed. They never made it far, no more than a couple of forms without the elf stopping his student to correct his footing, handholds, sword thrust placement, and more. He repeated throughout. "You must be perfect in your precision."

It took nearly an hour to complete the first cycle with the number of errors Ryker made. By the end of the routine, the warrior apprentice's shoulders burned under the weight of his blade nearly as much as his legs ached.

Aegnor moved from Ryker's side to stand before the man and found a rock to settle on, his silver eyes were focused on his pupil. "Again."

Ryker could sense beads of sweat dripping from his forehead as he went through the sequence of forms repeatedly for what seemed like a never-ending duration. Despite frequent interruptions from Aegnor, who was correcting his technique, Ryker could feel his master's satisfaction with the improvements he made during the second round. Aegnor nodded in approval as Ryker completed the second cycle. Once completed, though, he heard, "Better, now go again."

This continued till the late hours of dusk before Aegnor mercifully called, "This is enough for today." He tossed the man another round of salted meat. "Eat this. You need it to recover. Clean yourself up and get to sleep. You need to rest. We will repeat this routine each night until we arrive in Ravenford and likely beyond the rural city."

Ryker shuttered, thinking, *Yeah, this man is going to inadvertently kill me.* But despite the pain he felt, he swore he would not return home before his training was complete. If you could say one thing about the Marriock family, they finish what they started.

Ryker - Chapter 12 - Great Plains, Great Steeds

On the final morning before arriving at Ravenford, Ryker awoke to the sound of rustling pine needles and the gentle sway of dense branches as the morning breeze swept through. The night still clung to the sky in a losing effort to hold back the sun. As he pushed himself onto his feet, Ryker could feel his muscles shriek in protest with each movement.

Before he departed Stone Guard, Ryker assumed that any physical training would seem easy compared to the hard labor he performed daily on the farm, and this may have been true had he been apprenticed under any other master. Aegnor seemed intent on pushing the young man beyond his physical limits to try and break his apprentice. So far, Ryker had not succumbed to the grueling regiment, but he was only on day four of the apprenticeship, and his every movement shot pangs of agony through his body from foot to head.

Despite the excruciating trials, Ryker's determination only grew with each day. He was unwavering in his commitment to improve, to show Aegnor he was committed to success. Every painful step, every sword form correction, and every moment of discomfort only fueled his resolve to become a more skilled and disciplined student. The thought of gaining Aegnor's approval and mastering the art of death pushed him to defy the torment of his training.

He strode over to an ice-cold stream they had camped by and washed his face. The touch of the cold water was an elixir that shot energy through his body, causing him to shiver as droplets fell from his face and hair to his bare chest.

"We will be approaching Ravenford just after daybreak. We will stay for as long as needed to find steeds, but I do not wish to toil in this town. We will leave early tomorrow if we can successfully broker a deal," he heard his master shout from further in the brush.

Ryker felt better as his blood warmed during their morning jog. It was a pleasant pace when compared to the previous days. His muscles were still sore, but the movement loosened them quickly as heat suffused his limbs. He smiled to himself, noticing a significant improvement in his breathing as he nearly kept pace with Aegnor's long gaiting lope. He was shocked at the drastic impact that just four days of consistency in training had on his endurance.

As the sun finally crested over the horizon, its beams painted a beautiful picture of Ravenford at the base of the hills Ryker had, for so long, called home. The city looked strange to the young man as he and the warrior elf descended. After spending his entire life near Stone

Guard, a massive metropolis surrounded by high walls, nestled snugly into the pine-covered hills, he thought Ravenford looked exposed, naked even, where it sat on the edge of an endless plain.

The city was built where the forest faded into an ever-expansive grassland. Looking down from the hilltop, the plains were a sea of green chutes dancing in harmony with the delicate winds. The movements of the plants were mesmerizing. Ryker watched the patterns stream across the tall grass as invisible waves of air passed overhead. From their vantage point, the emerald green appeared as one large smooth surface, only broken by the trails of trampled stalks following dark figures galloping through the fields.

The city appeared to be composed primarily of large wooden homesteads, each enclosed with acres of unkept, fenced-in land. Some homes adjoined to barns placed within the property lines of larger residences. No wall was built around the town. The area was too vast to make it feasible to do so. To Ryker, this only heightened the sense that the residents in this place were vulnerable and exposed.

The two travelers slowed to a walk, now just over a mile from the entry gate. As they neared, Ryker began to understand that though there were no walls, the town was anything but unprotected. While the people of Ravenford were known for their Ravanian horses, it seemed that was not the only impressive breed that resided within.

Each of the four soldiers manning the pathway toward the center of the town was trailed by a hound unlike any Ryker had seen. The shoulders of the smallest dog reached well over his midsection. The tallest could almost see eye-to-eye with him while standing on all fours. The breed had short noses and powerful jaw muscles, causing their head to be far larger than any human or elf, and that was paired with droopy lips hanging over wicked-looking teeth set in a severe underbite. The dogs' coats seemed to vary, some being brindle, faun, or black with striped, white faces and feet. Their eyes followed the two men as they approached. Overall, the breed had a look of being far less intelligent than their station as guardians seemed to suggest they were. That lack of intelligence in their appearance was only outweighed by the intimidation they forced upon all in their presence.

Looking over the wooden fences of the properties lining the perimeter of Ravenford, Ryker could make out small lines of movements through the grass and saw that there was a group of monstrous dogs patrolling the interior. Each breath they took pulled the stalks of grass toward their large snouts. The beasts were so large he mistook them for horses from above.

As he and Aegnor approached the four soldiers, none of the men moved, but all four hounds sprang to their feet, dropped into a menacing crouch, and snarled, revealing their knife-like teeth. An audible threat filled the air in the form of deep barks. The shoulders of each beast rippled with power and anticipation, awaiting the word from a guard to attack.

"What's your business," one of the soldiers called up. "And why the hell are you stumbling into our city so early? I don't like talking to folk till after midday," the man added with a hint of annoyance. He still hadn't commanded the beasts from their aggressive posture.

"We are travelers passing through on the road north. We are looking to purchase horses to aid us on our travels. We will be leaving the city on the morrow, assuming we can conclude our dealings today," Aegnor responded politely.

The guard barely looked up from his reclined position. "Yeah, yeah, yeah. Go on through, and don't cause no trouble, or I'll send Daisy after you," he said, patting the back of the largest dog who growled and barked at them in warning, foamy saliva dripping from her maw to soak the dirt below. She settled on her haunches and licked at her salivating lips before grooming her dust-covered paws.

"Fair enough, sir," said Aegnor. And the two travelers walked into Ravenford.

The first stop they made was at a small inn one of the townsfolk directed them to. The building seemed quiet. Ryker assumed it was likely slow for businesses as most travelers would have begun to shelter up for the winter. As such, the two men had little trouble securing two rooms, planning to change and eat before beginning the search for their mounts.

And so, after their things were settled, Ryker bathed quickly with cold water, then threw on a pair of clean trousers, a fresh shirt from his pack, and a thick wool coat he would need since he would not be running to stay warm. Lastly, he strapped his sword to his side and his dagger to the opposite hip. With the scabbard secured to the belt, he was ready to head to the dining room. He felt refreshed, donning fresh clothes and being free from the thick layer of grime that clung to every crevasse. He headed out the door unconsciously patting his hand against the scabbard hanging from his hip. It was funny how, after a few days of dedicated practice, Ryker would no longer think of going anywhere without this blade. It offered him a surprising level of comfort, knowing the cold steel that obeyed his every command was so close and at the ready.

Ryker found Aegnor was already waiting within the inn's main room at a beaten wooden table near a large soot-stained fireplace; roaring and casting an orange glow about the elf. The apprentice held his hands over the flames as he settled into the chair opposite Aegnor, appreciating the heat on the cool winter morning. Aegnor had one mug in his hand and slid another pint in front of Ryker, who raised a brow and took a long swig. His mouth leaped in surprised joy as the light berry mead ran across his tongue. "I'm not normally one to drink mead for breakfast," Aegnor commented. "But it has been a hard journey. We can take a few minutes to enjoy a fresh meal."

A gravelly voice came from behind Ryker, startling the apprentice as it responded to Aegnor's comments. "Can't say any meal'd be fresh, mostly got some leftovers from the night before, but we got a nice bit of pheasant and pork from just last night. Can throw in some eggs and taters, too, if ya like." The voice came from a haggard-looking man with graying hair, an unkempt beard, and a severely hunched back from a long life of moving heavy barrels of mead. He was slowly walking their way from behind the room's polished wooden bar.

Ryker's stomach sang at the words of pheasant and eggs, and he blurted out instantly, "Fresh or not, a hot meal sounds wonderful, sir. I wouldn't mind pheasant and eggs one bit."

The man smiled, revealing stained teeth and a few gaps. "No need to call me, sir. I'm just a humble barkeep looking to serve my only patrons this morning. The name's Bennet."

Bennet turned to face Aegnor. "And for you, sir?"

"I will take the pork and potatoes, but I would also beg of you some information should you have it."

"That's no problem at all, so long's I know what you seek," the old man chuckled. "How can I help you apart from the beverages and food?"

"We are looking for a place to buy Ravanians. Last I traveled through these parts, I spoke to a man by the name of Cyrus. He was a fine breeder, the best I've met, actually. Do you know if he still operates in these parts?"

"Cyrus? Do I know if he's still in Ravenford?" The man seemed perplexed by the questions. "Well, of course I do. The man's about as famous as you can get from raisin' animals. The Queen herself has sent emissaries out to buy his finest. Thought you might actually be out on her bidding givin' yer look, sir…" He waited for Aegnor to confirm his suspicion. When he did not, Bennet continued, "Can't miss his place. He lives at the biggest farm, well it's more of a palace really, jus' at the end of the main town road. Turn left out the doors, then walk straight for a couple minutes. Can't miss it."

Aegnor nodded his appreciation. Once the barkeep left, the pair lounged in their chairs, content to sip their mead in silence as they awaited their meals.

After what seemed like an endless number of grueling days on the road, Ryker thought the roast pheasant and eggs he ordered might be the best thing he had ever eaten. Not to say he didn't appreciate the rations of bread and cured meat, but they didn't hold much in terms of flavor, and the bird was succulent, savory, and paired perfectly with the fried eggs. Stomach full, Ryker was inclined to nap. His sore body wouldn't have argued with a day of respite, but Aegnor, Ryker was coming to learn, did not believe in relaxation. After he finished off his roasted potatoes and pork, the two were back on the streets of Ravenford, and the training resumed on their walk.

"You are familiar with horsemanship, with riding, yes?" asked Aegnor, leading the way through horses and carts that were beginning to fill the dirt streets.

"I am. We have always had horses and other work animals on the farm. My father told us it was important to learn to ride and had us in a saddle from as early as I can remember. That said, I am a far cry from an expert. Generally, we had our beasts hooked up to plows," answered Ryker.

"Have you ever rode a Ravanian?" asked the elf, raising his brow in question at the young man.

"Rode a Ravanian? You must be mad! I have only ever been a simple farmer's son... Could count how many Ravanians I have seen on a single hand. I think Frenir gave one as a prize to one of his tournament champions once when I was younger, and before I got close enough to pet it, a couple of guards carried me off. I couldn't believe the size of him. Honestly, before seeing the dogs in this place, I don't think I have seen anything so impressive. I've heard countless stories of the great warriors who rode them."

The two continued through the city, getting further from the hills they had emerged from earlier that day. Eventually, they turned from the main paved city road to a smaller dirt road that led straight out through the plains toward what appeared to be a large estate.

Aegnor seemed pleased to hear that Ryker had heard tales of some of the most famous steeds throughout history. "The tales of the most famous Ravanians are often told through great feats of elves and men. What the stories often skew is the role played by the hero of the tale and the role played by the horse. Remember, these beasts live far longer than most human men and are stronger, in mind and body, than nearly any creature on Divinoros. Outside of a few races of dragon and lion, few animals are capable of hunting these creatures without a pack, and even those would rarely confront a Ravanian unless their circumstances were truly dire. Nearly any other prey would make for a far easier target. Even the foals remain vulnerable for only a few hours before they gain their legs, and once they do, they can outpace any other breed, with the exception of a couple of Sandshari bloodlines. And those Sandshari are diminutive when side by side with Ravanians. Which horse from the stories do you know best?"

"It has to be Ferenthor's steed. But I have only heard the ballad performed a couple of times and you are right. The horse plays a side role to its owner in the tales I've heard," Ryker said. "I don't recall the name of his horse."

Aegnor picked up again, his lips curling upward in a sly grin. "Ahhhh, yes, Ferenthor. The blasted fool. You must know of him forcing back an entire battalion of the northern raiders?"

Ryker nodded.

"It is commonly passed down through the generations in song and story. You may recall that these tales highlight the skill of Ferenthor on the battlefield, for he did instill fear in the hearts of his enemies for his prowess with a mace was told accurately, he was formidable, but more fame should be granted to the creature he rode than him for his great successes. His most famous tale, if you recall, is of the general's retreat at Golem's Pass. This only became a tale because he blindly led his battalion into an ambush. As you recall, the northern elves and human tribes of the north united in Reyvothia under a cruel human warrior who called himself the Child of the Flame." A faraway look crossed Aegnor as if he was thinking back to remember the scene.

He couldn't have been there, could he? Ryker thought.

"Yes, what a name he gave himself... the man was a bit vain, and the name lacked creativity if you ask me... Easy to call yourself anything related to fire if your hair shines as orange as the morning sun. Anyway, you remember it was the Child of Flame and his bezerkers who raided, burned, and raped their way through villages all along the northern shores of both the western and eastern continents. He killed some fifteen thousand men and women before he was defeated.

"In his reign of terror, he ruined countless villages, destroyed thousands of families... scarred the minds of his victims who survived his wrath. Not to mention, his destruction cost a pretty penny. He was indeed a fiery blight in the north. An orange smear across Celestra's pristine rule, and all who stood before him had been struck down with reckless abandon. They were so successful because of the brutal lightning raid tactics they deployed, and as you know from yesterday's lesson, it was actually the Child of Flame that caused Celestra to re-evaluate and begin to train a group of soldiers who were highly proficient in small mobile unit warfare, her new Elite's. Anyway, I digress, but we can begin tomorrow's lessons with what is called guerilla warfare tactics that evolved from the Child of Flame's very own.

"Now, back to Ferenthor, the issue in the north spread beyond the point of being a minor hindrance to being a major impact on food supplies, shortages began popping up through the countryside and all western Divinoros. In response, Celestra sent Ferenthor's company to eradicate the usurpers who had bloodied her land. I would have helped, but I was otherwise occupied at the time."

Ryker looked stunned at his master as Aegnor took a sip from his waterskin before offering it to Ryker.

"Now, as I was saying, the land, the populous, the empire was bleeding, and bleeding badly. The general populace under Celestra's rule felt that the raiders had successfully loosened her hold on the northern provinces, and many, including our dwarven allies, assumed that Celestra would lose in the north just as she had in the southern in the battles of the Oasis many years prior. Celestra needed a swift victory once she engaged with the enemy head-on. The Queen because of political positioning and Ferenthor's familial relationship with her strongest ally at the time—Lord Frenir— Queen Celestra was forced to send Ferenthor as her lead Commander despite his, to be kind, mediocrity between the ears. And to compensate for what she knew to be inadequacy in her general, she sent him with three fully outfitted battalions, all hard elves and men. All of them had proved capable of warfare.

"She knew the numbers would be overwhelming to her enemies based on scouting reports she received from spies who successfully positioned themselves in the Child of Flame's midst. But the Child of the Flame was no fool. He understood the Queen's position and her, at the time, weakening grip on the crown. So, he anticipated a show of overwhelming force and was glad to learn that force would be led by a fool.

"And because of this, in the first battle of the fjords, when Ferenthor marched his army without properly scouting the narrow mountain channels, the raiders sat in waiting, ready to annihilate their opposition. They had booby-trapped the channels with magical explosives and rigged tar bombs set to burn once rolled down the steep slopes of the fjord's mountain into the body of the Queen's army marching within the ravine. Ferenthor's force marched headstrong into the trap. Almost immediately, he heard screams from his men at the rear of his battalions and wails from those who were blown to pieces near the flanking fjord inlets. After miles of marching, the valley they had traveled through grew so narrow only four fully grown horses, that of a standard breed could fit through at a time. The narrow passages made it nigh impossible to turn the army and retreat, which was already rendered impossible as the narrow passage they pushed headlong into was now sealed off, filled with tar set alight with flame, blocking retreat. The army was effectively trapped and would burn by tar and magic. With nothing else to do, Ferenthor resumed the forward march but at an accelerated pace, a frantic charge.

"Fear gripped the army as the tar bombs continued racing down the ravine's sides, crushing soldiers and spraying boiling black liquid around them. Horror filled the heart of Ferenthor as he watched flaming arrows rain down from above, setting alight large pools of tar and burning large groups of his men alive. Dark smoke smelling of burning flesh filled the air, restricting Ferenthor's vision and choking his lungs. His soldier fared little better. Those close to Ferenthor said this is where the panic set in… but his steed never faltered.

"Without instruction, for panic had consumed his rider, and the smoke-laden air wasn't far from relieving Ferenthor of his consciousness, the Ravanian whinnied loudly. He communicated with the other horses that elven riders had sat upon, and they galloped at frenzied pace behind the steed. The horse navigated the narrow passages with great speed, the elves on foot sensing urgency and fearing the traps that ravaged the main body of the army followed as well. Without hesitation, the Ravanian altered course from channels with heavy blockades, but there was no clean escape. A force of thirty raiders were positioned in the only passage heading from the chaotic ambush. But thirty men or thirty elves matter little when faced with a frenzied Ravanian. He mowed down a path through them with ease and led the Queen's army from complete annihilation. Ferenthor did survive and ultimately led a successful battle. But it was his horse who gave him the opportunity to redeem himself."

Aegnor paused just once more, and Ryker was astounded once again. The tale, for one, had never been told in this light, and more than that, the apprentice struggled to grasp the length of time his mentor had lived.

"The issue that storytellers face is that the influence and intelligence of a horse is harder to believe, harder to portray, harder for an audience to relate to. So as these legends are handed down through the generations of your race, the majesty of the greatest Ravanians to have roamed these plains is watered down, and the truth of their genius and their impeccable instinct begins to fall by the wayside in order to push a more appealing and acceptable tale."

Excitement bubbled up within Ryker. He had never seen his mentor show such reverence to anything in the brief travels together. Not even the dragons, which popped up briefly in one of Ryker's history lessons two days back. "So, we are getting Ravanians and continuing north. Why do we need them?"

Aegnor smiled at his apprentice, mischief glinting behind his silver eyes. "There are many reasons. As I said, we are going to see an old friend in the Marbled Caverns, and I would like to show off the steeds and cause a scene upon our arrival. It bothers dwarves to be so ostentatious, and I find that to be… comical. But in actuality, the roads north to the caverns have grown more dangerous over the past few years. I have seen more and more creatures stirring that had long ago retreated to less populated areas. They are now reemerging near towns, not to mention the spike in civil unrest in the rural towns has led to more hostility and robbery along what have traditionally been safe travel routes." He looked at Ryker. "And if my suspicions are correct, things are going to get far, far worse before they have hopes of getting better. Our horses, you will see, will prove to be of far greater value than their inevitably steep price before our travels together end."

Ryker could make out a massive homestead a half mile down the road where the street they traveled came to an end. The building was two stories tall and designed as a barn, but the precision and quality of the craftsmanship to complete the structure were evidenced in the clean red paint covering the building, not a single corner peeling or worn away, in the wrap-around porch supported by thick white painted oak beams with zero bend in the wood, and with oversized iron hinges on the massive solid oak doors at the front of the homestead. Each door was wide enough to fit a cart through while standing twice the height of an elf. No other building in Ravenford stood half the size of this barn.

The doors silently swung open on their massive hinges as the two approached, revealing a couple of ranch hands leaning into the inside of the doors as they pushed them open. They were so large no one person could open both. As the seam between the oak doors continued to part, the gap between them revealed a well-dressed elderly man wearing a neat vest over a white tunic and simple tan trousers. He twirled a piece of straw in his hand as he swaggered over to his guests.

Contrasting the otherwise clean appearance, the man wore dirt-covered work boots and a large-brimmed, very worn hat. He flicked away the straw and then stretched his arms wide, a grin emerging from his neatly cropped, graying beard. "Welcome to Hawthorn Farms, gentlemen", he said with a thick accent Ryker hadn't heard before. "We breed the finest hoases in Ravenford right here, and that, my good men, means the finest hoases in the world ya see. Got a couple a freshly broken in Thoroughbreds, an'some beau'iful Quarter hoases as well. Come on in, come on in. I don' bite." He ushered the pair into the massive barn following shortly behind Ryker and Aegnor.

The inside of the barn spanned nearly a quarter mile, lined with rows and rows of large stables, some full, some empty, before finally opening to the massive plains on the far side of the building. Ryker's family held both horses in just one stable room at their farm, and that one was far smaller than the average size of the stables in this building. *He must breed some damned fine horses indeed to afford this.*

The space was bustling with activity. Throughout the rows of stables, men and women were carrying water pails, mucking stalls, and filling feeding troughs throughout the barn. The musky scent of horse sewage had been pungent since Ryker set foot in Ravenford, but here in the barn, there was no breeze to grant a reprieve from the onslaught to his senses.

Not that he was unfamiliar with the odor of large beasts of burden, but it was not something that got any more pleasant with time or familiarity.

There were also five or so dogs trotting with surprising grace through the bustling halls, pausing every so often to test the air with the twitch of their noses. "So! Gentlemen, ma name is Cyrus, Cyrus Hawthorne, that is. How may I be o' service today?" the man asked as he leaned back against a light-stained pillar at the face of an empty stable.

Aegnor, looking directly at the man, stated bluntly, "I want to buy two of your finest steeds. Nothing else will suffice."

"Two of my finest you say? Well, that'll cost ya it will. I 'spect that money ain't gon' be an issue based on the looks of ya," said the man, stroking his beard and looking Aegnor up and down with a brow raised in question. While the elf was dressed modestly, his attire was clearly of high quality if inspected under a careful eye. And Cyrus was clearly practiced in telling if his prospective customers had enough funds to afford his wares.

"Let me show you's two tha newly broke Thoroughbreds I mentioned," said Cyrus, who turned left to walk to the far wall of stables. He began walking but turned around with a puzzled expression when his newest potential customers did not follow.

'I told you, I want your finest. I am not here for a Thoroughbred. The road me and my apprentice travel will undoubtedly be trying, in the extreme. We require Ravanian's. If you are unwilling to part with any of yours, I can take my business elsewhere. Though I have heard the quality coming from Hawthorne Farms is superior to most, and that's why we wanted to do business with you," Aegnor noted.

"Right, right. My humblest of apologies, good sir. Most who come to me fo hoases can't afford such bea'ful beasts. Act of habit showing you the others I s'pose. Follow me if ya please." He turned straight toward the back of the barn to the open spaces beyond.

"We ain't able to stall the Ravanians in here ya see. Too much commotion about them. They're fine inside most smaller operations, but for whatever reason here, when I brought 'em in from the pastures, they wanted back out. Badly. Lost one of our best stable hands that day... Best to leave 'em outside to roam an run, it seems, don' try fightin' it much now. They grow better out there anyway." Reaching the outside space, Cyrus raised his arms gesturing to the vast expanse of land too big to see the perimeter of the enclosure with the naked eye.

"Now, if you looking for a Ravanian, *this* is the place to come. Have the largest selection of Ravanians in all of Divinoros here. Now, if ya ain't familiar with this breed, you don't get to just well buy one per se... The creatures are highly intelligent ya see. Must prove ya worth to 'em f'ore they'll let someone just saddle em up. It's a, well, a test ride, so to speak. Jus' mo a test for the hoase then the rida. They want to ensure they ain't burdened by someone unworthy of they service."

Ryker glanced up at Aegnor. He wasn't prepared for a trial ride from a Ravanian... He was familiar with horses, yes, but by no means did he consider himself to be an expert. Usually, the two mares at the farm were hooked up to equipment rather than saddled, not to mention how stiff and sore he was from the previous three days of training and traveling. Aegnor nodded in response to Cyrus's proclamations.

"We are prepared. This would not be my first time riding one. My apprentice, however, must learn to handle the beast quickly." Eyeing Ryker slightly skeptically, he added, "We will see if he's up to the challenge."

Cyrus nodded and let loose a loud whistle that split the air around them, sending the sound wave rolling into the distance. The three men stood for minutes before Ryker thought he could feel a slight shaking beneath his feet. In the distance, he saw a flock of pheasants rise from the tall grasses in a spastic cloud as if disturbed by the rumbling. The shaking continued to grow in intensity until Ryker could hear a thunderstorm of hoof beats growing into a torrent with each passing second.

He heard Cyrus shout over the noise, "You's two get behind me! The herd ain't gon' recognize you yet, and I'd hate for a good paying customer to be trampled b'for I get paid!"

Aegnor and Ryker shifted till they were standing behind the old man, who calmly clasped his hands behind his back, patiently awaiting the oncoming stampede. Seconds later, a dozen enormous horses stormed into sight from the tall grass. Each was magnificent. And absolutely massive. Their coats varied in color: chestnut, black, white, palomino, silver, and blue, each shining brilliantly under the clear sunny skies. The horse in the lead was pure black—hooves, mane, eyes, and all. He came to a stop abruptly in front of Cyrus, towering over the man and letting loose a booming whinny. The other horses in the herd seemed to follow his lead, echoing the call, stamping their hooves into the earth with restless intensity. Ryker struggled to keep himself from covering his ears at the noise. The shoulder of the black horse stood a foot above Aegnor's head. Ryker gaped at their sheer size, their clear power. He hadn't seen any living thing larger than the stallion standing before him, and frankly, nothing even came close. Not even the Ravanians that Lord Frenir possessed.

"Oh, quit ya fussing you big ol brute!" shouted Cyrus in mock admonishment to the horse's whining protests at being summoned. "I brough ya somethin Maximus."

Cyrus lifted his hand and patted the monstrous horse on the chest as he pulled a half-eaten apple from his coat pocket. "Here ya go, big heathen," said the old man, smiling and lifting the apple to Maximus. The black horse shook his mane, stomped his front hoof affectionately, and took the apple from Cyrus's hand more gently than Ryker would have thought a creature of his size to be capable of.

"I have a couple a folk here who are looking to take a couple of ya north, it seems," Cyrus said, still speaking to the horse. Maximus shook his head and snorted, lifting his chin as if to say, *good luck taking me.* The horses behind Maximus seemed equally displeased by the news.

Cyrus spun around and faced the two, "Alright, pick whichever you's wish. I don't keep most of my studs wit the main herd, 'therwise Maximus here might kill 'em, so all the beauties here are 'vailable for purchase. Jus' know, if you fail the test with one mount, the rest will also deem you unworthy as a rider. In which case, I'd be happy to show you's the other breeds." His gaze fixed on Ryker with the last comment.

Aegnor nodded and instantly strode up to Maximus, looking directly into one of the eyes of the great beast. He reached an arm up and stroked the neck of the horse. The motion seemed to settle the horse. "I will take you with me, Maximus. Your name will go down with the greatest of your kind. The adventures we pursue are not for the faint of heart. I think you will do fine. Should you deem me worthy, that is."

Aegnor took his attention from the horse to face the farm hand, "Is this one violent?"

"Well, let's jus say I had more than a fair share of folk think theys up to purchasing Maximus. Not one's stayed on long enough to settle 'em down though. Killed one man, too. But only when he tried to climb back on him after he don got tossed the first time around."

Aegnor nodded.

Ryker looked over the remaining steeds. Each was voicing protest at having a human potentially take ownership of them. All except for one gorgeous palomino, who stood toward the back of the herd, calmly grazing as if she was disinterested in the day's affairs. The mare was beautiful. Her golden coat shone in the sunlight, brightening into a gleaming white mane and tail. She was much smaller than Maximus. In fact, she seemed to be the runt of the herd but still towered over Agenor at her shoulder.

Ryker approached the mare timidly till he heard Aegnor bark, "Confidence, show her no fear. If she is to be your mount, you will not want to appear as some helpless boy unwilling to look her in the eye and approach with purpose. She is intelligent enough to know your intentions, so show her certainty."

Ryker straightened and looked the mare in the eye. As he neared, he reached his hand out toward the horse. She snorted and whinnied and pranced backward in two graceful steps. Ryker continued to hold her gaze and approach. This time, she allowed him to close the distance between them, snorting still but no longer retreating. Ryker rested his hand on the base of her neck and patted her shoulder. "What would you say to taking a trip? It's bound to be a grand adventure traveling with that one." Ryker spoke softly toward her. She whinnied again, shaking her head and whipping her mane.

"Ahh, she's accepted yur challenge, young master." Ryker heard from behind, "Ain't never seen anybody even get that close to 'er. Skittish one normally. Fastest damn horse I've ever seen, though. Must see something in you's to let ya try ya hand."

Ryker smiled at the mare, still patting her shoulder. He looked back to Aegnor, who nodded. "There is nothing I can teach you in this. It will be your will against hers... Make sure you win. It is a long run to the Marbled Caverns should you fail." With that, the silver-haired elf swung by the base of Maximus's neck up onto the animal's back. As soon as he touched down on his back, the horse reared on its hind legs and tore off into the plains, bucking and zigzagging in an attempt to break the death grip Aegnor had on the creature. The remaining Ravanian horses took off after the pair. All except the palomino, who shook her head and whinnied once again, stomping the ground impatiently.

"Well, let's have some fun!" Ryker reached up to the mare's neck and jumped as high as he could, pulling himself onto the mare's back. He finally got his legs around the back of the beast just as she reared up, snorted furiously, and tore after the rest of the herd. Despite the significant head start Maximus had, she caught him in no time. Ryker smiled, "Guess the old farm hand wasn't lying, huh, girl?" The cold winter air stung his exposed face as man and steed soared through a sea of green, trampling the tall stalks under thundering hooves. Just as she passed Maximus, the palomino turned hard to the left, nearly throwing Ryker over her side with a sharp movement. She didn't slow and soon left the herd far behind, even with intermittent bucking and sudden turns.

Land was eaten up rapidly on the back of a Ravanian. Eventually, the palomino seemed to settle, resigning to the fact that Ryker could be an adequate owner. With her sudden change of direction and bucking slowing, he dared to let go of her mane with one hand to look back toward the barn they had just left at most a minute ago. He was shocked to see he could barely make out a dark speck where the building stood in the distance.

A few more tumultuous turns that nearly sent Ryker tumbling from the mare's back jolted him back to the present task. He now not only needed but wanted to win this horse's full approval. But despite the importance of the occasion, a childlike joy filled him. He let out a shout, enjoying a freedom unlike any he had previously experienced. On the back of this horse, the world was his to explore. The palomino whinnied in response to his shouts of joy, as if she was glad at his glee. The feeling of rushing air through his clothes and hair and the thudding of his heart seemed to fall into rhythm with the frantic pace of the hoof beats below. Nothing could catch him on the back of the Ravanian, not on these open plains.

He admired the beauty of the plains, the new world he had just walked into early that day, but then he saw something approaching, fast, in front of the mare. A stream of dark gouges were forming through the tall grass and converging on them. Whatever approached was not large enough to be seen above the line of tall grass, but the palomino whinnied, seemingly nervous, and veered sharply to the right to avoid the oncoming disturbance. As she turned, Ryker looked back over his shoulder to see at least a half dozen additional lines approaching through the tall grass in the direction they had turned, and they were now on a collision course with the trails.

He could feel the mare growing panicked as she strove to outpace whatever was following them, but amazingly, the rifts being carved into the sea of green kept pace with them as other lines appeared, intending to cut off their retreat. Ryker looked back toward where he assumed Aegnor may be approaching from, but they seemed to have fallen much further behind than he had hoped. Help would not be here in time for whatever descended upon them. Then he heard a low howl, and ice gripped his heart. Wolves.

Unsure of how to proceed, Ryker released the mare with his right hand and drew his master blade. "When they come, we can face it together, girl," he shouted above the thudding of hooves and hard breathing, hoping the horse could understand. He unsheathed his blade none too early. From his left, a large, dog-like creature sprang from the grass, leaping toward the mare's neck. Instinct kicked in, and Ryker thrust his blade at the beast, catching it in the ribs before its claws or teeth could sink into the horse's flesh. She finished this one off as it fell, caving in the beast's abdomen with a hoof larger than Ryker's head.

Just then, two more wolves jumped from directly in front of the horse and rider. The mare was forced to stop suddenly, and she reared up with her front hooves to batter the creature's back. In doing so, Ryker was thrown to the ground, landing flat on his back. His breath left him in a rush, leaving him gasping for air as he scrambled to his feet, looking around frantically. He could hear the pack circling him and the horse. She spun wildly, whining and stamping down the grass nearby them, sending the pair of wolves that ambushed them back into the coverage of thick grass that surrounded them.

"Calm down, girl. We can hold our own." He took up a position near the mare's left flank and shouted again, hoping she could understand his intentions. I'll protect your sides. Just kick and stomp any that come for your head or back." She whinnied defiantly as if in agreement with the apprentice, an audible challenge to the pack that circled them. *We just need to survive until Aegnor gets here. He must have been following us.*

An explosion of activity crashed from the front of the pair. The Ravanian quickly stomped down on those two wolves as they rushed for her neck. Ryker heard their bones crack. The sound was soon accompanied by the dog's pained whimpering. He had no time to process the scene further as another wolf jumped at him. *Damn pack hunters.* He got his blade up in time to skewer the beast, but the weight of the wolf knocked him on his back again. Before he could scramble up, Ryker cried out in pain as he felt the jaws of a fourth animal clamp over his ankle.

White hot fire flamed at the site as long teeth sunk into bone, muscle, and tendon. Ignoring the pain, Ryker tossed the dead wolf to the side and swung the blade down hard on the back of the creature that was now chewing his leg. It dropped lifelessly as its spine was cleanly severed. The apprentice sprang onto unsteady feet. Ignoring the burning wound in his ankle, Ryker bounced on his toes and concluded the bones were not broken.

It was a good thing, too, as three more wolves were now stalking at the horse, avoiding areas she could easily reach with her hooves. The apprentice could see that one or two of the dogs had been able to rake their lion-like claws down the side of the horse, losing bright streams of scarlet blood trails down the brilliant golden coat. *Such odd creatures. I've heard of the Great Plain wolves, but seeing them in person. They look like a dog-feline hybrid.*

Ryker shook his head to clear his thoughts and hobbled into the fray, swinging his blade in broad fanning movements, warning the wolves that he and the mare would not be easy prey. He could see another three wolves creep into the patted-down prairie that had been leveled during the fighting. Just as Ryker thought the two might die here, he heard loud barking in the near distance. The largest wolf, an immense silver-blue beast with razor-sharp retractable claws, now fully extended on his paws and long curved canines that were visibly protruding beneath the lower mandible, raised his muzzle into the air and let out a short howl. All the predators that were previously circling their would-be dinner retreated into the tall grass.

Seconds later, Aegnor appeared astride the great Maximus, bursting into the cleared space looking like a demi-god on top of the father of all warhorses, with four of the Ravenford hounds in tow. The hounds sniffed loudly at the air and ground, briefly looked over the injured horse and rider, and tore off into the thicket after the wolf pack. The guard dogs were bred well and strong, and they would hunt this pack to the edge of Cyrus's property before turning back.

"Are you well?" Aegnor called to Ryker, "The dogs must have heard your Ravanian cry out; they came sprinting in this direction, and I convinced Maximus it would be worth our while to follow. Appears I was right," said Aegnor.

"Well, I've been better. They tore up my leg pretty… wait, what do you mean, my Ravanian?" asked Ryker, picking up on his mentor's choice of words. Aegnor was not one to make mistakes in his speech.

"Look," the elf nodded past Ryker's shoulder. The apprentice turned to find the palomino standing over him protectively, her ears twitching all around to pick up on any small sounds or movements in the grass. As he turned to face her, she lowered her head, pressing the crown of her head into his chest, nearly knocking him over. Despite the pain of stumbling back on his mangled leg, Ryker laughed and scratched her along the jawline.

"Guess fending off a pack of wolves is a good way to solidify a bond, eh, girl?" chuckled Ryker, drunk with excitement. "I thought you said only some dragons and large cat breeds can successfully hunt a Ravanian? Why did a pack of wolves attack us? We killed four of them at least."

Aegnor furrowed his brow. "This is… curious. Wolves prefer the Perampla Mountain region and the ice plains further north. They are rarely spotted this far south below the range. I do not know, but it is troublesome. Something must have forced the pack south. That or they sensed danger north of the mountains…" He paused, deep in thought, then said, "Come. Let us complete our transaction." Aegnor helped his maimed apprentice onto the back of the mare and then gracefully leaped to the back of Maximus.

When the two trotted back to camp, Cyrus's mouth fell agape at the site of the mare's side and Ryker's torn clothing… Ryker rested near the barn where two farm hands fetched pales of fresh water to help clean out the shallow claw marks along the mare's side, scarlet stains scratched into her golden coat. He decided Aegnor could complete the transaction without him as he set to caring for the palomino.

As he cleaned the wounds, thankful that they were shallow, he spoke to the horse. "Guess if you are coming with me, you will need a name. Doesn't seem like you've been given one yet. How about Lily?" The mare turned and eyed him. "Yes, I suppose you are right, that seems far too common…" She bobbed her head as if to agree with him.

"Melody?" The horse whinnied in disagreement. "Yeah, yeah, I guess that sounds a little too frail. You are anything but."

Ryker thought back to one of his favorite childhood stories of the great warrior elf, Eldacar, who forced the Demon King, Daemaron, to his banishment on the Cursed Isle with the help of not only the four Gods but also his horse. Perhaps the most famous horse in all history, a stallion

91

called Xanthus, but he was, well, a *he*. Ryker's mare would need a slightly more feminine touch. After all, it was clear to Ryker that though Maximus and the other male Ravanians he'd seen were magnificent, his mare carried a natural beauty the brutish males could never hope to match.

"How do you feel about Xantharyia? You're every bit as noble as Xanthus would have been... from what I've seen, I would think more so."

The mare whinnied excitedly, shaking her mane in agreement.

"Xantharyia it is," Ryker smiled and patted the horse on the side. He sat and leaned back against the barn. Now that she had her wounds cleaned, he needed to address his chewed-up ankle.

He ripped a fresh piece of cloth from the material the stable hands provided. He rolled up his pant leg to reveal torn flesh peeling away from his body in chunks, revealing the muscle and bone beneath. The wound was still bleeding, but the site was so swollen that the blood had begun to partially clot and stick together. Chunks of white flesh hung loosely from where the wolf's teeth had penetrated his flesh, but all in all, the damage could have been far worse. From what he could tell, there was no cracking in the bone, and his Achilles and other tendons seemed to still be fully intact. He cleaned out large dirt clumps caught in rips of flesh, causing fresh blood flow, and wrapped the damaged ankle to add support and stifle any additional blood loss.

As he stood back up, he saw Aegnor approaching. "How is she?" he asked, gesturing to the horse.

"I cleaned up the wounds. They were shallow and should heal quickly. She's called Xantharyia now," Ryker replied.

"The name suits her," nodded the elf approvingly. "And your leg?"

"Painful, but the damage seems to have only been flesh-deep. I can't feel any cracks or torn ligaments. I'll need to dress it properly once we're back in the rooms, but I was able to bind it up well enough for now."

"Then let us return to the Inn. Cyrus is preparing saddles and travel rations. Plus," said the silver-haired elf with a smirk forming on his lips, "If your wound isn't severe, we will continue your sword training, and we won't need to use the curative elixirs I carry. I like to conserve those for more serious wounds. It will be good to simulate an injury in battle without me having to stab you during one of our training sessions." He turned and strode in the direction of the Inn.

Ryker was shocked and shouted after him, "Hey! Was that a joke from the almighty Aegnor?" No response came from his master's retreating form.

"You are joking with me, right? You wouldn't actually stab me?" Again, no response came from the elf, and Ryker scurried after him. "Hold on now! I know I'm your apprentice and all, but come on...

Stabbing me for a training simulation of a battle wound? Aegnor, you can't be serious!"

Aegnor raised an eyebrow to the young man, and the pair bickered about training regimens the entire walk back to the inn.

Nienna - Chapter 13 - The Outsiders

Nienna and the three Elites Lord Sennin had assigned to the mission, Taniya, Joralf, and Kimo, were a week into their journey. To Sennin's credit, she found that the Sandshari mounts the soldiers rode easily kept pace with Zarou despite being a fraction of his size. The steeds were a marvel, an oddity, seeming to almost defy nature with the discrepancy between their visage and capabilities. Each stood slightly shorter than a typical quarter horse that most humans seemed to favor, nearly the size of a large pack mule. The diminutive size gave a rather commercial appearance with the tall elves mounted on their backs. That said, the thick stout mounts had no trouble keeping pace with Zarou's long bounding strides that ate up miles with fervor in the vast desert. Despite the seven days of travel, the horses still acted skittish around Zarou in an eerily similar fashion to how the Elites avoided her.

Nienna crested a large dune as the sun was setting. A row of lights stretching up two sides of a canyon wall were flickering in the distance, indicating the Narrows were only a couple hours from them on horseback. As no one from their group thought it wise to enter the city at dark, a city that had refused to communicate with Sandivar in the past months, the party found a location sheltered by large rocks that protruded through the sand to set up camp for the night.

Rumors had trickled south that the Narrows had grown dangerous in recent months. Intelligence reports Sennin briefed the party on before their departure seemed to indicate that an underground human-run organization was working to overthrow the elvish rule in the city. Many of the scouts reported the group were sympathizers of the Bankhoft family syndicate. Many went so far as to voice suspicion that nefarious activities within the city were funded by the Knife's own coffers. The information had unsettled Nienna, as she wished nothing more than a long reprieve from facing the Knife in person again.

I honestly wouldn't mind being on a different continent than that man. Perhaps I will go to Stone Guard after this errand.

Given these reports, Nienna decided on the safer course of action while traversing the city, despite the fact that it would likely take nothing short of a full battalion of humans to kill her and three Elites. The group would cross through the city in the morning hours tomorrow after a night's rest, ensuring they would be in and beyond the city while the sun still hung in the air. The passageways within the walls of the Narrows Canyon were not a place any elf wished to be stuck in at night. The people lived burrowed in the walls of the canyon like rodents, and the confounding tunnels stretched for miles. It was possible to be tangled up and lost for hours, days, even should you lose your way in the dark.

The four settled into their usual camp arrangement. The three Elites circled around a fire with her and Zarou setting up their own camp further off to the side. Neither party trusted one another, not entirely anyway. Nienna and Zarou worked alone. The presence of others unnerved her, representing a variable to this mission that was not under her direct control. And to the soldiers, they likely thought of her as little more than a professional killer, ready to snap and stab at any one of them on a whim. Which was only partly true, she thought resentfully... Yes, sometimes she would assassinate people, but only those who are deserving, and only when paid for it and paid well. She wouldn't attack her traveling companions without just cause.

Not many live by a code any longer in this world. These three are brainless servants to whatever elf is their appointed leader. At least I am able to choose my own path. Live my own way.

She could overhear the others chatting, mostly just small talk about the last time they had visited Turenian, why the three Elites needed a party leader imposed on them from outside their ranks by High Lord Sennin's order, and the best combat stories from their centuries of service. Nienna decided she should approach the group to prepare a plan for the following day. Joralf, the oldest of the three, stopped mid-conversation and nodded to the approaching elf in respect. She liked Joralf.

"Joralf," said Nienna, returning the nod. We should formulate a plan for passing through the Narrows in the morning. We will need some sort of story, a cover for why we are traveling north. Given the civil unrest we are seeing, it would be best to leave no trace or indication of our presence here. With the conflict between humans and elves, I want our profile to remain low and our presence to be brief."

Joralf and Taniya nodded their agreement, but Kimo, the youngest of the party, scoffed at her. He had been difficult when it came to taking orders or suggestions from the Ghost, annoyed to have one outside the Queen's command placed ahead of the Elites on a sanctioned mission. He spoke, his voice dripping with contempt. "We don't need a plan, *Ghost*. We are the supreme soldiers of Lord Sennin's army, the *Queen's* army. Perhaps you have forgotten in your back ally escapades, but Celestra reigns as supreme ruler over these parts. The humans will let us pass even if they are unhappy with our presence. Lady Elba wouldn't dare block us."

The pride of a handsome young elf who's only known the life of soldiering... I think it's dulled his wits.

"Yes, you are likely right. Not one soldier under Lady Elba would dare stand before us or deny us entry, but that is not what troubles me. Rumors have been trickling out of the Narrows for almost a year, rumors Sennin confirmed before we left on this little trek north. An organized coalition is actively working to overthrow Elba's rule and seize control of the city. They have been seeded and have had ample time to grow within the Narrows. Their actions are causing the human population to riot against the elven contingent station here under Elba's control. *Think, Kimo, though I know it's hard for you.*" Kimo was about to respond, but Nienna continued before he could cut in.

"Reports Sennin detailed to us may have indicated the skirmishes that have broken out have been quelled, but that report is over two months old, and since the uprising here was supposedly squelched, Sandivar has yet to receive even a single shipment from Turenian. The city is a hazy cloud of uncertainty in Sennin's otherwise deep and widespread intelligence network. No one knows what has happened since things inside the canyon went dark to the outside world. If I had to guess, the residents, and very possibly the city guard, won't take kindly to three of Lord Sennin's most dangerous soldiers striding through the front gates," remarked Nienna sternly.

"What, you're scared of a couple humans now, are you? Thought you had a spine assassin. Guess the rumors that follow you may be more fiction than fact," taunted the young elf. The older soldiers sat in silence, unwilling to interject.

This whole trip would be easier if they told him what a fool he was being. They likely think it's good to argue before we're in a dangerous area I suppose. Gods I hate working in groups.

Nienna stared flatly at Kimo but refused to take the obvious bait. "The group leading the rallying against elven leadership is said to be backed by the Bankhofts. I have seen firsthand the power that family possesses. Perhaps you have forgotten the fate of the elves who tried to march against them, Kimo? Though it wasn't so long ago, you were young then... I suppose you may not remember all the gory details. Those lowly humans you wish to disregard covered the desert in elven blood. I, for one, do not wish to join the ranks of our race that have died at the Bankhoft's hands." She continued to stare into Kimo's eyes, refusing to blink or look away until the dark-haired male shrugged and looked down, finally yielding to authority. Nienna curled her hands into fists and then relaxed her fingers as she exhaled.

Finally, with Kimo no longer pressing the issues the only other woman in the party chimed in. "I agree with her," said Taniya softly, breaking Nienna's train of thought. "There is wisdom in avoiding unwanted, unnecessary attention. We have been fortunate to avoid confrontation with bandits thus far, and we should minimize conflict on this mission to ensure we remain on schedule. Lord Sennin emphasized the criticality of success. If we can return to our families with no one the wiser, I would like to do so. As should you, Kimo; your wife is expecting a child, and I should like to think she will want you home in time for the birth of your first daughter."

Nienna waited for her to continue, but when she did not, the assassin nodded her thanks to the brown-haired woman. "Right, so we will need a good cover story."

The four continued to iron out the details of their lie for the next hour or so while Zarou prowled the camp's perimeter, rubbing his muzzle onto rocks to leave a scent to deter any would-be predators in the area. Another benefit of owning one of the most dangerous animals in Divinoros is that even the largest natural hunters would avoid the Sand Lion in all but the most uncommon circumstances, making camping anywhere in the world a relatively safe endeavor.

The party woke the next day just before dawn to break camp. The horses and Sand Lion were loaded with the riders' traveling gear. Nienna looked over her companions to ensure they were adequately equipped. The three Elites looked much less imposing, now stripped of their highly embroidered armor which had been marked with an encircled bronze dragon claw highlighting their status as Elites.

They now wore ordinary clothing and almost seemed to resemble common folk, as common as elves in peak physical condition could look, that is. However, under the scrutiny of Nienna's trained eye, it was clear to make out the defined muscles and lean build of each Elite under their loose-fitting commoner shirts, indicating they would be formidable opponents in a scuffle.

Additionally, though many people brandished weapons in the southern regions of eastern Divinoros, the master craftsmanship of the Elite's blades was obvious to Nienna. The final giveaway that there was more to the three than meets the eye with these elves, was the barely visible outline of hidden weapons that they had secured to their person. She only made one suggestion, knowing the party would refuse to disarm, even partially so. "Kimo remove your ring. You can't already be in a life bond for our plan to be convincing."

The dark-haired elf glared hard at Nienna, but she held his gaze until the man relented.

Nienna nuzzled Zarou with her forehead. "I'll see you on the other side, my love." Zarou purred his agreement before he turned and began running toward sparse woods that were emerging on the fringes of the desert. Zarou was heading to where the surrounding sand met the high cliff faces on either side of the canyon they now approached.

The travelers had decided that parading Zarou through the Narrows would be a poor way to avoid detection and remain innocuous in their traversal of the city. So, Zarou, rather than pass through the city with them, would find a place to scale the cliff face that stretched sea to sea on the narrow strip of land connecting the deserts to the main body of eastern Divinoros. He would meet them on the northern side of the city by day's end. Nienna hated parting from the partner of her soul. Though she hated the absence of the lions' domineering presence, they did this on occasion when the mission demanded it. She knew he would be okay.

The trip to the entry gates on foot took just over an hour. Although Nienna had passed through the Narrows on a handful of occasions, the town's visual appearance was truly baffling in its abrasive defilement of what could have been a beautiful canyon. She couldn't imagine why anyone would choose to settle in a place like this. A city that rarely saw the sun, given the only opening to the sky was a narrow split of earth that ran along the length of the canyon. The city was named after the fact that it was built within a great ravine that was over two miles long. The base of the canyon had a small river running through it, with many temporary bridges placed over the rushing water, allowing for safe passage across to each muddy bank.

No buildings were built along the river basin, it wasn't worth the cost. Regular flooding would surge through with enough frequency and force to knock down even the sturdiest of homes when thunderstorms rolled through the forests and highlands north of the city. Instead, the settlers here carved grand staircases that spiraled up through the walls of the canyon to the main city centers carved into the facade on each steep canyon wall, high above the basin. Permanent bridges of stone and thick rope sat suspended hundreds of feet in the air, connecting the two sides of the vertical city. On the walled side of city centers, the residents burrowed deep into the canyon walls, forming a labyrinth of tunnels hundreds of miles in length, connecting various homesteads encased in earth. In a word, Nienna would describe the city's structure as inconvenient or, despite its overall impressiveness, ugly. An ant hill carved by humans, the only real benefit of the orientation was that the residents were insulated by dwelling deep within the earth, which helped keep the Narrows residents comfortable even during the harshest winters and hottest summers.

The city was founded long ago, apparently one of the last safe havens above ground during the First War between demon and dragon, before the Gods ever touched this world. But it was not built into what it is today until valuable minerals, fashioned for the rich once harvested, started to be mined within the walls. Lucrative gem hunting drew the ancestors of its current occupants. Greedy jewelers and shady mineral dealings long cast a shadow of crime in the city. After the fall of Omnes, when all cities of Divinoros fell under Celestra's empire, the elvish rule put in place did its best to cover up the crooked blemishes staining the city's culture.

The first ruler set up the town as a major trade port connecting the capital of Divinoros to the desert cities, finally bringing honest laborers to mingle with the dishonest in such quantities that crime was suffocated to the point of near extinction. Still, Celestra's high lord minions never fully corrected the deep-seated ties to crime and corruption that permeated the people here.

The city functioned well enough for centuries, but recently, more and more of the old criminal tendencies slowly boiled up from the darker recesses of the Narrows, once again becoming prominent. Lady Elba, the most recent figurehead, was thought to be losing her grip on the primarily human population beneath her rule.

Word within the crime world, of which Nienna was privy, seemed to think an unknown organization was looking to overthrow the city, blocking the Sandivar Desert region from receiving any trade or supplies from Turenian by land. This would effectively cut off Sandivar's most important trade route and reliable path of needed subsistence. Snippets of Sennin's intelligence spoke of regular violent raids on transport carts. More often than not, these would result in murdered caravanners and, for some odd reason, Nienna thought, burned goods.

Why wouldn't these people steal the goods that were being carried? Sounds like amateurs or people just plain wasteful.

Sennin was equally duped as to the purpose of these raids other than to cause inconvenience. But before she ventured south, common thought in her circles was that once this organization had a firm grip over the city, they would leverage their position of power to negotiate a peace offering with the Queen where they would maintain control over the trade station under human rule. Nienna dismissed this as an impossibly naïve fantasy, having seen how the Queen responded to insurrections in the past with overwhelming forceful aggression.

The site of guards pulled Nienna from her thoughts and without hesitation, the slender elf plastered a giddy smile across her beautiful face and grabbed Kimo around the waist as they approached the southern entrance to the city. She leaned in toward him and brushed her lips against his ear. "Remember, Kimo, we're engaged for the day," she said in a stern tone, contrasting with the visual display of affection. Letting out a giggle, she pulled her face away from Kimo to wave to the guards stationed at the ramp headed to the main city base with one free arm, the other still firmly locked around her unwilling partner.

"Good morning, gentleman! It's a lovely day, is it not?" Nienna called in a high-pitched voice once within earshot of the guards. The hardened-looking human, outfitted in an all-black wardrobe, rolled his eyes and looked to the other guard. With an exasperated sigh, he turned to Kimo, completely ignoring the ditsy Nienna, and asked, "What's your business in these parts?"

Kimo grabbed onto Nienna's waist, smoothly spinning her in front of him in a shallow dip. Staring into her swimming blue eyes, he addressed the guard, "Well, sir, I am on my way to celebrate a life bond with this woman." Looking up, he faced the guard. "We are heading to our ceremony in Turenian. The two behind us are Reiyla and Amariso, my aunt and uncle. They are acting as escorts on our trip north." Kimo gestured to the two walking behind the "lovestruck" couple with three horses now playing pack mule.

The guard immediately let them through, neither displaying the slightest interest in hearing anything further from the pair. Once the party had passed earshot and was heading up the ramp carved into the face of the Narrows, Nienna raised her eyebrow toward Kimo. "Told you, no one likes to be around a couple in love… especially guardsmen."

The young Elite shrugged, only acknowledging the comment with a "humph."

The four travelers ascended the spiraling ramp carved in repeated concentric circles toward the primary level of the Narrows cliff-face cityscape. Once within the depths of the wall, the heat from the desert region was immediately dampened, the air grew moderate in temperature, moist with humidity, and all sounds of the rushing river were drowned out by the echoing of the travelers' boots and clacking of horse's hooves on stone. They soon broke from the seemingly endless climb, emerging to the sounds of muffled voices belonging to the city's residents.

While there was activity along the main terrace market, vendors setting up shops, mothers carrying baskets of groceries, there seemed to be a lack of the bustling energy that Nienna had grown accustomed to when traveling through the once highly trafficked trade center. The people who were about had their eyes cast down, occasionally glancing about nervously while they hurried about their business. No pleasantries were being shared amongst passers-by, no merchants shouted details about their wares, and everyone, Nienna noticed, was making a great effort to give the pairs of mean-looking guards that patrolled the market a wide berth.

"Something is off here…," said Nienna. Kimo looked at her quizzically; having never traveled through the city, he noticed no abnormality, but before he could comment, Joralf spoke up in a hushed whisper, "I sense that as well. Look around, Kimo. Where are the elves? Not only that but why do the people seem to fear the guards that should be protecting them?"

I didn't even notice... Where are the elves? There aren't many of our kind choosing to live in a city such as this, but there is generally a handful of elven miscreants can be found just about anywhere.

Kimo glanced around, taking in the concern, then commented, "It does seem... quiet." Taniya tilted her head as a small group of men dressed in all-black uniforms, marking them as guardsmen, strode past. Each man eyed the four suspiciously, making little attempt to hide their blatant observance over the party.

"Let's get away from the main open areas and head through some of the deeper tunnels till we get to the Northern gate," whispered Taniya. "I don't like how much attention we are garnering."

Just as she quit speaking, two guards stomped out of a storefront to their left. Their sharp gazes were fixed on them, and one shouted in their direction, "Ay pointy ears!" Nienna bristled at the comment. "Hold it right there!" The travelers glanced around. The three Elites made subtle shifts of their cloaks to enable easier access to their plethora of hidden weapons. Nienna remained calm. This was hardly the first time she had had a run-in with a city's guardsmen. She forced her gaze to meet Kimo's eyes sending him a silent message of refrain, and then broke out into a dazzling smile that she had used to make men nervous around her in many tight spots before.

"How may we help you, gentlemen?" Said Nienna in a sweetly pleasant voice as she spun toward the guards on her toes and reached out a hand to tangle her fingers in Kimo's. She was transformed into every bit the dotting excited bride-to-be.

"We don't have many of your kind walking these streets anymore. The elves have taken to greener pastures. We don't want any more of your kind coming this way either," said a tall bald man with the build of a bull-ox. He stood next to an equally impressive man who had long dark hair matching the color of his uniform. *These men look like they were built to combat elves.* Nienna's luminous smile and charm seemed to sail right past the pair of guards to no effect.

Both men's eyes were bloodshot, a familiar visage on the face of humans overly fond of drink, but they lacked the pained expression that often accompanied the drunk. Nienna could also make out thin black tendrils that appeared to be reaching around the perimeter of the whites of the eyes, comingling with the red, as the dark veins stretched toward their brown-colored pupils. The tendrils stirred up fear in Nienna as they seemed to wriggle and move, straining to reach the iris of these men to snuff out the little bit of life in their cold gaze. *The darkness followed me here from the Badlands.* "What is your business in the Narrows?" the long-haired guard asked.

"We don't mean to stay any longer than required. We are just passing through on our way towards Turenian." Kimo said through tightly clenched teeth, rage clearly forming on his face.

Before he could follow up his comment Nienna cut in. "I am entering into a life bond with this one at the end of the month! My aunt and uncle are accompanying us from Sandivar." Nienna brushed her thumb over Kimo's knuckles as she recited their fictitious betrothal in a giddy voice. Kimo, who had stood staring hard at the two guards showing no affection to his bride, finally snapped into his role at her touch and broke into a broad smile, wrapping his arm around Nienna.

The bald man looked over the travelers, his eyes landing on the young elf. "I have no love for your kind, and frankly, I do not believe your little façade. We will escort you to the northern gate to ensure you do not stir up any... trouble on the way out." The man gestured to the left toward a small walkway carved deep into the wall of the Narrows. By now, the market disturbance had resulted in two other large sections of guards having made their way toward the cause of the ruckus. Ten more men now stood watching the exchange. Nienna, not liking their odds in a fight against so many, motioned for her group to follow the escorts into the walkway.

The tunnel paths were lit by evenly spaced torches set in iron sconces. The smoke blackened the wall surrounding each flame, creating a dark smear at the center of the orange glow cast out by the flame of each torch. The walls within the tunnels were spaced just wide enough for the horses to be led one at a time. The party was slowly winding further and further from the main market area into the depths of the carved labyrinth that made up a large portion of the city's footprint. Nienna was not only unsure of how long it would take to reach the northern gate, but it wasn't clear if they weren't being directed in the proper direction or to some worse fate by their human escort.

Nienna hated being underground. She could feel the weight of the oppressive stone around her. The only reprieve in the solid, picked-out stone tube was the intersection of additional tunnels or the wooden frame of an unmarked door—small entryways to the homes of the people who lived in the Narrows. She could never understand the desire to live like a grub burrowed under the earth.

People, humans and elves alike, were bred to relish in all the beauty that life has to offer. That is impossible for those who live huddled in the soil like ground worms, fearful of birds should they breach into the open air.

Plus, she didn't fully believe beings could live without sunlight. Not even the dwarves lived in this way. Their grand city was crafted to emulate the world outside while emphasizing the world's beauty beneath.

102

It was no crude tunneling like what they now walked in for what seemed like hours already.

The long-haired man marched at the front of the group, guiding them silently while the bald man took the rear. Nienna stood at the front of the elven party with the three Elites guiding their mounts directly behind her. She could make out the other guard walking behind them whenever she turned to look back at Kimo, who trailed directly behind her. The light may have been playing tricks on her, but she swore that more guards had joined the rear of the party alongside the bald man, but they faded in and out of her view just as the flickering shadows that painted the walls in the ever-changing torchlight.

Even more unsettling, the long-haired man continually curled his head backward; she could make out his eyes just beneath strands of long hair that obscured most of his face as he continually glanced in her direction. Though dark, she thought his eyes grew more shaded with each passing look, the inky black tendrils growing in length and thickness as they drowned out the whites of his eyes. *Something's not right,* she thought definitively, *we're being led to slaughter.*

Nienna whispered just loud enough for Kimo to hear, "I have lost track of where we are, but we need to find a way to leave these guards behind." Kimo nodded his agreement and communicated with Taniya and Joralf, who brought up the rear.

"What is our next move," she heard Kimo ask. "They are ready to go on your signal."

"Wait till he," Nienna nodded to the long-haired man in front, "takes another turn out of eyesight, and I will take care of him. You stop as soon as I am out of sight. You three subdue the guard at the rear. Be cautious. I think more guards may have joined our little escort. I don't know, but something, well, something is going on with these men. They are more than simple guardsmen."

The young Elite nodded again, an indication of his agreement, and relayed the information to his companions silently. The elves had long ago developed a technique to communicate telepathically through careful channeling of their innate residual magic that was inherent in all higher beings to various degrees. It wasn't the same as wielding one of the gifts of the Gods that the magi possessed, but elves who were intimately familiar with one another could use their minds to speak silently. They couldn't use words, merely portray intention. It was a skill all Elites trained in. This was not easy, however, as it required both parties to trust one another entirely as the mental synergy exposed the individual's secret thoughts and innermost feelings during the mental entanglement. Not to mention, if you were not very familiar with those you conversed with, misinterpretation of thought projections would be common.

Joralf, Kimo, and Taniya had trained together for many decades and integrated the technique into standard combat scenarios for years. Given the nature of her profession, Nienna refused to expose her mind to anyone, but she was practiced at protecting her own mind from exposure against all but a mind mage.

Shortly after Kimo indicated the team was informed of her plan, the long-haired guard turned to the right down an adjoining hallway, briefly obscuring his view of the escorted party. Nienna, without hesitation, burst into action.

Slipping free two of her smaller daggers hidden beneath her cloak, she rounded the corner at a dash, ready to stab down on the man. His back was still turned to her, and with practiced efficiency, she sank the blades into the base of the man's neck, on either side of his spine, with satisfying smoothness. She intended the blades to sever vital arteries, granting the man a swift death. Instead, he grunted, whipping his head around in surprise as if stung by a bee.

He trashed with his arms to grasp at Nienna. Unable to get a hold of the woman, he felt for the rocky wall and began slamming Nienna into the rough tunnel. He forced her repeatedly into the jagged surface with more force than the well-built human should have been able to muster. The impact against the sharp wall shook Nienna violently, but the harsh movement simultaneously widened the wound in the man's neck.

Time was on her side, though. Soon, the flailing man's strength won out. After a harsh impact setting stars to dancing in Nienna's eyes, he was able to grab the Ghost by the arms and toss her over his shoulders. The move sent her sailing through the air. In an open space, the elf could have contorted to land on her feet, but being confined in a tunnel, she ricocheted from the ceiling to the floor before finally rolling against a wall, where she rested in a tangled heap.

She was able to get to her feet as the man stumbled toward her, his eyes now black as night. He faltered, unable to overcome the torrent of viscous black fluid, smelling of rotted flesh, pouring from the gouge in his neck. Before he could reach the elf, the black tendrils drained from his eyes, revealing the panicked eyes of a dying man. He fell to his knees and then toppled over in a still heap as death snuffed out his last spark of life. Thankfully, the mortal wound ended his life before he could finish his display of strength on Nienna.

Breathing heavily, Nienna ran back to the rest of her party, using the wall to balance herself. Her vision contorted with the ringing between her ears, courtesy of the slain long-haired brute. She saw a swarm of chaos as she rounded the corner. The horses were in a fray, with Kimo attempting to calm them, hoping to move the three steeds away from where the other two Elites were fighting the bald man.

To her surprise, Joralf and Taniya hadn't been able to subdue him. In fact, it almost looked like the pair of seasoned soldiers were the ones nearly overwhelmed. As she approached, she saw why. The man's eyes were black, and while he held no weapons, each time Taniya or Joralf struck out, a tentacle of darkness would materialize from the deep shadows behind the human to intercept the elves' advances. New limbs were materializing all the while, shimmering into dark points of lethal existence from the intangible darkness beyond, stinking out against the Elites with speed the elves could barely avoid.

Nienna pressed against the side of the wall and pushed her way past the horses to assist her companions. As she passed, she saw Joralf lunge toward the man with a lightning-fast jab of his sword. Two shadowed arms appeared from opposite sides of the bald man and wrapped around the blade. The shadowy arms strained, and the sword shattered under the force of the mysterious power this guardsman wielded.

Just as the sword splintered, two new arms shot forward and pierced through both shoulders of Joralf, shattering bone and tearing through muscle and tendon. Bloody mist hung in the air as the shadow limbs became visible from the elf's backside. Joralf screamed in pain as he collapsed, the howls fading into muted groaning agony. Taniya screamed in rage, knowing she may have witnessed the end of her friend, and began unleashing a fury of attacks, all parried by the laughing guard.

Nienna knew the Elite's close combat could rival her own, and the guard seemed to welcome any additional challengers. So rather than join the fight, she retreated till the bald man was only focused on Taniya.

I just need to find my opening.

She reversed her hold on her dagger and then released the blade with expert precision. The shining steel rotated past Taniya's face, nearly nicking the elf's ear before emerging through her billowing hair to land with a dull thump in the bald man's head directly between his eyes. He staggered back, his face frozen in an expression of surprise. As his guard dropped, Taniya took full advantage. The Elite brought forth her sword in a fast, powerful stab that pierced through the front of the man's neck, causing the guard to burble the rotted blood—the same as Nienna saw pouring from the guard she had slain—through his gaping lips.

A wet, sucking squelch accompanied Taniya when she yanked her blade free of its fleshy home before she brought it about in a perfectly executed horizontal strike decapitating the monster dying before her. As the dark liquid left the body in large spurts, the corpse withered and decomposed as if the rotted substance within was what kept him alive in the first place. "What in the name of the Gods was that?" lamented Taniya as she dropped to her knees and bent over Joralf, checking his pulse.

105

"I believe I have seen this magic before, or at least something very similar. In the Badlands, wielded by the Bankhoft leader. The Narrows have been taken from Celestra, I imagine," responded Nienna, astounded by the circumstance she found herself in. "The Knife... He is spreading his influence, and the Narrows will cut off Sandivar from any ground transit or troops. A war is beginning... And I don't believe Celestra has any clue who her true enemy is."

She filed those thoughts away. Right now, major geopolitical maneuverings were not her top priority; survival was. The two healthy Elites seemed shocked by the forces at play, but centuries of training kept them moving, and Nienna commanded her team more naturally than she would have thought herself capable.

Keeping her calm demeanor despite her internal panic, she issued her orders. "Kimo, help Taniya treat Joralf and strap him to a horse's back. Move swiftly; we must get out of the tunnels before more of these monsters find us. We were not quiet."

There was no argument as the two untouched Elites careed for their injured companion. Nienna closed her eyes and recounted the steps they had taken thus far. The party, she believed, had been led primarily west, moving deeper into the canyon wall. Now, knowing that there was powerful magical, possibly divine, opposition awaiting them should they choose to step foot back into the open market, Nienna thought their best bet was to weave through the labyrinth of passages toward the Northgate and hope to avoid any additional unwanted attention until that became an inevitability.

Once Joralf was safely secured to the back of his mare, the party trudged through the haunting passageways, Nienna silently praying to the Gods that she led the party in the correct direction.

Nienna - Chapter 14 - Fleeing North

Nienna had long lost track of how long the party had been stumbling through the maze of tunnels. With only the number of steps they took available to gauge the passage of time, they could have been navigating the labyrinth for a couple of hours or half the day.

To make matters worse, Joralf's condition was rapidly declining. Beads of sweat covered the fever-stricken man. The heat radiating from his body was only growing worse as signs of infection began to appear, evidenced by swollen black veins around the site of each wound. Nienna tied a cloth around her face to mask the rotting stench that now trailed the party, growing worse step by step.

As the minutes passed, his groans of pain grew louder. Soon, Nienna thought, she would be forced to gag Joralf to reduce the risk of drawing the attention of patrolling guards or residents who were moving about the tunnels. She had no way of knowing when the two bodies of the slain guards would be found, but once they were, she had no doubt the entire city guard would be on the lookout for the strange group of elves.

They traveled at a hurried pace, and after an excruciatingly long day, Nienna finally caught a glimpse of a doorway leading out into the fading light of dusk. She held up a fist, and Kimo and Taniya halted immediately, the horses they led following suit.

"I see a way out of this hellhole," Nienna said in a hushed tone. "It looks to be nearly nightfall."

Joralf let out a groan of pain followed by a terrible scream. His body then went limp, only briefly, before spasming in tightness as his body seized up, protesting the agony he felt from what appeared to be some unknown toxin tightening its stranglehold on his life.

"Move back now!" Nienna ordered in response.

Once they had retreated further from the cavern's entrance, Taniya ran to the horse that held the man and ran her hand over his face in an attempt to comfort the severely wounded elf. The seizure ended, and Joralf once again went limp, eyes wide open but plain white as the irises rolled back into his head. The team needed to move quickly. None of the healing tinctures Taniya carried had worked to improve his condition. They needed to find a healing mage if they were to have any hope of saving him. *And a slim hope at that,* Nienna thought. Nienna would never voice this to her companion, but based on Joralf's condition, there was no way he would make the arduous journey that still spanned between the Narrows and Turenian. She simply wished to get him out of the city to find a place to bury the man in peace once he passed into the void beyond.

Nienna looked back toward the entranceway leading to the open space. She saw a group of four guards appear in response to the loud incident from Joralf, peering hesitantly into the corridor. She overheard their conversation. "Someone needs to check that out."

"Send in Dougfrey, he's the new guy…"

"What?!... Why me?! What could I do against four elves? We need one of the Gifted with us…"

"Well, Doug, we ain't calling a Gifted without knowing the intruders are in there."

"Well, let's just keep moving then. Pretend we ain't heard nothing! I ain't going in there alone. Plus, they'd have to get by the barricade anyway. What good is me sacrificing myself?"

With that, she heard shuffling feet as the four moved away, chastising the man they called Dougfrey until their voices were too far away to make out.

Nienna turned to her companions, "Gag him." Taniya looked aghast, but before she could attempt to rebuke their appointed team leader for her cruelty, Nienna continued, "The guards heard him. If they hear him again, they will send in a scout. We must retreat and be silent. We will escape in the night. It won't be long now. We can treat him once we are gone." Though Nienna knew the man to be beyond the point of help, her word reassured her companion.

Taniya nodded, though the fury in her gaze remained. Nienna believed the anger to be directed at the situation rather than the harsh orders she had to give, so she brushed off the gaze as inconsequential at the moment. She knew that Joralf and Taniya had spent the better part of five hundred years at each other's side, and it was clear that she cared greatly for the man.

The group returned the way they had come, waiting for the nightfall's darkness as the Ghost had suggested. Once Nienna assumed enough time had passed, she motioned to the others to follow her back to the mouth of the gate to the outdoors. In a hushed tone, she called to Taniya and Kimo, "I am going to scout. You wait here." As silent as an owl in flight, she moved closer to the tunnel's exit. She was the Ghost. Recon and assassination are where she excelled. She could move about in the night far more effectively than the clumsy Elites could manage, and as such, she would tend to this portion of their escape alone.

Orange torchlight painted the floor just outside the doorway of the tunnel the Ghost now crouched in. She assumed the outside of this tunnel's entrance was lit from the two sconces bolted to the wall adjacent to the tunnel's opening. Thinking about how she had many times required a clever escape from a barricaded location, she assumed there would be a pair of guards stationed at each opening to the deeper caverns. This proved true as the assassin could easily make out shadows of two men in the flickering torchlight, one to each side of the mouth of the tunnel. She was unable to make out any other guards moving about in the open space beyond.

With the situation requiring swift action, the Ghost did not hesitate in her approach, unsheathing one of her long daggers and pressing her thumb against the edge of the blade to quiet the slide of metal as she drew the weapons. She dropped into a crouch and sidled up to the doorway along the right wall. Once she saw the frame of an armored guard near the edge of the left door frame, the Ghost descended upon the man, silent as a shadow emerging from nothingness, a wraith of death. *Kill in silence,* she thought.

Without hesitation, the Ghost stabbed the man through the side of his neck and pulled the blade out the front of his throat in a singular movement, severing the man's vocal cords. As the blade freed from the neck of the first guard, blood sprayed in a broad arc as the elf spun and buried the long side of the same blade into the front side of the second guard's throat before he could react. She grabbed both men before they crumpled loudly to the floor and slowly laid them down to avoid commotion.

She wiped her blade on one guard's jerkin before sheathing the weapon to grab both men and pull their bodies back into the depth of the tunnel she had just emerged from. Depositing the corpses with Kimo and Taniya, she said, "Take these men further back. They were guarding the door." Kimo looked at her, astonished. There had not been a single sound made, not even as the assassin dragged two limp corpses through the hall. She was a practiced killer, after all. The Elites gave her a look she was all too familiar with, surprise and fear.

"I will be back for you in a quarter-hour. I need to plot our escape route. Wait here," said the Ghost. And she again immersed herself into the shadows of the tunnels as she moved toward the main plateau of the Narrows.

The scouting mission went as expected. As she exited into open space, she saw the spiraling descent to the Northern gate, guarded by two more guards, no more than a hundred yards from the tunnels the Elites now hid.

Thank the Gods we went in the right direction.

The open market space in front of her now seemed abandoned. No residents milled about, and no taverns emitted boisterous tunes from bards with drunken patrons singing along. The only activities were groups of guards outfitted in black marching on patrol.

The assassin crept toward the spiral stairs that led down to the northern gate, using the shadows and vacated storefronts to disguise her approach. To the right of the descending entryway, where the guards stood in waiting, was a large overlook. This point allowed viewers to see an unobstructed view of the paths leading up to the Narrows and the northern gate that now stood closed.

Making her way to the overlook, the Ghost quickly took in the reinforcements stationed below the overhang at the northern gate. She counted at least twenty armed men facing toward the city on ground level. Clearly placed to ensure no parties left the Narrows rather than being concerned with what may come in. There were also two fifteen-foot watch towers with a pair of archers atop each post. The towers stood to either side of the northern gate's main road. Sneaking through unnoticed would not be an option.

In front of the twenty men was a hooded figure. He was pacing back and forth, instructing the gathered guards. Nienna could not hear the voice or make out any features from the distance she was observing, but she did notice one thing about the man that was unmistakable. He held an unsheathed dagger that appeared to be about a foot long. The blade seemed to swallow the light around it as if emanating darkness deeper than the surrounding night.

How could the Knife be here? thought Nienna, as fear began grabbing her chest, cascading her heart into rapid thrumming. The Ghost took a deep breath to calm her nerves. *Observe and make a plan.* She continued to watch as the Knife raised his arms to the concise battle cry emitted from the small group of guards, each shout accentuated by the sound of swords banging against shields. Once the chanting ceased, one lone guard stepped up toward the leader of the Bankhofts, kneeling before him. The Knife reached out and cupped the kneeling man's face before using the dark dagger to draw an extended cut down his arm. With no hesitation, he reversed the grip he held on the blade and brought it down into the shoulder of the kneeling guard at the base of his neck. The guard howled in pain as shadowy tendrils flowed from the Knife's wounded arm, arcing toward the sky before descending back down toward the blade embedded in the guard, like lightning to a rod.

As soon as the spiraling shadows touched the blade, the screaming ceased, and the guard went stiff. His arms extended behind his rigid torso, his head pulled back in a soundless cry. Then the Knife pulled the blade free of his neck. The tremors in the guardsmen's body ceased. He stood, bowed to the Knife, and then retreated to the line of guards as if he had never been harmed. The man moved with more confidence than before, and the assassin could make out what appeared to be shadows swirling about him on the ground. *This must be how the Gifted are born. But how could the Knife be here? Nothing could travel as fast as Zarou and the Sandshari.*

The answer came quickly. The Knife saluted the group, then used the dagger to carve a deep rivet through reality itself, creating a rift, a portal that pulsated with dark otherworldly energy. As the Knife stepped into the portal, his form blurred into a faint echo of his presence until the rift knit itself back together, erasing the trace of the corrupted man. In his wake stood awestruck soldiers amidst the newest Gifted the Knife had created.

Nienna had never seen anything like that in all her days traveling across Divinoros. A man with the power of a God could now seemingly open portals at will to travel to Gods knows where in the blink of an eye and create soldiers superior to Celestra's Elites. *My, how the world has changed these past months.*

This must be how he was able to take over the Narrows without a whisper of his action reaching the ears of Lord Sennin. Now, in the eyes of the Ghost, there was no question of who the primary power in the pivotal trade city belonged to. The Bankhoft family now controlled the Narrows. Their influence in this world was expanding, and no one was any the wiser of his actions. No one other than Nienna. *The elves in power have grown arrogant. They never would assume humans to have such power, and in their complacency, the clever have slowly chewed away at the firm grasp we elves have held on Divinoros for so long. The Knife is loosening their clenched fist one finger at a time.*

Her recon complete, the Ghost retreated to her companions where she relayed what she had seen. Both Taniya and Kimo looked toward her with newfound admiration and respect, as not many could walk freely in such hostile territory undetected. But as she relayed her intel, Nienna could see they feared the prospect of facing another Gifted in combat, though neither would admit this to her. With no time to waste, she laid out their escape plan. Once finished, Kimo nodded to her. "It's as good a plan as any." And with that, they went to carry out her orders with a swiftness that spoke highly of the Elite's disciplined training.

Nienna left the tunnels ahead of her companions. She would eliminate the two guards covering the passage to the descent without being noticed. Once they were dispatched, Kimo and Taniya would lead the horses to the descending tunnel out to the north gate. This is where things could no longer be subtle. On the descent, the Elites would mount their steeds and lead a charge to kill the guards on foot, while the Ghost would eliminate the archers positioned in the abutments at either side of the gate.

Kimo and Taniya were aware of the guard who was likely converted into one of the so-called "Gifted." So, the plan was to eliminate as many common guards as they could on their initial charge so the three elves could then converge on the real threat in unison. The fight would be brutal, but the Ghost seemed confident the three could overcome the force below, especially if they were able to isolate the Gifted before engaging him in earnest.

The Ghost's lengthy resume in successful espionage and silent assassination was evident as she quickly dispatched the two guards watching the descent without raising the slightest alarm.

The party was soon down to ground level, and as they exited the tunnel, the elves heard shouts being called from the northern gate as the Gifted was organizing his men to form rank and keep focused. *They must have heard the horses on the stone.*

As the certainty of martial conflict approached, a calmness overtook Nienna. *I will enjoy killing these men.* The Ghost smiled menacingly at Kimo and Taniya, who looked between each other with concerned expressions at the gleeful assassin.

"How kind of them to line up our targets. This should make things easier." Nienna surveyed the landscape, and the enemy lined out before them. "Feint a charge to hold their attention, but don't get within range of the towers until you see the first archer fall."

Kimo and Taniya did not need to be instructed twice. They immediately mounted their horses, nodded toward the Ghost, and rushed at the enemy swords in hand, leaving the Ghost and their wounded companion near the exit of the descent. They didn't rush head-on; instead, they taunted the line of human soldiers, pulling the attention of the archers and soldiers as they buzzed about their established position.

Night had fully descended, and the riverside landscape was now cast into deep shadows dancing within the canyon ravine to the tune of flickering torchlight. The only other light to fall on the area were soft slivers of unimpeded starlight mingling with the orange hue of the lit torches. The Ghost scouted her path, well accustomed to working in minimal visibility. Once she settled on a route, she was quick to slip into the shadows.

The assassin rapidly crept along the perimeter of the soon-to-be battleground approaching the left battlement. The two archers stood one with a torch in hand, the other his bow ready to draw, both squinting out at the two riders on horseback brandishing their weapons just out of their range. Well trained, neither bowman fired, not wishing to waste a shaft.

The Ghost approached unnoticed, creeping amongst the shrubbery and debris cast from the river during one of the many floods in the area, until she was no more than a good stone's throw from the tower. She slipped two throwing knives from her corset sheath before whipping the blades in the direction of the two men. With deadly accuracy, she buried the blades under the jawline of both men. Not a sound was made as the bodies stiffened slightly, before folding over the banisters, momentum carrying their bodies over the rails, sending them crashing into the ground with a loud thud of heavy metal impacting sodden soil.

The guards nearby turned and, seeing the crumpled forms of their companions dead, began to shout a warning. Their tight formation crumbled as many turned to face the battlement looking to see how the men had died. With the formations deteriorating, Taniya and Kimo spurred their Sandshari steeds toward the fray. Seconds passed before the charge was recognized and then chaos ensued amongst their ranks.

As the guards struggled to reform order, the Ghost unsheathed three additional throwing knives and crept along the backside of the panicked guardsmen now focused on the brazen charge.

Still sticking to the shadows, she closed in on the second tower of archers who had begun firing arrows rapidly at the elves on horseback. She quickly threw two of the knives, listening for the dull thud that indicated each knife had found its target. As the bodies tumbled from their perch, she hurled the final knife at the back of the Gifted with enough force to bury the blade down to the hilt in the man's skull.

Her aim was true, and she watched the rotation of the blade, metal gleaming in reflected torchlight as it carved through the surrounding darkness. The Gifted would fall, and this skirmish would end quickly. She almost smiled just as a common guard shifted his weight, stepping directly in the knife's trajectory. Fury rose in Nienna's chest as the blade dug into the side of the man's neck. The human fell to the ground screaming and clutching at the fatal wound, his hands feebly attempting to quench the flow of blood that spurted past his fingers.

"Well, not where I wanted that to go... at least they broke ranks... that should make it easier for..." An enormous crash filled the night as Kimo and Taniya slammed full tilt into the formation of men. Soldiers fell under the powerful sword strikes delivered from horseback, and the well-trained steeds kicked out with hooves and stomped upon fallen injured men, crushing bones and rupturing organs underneath hooves. *Small but furious Sandshari are.*

The going seemed surprisingly easy until a blood-curdling scream echoed from a figure now hunched in the middle of the remaining guardsmen. The Gifted's limbs began contorting with the accompaniment of loud snaps; pained whimpers preceded his head, ripping back in a vicious guttural laugh as he slowly stood, revealing solid black eyes.

Dark obsidian spines erupted through the man's skin, covering his forearms, shoulders, back, cheekbones, and brow in a spiny obsidian-like carapace. Nienna could see sharpened spines also running along the sides of his legs at an upward angle. The carapace turned the Gifted's visage into something resembling a spiny reptile and human crossbreed born with violence and hatred in its black eyes. He reached out an open palm to his side as if to bask in the newfound power. The Ghost could make out bloodied hands where claws of obsidian had pushed through the tips of what were once ordinary fingers, now lined with jagged black

113

stone protrusions. They were hands belonging to a monster that haunted children's dreams.

He looked like a beast spit up from the underworld, a deadly spined figure forcing its appearance from the corrupted body of a broken man. He continued to hold his arm to the side and opened his palm. Nienna watched as a javelin formed in his open hand, condensing from a swirling darkness that released from his core. Not wishing to wait for the javelin to fully form, the Ghost charged at the man, unsheathing her blades as she sprang at him. She intended to bring down both blades in a devastating overhead blow.

She was too slow. The Gifted moved with speed that matched her own. Maybe exceeded it. He spun, catching her by the throat with his empty hand. With a strength that should have only been possible amongst the beast and fey folk of Divinoros, Nienna was slammed into the ground by the vise grip on her neck. Then she was airborne, thrown aside as a child would toss a ragdoll. The monster then spun to face the Elites. Without hesitation, the javelin was hurled directly at Kimo, who could do nothing more than watch, eyes wide, as the weapon of darkness lodged into his abdomen with such force that he was knocked free from the horse's back

He stood and screamed in agony as he yanked the weapon from his midsection. The javelin dissolved once it was no longer wedged in his body. Blood and gore fell away to the ground as the weapon vanished. Kimo fell into a fierce battle rage, adrenaline and fear masking his pain and allowing the elf to continue striking out at the handful of still-living guards.

Likewise, the Ghost paid no mind to her wounded companion, as a lack of action would only worsen the situation the traveling party found themselves in. The assassin struggled to her feet before rushing to strike at the spined monster with both daggers once again. Her first attack was a two-handed cross strike, but the weapon merely glanced off the spines on its shoulders, fracturing away a number of the stone protrusions. The only success of the movement was to bring the full attention of the monster to herself. The creature fixed its dark gaze on the she-elf. Reaching both hands to the side, he manifested two additional javelins of darkness; he hurled one toward the Ghost immediately with a speed that impressed her.

It wasn't fast enough to catch her, though, as she spun to the side and stepped in closer to the creature. The sailing javelin passed inches from her neck before burying itself in between the shoulder blades of one human guard who was too close to the fight between an elf and a supernatural force. The circle of soldiers around the Gifted grew wider at the sight of friendly fire. The men opted to move closer to their comrades being slaughtered by the two Elites rather than stand near the raging Gifted.

Nienna emerged from her spin around the thrown projectile with a vicious side slash at the colossus's knees, but the blade was again deflected by the obsidian spines that now seemed to cover the entire monster. She pressed her attacks, stabbing and slashing in a complex barrage of feints and stabs. The Gifted blocked most blows, but its skill level was clearly below that of the infamous Ghost.

Lack of skill, however, was made up for with durability and raw power. Each landed strike merely glanced off the hell-born beast. Inexperienced against such a foe, the assassin made her mistake; she stepped in close to stab at the Gifted with all her force, hoping to break through the obsidian carapace, but as she did so, the monster dropped his javelin and caught the Ghost's blade with one hand. With the other, he seized the elf around the neck again and lifted her clean off the ground. The monster yanked the long dagger from her grip, tossing it to the side as Nienna feebly kicked at the creature.

A gravelly voice filled the air as the Gifted spoke to her, "Pesky little elf. Even you cannot match the power handed down from divinity. Even if you happened to be victorious today, I am but a sliver of what is to come. I will do you the service of killing you today to keep you from witnessing the horrors on the horizon."

The spine monster slammed the Ghost to the ground, then straddled the she-elf, wrapping both spindly hands around her neck. Squeezing with immense force, he slowly choked the life from her squirming body. She fought voraciously, bloodying her fingers as she clawed at the backs of his spine-covered hands and pounded useless fists against the man's chest. She tried to throw the Gifted off her by thrusting her hips, but he seemed to weigh a ton and barely budged as her legs gave way to flailing. She tried everything to relieve the force that was attempting to pop her head like a melon. Her mouth opened and closed. Nienna struggled for precious air.

I'm not yet ready to die.

Her vision faded, her oxygen-starved brain growing closer and closer to ceasing function.

Just as she was about to lose consciousness, a massive creature soared overhead, slamming into the spindly monster with enough force to throw the magically enhanced human from the assassin. Nienna coughed and sucked in air through her ravaged windpipe, only succeeding in spurring a wave of violent, bloody coughs.

Once the dark perimeter of her vision faded, her heart soared as she saw a massive feline standing over a crumpled, thrashing form. Zarou had the Gifted pinned beneath one paw, roaring in fury down at the struggling form. She smiled. It was a sound she imagined could make even the Gods tremble.

With his other free arm, Zarou raked deep gouges down the struggling beast's back, sending blood and gore sailing from his paws as he mauled at the man over and over, tearing through his carapace, spine, ribs, and organs with ease.

While Nienna lacked the strength to cause damage, Zarou easily cracked through the obsidian carapace like a snail's shell, freeing the same rotten blood she had freed from the Gifted in the tunnels. Soon, the surrounding landscape was soaked in gore. The monster's screaming and writhing soon slowed to a halt. As the last few remaining guards noticed the most recent addition to the scuffle, they dropped their weapons and fled back to their safe haven in the Narrows.

The giant sand lion was not yet finished with his prey. Nienna knew Zarou's history of decimating any being that threatened her. He would hunt for food and kill concisely, but when Nienna was threatened, he killed with demonstrative intent. This was not the first time he had brutalized one that attacked his lifelong companion.

So, with a final roar, Zarou leaned over the twitching figure, snarling. The Gifted that had, just a moment ago, seemed so daunting lay limp. Zarou bit into the man's head. The skull cracked loudly under the immense strength of Zarou's jaws, and the body went fully limp. With a final show of force, Zarou shook his thick neck, and the head separated from the wrecked carapace body. Grey gore spilled from the fractured head as the lion dropped his kill to raise his head to the night sky and lose a final deafening challenge at all who remained in the Narrows, relishing in his kill.

Nienna struggled to her knees as the scaled lion strode over to her and nuzzled the elf. "Thank you," Nienna wheezed as she pressed her forehead against the giant sand lion's forearm. She stroked his maw, ignoring the chunks of flesh that clung to the lion's face. She was met with a loud purr of affection, and despite everything, she felt safe once again.

"I'm not leaving you again… ever… you go where I go, or we don't go at all." Nienna was met with a sandpapery lick of agreement along her upper arm.

The shock of being seconds from death was near to overwhelming Nienna, but the feeling soon passed as she knew time was of the essence. *Responsibility is unforgiving. Emotions can be dealt with later or ignored. Now, I must deal with what's in front of me.* Nienna looked over her shoulder at her companions, wondering how to address the situation. Taniya looked reasonably well, only taking minor cuts to her forearms and legs during the foray. She was tending to Kimo, whom she'd helped down to a laying position. Kimo looked to be in far worse condition.

116

As Nienna approached, she could see that Taniya had removed the section of clothing from around where the javelin had punctured Kimo's midsection. The entry site of the wound looked to be festering in a similar fashion to Joralf's shoulders. Nienna could smell the rotting stench of black puss that was already oozing from the gut wound. The skin surrounding the puncture was swollen and red, interlaced with bulging black tendrils growing and spreading to the healthy surrounding tissue.

Taniya ruffled frantically through the saddle bags strapped to her horse. She pulled out a vial of clear liquid along with clean rags. Nienna grabbed her arm, "We need to leave now. The guards will have already found reinforcements and could be upon us any second."

Taniya yanked her arm free and glared at Nienna without a word. Kneeling back by Kimo, the elven woman said sternly, leaving no room for debate, "I will not let him die. If you wish to leave sooner, then help. Go get a torch and begin heating the end of my blade." She wiped the tip of her sword to wash away blood from the humans she had killed. "Once the blade is heating, go retrieve the mount carrying Joralf, tie his horse to the back of mine. We will need to ride with haste if we hope to reach Turenian to treat him, along with Kimo. Even still... I do not know if we will make it in time."

Nienna nodded and did as she was instructed; she owed the woman that. *That is a terrible gut wound. That would spell death for all had it been a normal javelin that pierced him. With no healing mage, of course, death awaits with the wound coming from that dark weapon...*

As she placed the clean blade over the open flame of a torch, she saw Taniya working frantically. The Elite had squeezed the outer ring of the wound, forcing more and more of the black pus from Kimo's abdomen. The liquid bubbled and was absorbed into the earth once it was forced from the living body. Kimo screamed as the pressure was applied but soon fainted under the treatment, the pain too much to bear while conscious.

"Get Joralf," Taniya said to the transfixed assassin. Nienna had been staring at the growing pool of black liquid. Nienna nodded and moved to where Joralf's horse had taken up hiding during the scuffle. After gentle coaxing, she was able to take the horse's reins to lead the beast and unconscious elf back to where Taniya was rapidly tending to Kimo's abdomen. As she was turning the Sandshari back toward her remaining companions, she saw specks of torchlight marching along the main level terrace toward the ramp leading to the Northern Gate.

"We must hurry. Reinforcements are near," Nienna shouted over to Taniya as she tied Joralf's mount to Taniya's saddle.

"I am nearly done," came the reply as Nienna approached to check the progress. Taniya had finished squeezing the javelin's impact site. No

117

dark tendrils webbed the elf's abdomen after the treatment, but the aggressive squeezing had angered the skin, which had grown puffy and still bled rapidly—a sickly color of rotten blood rather than scarlet red. A sizzling sound penetrated the silent party as a clear liquid was poured into the wound.

"This is a purifying potion developed by the northern elf ice tribes. I have seen it can clear out the nastiest infections of rotted battle wounds. Unfortunately, it does not stop the bleeding." With that comment, Taniya seized up her red-hot sword and pressed the flat of the blade forcefully into the wound. The smell of burnt flesh filled the air as the site was cauterized. Surprisingly, after the putrid scent of the dark puss, the burning flesh didn't seem bad.

"Help me lift him," Nienna said as the sound of marching crept into the range of hearing. "We need to leave now."

The two she-elves lifted the unconscious Elite. "We need to strap him to Zarou. You can't lead both mounts, and neither will allow themselves to be tied behind a sand lion," Nienna said.

With that, the unconscious Elite was tied to a clearly unhappy Zarou, who had expected to be ridden by the partner of his soul. Nienna thanked Zarou, understanding his displeasure, before jumping on Kimo's steed and galloping off into the night.

Baelin - Chapter 15 - Aftermath of Eradication

Months of traveling north would soon culminate in our final stand against Omnes's minions of death. Most of our force had died violently before ever reaching the frozen plains. Thousands. Tens of thousands. All dead at the hands of a cruel deity intent on controlling this world.

There was more than one night I wished to be counted amongst those already fallen. Their lifeless fate was less cruel than suffering the trials still to come. The constant physical pain of my wounds was one thing, but healers and potions were able to alleviate most of that pain. At least, they were up until a month ago. That is the point that we lost our last life mage in a particularly violent battle. And the enemy seemed to know. Seemed to target the life magi.

After that point, we became reliant on a depleted stock of healing potions and traditional mundane medicine. But the physical pain is not what leaves me so wary. I have grown mentally and spiritually exhausted. There is a wearing effect on your mind after seeing countless of your kind torn apart in front of you, just meat forced through the grinder of an unyielding enemy. There is something innately wrong in growing numb at the site of your friends spilling their innards in front of you, growing numb to the site of watching life fade from once bright, gleaming eyes.

No matter how many of our enemies we kill, more seem to replace them...

We know not where they are born, and I have grown disheartened by their never changing numbers. Each battle brings fresh waves upon us. I rarely sleep now. My thoughts haunt me. I should have stayed with my wife, with my children. If we're all to die, would it not be sweeter to perish in the arms of loved ones?

I would have thought it a miracle to have survived as long as I have, but can you call living in constant horror a miracle? No, you cannot. Now I seem to exist only in a twisted version of hell, struggling to grasp the last strands of hope that we may emerge victorious...Those strands become more fleeting by the day.

But I digress, detailing the torment in my mind.

I wished to record events of the war when I set out, and that is what I shall do. Ten thousand of the remaining army had finally made it to our final stop of Reyvothia. Standing orders are to make camp in the fallen city and march on the Rift at first light, a journey through the frozen plains sure to claim additional lives. I have grown quite close to my team, and through the loss of my betters, I have even been promoted *to colonel, the highest-ranking soldier remaining in General Celestra's battalion. As such, I have the time to make this entry as camp fortifications and tents are erected. That being said, this is all I can write for now. With our numbers depleted as they are, everyone is expected to contribute.*

Baelin sat upright in his chair, running his hand through his beard in contemplation and silent hope. So far, the journal has primarily been a first-hand account of how King Kei-Tel Turena managed to minimize losses to the Dark God Omnes while marching on the Rift.

There had been little detail in the way of religious theory on how the monsters and God had been summoned. Still, the journal had proved beyond exceptional in evidencing how the elf army fared against their mighty foe and how the horrors of battle could warp and wear down a person's mind.

Despite the lack of a major breakthrough, Baelin was hopeful that Durenthi would survive to provide an account of the final battle and also the aftermath of the conquest revealing some new details hinting at the origin of Omnes landing on Divinoros. Flipping through the remaining pages, he was relieved to see the same black ink scrawled through the back binder of the book. The story was not yet near its end.

The night passed by without incident. We were all surprised by this, being so close to the source of divine power in this world. We were grateful, nonetheless. This may be my last entry should the Gods choose to claim my life the next time we sacrifice ourselves at the hands of the Dark God. We have only a week's march before we arrive at the gates of Omnes; the Rift draws near. If someone unknown finds this, please return it to my family in Turenian. The Bari family owns a beautiful baked goods shop in the main city square. They, and I, would appreciate the gesture.

Knowing full well that Durenthi survived this battle, having flipped through to the final pages of the book and still seeing his scribbles, Baelin continued on, skipping over text detailing the travels north and the final battle.

I saw him fall. Our King is dead. Had it not been for Captain Celestra, the army may have fallen into chaos after he died.

My memory of the battle is blurred even though it happened no more than a few days before making this entry. I was amongst the last remaining forces who attempted to hold out against hordes of krakenshi and the giant serpentine monsters. We fared well, at the start, at least. But once the serpentine warriors were released... the battle descended into messy scrambling, as all martial contests eventually do.

When I close my eyes, I see rivers of scarlet carved in snow, littered with broken bodies and discarded innards of my kin. The brutality of the towering human-like serpents quickly scattered our defensive

120

formations through broad swings of war hammers as large as the pillars in our dead King's throne room.

I was hit with a glancing blow from one of those that sent me sailing through the air. Luckily, I was fighting alongside a formidable team of warriors who were able to distract the creature as I struggled to regain my bearings. As I stood, I recall time seeming to slow as I scanned the battleground. Funny how pain seems to elongate time. How it wishes to keep you within its grasp to experience the moment for far longer than should be permissible.

I remember seeing swarms of krakenshi buzzing between groups of soldiers, biting, clawing, and tearing through any unprotected flesh with ease. The massive snake creatures carrying obsidian war hammers slivered through the swarming masses, smashing through groups of soldiers. Defeat seemed inevitable as wave upon wave of new combatants made quick work of large sections of soldiers.

But any who discount the might of an elf must do so at their own peril. There is a reason the Gods had recruited our race to help them rid the world of demons so long ago. We are magical beings and possess a great power within us. Despite a disgraced God throwing all the divine power he could muster at us, we refused to break, and in that, I hold immense pride. I saw one snake giant fall and, in seeing that, jumped back into my own battle with a renewed determination.

Then, from my peripherals, I saw two figures standing face to face at the edge of the world. One was elegant, tall, dressed in shining gold and silver armor, silver hair flowing down his back with a two-handed grip on his acclaimed glaive. The other was a massive, bulky figure encased in a seemingly impenetrable suit of obsidian armor. Gold radiated from the two eye slits of the solid helm, and a massive pure black broadsword was held in each hand. Behind the figure, a long cloak of shifting shadows billowed behind him despite the lack of wind.

I was unable to watch the beginning of their fight as I was in the middle of one myself, but the glimpses I caught showed two masters of combat, two harbingers of death. I could not believe that the heavily armored figure moved as quickly as our King, but he did... seemingly with ease.

I was forced to refocus on my own fight to avoid being shattered by the massive war hammer of the snake creature I fought. Eventually, we were able to subdue the monster, successfully lodging multiple glaives deep into its back. Once collapsed, my team hacked at the neck of the creature like lumberjacks attempting to fall a tree. After the beast had been fully decapitated, I turned back to see how my King fared.

King Kei-Tel had managed to knock one of the broadswords free from the Obsidian Knight's hand. But as the King wheeled to deliver another strike, I saw the knight pull a dagger—an obsidian dagger, pure *black. He plunged the blade into the abdomen of our King in a frenzied flurry of blows.*

I saw the knight walking, gesturing to the army of krakenshi that continued to pour from the wall of mist hanging above the Rift. The Obsidian Knight plunged his sword through Kei-Tel's chest, and in that moment, dread pierced my heart, as cold and as fierce as a metal blade. But the great Kei-Tel possessed the will of a God himself, it seemed. As the Knight turned his back to the King, Kei grabbed the figure and pulled him over the edge of the Rift. I remember seeing the obsidian dagger sail through the air and land on the edge of the massive crevasse next to a stone where the Knight's shadow cloak caught and ripped. The two fell over the side, leaving no indication they had been there other than that dark obsidian dagger and a ripped piece of cloth that clung to the rocks at the edge of the Rift.

Celestra was at the spot in the blink of an eye, shrieking at the loss of her King. As she wept, the monsters seemed to collapse around us, losing direction, purpose, and sustenance. The flesh of the beasts began to rot, dissolve, and peel from their limbs as they dissipated into puddles of black viscous fluid that trickled back toward the shroud of mist as if a gravitational pull summoned them home.

Baelin raised his eyes from the book in deep thought. He hadn't come across any evidence suggesting that there were any artifacts left from Omnes. He didn't yet know how this tied into what he already knew or if the detail was important. But this was a new avenue in his research he could chase down. This was the clue, the spark Baelin had hoped for in his hunt to thwart any return from the Dark God of Power. He was close to the end of the journal, but he flipped the page in anticipation of what other secrets the document may tease at.

The days in the immediate aftermath of the final battle with Omnes's forces were slow, quiet, and mournful. The few remaining soldiers didn't boast jubilantly as many victorious armies in the histories of our people would. There was no celebrating the great victory over their immortal foe. For of the mighty force that left Turenian so many months ago, just a handful survived the campaign, not even enough to form an entire battalion. And those of us who did survive, I fear, will forever be haunted till the day we join our fallen brethren in the afterlife. Our minds were broken despite our great victory, for there is a difference between war and surviving a slaughterhouse. Elves live a long time, but I don't believe I will ever recover from the horrors of this campaign, even should I live a thousand years more.

As I said before, the journey was slow and silent. Celestra took the initiative in plotting our route back. Rather than travel south along the entire western continent, we would travel southeast to the city of Veilenthia. We had no indication of how the city had fared, but our hope was to find multiple ships that could be salvaged to sail back to Turenian. The trip from Veilenthia across the Aeronian Straights would have cut nearly half a year of travel time, and we would all be grateful to return to our families sooner.

We encountered no issues. No bandits had survived the onslaught of dark monsters pouring from the Rift. At least none this far north. Now that no monsters remained, the familiar sound of birds calling and crickets chirping grew in consistency and volume, bringing back a semblance of normalcy to the devastated country we trudged through. The evil followed Omnes to the center of the earth when Kei-Tel pulled him into the Rift, it seemed. So, there were no issues. No issues until two nights back.

Celestra had commandeered the two items that the Obsidian Knight had left behind, securing the cloak and the dagger in the only cargo trailer the small travel party had possessed still in traveling condition following our final battle. All the soldiers were explicitly instructed to keep a distance from the wagon, but power, it seems, even the potential for it, has a way of fracturing one's resolve, especially those whose minds are already broken.

Power is a consistent curiosity poking at your fortitude and restraint. If there is a crack, the desire for it will weasel into your mind. I... Well, I am no different. I wish to have the power to prevent any monstrosity from killing myself or my family in the future. And if there are tools to ensure this outcome, I will use them. I will use them without any regret upon my consciousness.

As stated before. Our remaining army, more so a small group of soldiers than an actual army at this point, was exhausted. Thankfully, there was little need for camp watches as guards and assigned lookouts rarely stayed alert and awake through their shifts. The guards placed to watch the cargo wagon were no different than the rest, and they were unable to maintain a vigilant watch through the night as sleep and exhaustion eventually won out.

I wanted a better look at the items touched by a divine power, so I stayed awake late into the night until the wagon guard finally nodded off. With that man asleep, I was able to sneak into the wagon containing the cloak and dagger. I opened the larger of the two crates within the wagon, revealing a cloak that seemed a shade darker than the blackness of a cloudy night. I could feel, no, I could sense, almost as if it was an innate understanding I held in the deepest recess of my soul, that this object possessed an immense power, and that power was dangerous. But it was a power that could be wielded.

Without thinking, I reached my hand out and touched the cloak. It reacted immediately, and a rippling blast of ethereal energy, born from *the large fragment of a shadowy cloak, pulsed through our camp, leaving wisps of black tendrils flowing through the air.*

In a rush, the floating strands of darkness pulled into my body and then disappeared. I was left in the back of the wagon, frozen in shock as the camp stirred to life, seeking out the source of the concussive commotion. I heard the wagon guard stir and rush toward the back of the wagon covering. Without thinking, I conjured a full cloak to form from the shadows and darkness around me making the fragment of cloak whole once again. I pulled the material over myself and pressed into the far corner of the wagon. The flaps at the back were ripped open by the guard. I saw him clear as day, but his gaze passed over me as he scanned the inside of the cargo wagon, as if I had grown invisible. He let the flap close, and I slipped out behind him.

I didn't stay in the camp that night nor any night thereafter. The elves were looking for the source of the disturbance, and while I had avoided detection to that point, I did not have the confidence that I could avoid Celestra's scrutiny over the coming days. Not looking for a conflict with those of my own kind, I fled, disappearing into the woods of the Perampla range.

Baelin jolted upright. He had been looking for some source that still connected Omnes to the physical world. He had been looking for a reason that the Shroud hanging above the Rift remained rather than dissolved as Omnes monsters did. He now had a new hypothesis of how this had happened. These items that remained in control of Divinoros's mortal entities acted as a tether for the God to act in this world through mediums that possessed the artifact.

Ryker - Chapter 16 - Competing with Superiors

The air rushed from Ryker's lungs as he landed hard on his back. Again. "That was better!" called Aegnor with a rare smile as he lent a hand to help his apprentice back to his feet. Ryker stood bent over trying to regain his breath as he struggled to keep the contents of his stomach from making a reappearance.

"You know, you keep telling me I am improving, but I feel like I have been losing in these sparring sessions faster and faster each time we duel." Ryker pressed his ribs gently, checking for any signs of cracks or serious injuries. "And losing them more painfully, I'd have you know. I mean, I'm all for intensity in our training, but I think the last kick may have cracked my sternum," groaned the apprentice as he stretched out his back trying to ignore the various points of pain in his chest and arms where Aegnor had beaten him thoroughly today.

"You are correct; you are losing faster, and as we continue to progress in your training, the lessons will become even more painful than they are now. Now, I must hold back, lest you would have no time to learn. And pain, young Ryker, is a highly effective tool when learning martial skills."

Ryker, now bent over as he recovered his breath, shot an unamused gaze at the silver-haired elf who seemed to be enjoying the repeated dismantling of his apprentice.

A sentiment that was cemented by the elf's next comment. "The best way for you to avoid the punishments in these sessions is to stop letting me hit you and to start winning." Aegnor smiled again as he sheathed his blade and lowered himself to a rock on the outside of the pair's camp.

Xantharyia and Maximus were left untethered on the far side of the encampment, watching the man and elf as the two practiced increasingly difficult sword forms and then fell into combat training. The horses would roam and eat as they pleased, but the mare seemed to enjoy watching her rider spar with the elf nearly as much as Aegnor enjoyed schooling his mentee. She would loose neighs as if she were laughing at Ryker's mishaps or stomp in congratulations when he managed to land a rare blow. His bond with her had continued to grow over the weeks they had traveled together, and he already cared far more for the horse than the beasts of burden that he'd shared a lifetime with on the farm. *Travel and adventure seem to forge bonds deeper than the mere passing of time can hope to create.*

He could tell Xantharyia possessed an intelligence beyond that of a normal horse, allowing the pair to form an almost unspoken form of communication that they each grew more fluent in by the day. This allowed them to foster trust between man and animal. As the weeks passed, Aegnor regularly incorporated training from horseback. Despite Ryker's leaps in competence, it was clear he had more to learn about riding and doing battle from horseback than swordplay on foot. Nevertheless, Aegnor assured him each day that he was making large strides in improvement.

Ryker and Aegnor had continued their path north toward the Marbled Caverns the night after the horses had been purchased. They'd been on the road for months now, and Ryker quickly became accustomed to the new training routines. Aegnor wasted no time in establishing them. The morning would begin with a ten-mile run before the two would mount their steeds, followed by rigorous questioning on the geography of Divinoros's two continents, the history of the elf's empire formation, and current political maneuverings by those in seats of power, as well battle tactics against various potential enemies in a broad array of scenarios pulled from Aegnor's own ancient history and personal experience.

Each evening would start with meditation, sword forms, sparring, and even more forms. Ryker had begun to notice rapid improvements to his physical conditioning, mental capacity, and combat strategy, not to mention a steep improvement in understanding what seemed to be, at first, inconsequential political undercurrents of individuals far exceeding his social class. But, despite the leaps Ryker made, he was still eons away from matching Aegnor in speed, strength, or wisdom, borne from a gap in centuries of experience between the pair. Ryker wondered how he might ever hope to equal the elf in combat skills, doubting years of dedication would prove sufficient. After this evening's thrashing, he voiced this to Aegnor as he settled himself on a nearby boulder.

"I know you meant to train me to fight powers greater than humans. At this point, I feel confident I could match most, if not all, of the human soldiers in the Queen's army with the sword. But how can I ever hope to be your equal?" the apprentice asked.

A distant look took hold of Aegnor as if he was searching the recesses of his expansive memory. "You will need to find your own way. I can train you in fundamentals and help point you in the right direction, but ultimately, the tactics I employ with my glaive and my sword will never suit you. Not perfectly, anyway. We have different strengths, so you will need a different style, your own, that you will begin to create the more you practice. I remind you that the reason I decided to train you—one of the reasons, that is—is because you showed an aptitude for

126

creative thinking in a critical situation. The other… well, let me point you in a direction I know you will need to head." The elf stood and walked to his saddle bags, removing a waterskin from it. Taking a long pull, he tossed the skin to Ryker.

"I met a man once, nearly three decades ago. I was hunting information on behalf of the Queen, and this man, I thought, may be privy to questions I needed answers to at the time. At the very least, he could be used as a key to access the information I sought. I stalked the man for days, as he was rarely alone, keeping company with various guards and soldiers. After the third day of following him, I was able to finally set up an ambush as he went out on a hunt. He was hoping to find fresh venison for his newly founded family. As you can imagine, I felt very confident in my ability to subdue the man despite the fact he was a decorated soldier leading a company of Elites in Sandivar. An uncommon feat for a human, I might add." Aegnor settled on the ground, leaning back against a fallen tree.

"He was a human, after all. But, alas, my confidence was mistaken. I attacked the man at full force, though my plan hadn't been as intricate as I may have developed should I have understood the true extent of his capabilities; it should have been far more than required to subdue one human. So, despite the ferocity with which I struck him, he defended himself against me easily… Maybe not easily, but effectively, at the very least. He implored a strategy I had rarely seen in my many centuries on this planet, and never had I seen it deployed with such mastery. You see, he fought with two swords, though rather than using them in unison, each seemed to move about him in coordinated yet autonomous motion. Independent bodies of a unified mind that could split its focus. One unifying objective—different paths to get there. It was impossible for me to discern a pattern I could break."

Ryker cut in, "I thought fighting with two weapons was typically a mistake. Oftentimes, it's just for flashy showboating over practicality."

Ryker knew Aegnor had grown used to his apprentice interrupting lectures with questions. He suspected the elf did not mind this, knowing the apprentice he had chosen possessed a questioning mind.

"Yes, you are correct, in most cases, but not for this man. His arms, though moving, striking independently of each other, seemed somehow married to his footwork. Each movement was precise, eloquent, and deathly effective. It was… a masterful display of swordsmanship I have never seen matched. He may have been slower than me, but the discrepancy in speed did not matter; I felt as though I was fighting two sword masters at the same time. Regardless of how much I pressed my advantages in speed or strength, I found he had a counter to my attacks." Aegnor rubbed his chin as if contemplating continuing in his tale.

"Eventually... he disarmed me. It was at the same moment I was able to pry one of his blades free. Regardless, it was the first time in over a century that someone had disarmed me. I was, and still am, aghast that a human, a *human*, had been the one who managed to outdo me. Ah, I won't admit to being outdone, let's say, a human who *matched* me. This was a feat that should have been impossible against an elf with my training and experience, yet after a few minutes of blindingly fast combat, I stood before the man unarmed while he stood holding his one sword. We consented to call that a stalemate. I did not get answers to the questions I sought that night. The man did not take kindly to being attacked while he sought food for his family. This I understood and respected. It is a noble cause to look after one's own, and I did not wish to come between this man and his. When I had set out that night, I had never intended to kill him, you see, and after a long explanation of who I was, what I was after, and that I intended no long-term harm, I offered to help the man on his hunt, which he accepted."

Ryker nodded. "Wow... bested by a human..." Aegnor shot Ryker a warning look, causing Ryker to correct himself quickly. "I mean matched by a human. And a human without magic? Impressive."

Aegnor seemed to accept the correction: "We need to cover magic in our upcoming lessons... Anyway, on this hunting expedition, I helped the man kill two deer, enough to feed his family for a month, with some to spare for his neighbors. As a reward, he shared the secret to his skill with the blade, a secret I have yet to crack, but I hope you will succeed where I have failed.

"His technique is your path to competence. Then, to excellence. I recall that he had attributed his ability to a mental state where he could split his consciousness. He had an effortless awareness of movement, a balance between his mind and body. He explained that in this state, he would allow his limbs to react independently as if his mind were split into two separate nodes of awareness inherently connected to the other. This allowed his body to react and respond to stimuli from two nodes at once. He turned each limb into an independent weapon with one goal. So, with two weapons, depending on his position relative to mine in the fight, he employed the most efficient moves with either his right or left arms, countering any speed advantage I might have had being elven born."

Aegnor took another sip from the waterskin. "You, I hope will find a way to replicate this strategic approach, to react without thinking, choosing actions that require the least movement and effort while wielding two weapons in their most efficient manner."

"Wait, how am I supposed to even begin accomplishing this." said Ryker, throwing his hands up and shaking his head, "splitting my mind but acting in unison... That sounds absolutely preposterous. How in the

128

hell can I learn this? It's not something you can do. How do you expect to teach me? I am supposed to separate my mind into two separate states of consciousness but then also have them connected as one... so... not have them separate... Aegnor, I am just gaining adequacy of fighting with one sword..."

Aegnor scratched at his chin in thought. "I have had the same questions myself, but I like to think my inability to grasp this concept is because I was already too ingrained in my own training and style by the time I met this man. I never had any need to master the strange technique, as my martial skill surpassed nearly all in the world even then. You, on the other hand, are rough, well, very rough." Ryker started at the insult, but his master wasn't done.

"Rough at best actually... a block of stone that a great artist has yet to even pull up from the quarry to begin shaping. We are just now trimming away at the edges, just beginning to shape you into a force to be reckoned with. I think we will need to begin incorporating this concept of this split consciousness into your training early, and this, coupled with general guidance, will set you up to accomplish great things, should you perfect it. To start this process, we will begin to explore this line of thought through training in meditation. This was the only direction I received from the swordsman. To begin to understand the connected duality of the mind, you must be able to maintain complete focus on two different lines of thinking. Moving forward, we will incorporate dual-weapon swordsmanship into our nightly sparring. You will fight with both your sword and dagger in hand until we can find you a second sword as worthy as the one you now carry. We will also have a different objective while meditating. You will focus on your surroundings, capturing sensations of the environment you are in with complete focus. At the same time, I will question you in mathematics, the arts of science and magic, and geography. As you think through those answers, you must not lose focus on your surroundings, for I will question you on that as well. As with everything, Ryker, you will master this through strenuous, dedicated training."

Ryker leaned back, lying flat on his back with his arms behind his head. He winced as the bruised cartilage and muscle between his ribs stretched out with the movement. "You know, this sounds convoluted at best, but at this point, I am willing to try anything to smack you around a little, even just once, in one of these little sparring sessions. My body has turned into one large bruise since we began traveling together, and you seem to be enjoying that far too much for my liking."

Aegnor shook his head in mock disapproval but indicated for his apprentice to sit up and begin his meditation.

As it turned out, reaching a state of split consciousness was just as difficult as it sounded. Ryker repeatedly lost focus on his surroundings, misheard Aegnor's questioning, or answered questions that were not asked. Despite his failings, Ryker was not perturbed. If he had learned one thing from his travels with Aegnor, nothing comes as easy as he would have liked, but if he worked at it, massive improvements would be made. Maybe one day, great things truly could be accomplished as he built on the foundation he was now crafting.

Ryker went to sleep in bright spirits that evening. He had been unsure if he would ever be able to match the skill of his master with the blade, but he now knew it was at least possible. *If another human had been able to best him in the past, maybe I can get there in the future.*

Ryker - Chapter 17 - Morality in Death

The morning commenced with Ryker sitting in meditation before the sun rose. He directed his focus to visualization, mentally picturing every movement of every sword form he had learned. In his mind's eye, his body executed the series of techniques with expert precision, each step and strike unfolding with meticulous detail.

He liked to start his meditative state with this practice, as the clarity of his movements in his mind helped him refine his skill and identify errors he made on the previous day of training. After building up steam, he attempted again to enter the state of split consciousness. He had no success. He found his mind struggling to grasp two concepts with full attention at once, as he attempted his visualization exercise while also sifting through the history lesson Aegnor had grilled him on the night before; the first reform of the Selection after the first human revolts against Queen Celestra. As he tried to encapsulate two separate lines of thought and focus, his conscious mind would quickly wash away any barrier built between the streams of thought, congealing into a single lane of focus.

After an hour, the sun nearly eclipsed the horizon. Ryker re-saddled Xantharyia but did not get into the saddle as he bent at the hips to stretch his legs in anticipation of a run. "You know, I don't understand the purpose of needing Ravanians, not that I don't like having Xantharyia, and I wouldn't give her up for the world at this point, but if we don't ride them throughout the day... Frankly, I think a well-trained pack mule may be able to keep pace with me as I am," the apprentice complained.

"Ahhh, well, if you were not born to such a pathetic species, we may not have to work so hard on your physical conditioning. Maintaining a barely acceptable level of endurance in your kind is a lot of work. The horses will prove their worth, no question, though I imagine they are growing tired of having to plod along each day at such a feeble pace, that said why don't you try to run a little faster this morning for their sakes," the centuries-old elf shot back in Ryker's direction, amusement dancing in his eyes.

"Okay, okay, old timer, I get it... I'm pathetic. I'm weak. You're sculpting a rough block of stone. Let's skip the rest of this lecture and get a move on huh?" Ryker breathed into his hands, rubbing them together to fight off the cold that crept into his fingertips during the morning's meditation, "I'm freezing. Think winter might finally be fully upon us."

The two had grown familiar over the past month, and Ryker had been surprised to find the elf so willing a participant in his constant banter, a practice which was commonplace on the Marriock farm. He

131

thought the elf enjoyed it. Ryker imagined there were few people, if any, that would talk to him in such a casual manner.

"You are right," Aegnor replied. "The morning frost has grown more consistent the further north we've gone, and the grass is well into hibernation. The color of the plains is fading back to gold as the grass prepares to weather the full brunt of winter. Hopefully, we reach the Granite Tunnel Entrance on the south side of the Perampla Mountains before the first snowfall. The plains provide nothing for cover if we are caught in a blizzard. But you are right. Let us run and be warm." With that, the two were off on their normal routine.

Their travel routine persisted uninterrupted over the next couple of hours. So far, the journey had been easy since Ryker's encounter with the wolves that won him Xantharyia's trust. The pair had not come across any dangers or perilous creatures, and he questioned whether Aegnor had been exaggerative in the possibility of threatening situations being prevalent throughout the land. So when the pair noticed smoke rising in the distance, Ryker turned to his Aegnor in surprise and asked, "Think that might be a merchant caravan cooking? I wouldn't mind a freshly cooked stew in this cold." Aegnor did not respond, his gaze locked on the rising plumes of dark black smoke, an unnatural smear against a clear blue sky.

"That is no cooking fire. Far too much smoke."

The pair mounted their steeds and maintained a steady trot onward. Ryker saw Xantharyia's keen ears twitching in agitation, a clear sign of her concern. Moments later, the pair heard screams cutting through the cold silence. Aegnor did not waste a second, thrusting his heels into the haunches of Maximus to spur the great black horse forward at a speed his size would suggest to be impossible. Ryker followed suit, and the lightning-fast palomino quickly caught Aegnor despite his head start. Aegnor shouted in the rushing wind, "Raiders have been in the area. There may be women or children alive. Fight to kill. Remember your training. Do not pull your blows."

Anxiety instantly clawed into Ryker's stomach. *I have never killed a man before.* Regardless of his apprehension, the nerves brought clarity to his focus as adrenaline coursed through his veins. The apprehension he felt at using steel to end a man's life evaporated as the pair grew closer to the commotion.

The screams grew louder; panicked shouts of agony and terror cut sharply into Ryker's ears. Anger welled with each scream, loud enough to split through the wind that was rushing past his ears before being abruptly cut short. Finally, the pair grew within an eyeshot of the carnage.

The apprentice saw three large merchant wagons, two toppled over in a blazing wreck on the side of the cart path. The two knocked over were set alight, the final cart remaining upright and largely undamaged. There were numerous figures collapsed around the caravan, unmoving limbs outstretched at odd angles, some having the appearance of porcupines, multiple arrows protruding from the motionless bodies. He did not have time to count the fallen as he could still make out the screaming of people actively being murdered.

More disturbingly, he could now hear laughter. Making his way past the burning wreckage, Ryker saw a group of nearly twenty men encircle a woman and two girls who must have been the woman's children, no older than Ayden had been when Ryker left the farm. Ryker felt true rage within him as he saw the group beginning to shove the women and girls, ripping at their clothing whenever their hands fell on them, jeering with cruel intent.

The men were so enthralled with their sinful indulgence, their grotesque violence, that they did not pay notice to the thundering hoofbeats of two Ravanian steeds until Ryker was within thirty paces— a distance that Xantharyia closed in a matter of seconds. Faster than the men could draw their weapons against Ryker's unsheathed blade.

Xantharyia crashed into the men with the force of a catapult. Her bulk crushed three men on impact, brutally maiming and breaking the bones of the raiders. They were all mortally wounded, if not outright dead on impact. Ryker brought his heels in with force against her side, and Xantharyia responded just as they had in their training by rearing up and kicking out her front legs. She caught a fourth man in the head with her hooves, leaving a crater in the man's skull so large the gray flesh within his head oozed from his cranium, mixing with his blood and dirt after he collapsed.

As she settled back to all fours, Ryker did not delay in dealing his own deadly justice, bringing his blade down hard into a man's neck. The perfect blade met a thick resistance Ryker fought through before he heard the thud of a head hit the ground, the body following. He killed three more men before he was finally pulled from Xantharyia's saddle by a behemoth of a man dressed in dark red stained leather and wolfskins, his rotted black teeth visible in his grim snarl.

Ryker slammed to the ground hard, and before he could struggle to his feet, the giant man brought a mighty war hammer down toward Ryker's chest with an overhead swing. He rolled to avoid the blow, although it was unnecessary, as Aegnor had finally joined the fray, noted by his iconic glaive erupting through the man's belly, sending a mist of blood over the apprentice. The giant curled over, grasping at his stomach as Ryker got to his feet to finish the man off. But Aegnor did not waste a second, and he followed up the strike to the abdomen by driving the glaive down a second time, impaling the man through the back of his head with enough force to send the end of his glaive point through the

133

brain and out his eye, dislodging the flesh orb from its intended resting place.

Within a half-minute, the pair and their horses had already killed or disabled eight of the raiding party's members. The remaining criminals were now prepared, however, and had their weapons unsheathed. By this point, the woman had been able to usher her children out of the fray using the chaos to mask their retreat, and the trio now cowered beside the wagon that had yet to be set ablaze.

Ryker smacked the rear of Xantharyia to send her away. She had been whining and prancing nearby after he'd been pulled from her saddle, and Ryker did not wish her to be needlessly injured in the remainder of this skirmish with the red-cloaked bandits. Aegnor followed suit and dismounted Maximus, holding his glaive against the ground leisurely as if it was nothing more than his walking stick on a morning stroll.

One of the red-clad men waved his sword in their direction. His fuming expression set his face to such a hue it now matched the red of the fabric he donned. "You shouldn't 'ave made this yer business, you fools. Now," the crook raised his arms to the side in a showboating gesture, "we're gonna kill you and then finish taking our fill with those nice ladies before we decide they're used enough to slit their throats. I can see one of you is an elf, but that don' matter. See, it's still twelve to two."

In a flash of movement, Ryker saw his master reach into his cloak. He unsheathed all four throwing knives from his bandolier before releasing the four in a single quick movement that lasted no more than a blink of an eye.

The apprentice heard a rapid succession of dull thuds as each blade found its mark, sinking into the flesh of four different raiders grouped at the center of their ranks. Not all were killed instantly. Throwing multiple knives at a time did impede the elf's accuracy, but they were no longer in fighting condition. Two were dead; one was writhing in pain on the ground, grasping at his groin, struggling to quench the outrush of blood at the site of the wound, and the final man was limping, having pulled the knife out of his body from directly above the kneecap.

"I will take the group to the left," said Aegnor, nodding toward the larger group of five men, including the leader of the bandits. "You take the three to the right. Remember, strike to kill. These barbarians deserve no mercy."

With that, Aegnor erupted into a flurry of movement. Ryker was sure the elf would dispatch the group of men rapidly. He was less confident in his own fight. While Ryker had been gifted with the sword before he gained his apprenticeship and rapidly improved with guidance

134

from the world's most famous weapons master, he still had never been in a true fight to the death with even a single opponent, much less three.

His nervous energy continued to claw at his stomach, focusing his attention. Despite the nerves, he unsheathed his dagger with his left hand, raised the longsword in his right, and approached the raiders. He stepped cautiously forward to the trio of hard and cruel-faced men. He held no apprehension in killing these men, for they deserved a fate worse than a swift death. As he approached, the wounded, limping man joined the enemy's ranks as they spread out, attempting to flank and encircle the apprentice. *Don't allow yourself to become surrounded. The longer this fight lasts, the more likely I can fall victim to an unseen blow. Attack viciously, attack ferociously, attack with intelligence,* the apprentice thought as he prepared to engage.

Before the raiders could fully encircle him, Ryker struck out savagely with a flurry of attacks at the wounded man, catching him unprepared. With the man's movement hindered, he was unable to shift his footing backward, throwing the power and speed of his parry off. He could only block two of the slashes the apprentice levied at him before the third strike, a stabbing movement with his sword, caught the man in his hip above the already injured leg. He let out a deep groan as he dropped to a knee. A sound that was silenced as Ryker buried his dagger in the nape of the man's neck, twisted the blade, and pulled the knife free with a sickening sound no different from slaughtering a pig.

Concern flashed among the remaining bandits as they exchanged glances. The boy before them had efficiently taken down one of their own; even if the man was injured, the speed of his actions left them little time to react or come to their comrade's aid.

"He's quick," called one of the men. "We still got numbers, though. Attack him at once; don't let him isolate you." The three nodded at that. "Now!" the man in the center called, and all three bandits jumped in at Ryker from his sides and in front of him. Allowing Aegnor's lessons to guide him, Ryker quickly shuffled back and circled to his left as the three men approached the location where he previously stood.

When men converge at once with no coordination, they will lose the advantage of spacing. Use this if you are facing multiple adversaries at once, Ryker recalled Aegnor instructing. He was able to flank the man on his far left, rendering two of the three men inconsequential as they were now stuck behind their companion. Ryker exchanged blows with the man as his other partners attempted to get back into an advantageous position on either side of the apprentice.

Ryker exchanged a number of blows, and with each strike, he grew more and more focused. As he took a breath between a parry and stab, Ryker noticed a quiet in the air as his mind began to tune out the distant periphery, drawing his focus to the closest dangers. Despite this, Ryker remained aware of his surroundings, rapidly ingesting and interpreting information, relaying details of consequence to his conscious area of focus.

He could hear the ragged breath of the man directly in front of him, saw the bandits struggling to reposition themselves around him, saw Aegnor standing amongst a circle of dead men, turning to watch his apprentice under a keen eye, and he saw the woman in tattered clothing watching the pair of travelers with an unspoken appreciation and unmasked fear in her eyes.

Ryker was unable to kill another before the three bandits managed to get back into position. This time, the men flanking Ryker succeeded in getting further behind the apprentice, making it harder for Ryker to keep an eye on all three bandits at once. Ryker crouched low, swinging his longsword back and forth in long, low arcs to keep the men at bay and rapidly pivoting like a tiger in a cage. While he managed to keep them at bay, there always seemed to be one man out of his line of vision. He soon felt the pain of a blade cutting deep into one of his calves. He remained standing after lashing out at the man who scored the hit, pushing him further back.

He heard Aegnor call. "You are not making use of the dagger. You are concentrating on only one combatant at once. Fight with both weapons, broaden your focus, split your attention, or you will be cut down."

Ryker did not believe the elf was going to let him die, but he wasn't completely sure he would step in unless Ryker was gravely wounded. Taking Aegnor's advice, Ryker stilled his wild thrashing and focused his gaze on the man before him. He held the man's position in his gaze with all his focus, but he managed to break his mind into a second point of focus that relied on the information in his peripheral vision paired with his hearing to track the movement of the soldiers on the left and right.

He heard gravel shift to his right. He assumed that the man there was lunging toward him. Ryker's right arm reacted instantly. He brought his sword up to parry the blow he believed was coming while his gaze remained fixed on the man in front of him. The clang of metal on metal resonated through the air, indicating his assumption was correct. The man on the right backed up after the failed attack, just as the man on Ryker's left advanced.

Ryker heard the bandit grunt with effort as he jumped toward him. He heard no footsteps and assumed the man jumped, prepared to bring down a powerful overhead strike. Again, Ryker predicted the move correctly, and as he brought the sword down toward Ryker's head, he stepped back so the blade passed in front of his face so closely he could feel a slight breeze against his sweat-covered skin as shimmering steel

136

passed by him. The momentum of the swing carried the blade down until the tip of the sword thudded into the earth.

Ryker brought up his left arm, slashing through the back of the man's shoulder, his razor-sharp dagger easily severing the muscle and tendon it bit into. The cut was deep, and the man lost the ability to lift or use the maimed arm. He screamed out in pain, but Ryker quickly alleviated the man's pain as he followed up the slash by bringing the serrated back side of the weapon across the man's neck, ripping open a gash in his throat that his grasping finger had no hope of sealing while he squirmed on the ground.

Ryker sensed panic now flooding from the last two raiders standing. It was pungent, their fear, in an almost tangible way that Ryker thought he could see, smell, even taste in the air. In their panic, they both attacked Ryker in earnest, wild, brazen and—luckily for him— uncoordinated attacks.

A flurry of motion approached Ryker from his right side and the front. The men were not used to fighting an enemy who had the skill to fight back.

They preferred to target innocent, unprepared travelers and women, the vile humans.

It was clear their training did not prepare them for an equal fight. They were used to ambushing weakly guarded caravans using surprise to kill the men off before raping and murdering any women and enslaving the children should they wish to keep them alive.

Ryker proved to be more than a match for the two. In his current state of battle focus, he maneuvered his dagger and sword in separate yet coordinated movements, swiftly dispatching both men. As the man in front stabbed at his chest, Ryker stepped around the blade. He was not fast enough to go completely unscathed, though the cut across his chest was shallow. He brought his longsword in a low slash and felt the satisfying thud of steel into bone as the blade cleaved through the man's shin. His screams were cut short as he fell. Ryker caught him below the chin with the dagger in his left hand.

As his life ebbed out, the apprentice *felt* the air behind him split. He ducked his head and felt the wind of a would-be decapitating blow pass by. Knowing where the man must be standing, Ryker reversed his grip on the longsword and drove the point back with as much force as he could muster. He heard a grunt as the final raider's body stiffened and slid off the blade, crumpling to the ground to die.

Once the men were dead, Aegnor approached. "You did well."

Ryker did not comment. Coming back into a more present state of mind, he surveyed the ground around him, soaked in blood and lifeless men. He was appalled by the brutal nature of which he had just killed so many. *I've been a hunter and a farmer... I've killed so many today... so*

137

much death. In his shocked realization, he wiped his blades clean and sheathed them before attempting to wipe the blood from his hands on the jerkin of a fallen man.

There is more blood on these hands after today than many in the Queen's army. He did not regret their deaths. They had this coming. These men were sick, twisted, evil. They deserved the justice of cold steel, but he wasn't sure he liked to be the executioner. Men who committed murder, rape, and slavery deserved a slow demise, yet they were swiftly dispatched with a sense of justice. Still, he had taken a life, and the gravity of such a deed weighed heavily on his mind now that his blood had settled. He turned and looked to the silver-haired elf who held Ryker in a discerning gaze. "I… I just killed… I killed them all," Ryker mumbled, a confused expression on his face. "I didn't feel a thing when I did it."

"Aye. You gave them better deaths than they deserved," said Aegnor with no hint of remorse or empathy in his tone. "Go see to the woman and child."

Ryker did so, walking to where the woman and young girls were still cowering beneath the only wagon. The small girls were hugging the woman with their tear-streaked faces buried in her breast. Both were crying, but the woman seemed to steel herself as Ryker approached. She looked at him with fear and thanks in her eyes. When Ryker reached the edge of the wagon, he knelt down. "It's okay," he said, holding out his hands in a placating gesture. "You are safe now. Are you hurt?"

The woman shook her head but still did not consent to speak. One of the young girls no more than ten years of age turned her head from the woman, and Ryker could see some of the fear leave the child's eyes as she realized he did not wear the ragged red clothes that seemed to be the mark of these raiders.

"My name is Ryker. I am from Stone Guard and am traveling north to the Marbled Caverns. I am training as a soldier with Aegnor the Great. I am sorry for your misfortune, but I am glad we arrived when we did. What is your name?"

In a voice barely louder than a whisper, the woman said, "I am Freydna. These are my daughters, Elaina and Yaesna."

Ryker offered his hand to the woman. She recoiled back further under the wagon but quickly relaxed as Ryker said, "It's okay. Let me help you out of here, and we can get you some water and food." Freydna took his hand in one of her own while keeping the other arm firmly grasped around her daughters.

Once liberated from the wagon, Ryker beheld Freydna's garments, shredded and tattered, exposing her form in a manner that unveiled more than Ryker had ever glimpsed of a woman. A flush of both embarrassment and fury tinted his cheeks as he grappled with the injustice she had endured. He quickly removed his cloak and placed it over the woman's shoulders. She covered herself and whispered a quiet thanks. "Let me get you water. I will be back shortly. Please stay here. You don't need to see..." Ryker trailed off as images of ripped-out throats and spilled innards of the raiders filled his mind.

He left the woman seated against the wagon wheel and walked back to where Aegnor stood alongside Xantharyia and Maximus. "The mother and her children are okay," he told his master. "Her name is Freydna. I will grab water for them. Do you think we can spare any of our rations?"

Aegnor nodded his approval. "Of course. Keep enough food for us to eat tonight and in the morning. We will hunt for the remainder of our travels. They will need it more than us, I imagine." Ryker appreciated his master's willingness to give more to the needy and helpless women despite the inconvenience and time it might add to their journey. "Come back here once you have tended to them. We are not yet done here."

After doing his master's bidding, he returned to the scene of the fight. Ryker glanced around and saw that Aegnor had pulled the dead into two piles. One pile consisted of the men lying dead as a result of the confrontation between Aegnor, his apprentice, and the bandits. The other pile contained the victims who were slain in cold blood by the ruthless bandit group.

The silver-haired elf now stood motionless, his back to the mounds of bodies, staring coldly at three men positioned shoulder to shoulder on their knees in front of him. Ryker could make out throwing knives still protruding from the groin of one. The others appeared to have taken horrible, though not life-threatening, wounds from the horses. The men swayed and groaned in agony as pools of scarlet formed around them. They looked nearly lifeless with their pale complexion and hollow gazes.

Ryker approached his master and stood beside him. Without breaking his gaze, Aegnor ordered his apprentice to action. "Kill them." He said it in a level tone, no excitement, no mercy, no emotion at all.

Ryker furrowed his brow. "Master... Aegnor... I cannot kill these men. They are unarmed, kneeling before us, unable to defend themselves. I do not regret killing the bandits while we fought, but I am not an executioner. I cannot do this."

The elf's gaze hardened as his apprentice refused the order, and the icy gaze was turned on Ryker. He stared at the apprentice for a long period of time silently. He looked terrifying, with his silver eyes boring down upon him and silver gray hair billowing in the wind. The hair and eyes simmered in stark contrast to the dark charcoal gray cloak and dark armor now blotted with darker bloody spots.

139

He had never seemed so imposing as he stood over his apprentice, looking down at him. "You must get used to vanquishing evil, boy." The elf spoke with a definite twinge of disappointment and annoyance in his voice. Ryker still did not move. Aegnor continued, "You have set out on a path to fight with me. Where we go, we go to combat the darkness that plagues this land. To pull its roots from the soil of Divinoros. You will take more life before yours is over if you continue on this path with me. If you do not slay the monsters that walk this earth, then any blood they spill will be on your hands. And make no mistake, these men are monsters of the worst kind. They have slaughtered countless people here today," Aegnor spoke icily, gesturing to the pile of dead merchants. "Worse than that, they were going to rape and murder a helpless woman in front of her daughters. Young girls who would be enslaved and abused until that same abuse that was to befall their mother claimed their lives. You wish to let these men live? Frankly, they deserve a worse death than a swift one by your sword."

The words rang true in Ryker's ears. He dropped his head. "You are right. They should be killed." He gazed over the kneeling men. Each one of them was begging to be spared. Mumbling for forgiveness and mercy. Mercy they did not deserve. They deserved slow, painful deaths. "I just... It feels wrong to do it this way. I'm with you to learn the ways of the sword, to become a warrior. This is different. This is simple execution."

Aegnor shook his head and grunted in frustration. Then, with a flash of movement, the elf unsheathed his long sword and brought it horizontally at the first man's neck. The force behind the swing carried his blade cleanly through the neck of the first and second man. The heads thudded against the ground with heavy impact.

It was no easy feat to lop off a man's head, much less three, and the blade lodged halfway through the third man's neck before Aegnor yanked it free and completed the decapitation. The elf turned back to his apprentice. A splattering of fresh blood now painted the elf's otherwise perfect face. He looked frightening. "You disappoint me. You are weak." Without another word, the elf strode back to his Maximus and took the reins before he began walking toward the survivors Ryker had seen to earlier.

Ryker stood on the spot, staring at the three headless bodies that collapsed before him. He felt sick. The men deserved it, but he had never witnessed such violence. This was a side of Aegnor he had not yet seen, and it scared him. He knew the elf was right, yet the vicious act he witnessed here had him questioning the morality of his tutor in a way he never had before.

Nevertheless, he found himself devoid of alternatives on how to deal with these men, save for a swift death. Turning his gaze away from the grim scene, Ryker strode towards Xantharyia, his mind consumed by thoughts of home. Doubts crept in, wondering if departing home in the first place had been a mistake.

Ryker - Chapter 18 - Onward

After securing Xantharyia and composing himself, Ryker gathered the three fresh corpses, adding them to the mound of fallen caravan raiders. With the task done, he approached the place where Aegnor conversed with the mother and her children. Freydna was profuse in her thanks to the elf and her apprentice, having partially recovered from her ordeal, repeatedly blessing them for saving the ill-fated trio.

Ryker learned that the family was traveling southwest from the coastal city of Veilenthia to Stone Guard. Her husband had passed from sickness a month ago, and she and the children were headed to the city to live with her brother. Ryker was shocked to learn that the woman's brother worked on the Marriock Farm, and she planned to do the same.

"Well, we just traveled from that direction, and we were free of any disturbances or trouble along that route," commented Aegnor. "My apprentice and I are headed north to the Great Marbled Caverns." The woman looked conflicted, as if she were inclined to ask to travel with the pair.

Ryker jumped in before she could ask the question. "You can travel with us if you like. Although it is in the opposite direction you intended to head. Also, I know the owner of the Marriock farm well... He is my brother. If you continue on, tell him you crossed paths with me, and I wish you to be incorporated into the team there. You should have no issue finding work."

"That is kind of you," said Freydna. "Despite my inclination to stay with you, I... I think we must continue our path to Stone Guard. I have heard the roads are getting more dangerous the further north you travel, and I do not wish to burden the pair of you with three helpless souls when it comes to a fight. Be wary. We had begun to get strange reports of disappearances occurring among some of the villages north of Veilenthia. Some entire villages had been destroyed and attacked in the night." She hugged her daughters close after placing their hands over their ears as she described the recent events near her hometown, hoping to spare the children any further distress. Unfortunately, after the day's events, Ryker believed this to be a futile effort. "It sounds like fleeing south is our best bet."

Ryker and Aegnor nodded. The two helped outfit the last wagon to the horses the bandits had tied up in a patch of aspen trees nearby. Ryker walked Freydna through the process of tethering the horses to the wagon as well as how to strap on a saddle should a wheel of the wagon break on their journey, forcing them to ride on horseback.

Aegnor took to loading the wagon with any relevant goods, along with two swords and a bow from the dead bandits, placing the acquired items in the driver's seat where Freydna would be able to access the weapons quickly should the need arise. Aegnor and Ryker nodded their farewell. Ryker asked Freydna to relay a message to his brothers that he was okay and traveling north before he set off to retrieve the Ravanian mounts. The woman and her children departed.

The pair rode in silence for a long time. Ryker was unsure how to start a conversation with the elf after seemingly disappointing his master by refusing to kill unarmed men. If he was being honest with himself, he was also disappointed in his inability to do what was necessary and provide justice to the poor, innocent people slain. But the act felt like murder, not fighting against evil, and he wasn't sure he wanted to grow capable of such acts.

"I'm sorry," Ryker muttered in a voice barely above a whisper. Aegnor did not respond. "I should have acted. They deserved execution. I just... I didn't have it in me. I hadn't killed anyone before today. And I do not like the thought of loping off the heads of unarmed men or women."

He heard the elf sigh. Aegnor turned to look at Ryker as they rode, and there was a weariness, a tiredness, in his gaze. "I have lived centuries, Ryker. There are few on this planet that are older than I. I have confronted evil in every corner of this world. In every fashion and form evil has to offer."

Aegnor grew quiet, contemplating how to continue. "I was not yet born at the time of the great war against the Dark God. Many proclaim him to be an *evil* god. While his actions are devastating, I do not know that I could call him evil. He acts in his nature, seeking power and destroying inconsequential beings, well, beings of no consequence in his eyes, to obtain more of what he is: *power*. I have seen minor demons, undoubtedly wicked and cruel. Those who manage to slip into this world from where they were long ago locked away seek to cause chaos as their creator, the Demon King, deemed them to. Again they are acting in accordance with their design. A cruel and wicked design."

Ryker wasn't sure what Aegnor was getting at, but he remained silent as his master continued. "Those divine entities don't surprise me any more than a sand lion hunting gazelle or a wolf killing a farmer's sheep. They all act within their nature. That is not to say those foul creatures are good; they spread cruelty and danger further and wider than any mortal or higher race ever could, but I understand why they do what they do. Their actions are guided by a purpose coded into every fiber of their being."

Aegnor looked at Ryker seriously now. "Regardless of how frequently I see it, what shocks me every time is the act that man, elf, or dwarf is willing to commit against another of their kind. The greatest evil and wrongness I have faced is just that—acts of true evil committed

143

by man or woman. Mortal beings who have the potential to choose any path in life, to choose their own purpose, but devolve into a path of laziness, thievery, murder, and treachery. Such frail souls, opting for the easy path of ill-gotten gains instead of the honest toil for wealth. Instead of extending a helping hand, they choose to oppress their neighbors, seeking to inflate their own sense of importance at the expense of others. And worst of all, what we just witnessed, rather than to pursue a path toward closeness with a family, to develop loving relationships, they seek to take simple pleasures from those unwilling to give it."

Ryker nodded his head.

"For centuries, I have seen many stumble down this treacherous path. People who repeatedly choose their needs and their wants despite the pain and despair they cause others. I will kill as many of them as I can, for they bring nothing but pain and terror into our world, and they, unlike Omnes, unlike the demons or the dragons of old, have a choice to do good in this world. Now, you may wonder what makes me the determiner, the exactor, of justice, to which I would respond with the fact that I deal with objective truth. And only in a situation where I witness firsthand the accounts of a horrid act. A wrong that is impossible to dispute. Rape, murder, and enslavement are the worst acts a mortal being can do unto another. When I see this on my travels, I exact a quick justice. This will never change." Aegnor looked to Ryker. "Do you understand what I am saying?"

Ryker nodded slowly. He appreciated that Aegnor would go to such lengths to explain to him the action he had just witnessed. "Do not apologize for not killing those men," Aegnor continued. "My disappointment was not directed at you. I have grown tired in my old age. The disappointment of seeing our kind repeat the same mistakes leads me to a mindset of anger and quick temper. I am not disappointed with you, and I was wrong to call you weak. You are anything but, seeing as you have the audacity to stand up to me. There will be times, though, when, despite your desire to keep your hands free of blood, you will need to kill. Part of my training will be to dull you to the remorse many feel in the aftermath of such a warranted action. This is not because killing others is a trivial deed but because those we slay in our travels will deserve a fate worse than death. I will not have you hesitate in a moment of need. I will not ask you to play the role of executioner again. However, I will not spare any who commit a similarly violent act against another."

Ryker saw Aegnor looking in his direction. The tiredness still showed in his eyes. Ryker thought about what he had said. It was hard to comprehend the greatness of his master and impossible to grasp the full context and impact of what he was saying. He had lived Ryker's life span more than twenty-five times, and, being that old, it was little surprise he would see the world in a somewhat different light than Ryker. There was wisdom to his words, though, and Ryker would hang on to that. What the apprentice found interesting was he didn't disagree with the silver-haired elf in his stance. The only difference between the two was that Ryker had just killed for the first time... well, the first seven times, and Aegnor had slain thousands, growing numb to the act over his long centuries on this world. Ryker nodded to the elf, glad to possess understanding behind the frightening visage of Aegnor, The Executioner. With the tension passed, Ryker decided to change the subject.

"You know. I was thinking. I saw you standing to the side after you'd handled your half of the raiders. Thanks for the help, by the way... But the first thing I thought was, damn, that armor looks good." Aegnor laughed. Ryker raised his voice lightheartedly, "No, no, no, you can't just brush by this. If I'm going to be traveling with you, I can't be looking like a second-rate sidekick... I was thinking the dwarves could probably outfit me with something nice... You think?"

Aegnor raised his eyebrow, and the two began to laugh. "We shall see when we arrive in Marbled Caverns if we can't commission a suit of armor for you. I also noticed something in your fight. It appears you made some progress with splitting your point of focus, yes?"

Ryker dove into how he was able to maintain the state and the areas he felt he could still improve. Aegnor nodded as his apprentice continued. While he remained silent, Ryker could feel the wheels turning in the elf's mind as he thought through new wrinkles to incorporate into their training regimen. He also thought he caught a glimmer of pride in the gaze of the ancient elf as he listened to his pupil. As the conversation slowed and the pair began looking for a place to camp for the evening, Ryker asked Aegnor, "You know, you mentioned the nature of demons and said you came across the spawn of the Demon King in your travels. What can you tell me about their kind?"

Aegnor dismounted Maximus. "Demons are the only beings apart from the dragons that frighten the Gods. Even the Gods' combined might was not enough to defeat the Demon King in a contest at the height of his powers. This is why the elves' assistance against them was required. His spawn, the Demon King's, that is, are similar in likeness to himself, offshoots of his very being that are summoned beyond the prison Daemaron has been locked in since the time the Gods descended upon this world and waged a ferocious war against him. We will discuss their kind in our lessons in the morning. They are not creatures to speak of in the dark."

145

Captain Malfius - Chapter 19 - Necessary Action

Lord Sennin sat drumming his fingers on his desk within his grand office. It had been over two months since Sandivar had received any trade from their neighbors to the north. Typically, Sennin would expect a minimum of six large caravans coming down from the elves' capital city in that time. Sandivar's citizens, his loyal subjects, relied on Turenian for many of the necessities and luxuries enjoyed throughout the new desert oasis: food, wine, furniture, and linens were the main goods to be carted south. In turn, Sandivar would supply the Turenians with precious metals, minerals, herbs, and exotic meats from wild animals that roamed the great deserts.

As High Lord Sennin's gaze scrolled across the treasurer's report on his supply reserves, he felt the pit of worry in his stomach grow. It detailed low levels of fruit, grains, and herbs that were available to his residents, far below where he had hoped to see them.

Two weeks after the traders and merchants ceased to show in his city, Sennin was forced to open his doors for the residents of Sandivar to purchase materials from his vault of excess supply, and if the figures in front of him held true, it was an excess that had been rapidly depleted to the point of concern. If new supplies didn't come soon, the High Lord would be forced to ration what little he had left until he could send a fleet around the southern desert peninsula to a port city just east of Turenian, but the journey around was a long one—perhaps too long.

The High Lord was frustrated with his willingness to part with such large quantities of his reserve supply. If he was honest with himself, he knew he should have started rationing far sooner than now, but it seems the centuries of peace had dulled his sternness. Still, with steep rationing and increased consumption of the sand monitors and large desert tarantulas that frequented the area, he figured his population could survive for three or four months without resupply... maybe four months, and those would be hard months. *Even optimistically, this would not leave enough time to sail around the peninsula and back with holdover supplies.*

Senin called out to his manservant, a human named Alfiry. "Have we received any response from Lady Elba?"

His servant's answer came in an ever-professional, flat tone. "No sir, our first correspondence sent three weeks back asking about travel through the Narrows never received a reply. Strange, given that more than enough time has passed for us to have heard back. The second letter appears not to have been received either, as that was sent two weeks back requesting emergency reserves while we waited for the next caravan of goods from the Queen. The final letter we sent was four days back and we would not yet expect a response. However, given her apparent lack of concern about our predicament, I believe another course of action must be pursued. It appears no help or explanation will be received from the Narrows."

Sennin drew his hands over his face as he leaned back in his chair and issued a deep groan. "Well... by the look of things, we don't have long before our people grow frustrated with us. I truly do not wish to place a rationing on the city, but I fear we must. Prepare a bulletin and begin dispersing the news. Before that is released to the populous, we should send word north to Turenian. Send me Captain Malfius."

Alfiry looked at Sennin with a small frown on his face. "Sir, we have our full fleet of your loyal Elites available at the port. Should we not... send another rather than that, well, speaking frankly, madman?"

Sennin stood, annoyed with the cheek he was getting from his servant, "Yes, Alfiry, I am aware of where *my* fleet is stationed. I would happily, more than happily deal with them than Malfius, but we don't have time to sail around the southern peninsula to the eastern ports."

Alfiry went pale, catching what Sennin intended to order of the man, "Yes, sir. I will send him in right away and prepare the bulletin just after." With a slight bow, the man departed to do his master's bidding.

Lord Sennin paced around his office, his hands clasped behind his back. His long sandy hair hung in a clean ponytail along his back. He thought through how to tell Malfius these orders.

No man had willingly sailed directly from Sandivar to Turenian in over a thousand years. To do so meant navigating the Cursed Isles. A haunted place. A place that sparked madness. A place that corrupted the mind. No man had made it through completely unscathed. Malfius was a testament to that. The least daunting thing about the archipelago was the fact the natural terrain was not suitable for sailing, given the sea in the area was connected through the archipelago in many shallow channels, with large dark moss-covered rocks jutting through and near the surface as if a great golem had thrown boulders into the shallow sea a more than a millennia ago. To make matters worse, a dense mist clung to the region in perpetuity. Men who'd survived a trip into the mist compared it to entering into a different world of shifting gray haze and absolute silence. Silence until the voices started talking, at least. The real threat of traveling to this place is that it is home to the greatest terror that still haunts the earth.

It is said that these islands are where the four Gods, with aid from the elves long ago, many generations before Sennin or even Sennin's father had been born, were able to finally defeat Daemaron, the Demon

King, in a fight that shattered a solid landbridge between the eastern and western continents into the archipelago that remained.

In this distant era, thousands of years before the war with Omnes, Divinoros was under the dominion of Demons and Dragons. The relentless power of these adversaries, coupled with the intensity of their conflict, transformed the once-thriving planet into a desolate wasteland. Humans, elves, and dwarves cowered in the face of the overwhelming might of these titans. In these dark days, the bipedal species, along with every other, were broken under these forces, living like rodents, with the only goal in life being to avoid being seen and squashed by foes possessing such might even the Gods dared not intervene.

It was not until Daemaron finally defeated the last of the arch dragons, effectively ending the great war that loomed over Divinoros, that the Gods made their move, capturing and imprisoning Daemaron. But the Gods did not bury him deep enough, it seemed, for his influence still permeated from islands. From some deep cage, residual power spilled into the area like sulfur leaking into a hot spring and burbling to the surface above. Few merchants had braved the passage, and all who had attempted it or ventured into the area upon order were never to be seen again. All save one. Captain Malfius.

The office doors burst open as an odd-looking elf strode into Sennin's office. He was tall even for an elf but did not possess the beauty and graceful movement most of the race boasted. His face sat in a permanent grimace, his red hair was cropped short, and he looked an untidy mess beneath the three-point captain hat of Lord Sennin's navy uniform.

The rest of his attire was… call it, a unique take on the naval fleet's required garb. His well-tapered sailor's coat and trousers were disheveled and wrinkled. He cut the pants short above his knee, revealing hardened muscle and tattooed skin, and the coat was rolled short above the elbows, revealing the same tattooed body with corded muscles hardened by life on a ship, rippling beneath the inky skin.

Sennin once asked him to explain the obvious deviation from the standard uniform and the tattooed sea-beast that covered his skin from ankle to jawline. Sennin recalled being met with a particularly informal laugh and slap on his shoulder along with a cheerful. "Can't sail like the wind if yer clothes are draggin' in it! And the ink is to blend in with the beasts that haunt the waters! Won't eat ya if they think yer one of 'em eh?"

It wasn't much of an explanation in Lord Sennin's mind, but there was no questioning that Malfius could sail with an expertise unmatched in open water. Sennin wouldn't alienate such an asset just because of a bit of strangeness. He and his human crew sailed circles around the rest of the navy on individual missions, much to the chagrin of the other, more traditional, boat captains with elven crews.

Despite the appearance and utter lack of decorum, Lord Sennin did enjoy the company of the rough sailor. The High Lord also knew that Malfius was the only man who could reliably courier a message to Queen Celestra. He could not risk his messenger birds being intercepted as the rested near the Narrow's, which had become a black hole in communication and trade network.

"High Lord Sennin, how may I be of yer service," Captain Malfius called, brushing his coat out as he bowed deeply. Once he stood, he broke out into a broad smile that was missing some teeth, though the ones that were in place were in surprisingly healthy condition. He reached out and clasped the High Lord on his shoulder. "It has been quite some time since we last chatted, sir. I 'magine something mighty nasty has stirred for you to look to the fine seamen of the Grim Siren."

Lord Sennin gestured for the elf to sit on the couch in his study and settled down in a chair opposite. "May I offer you any refresh…" Lord Sennin trailed off as Malfius produced a worn silver flask and took a long swig.

"No refreshments needed, kind sir. 've learned to always pack my own! Lest I get caught with dry lips, ya see," chimed Malfius, taking a swig from his flask.

"Well," said Sennin, holding back a chuckle at the brazen behavior. "You are correct in your assumption that the city is in dire need. We have not received any shipments of trade from Turenian in a couple of months. Despite sending multiple messages to Narrows, we have gotten no word or explanation from Lady Elba, and the impact on our food supply has been hard to bear. Our royal reserves are rapidly being depleted to a concerning level… A level where action must be taken swiftly unless we want our people to starve. So," Sennin paused and fixed his gaze on the ginger elf. "I wish you and your men to sail North to Turenian. I am drafting a letter to Queen Celestra detailing the situation. I also need you to bring back as much cargo as your boat can carry on your return trip with her response."

"Ah, a few months in the open sea. That sounds like a mighty relaxing mission for us. Consider it done. But jus' know, even with the speed of 'ol Grim Siren, it will still take over a month, closer to two most likely, just to get to Turenian sailing 'round the peninsula. Not to mention the overland travel once we've arrived," commented Malfius.

High Lord Sennin held the man's gaze but did not speak. Captain Malfius's expression changed as the realization of what Sennin wanted of him sunk in. "Wait a minute." Captain Malfius shot to his feet. "You said sail north, not around! No, no, no, you can't be serious. You intend to send us through the Cursed Isles? Tis a death wish, sir! How could you ask this of my men? No one makes it through the Isles alive."

Lord Sennin kept a cool voice and expression despite his surprise at the outburst from the sailor. "I understand you have made it through the isles alive once before, Captain. Am I mistaken?"

"No, yer not bloody mistaken! The scars still linger in my mind they do. They claw in deeper at night, pulling my subconscious into haunted dreams, you see!" Malfius was shouting now. His hand, which dove into his coat pocket only to emerge holding an open flask, began shaking. He still managed to tip the flask to his lips without wasting a drop.

The hand grew still as the liquor soothed his nerves. After a long drink, Malfius settled to rest his gaze on Lord Sennin, but rather than looking at him, Sennin felt the sea captain's gaze pass through his being. He continued in a hushed voice. "The sounds from that place still haunt me. My crew went mad on the passage, ya see. Some jumped overboard to be broken on the rocks beneath the sealine, others went crazy and attacked their fellow sailors, and some even attempted to set the ship afire. All the while, amongst all the chaos, the mist laughed at our agony. It enjoyed the chaos ya hear, it longed for more of it, and the mist was not disappointed. One by one, the crew broke. I watched their minds fall apart, and just before I lost mine with them, we cleared the haze. I swore I would never return, and I don't plan on changing this now. I lost most of my crew that day, and ain't learned nothing since that makes me believe I could ever keep them alive if I ventured in the isles again. Please, sir, don't order me there."

Lord Sennin could discern genuine fear in the man's eyes as he spoke. He despised having to make such requests, but the pressing need for food among his people left him little choice. Before he could respond, a she-elf burst into his office. Lord Sennin did not know her by name, but she wore the uniform of an Elite scout. She bowed as she regained her breath.

"Sir, I beg your pardon for any intrusion, but this is urgent. My team has been scouting further out into the desert near the Badlands. There had been a sandstorm in the area, but this storm seemed to move, well, oddly, rising from the earth around the fallen Oasis. It has not dissipated in days."

Lord Sennin stood, cutting the woman off. "I hope you didn't barge your way into my office to tell me the weather. Get to the point, soldier!"

The elf nodded. "There appears to be a human army amassing in the deeper recesses of the fallen Oasis. We do not have an exact number. All scouts sent in close were killed by... something in the sand. We believe they mean to march on Sandivar, sir."

Lord Sennin went pale. He turned to Captain Malfius, "I am sorry to ask this of you, Captain, but your ability to navigate perilous seas could mean the survival of a city. Without your success, I fear this battle could prove fatal to the Queen's final stronghold in the desert. Can you do this for me, for your fellow kinsman here in Sandivar? The kingdom as we know it may just depend on your success."

Captain Malfius looked between the scout and his High Lord, clearly in shock at the day's change of events. He stood, took another swig off his flask, and nodded to Sennin. "I will prepare my vessel to depart before the day's end."

Lord Sennin stepped forward and clasped the sailor's forearm, "May the Gods favor you. I will send you a letter to bring to Celestra, letting her know our situation. It will be delivered to the docks within the hour." With that, the Captain departed, and Lord Sennin turned to his scout. "Send for the generals. We have a war to plan for."

Nienna - Chapter 20 - Slow Death

"We cannot keep this pace," Taniya shouted from behind Nienna after Kimo's unconscious groans increased in volume and frequency. Fleeing the Narrows had not been kind to the injuries both elven men had sustained, but Kimo's quick regression was particularly startling. Nienna had seen the healing solution applied to men and women in the firm grip of death, only to see them spring back to health in short order. *Why is it not working on Kimo and Joralf?*

The two women had been riding hard for over half a day, fleeing The Narrows at reckless speeds as they pushed their horses to their limits, striving to put as many miles as possible between them and any Gifted that may have lingered in the city. The insides of Nienna's legs groaned in agony from the constant drumming against a leather saddle and, were she honest with herself, she'd be glad for a brief reprieve.

The sun had risen and was beginning to set once again. The party only stopped to check on the wounded Elites briefly and to relieve themselves once. At Nienna's word, the great lion led them from the main road connecting The Narrows to Turenian, a journey that would take more than four weeks, plodding into the depths of the ancient Feyrenthia Forest. This was the oldest untouched stretch of land in Divinoros, commonly known as the Fey Forest. It was an area few ventured deep within voluntarily, so as the giant lion led his exhausted companions off the main path, Nienna felt sure they traveled further away from the threat of the Gifted that could be in pursuit from the Bankhoft-controlled Narrows.

The anxious energy and adrenaline that saturated the elf's blood began to fade as the feeling of safety blanketed her, allowing her mind to wander. The thoughts sent Nienna's head spinning from the implications of the crucial trade city falling into overtly hostile hands.

How could he have taken it in such silence? There were no whispers that Lady Elba had lost The Narrows.

She had no love for Celestra or her kingdom, but she disliked the prospect of how she would fit in a world under the control of a cruel human twisted by some malignant, malevolent force. Though she couldn't blame the root of the Knife's hate after years of humankind being crushed under the thumb of the elven rulers, she would fight against them to maintain her way of life. He had gone too far in his attempt to balance the power gap between their kinds, and in doing so, one thing was clear to Nienna: *The Knife had created a very powerful enemy in me.*

Once the party was securely nestled amongst the thick moss-covered trees, Nienna called out for Zarou to stop and slid from the saddle of

Kimo's horse. Despite the tightness in her legs, she wasted no time in rushing to Zarou, immediately untying the dying elf strapped to his back. The Elite hung limp, still dangling unconsciously, only held in place by the firm straps Nienna tied about him and secured to the saddle. Nienna felt a pang of anger toward the unconscious Kimo. Although it was no choice of his own and was necessary, she did not like anyone but herself riding on Zarou's back. She would reclaim her seat now that the elves were safely tucked into the dense forest and protected from the enemy, despite the inconvenience this would be for Taniya who would then need to lead two horses behind her own.

The Feyrenthia Forest was a beautiful landscape of lush, dense woods. Large dark green leaves covered the canopy of thick trees, their thick, low-hanging limbs extending wide from their trucks, giving moss and vines plenty of surface to grow and effectively blocking out a majority of the sun. In doing so, the forest floor below was cast into cool shadows.

The air was humid, and the ground was littered with decaying leaves, colorful flowers, and coiled vines bunched at the base of the long tendrils hanging down from the tree branches above. Suspended in the air along the vines were vibrant flowering fruits being harassed by yellow bumble bees the size of a child's fist. Large swarms of the bees flocked between the fruits as they raced one another to the fresh nectar of unmolested flowers. It was a beautiful display of symbiotic life between insects and plants. Beauty was a word that seemed to be in contrast with such an eerie place. Wildlife filled the forest with a cacophony of sounds as insects chirped, lemurs howled, and the songs of camouflaged birds filled the warm air. Nienna knew the forest housed dangers, a variety of predators that could prove a threat to the injured group. Luckily, Zarou, regardless of landscape, was one of the most dangerous predators to stalk the planet, a true apex, and all but a few creatures in this place would avoid them simply because of his presence. *All but the supernatural, that is,* Nienna considered.

After placing the Kimo down, Nienna rushed over to help Taniya unstrap Joralf. Nienna laid the man next to Kimo. Neither moved. Nienna looked to Taniya, seeing tears forming in her eyes before the swell of liquid broke like a dam, sending the clear fluid cascading over the edge of Taniya's lids, tracing glistening lines down her cheeks as her body convulsed with silent shutters of grief and agony.

Nienna's heart sank. *They are beyond the point of any help... Maybe a healing mage could help, but they won't make the night much less the journey.* Despite this, it was clear Taniya would not yet accept their fate,

"Go, get your medicinal supplies. I will check their pulse," Nienna said softly, dropping to a knee and pressing her finger into the crook of Kimo's elbow to feel for a sign that his heart was still beating life

153

through his veins. She could make out a weak pulse and smiled down at the once handsome face of the young, brazen, elvish soldier. His face was now fixed in a pale expression of pain. She moved to the older Joralf and performed the same procedure, feeling the joint of his elbow. Five seconds passed. She adjusted her grip. Ten seconds passed. She felt up under the jaw of the grizzled war veteran. Still, she felt no pulse. "Taniya, Kimo is barely hanging on, and I cannot feel Joralf's pulse!" Nienna held her wrist in front of Joralf's nose and mouth and felt no breath.

Taniya rushed over, carrying a wooden box and fresh linen strips to wrap the wounds of her companions. She pushed Nienna out of the way to kneel next to Joralf and instantly opened his jaw, forcing breath into his lungs with her own mouth. After two breaths, she began to press into his chest, trying to restart the heart that appeared to have retired from its laborious duty.

Nienna watched in silence as Taniya repeated her procedures: breath, breath, compression, breath, breath, compression, breath, breath, compression. Nienna made no sound but prayed silently to Vitala, but after a couple of minutes, Taniya relented. She sat back, tears falling down her cheeks in heartbroken streams: "He... He is gone."

Nienna felt for the woman. She had not known Joralf well, but she knew that Taniya had known him, trained with him, and lived with him for decades. She couldn't be sure but based on her limited interaction with the trio of Elites, Nienna had thought he and Taniya may have been lovers at one point, and at the least, they had seemed very fond of one another. Beyond that, Nienna found him to be level-headed and kind; his death was a loss not only to Lord Sennin and the Queen's Elites but also to all who knew him.

Taniya pressed her forehead against the dead elves and grasped his hand firmly in her own. She muttered something inaudible to Nienna's keen ears, then kissed his forehead before her training told her to move on and tend to Kimo.

Taniya took only a second, breathed deeply, and wiped her face free of tears as she tried to gather herself before she started her work on Kimo, hoping to keep the younger elf from falling into the same fate. "We will need to dig a grave," Taniya said in a hushed tone. Nienna nodded her agreement and placed a hand on the other woman's shoulder as she started to tend to the younger man. Nienna watched as Taniya unwrapped a gruesome-looking wound in Kimo's abdomen.

The black tendrils emanating from the javelin wound had resurfaced, appearing even more ominous than before, signaling a troubling development. The site was oozing a foul, viscous black liquid. As the wound was exposed to open air, an overwhelming scent of rot and viscera filled the area. Taniya and Nienna reeled back as the smell of decay entered their nostrils, forcing both women to tie cloths around their faces before they could properly assess the site of the javelin puncture. His veins around the wide puncture site showed as a dark black beneath his alabaster skin, creating a dark map of where his veinous tissue was carrying whatever toxic agent the Gifted infected him with.

"I'm going to need you to hold him down if he wakes up. We need to remove this infection from the wound site as best we can and hope that gives him time. I don't know what this could be. Wound rot typically takes days to set to this degree. That damned monster must have done something to accelerate the rate of decay. It's almost acting like a sort of poisonous accelerant, but it should have cleared up after the cleansing solution we treated it with... We need to get him to a healer's clinic. I don't know how else we can help him other than periodically cleaning the wound and praying he can fight off the infection," Taniya said quietly. She didn't take her eyes off her patient as she tipped a clear liquid healing potion from a glass vial into the wound.

As soon as the potion touched the exposed flesh, the skin bubbled and hissed. Kimo jolted upright, pain yanking him from a fitful unconsciousness to an unhinged state of wakefulness. His back arched, and his eyes went dark. His mouth clenched in an angered growl.

Taniya fell back from the man, fear and concern plain on her face, but Kimo soon collapsed back down to the cool ground, once more unconscious. Tears welled in Taniya's eyes once again, but she turned toward Nienna, her voice quiet but offering no room for debate. "Please dig Joralf's grave. I will do what I can here." Her voice broke at the end as she fought to speak over a sob that was welling within. Nienna nodded and turned from the woman, knowing she now accepted Kimo was dead. Not yet, but in the coming day, hours, maybe even minutes. She bent by the corpse of Joralf, hefted him onto her shoulder, and walked past Zarou. She brushed his shoulder as she passed the sand lion, beckoning for him to follow her as she walked deeper into the forest.

With the help of Zarou's ferocious claws, the pair was able to gouge a proper grave in the dirt quickly. Far faster than she could have alone, even if she'd had a shovel. Once they had laid the body in the grave and covered him in a thin layer of dirt, the pair walked through the forest to gather rocks to place over the body. This was a tradition Nienna had seen the dwarves partake in, though they would cover their dead with beautifully polished granite and marble stones rather than an odd assortment found in the depths of the forest.

The mystic of this particular dwarfish ceremony had once been explained to her that all creatures were carved from the earth by the touch of Vitala, and so in death, they were returned to her. While many other components make up bodies, each species has core minerals that tie us to the place the Gods forged life from. When members of their

155

tribes passed away, they were encased in minerals as a gesture of gratitude for the body that the Gods had lent to the soul. This act was performed in the hope that expressing thanks in this way would help Vitala accept those souls in death. Of all the death traditions she had witnessed, she thought this the most beautiful. Joralf was a kind soul; she had no reservations that Vitala and the other Gods would accept his with open arms, but she wanted to make this gesture out of respect for her fallen comrade and to ensure he received a smooth transition to life in the heavens in case the dwarf's practices proved true.

Once the grave was completed, she returned to where she had left Kimo and Taniya. She found the woman leaning against a tree near Kimo's limp body. She stared into the depths of the forest in front of her. She didn't look at Nienna approaching, but as she neared, she heard the woman say, "What are you taking to the Queen that could be worth this?"

"You know we transport an old manuscript, but I can't tell you of the contents it contains," Nienna responded as she collapsed near the woman, leaning back against the massive frame of Zarou, who settled behind her. "You can feel it though, can't you? There is a war coming to the elves. This fight was bound to happen regardless of where Sennin sent you. The only question of this fight is when, where, and who will stand atop the broken corpses of the loser. I fear this is only the start, Taniya."

Silence persisted for a short minute. "Kimo is dead." Nienna felt a jolt of pain before overwhelming sadness filled her. She tried to speak reassuring words, but they caught in her throat. Taniya continued, "His heart gave out while I treated him. His last day was spent in agony and pain after following a woman with no right to lead him. But even still, you can't tell me what this mission is, can't hint at what those monsters who killed my brothers in arms were or how they got such power. The price of two lives, two lives of great elven men I have known for decades, doesn't buy even an attempt at an explanation from you."

Her words cut Nienna deeply. She was about to apologize, even explain that she was sworn to silence on the details of the assignment Sennin placed upon her. But before she could get a word out, Taniya shouted, "Stop. I don't care what your reason is for your silence, but I guess the rumors are true. The infamous Ghost is truly a heartless form in the body of a beautiful elf. I thought I might like you when this little venture started out. I'm usually a good judge of character. It appears in this instance I was wrong," Taniya shrugged. Nienna thought she might continue to berate her, but the Elite remained silent and stared off into the distance as her once regal form shuttered with throbs of loss.

Nienna's stomach sank at the words of the typically kind woman. She wanted to remedy and comfort her, but what could she say at a time

156

like this? She had worked by herself for so many years, and her only companion throughout that time was the ever-loyal Zarou. It was a good life; she accomplished many things in her time in this world, but she had grown to feel lonely over the last few centuries. It had been ages since she spent time with anyone she considered could be a friend. Taniya was the closest thing she came to making one in recent memories, but it seemed as though that had ended with Kimo's final breath.

Taniya stood and, without looking at Nienna, stated, "I'm going to bury him." She loaded the elf onto her shoulder and walked from the clearing they had stopped in.

Dusk had cast the forest into shadows. Nienna wasn't wary of the forest as she leaned into a cat weighing over a thousand pounds, lost in her own thoughts. Well, she wasn't wary until a blood-curdling shriek pulled her from her thoughts faster than jumping into freezing water.

The scream had come from deep in the forest and was followed by the pleading of a familiar voice. Taniya's cries rang through the forest of shadows.

"What is this? Stay back! Stay back! Oh my... Oh my Gods, what has happened to you? Arghh!" The final scream was cut short, and the forest fell into absolute silence. The birds quit singing, and the bugs quit chirping. There wasn't even a breeze to rustle the foliage.

Nienna - Chapter 21 - The First Defilement

Nienna was on her feet. Her pulse quickened as anxiety weaved through her body till its cold grasp found firm purchase around her heart. She unsheathed her daggers; the distinct sound of sharp metal being drawn over the leather resonated sharply in her ears in the now silent forest.

She paused for just a moment, straining her ears in hopes of picking up the slightest sound, but after hearing none, she set off in the direction of the scream. Nienna moved silently, a phantom in the woods, following the path Taniya had taken as she left the clearing. Without command, Zarou disappeared into the foliage off to her right in a maneuver the pair had practiced hundreds of times. The cat intended to stalk through the forest after Nienna, out of her line of sight, but he could follow her easily enough by tracking her scent. Having a separation between the pair meant it would be more difficult for any enemy to catch them in a single ambush.

Dusk was rapidly giving way to night, and soon, the landscape was illuminated only by scattered slivers of pale moonlight that snuck past the dense foliage above. Shadows danced in her peripherals, and the motion of branches and leaves swaying in a gentle evening breeze frequently caused Nienna to freeze in suspense.

Gods damn these trees. Their low branches take the shape of monsters on the edge of my vision. Focus now, find Taniya.

She took each step carefully to ensure she did not disrupt the stagnant, heavy air suspended in an unnerving silent backdrop to the night. But Nienna had spent centuries working in the dark and she refused to allow the increasingly haunting feel of the forest to rattle her into a careless mistake. She followed the cracked twigs and tramped down foliage that indicated the path Taniya had taken Kimo's body. She finally ended up in a small clearing where the woman had clearly been digging a shallow grave for her companion. She furrowed her brow.

Where is Taniya and where is Kimo's body?

To the left of the shallow pit, a large patch of leafed bush limbs was folded and crushed. This was where Nienna guessed Kimo's body had lain temporarily as Taniya set to digging at the earth, but the body was no longer there, and Taniya was nowhere to be seen.

"Taniya?" Nienna called in a hushed tone that sounded like a shout in the silent night. "Are you somewhere nearby?"

No response came.

"Taniya?" The Ghost worked her way around the pit and noticed a pool of dark liquid reflecting the stars above. It was a substance she was familiar with, and as she knelt to take in the surroundings, she noticed the faint scent of iron hanging in the air. She dabbed the puddle and rolled the fluid between her fingers, confirming beyond any doubt that the liquid was elven blood. Her heart sank. *Where is Taniya? Where is Kimo's body? Something out here has taken them.*

A trail of blood smattering alongside long drag marks caught Nienna's eye. It looked as if someone in immense pain, unable to support their weight properly, was limping heavily and dragging a body beside it. A spark of hope kindled.

She might be alive, she must have dragged Kimo's body away from whatever attacked her.

A rustling sounded from the deep shadows behind a thick patch of vine-covered trees to Nienna's left, causing her to wheel about. She leveled her short blade in that direction, staring into the dark, trying to discern what had made the noise, and was met by a pair of massive gleaming eyes. A sigh of relief passed through her lips. It was just Zarou keeping watch over his companion.

She nodded toward him, grateful for the presence of the beast. She would never have forged her infamy as the Ghost without the assurance the lion's presence afforded, just as he would have likely been hunted and killed before he reached adulthood without her care. He bowed his head in the direction of Nienna's inspected trail, confirming her suspicions that this was the direction they needed to investigate.

Now sure of where to direct her search, the Ghost hurried along the path of the drag marks. If she found Taniya fast enough, then maybe she could keep her alive. Based on the size of the puddle of blood, she knew this to be an unlikely outcome, but she disliked the idea of all three of her traveling companions perishing prior to completing their mission. So, regardless of the odds, she couldn't leave her last remaining companion. Despite this, a strange knot of dread and apprehension begged her to abandon this search.

She moved quicker now; the urgency in her steps did not allow her to keep absolute silence as she followed drops of blood and strange loping drag marks. She had nearly resolved to give up the search, to jump on Zarou and flee, when she made out two shapes huddled together no more than fifteen feet from where she now crouched. The two forms were partially obscured by the mossy bulk of an ancient trunk. Something wasn't right. Her knotted stomach kept her from calling for Taniya immediately.

There was a still figure hunched and unmoving. Nienna had thought that must be Taniya but it struck a distinctly un-feminine figure hovering above a still form lying on the ground. The lying figure had long flowing

159

hair obscuring half the woman's face. The exposed portion showed a lifeless eye staring directly at where the Ghost was hidden, a deadly warning from beyond the grave begging her to flee far from here.

Nienna stared in horror. Blood dripped from the corner of Taniya's open mouth. Her limbs were twisted in abnormal directions, evidencing the cruelty and violence with which she was killed. The other figure was still. Unmoving. It was staring down at Taniya while looming above her silently. It made no more movement than a gentle swaying from side to side.

He was contorted and disfigured, and despite his skin looking like an oversized suit draped over a skeleton, it was unmistakably elvish in form. The looming figure was Kimo. *At least it had been Kimo*, Nienna thought. The man did not move or speak. His still sway was only broken apart by a heavy, silent panting and random spasms of his neck and limbs, accompanied by what sounded like gurgling pain. Suddenly, his head snapped violently to the side, then backward. He seemed to rest a moment, twitching again before the aggressive convulsions of his head resumed.

The respite between these fits shortened as the thrashing increased in frequency and intensity until a loud snap accompanied an aggressive cranking of his head directly backward. His neck had broken under the force, proven by the site of his head lulling forward until his chin rested on his chest. A sharp point of broken vertebrae was now visibly pressing through the loose flesh against the taught skin where the head used to stand. Nienna brought a hand to her mouth to hold in a scream or upheaval, whichever came first.

What is happening to him?

Kimo dropped to a knee, his head slumped lifelessly against his chest. His body spasmed, and an involuntary grunt emanated from Kimo's body. It could not have been an intentional sound, just air being forced from his frame as his innards were crushed and contorted. A deafening crack sounded as two large black arms erupted from his rib cage. Ribs and skin were split open in a bloody mist behind the force of the alien extremities.

The limbs continued to grow in size and forced the exit wounds wider till the protrusions found traction on the earth beneath the elf's body. Nienna gagged. She wanted to look away from the grotesque scene, but the horror of what unfolded before froze her in place, her eyes fixed on the distortion unfolding in front of her. Kimo's body then began trembling with unnatural speed, sending his head shaking side to side, a pendulum bouncing against his chest. More snapping accompanied bone breaks, louder than snapping tree limbs in harsh storms.

Before she could decide any course of action, the base of his neck bulged as *something* beneath the broken spine protrusion pushed against the skin. Nienna's heart stopped. *There's something inside of him!*

The thing probed and prodded, pressing against the loose skin until the flesh ripped apart and a long, dark head forced itself free to take the place of the elves' own. It was smooth, pure black, darker than the surrounding shadows, with three red eyes on each side of the head that gleamed like embers in the night. Razor sharp teeth were visible as the newly hatched monster sucked in air through its opened mouth and proceeded to chatter its teeth together as if to test the deadly power they possessed. The lower jaw was separated into two mandibles lined with rows of serrated, knife-like teeth.

Nienna's focus again was drawn to the gory scene of Kimo's head that was now hanging limply onto what used to be an elvish body by bits of skin. It was swinging violently from side to side as the creature spread its maw wide and began to shriek over and over. Its cry was a violent, terrorizing sound that cut through the icy silence previously dominating the night. The shrieking continued incessantly as the beast struggled against the fleshy shell encasing its form. The head of Kimo finally pulled free from the strands of skin and hit the ground of the forest. The sight was now too much for Nienna, who swallowed down the bile as it swelled up in her mouth to avoid making noise.

The abomination started trashing and dragging itself by its two fully formed limbs in circles around Taniya's body. Four more limbs, an additional pair to each side, with razor-sharp claws ripped free of the elvish torso. The horrible sound of tearing meat, common in a butcher's shop but appalling in the present circumstance, reached Nienna's ears as more and more of the elf was replaced by a monster that emerged from within his body.

Soon, the only trace of what had been Kimo was bits of flesh and broken bone, scattered limbs soaking in pools of blood. Nienna's vision faded and sharpened as her mind struggled to grasp the reality of what she saw... *Blood, so much blood.* The viscous fluid covered everything it seemed, smeared on the trees and dripping from the leaves of the witnessing plants in the vicinity of the carnage.

Despite her shock, Nienna knew she had seen this creature before. She had studied this beast, or a form of it, in her favorite accounts of historical war. It was present when her mentor taught of the great King Kei-Tel or encouraged her to read the many accounts of the wars and strategies that took place in various battles Kei-Tel waged. In the place of what had once been an elf stood a living image of the beast's Omnes, which had long ago been released on Divinoros to wipe out all living beings. The newly formed krakenshi roared triumphantly into the night

161

sky, reveling in its newfound freedom. The Ghost trembled at the thought that Omnes once again had taken a step into this world.

She backed away from the scene, her only desire to run to the Queen and warn her, for Celestra would need to raise an army. The mightiest army seen since King Kei-Tel unified the elven cities in his campaign against the Dark God. Nienna was horrified to have her suspicions of the Bankhoft family concretely confirmed in the worst way. It seemed that the Knife possessed the power of Omnes. There was only one thing that mattered now—surviving so that Queen Celestra would not be attacked, unaware of the dark powers brewing in the south.

She turned to run, ready to abandon stealth for speed, but as she spun, she was tackled with immense force, sending her rolling in the direction of the hatched krakenshi. She hit the ground and rolled back to her feet, surprised to see the form of Joralf staring back at her through lifeless eyes. Shards of rock stuck in his skin and his fingers flayed and clotted with dirt. Wounds on his hands from the dead man having clawed his way free of the grave in which she buried him. Stale blood dripped slowly from the wrecked hands of a once great man.

Facing Joralf, she knew the monstrous krakenshi born from Kimo was now to her back, and one still unborn stood in front of her. More unnerving, she no longer heard the fully emerged krakenshi shrieking. She did not want to be attacked by both creatures at once, so she whispered a silent prayer to the Gods that Taniya's body would hold the attention of the six-legged beast behind her while she dispatched the one residing in Joralf.

Omnes must have been the God to receive this prayer, however, as she heard the krakenshi behind her shriek once again. Nienna glanced to the side in time to see a flash of movement in the trees beyond where the monster stood and knew she did not need to worry about the krakenshi just yet. A deafening roar drowned out the high-pitched screech as trees cracked under Zarou's rushing mass. The lion lunged through narrow gaps in the trees to attack the Dark God's wretched spawn. He hit the krakenshi with enough force to shake the world around the Ghost, who now refocused on the dead man standing before her.

Joralf's lifeless eyes showed no fear or surprise as he looked at the she-elf approaching him with two gleaming blades. His body convulsed and twitched, just as Kimo's had, even as she stepped toward the elf to attack him. The upcoming transformation made the movements of Joralf clumsy, and the Ghost seized the advantage.

She cut off the man's head with one of her daggers but remembered the rolling head of Kimo… She wanted to ensure no monster would rise from this corpse. With three vicious hacks, she cut the man just above the midsection at his waist just as two black arms pushed through Joralf's chest cavity before she hacked through his chest once again.

162

Once Joralf's body lay in three large pieces, severed by her daggers, the twitching ceased.

The Ghost wheeled around to face the battle of two goliaths that continued to shake the forest floor. Zarou initially had the upper hand, being far larger, far stronger, and was nearly impervious given the fact that his scale acted like fine armor protecting him from the slashes of the krakenshi's many legs.

He had managed to score massive wounds in the beast's side that were now leaking globs of foul-smelling dark liquid that fizzled into smoke as it touched the ground. But the God-spawn was recovering quickly from its surprise at the lion's attack and soon began to use the tight spaces between the trees as an advantage in combat against the far larger opponent.

Zarou's forceful swipes were now shattering trees instead of finding purchase on the krakenshi's foul form. Despite its savage wounds, the krakenshi launched an effective counterattack, utilizing a highly mobile tail that culminated in a spear-like point. Most of the attacks reflected off the lion's carapace, but if the fight continued much longer, Nienna knew the tail would eventually find a small chink between Zarou's scales by luck, if nothing else. The Ghost refused to let the Knife, his minions, or the power of a God he served claim the life of anyone as dear to her as Zarou.

So she joined the fray with vigor, and the pair of seasoned mercenaries fell into a practiced dance of death that they had perfected long ago over centuries of fighting alongside one another. Zarou lunged repeatedly in an attempt to bite down on the krakenshi's neck. It dodged the blow, exposing its side where Nienna would cut with her long daggers. The monster responded by lunging at the elf, attempting to catch the smaller prey in its oscillating mandibles, but as soon as its attention departed the lion, Zarou pounced over the creature, sinking his claws deep in its hindquarters. His claws were long enough to sink deep into the flesh of the monster, and with an overwhelming force, he pulled away one of its six legs at the joint, ripping the limb from his body.

The krakenshi screamed in pain, seeming to realize its fate of being caught in the middle of two killers that could not be overwhelmed. Desperation set in. The beast lashed out wildly in a last-resort attack that was focused entirely on what it saw as the weaker foe. Nienna.

The monster lunged at the Ghost, its limbs flailing frantically in a reckless offensive. Nienna attempted to duck by spiraling back between trees but was too slow. She let out an involuntary whimper as one of the krakenshi's massive talons cleaved a large gash from her navel to her side. As she fell back in pain, she noticed a massive shadow blot out the moonlight as her sand lion leaped after the monster. He landed on its back, clamping the most powerful jaws in all Divinoros around the base

163

of the monster's skull. With a sharp flex of his jowls, the skull cracked. The red light faded from the beast's eyes as it crumbled to the forest floor and deflated into wisps of darkness that stood out as a deeper black even in the shadowed night of the forest.

Nienna struggled to her knees. As the adrenaline faded, the realization of the night's events hitting her, she started to sob. At the pain in her abdomen, at the death of her companions, and at the fear that was stirred by the grotesque violence the night brought upon her.

This evil is too great to be inflicted on mortals. These creatures are far too potent for our world, they needed to be sent back to the ethereal plan from which they were born.

She should not be responsible for keeping these powers at bay, yet she was unknowingly summoned to the very center of the next great war on Divinoros for what she believed to be a routine job from a respected High Lord.

She reached down to her abdomen and her hand came away warm and wet, slick with scarlet blood that poured from her side. She did not know how she would finish her journey; she only knew she must complete her quest to the Queen.

She tore her clothes to form a makeshift compress and bandage, which she painfully tied over her midsection, hoping to restrict the flow of blood.

Hopefully, only a wound from the Gifted fester as Kimo's and Joralf's did.

After struggling to her feet, she climbed onto Zarou's back and weakly grabbed the reins. She trusted him to care for her and to complete the travel north to the elven capital. Before they made it a quarter mile, Nienna's world went dark. The flow of blood from her midsection refused to be abated. Without a word, she tumbled from the back of the Zarou. The great sand lion circled her and whined in concern, nuzzling her over and over, urging her to get up so he could usher her to help. Try as she might, she couldn't get her limbs to obey.

The last thing she saw before the fading starlight above flickered out was a strange pair approaching Zarou. She couldn't make out the language, but Zarou appeared to acknowledge them and the strange words spoken to him. They appeared to be mother and child, but the child, strangely, was clearly leading the way.

As she neared, the features of the pair came clear; the woman was old, healthy, and fit, but lines earned from years of hard life were plain on her kind face. On her back, she wore a cloak that seemed to fall in and out of the surrounding shadows that dominated the woods.

The child was no child at all; her hair hung low on her back, dark green in the starlight, framing a narrow face with eyes slightly larger than that of a human or elf. Her eyes gleamed the same color as her hair

164

which was held into place by a simple circlet of woven vine. As she knelt by Nienna, she reached a long, slender finger to brush her hair from Nienna's sweat-soaked brow. Her skin was pale, gray almost, and from her fingers, long dark nails protruded. Nienna looked into her large green eyes and thought she heard words in her mind: "*Rest, daughter of the night.*"

She spoke words Nienna didn't understand, and then her world winked out.

Ryker - Chapter 22 - History Lessons

Blood spluttered and sprayed between the Ryker's fingers as he laughed, cradling a broken, bloodied nose. He sat on the ground, tears misting his vision after taking a blow from the hilt of Aegnor's sword straight to the bridge of his nose. The apprentice sat on the ground, tears and blood surging as he cracked the bone back into place. The pain wasn't enough to wipe the scarlet smile that clung to his face. He imagined Aegnor's expression of disgust at the visage of the laughing fool splattered in crimson.

Through his hazy vision, Ryker could swear he made out Aegnor breathing hard. However, when the water had cleared from his eyes, his master stood as elegant as ever, looking down on his apprentice's face in a frown of disgust, much like what Ryker had imagined. While the master hid his strain from the effort of their duel well, he was unable to hide the slight twinge that tugged at the corner of his mouth, bringing his lips to a quick smile.

Ryker had clipped the elf's tunic this time.

I clipped the great Aegnor's tunic!

The apprentice kept the cheering sentiment in his own head, for, of course, shortly after the marginal success, he was flattened by a series of lightning-fast offensive movements, one being the particularly violent strike to his face.

The apprentice sprang to his feet, feeling energized from the duel regardless of its intensity and the swelling pain in his face. He wiped the blood from his nose on his shirt, groaning from the sharp pain that accompanied the movement. "Gods damn, this hurts! Really, you had to break my nose just because I cut a bit of fabric?" The accusation was made in a jesting tone. "Doesn't seem quite the fair rebuttal, Master."

"Ahhh, but you are wrong twice in this line of thinking here, young apprentice. One, this is absolutely and unequivocally *fair*. You would need to spend nearly a full year of your previous farmer's salary to obtain such fine linen the likes of which you just cut… and I like this tunic. In fact, I wore it specifically for today. You see, the Dwarf King appreciates finer things in life, but we differ in…. Shall we say tastes, so I intended to wear the finest garb I carry for the introductions." He raised his arm to see the minuscule tear on the upper arm and shrugged as if to say it wasn't bad.

"Secondly, when in your life have you been given a fair punishment? Fairness is something that does not and should not exist in life. You do not receive fairness from others until you are able to adequately defend what is yours from those who would take it. Until you can do that, the more skilled will batter you as they please. Though this is not *right* or good, it is most certainly *fair*."

Then Aegnor swooped in an exaggerated bow. "Luckily for you, I am kind enough only to break your nose rather than claim your life, and I will prepare you to defend yourself against those who would not show such constraint."

Aegnor took on a more serious tone of praise now. "Not to mention, you are well on your way to overcoming the *unfair* obstacles against opponents that will be stacked against you as our journey progresses. You have grown far more competent. You have succeeded in conquering those shortcomings, and legend awaits you. Fairness and equality everywhere in the world mean nothing. Nothing is more important than the reality that all have opportunities regardless of the situation we are raised in. It is not fair you were born human and I elf, but despite our difference, you have succeeded in cutting my tunic this morning. Seize whatever opportunity is presented or join those who are too lazy or scared to do so and join them in begging for more *fairness*." Ryker nodded his ascent before Aegnor continued, "Now get up and clean yourself off. You're bleeding all over yourself." Aegnor made a show of looking in disgust at the still stupidly grinning Ryker, "We're meeting a king today! You must look respectable."

Ryker shook his head and laughed before saying in an unpleasant, nasally tone, "I understad, wha you say is true. Still... this is going to be awfully paiful the ext few weeks."

Aegnor nodded his agreement. "Yes, and it is a good lesson as well. The more often you experience pain, the less it impacts you in the future. People have grown soft and quick to cure any small ailment with magic or tincture. You must grow used to pain's company so you do not falter under its presence in more pressing times."

With that, Aegnor strode to ready the Ravanians for the last leg of their journey into the marbled caverns while his apprentice shook his head and turned to get washed and changed.

With morning training complete, Aegnor and Ryker rode astride Maximus and Xantharyia, steadily approaching the end of a short ravine that wound through the base of the Perampla Mountains to the southern entrance to the Marbled Caverns. "We have a short ride until we arrive at the gates of the Dwarves' Kingdom. I promised you lessons weeks ago on demons, and I fear I have been negligent in fulfilling that promise."

Ryker turned his head to face Aegnor. "I didn't want to press you on the topic. I trust your judgment on what needs to be prioritized in my lessons." Despite his words, excitement whirled in the apprentice. He had heard tales of demons terrorizing towns, killing in bunches before being driven off, but he knew little of their origination.

Aegnor expressed his appreciation with a nod at the words, clearly pleased to see progress being made with his student. "Well, today I shall tell you of the Second War. The tale of Divinoros's history is largely a tale of death, destruction, and sorrow for our people. Since the beginning of time, elves, dwarves, and humans have walked the earth. But in that beginning, we were little more than ants, cowering among powers and beings far greater than ours. We struggled for food and shelter. We had no kingdoms, no towns, nothing. In the beginning, the world was split between two great forces: the chaotic domain of the Demon King, Daemaron, and the rageful dominion of Dragons ruled by Drakkonian. The story of the demons is incomplete without knowledge of dragons and the First War that was waged between those two titans. I will tell you more about dragonkind and their downfall another time, but for now, just understand that these two kings were the most powerful beings that had ever stepped foot on Divinoros. Their might was such that even the Gods dared not come to this world to interfere in the First War, the war between these two."

Ryker jumped in, "I thought the Gods created this world, though. What do you mean they wouldn't come to this world?"

"A fair question. One that I can only answer with speculation unless I have the opportunity to speak to one of the Gods myself. But I believe they did create *this* world, seeded the life we see today, and forced it to flourish on the lands they established before retreating to the ethereal plain of existence to see to other Godly concerns or to simply watch our world grow. This only occurred once the titans had been… diminished. Despite that conjecture, the fact remains that both Daemaron and Drakkonian contained such power that they could have slain the four Gods with ease should they have entered Divinoros at the height of their powers. So, summarizing centuries of bloodshed and wars of such ferocity that their fighting gouged the craters that now make our oceans and pyres that make the mountains, Daemaron ultimately prevailed over Drakkonian and his legions of archdragons. In doing so, he weakened himself considerably. To fight for the sole rule of Divinoros, he spawned extensive forces of lesser demons that fed off his power."

Ryker cut off his master, "So spawning lesser demons weakened the Demon King to a point the Gods could return?"

"Precisely, but only because the dragons eradicated such a number of these ethereal beings, Daemaron was permanently weaker. Following the First War, Daemaron no longer possessed an overwhelming advantage in strength over the four Gods. Not him alone, that is. The issue remained that though Drakkonian had slain legions and legions of lessor demons, the Demon King still possessed a mighty army of his own offspring. And the Gods, well, despite overwhelming odds, they knew they could still not contend with his combined might alone. Now, you may question why the Gods cared that the world was run by demons, and the question would be justified. I believe there were many reasons, one being that I imagine supreme deities to be highly vain in nature, unable to act against their own nature. Omnes was unwilling to admit that others may possess greater strength and influence than their own. Vitala had likely long been tormented to see hundreds and thousands of creations she'd build to settle here being slain callously and offhanded by Daemaron, Sapiena eager to test her supremacy in strategy. But most importantly, Comporian wanted to show his compassion to our kind, to save us from eternal pain, suffering, and death in this world, and a desire to restore Divinoros to *balance*. And so, the Gods descended to our world."

Ryker was astounded by the tale. He could not believe there was a force stronger than the Gods. He had heard of Kei-Tel's assault on the Rift, and he couldn't picture a force more powerful than the one Omnes released.

"Despite their inability to act against their very nature, the Gods were smart. Knowing they stood little chance in a fight against the Demon King on their own, they recruited the help of the three major races that still cowered throughout Divinoros. First, they recruited the dwarves, as they were the only species to develop a larger settlement, given their propensity to burrow in the earth and live underground away from prying eyes. With the Gods' help, they created the initial footprint of the Great Marbled Caverns. Once this was built, Omnes, Vitala, Sapiena, and Comporian sought out all humans, elves, and dwarves, summoning them to the underground city. The people that were brought were broken and scared. All they have ever known was death and chaos, casualties in a war that was not their own."

Ryker shifted in his saddle and stroked Xantharyia's neck as he continued listening to his master's lesson. "These were not people who could stand against the might of Daemaron in their current condition. When the Gods proclaimed their vision of restoring peace to the world and defeating the Demon King, the dwarves refused outright to join in any fight. They preferred to hide in the soil, avoiding conflict in the world above. The humans refused. They hadn't lived long enough to understand that things would not eventually change under the rule of Daemaron now that one titan was slain. But the elves... They remembered the centuries, the millennium, that the First War consumed. Some elders living amongst their people were alive as long as the First War had lasted. They understood the need to stand against the Daemaron if their people ever wished to survive and live without fear on the surface of this world. So, they agreed to aid the Gods in their war. And in doing so, they received the Gods' favor. Each God granted a portion of the population certain gifts they would need in the coming war, and with these gifts, the first magi were born. Omnes granted the elves power magic, control over fire, lightning, and wind; Vitala granted life magic, the ability to heal and grow; Sapiena gifted wisdom magic, the ability to read thoughts, break into minds, and compel beings with a whisper. Only Comporian withheld giving any gift to the mortal world."

Ryker again jumped in. "Wait, wait, wait. But humans can use magic, too, and dwarves. If this was the birth of magic, why can the other species use magic today?"

Aegnor grinned. "Well, I think you might be able to figure this one out. Despite being of different species, dwarves, elves, and humans are all compatible in mating. Beauty is not a monopoly held by one race; love and lust can be compelling emotions." Ryker's cheeks heated at the obvious answer to his question. "Do you mean to tell me you have never thought any of the royal elven women that you have seen in Frenir's company beautiful?"

Ryker's ears went red. He had to admit that some elves possessed an uncanny beauty. "Yes, there are many who are."

Aegnor chuckled at his apprentice's embarrassment and continued, "Anyway. With the gifts granted to the elves, the Gods planned their assault on Daemaron. His kingdom sat on a stretch of land that used to connect the continents of Eastern and Western Divinoros. The war was so violent that the land bridge was shattered, leaving only the Cursed Isles behind."

Ryker nodded. "But if Daemaron was destroyed in the Second War, how can a demon still be summoned?"

Aegnor looked at Ryker intently. "Daemaron is not dead, Ryker. He was, still is, too strong for any being to kill him. Maybe Drakkonian could have, but the Gods could not. They built a secret prison beneath the islands where Daemaron sits chained to this day. Most believe he has been eradicated, a lie told to assure the population they are safe from his influence. The fact that he lives is why I was hesitant to tell you this history. It is not knowledge that should be commonly known, so guard the tale well."

Ryker nodded. He couldn't fully grasp the implications of this lesson, but he was uneasy with the thought that an all-powerful being rested in his world. A being that could easily shred the Queen's forces should he break free of his bonds.

Ryker - Chapter 23 - Into the Mountains

As the lesson on the ancient history of the Gods' activity throughout Divinoros came to a close, the pair came into view of a strange-looking cliff face in front of them. The narrow valley road they traveled came to a dead end at a large thirty-foot basalt column cliff face that faded into a steep Graystone wall rising nearly a hundred feet in the air before the normal steep incline of the Perampla Mountains resumed skyward.

The columns of dark basalt stone had strange hexagonal shapes and rose in a series of columns that were shorter on the outside and larger on the inside, creating the shape of a dark cathedral front. The two innermost columns met at a point far above Ryker's head framing a solid stone gateway around the lighter Graystone making up the massive wall.

The scene was strange, clearly resembling a gateway, but the cliff face was undoubtedly a solid mountain it appeared. Some runic alphabet was carved into the basalt columns that rose around the frame of the polished Graystone slab, inscribed ancient words that rose and fell along the entirety of the archway.

"We are here," Aegnor noted, reigning in Maximus.

Ryker nodded, bringing up Xantharyia on his right.

Strange, though, no door or seam is visible. I wonder how we enter.

"This is incredible…" Ryker murmured, mesmerized by the stone formations. "Is that the language of the dwarves inscribed into the basalt?"

Aegnor nodded. "Yes, it details the history of the dwarfish people. And it warns visitors that—beneath these mountains—they are under the unquestioned authority of whoever sits atop the granite throne. Enter here and abide by their laws. No leniency will be given to those who travel below regardless of ignorance of their customs."

That warning seemed to make sense to Ryker, but seeing the different alphabet from the common tongue piqued his curiosity about the trip under the mountain. "Master, if this is dwarfish writing, I imagine there is also a dwarfish dialogue. Can these dwarves speak in a common tongue? Or am I going to be unable to communicate with them during our business here?"

Aegnor was scanning the foliage growing around the massive basalt and Greystone obstruction that lay before them as if looking for a way beyond the impasse. "No, no, the dwarves are a well-cultured people, despite their lack of interest in leaving the confines of the earth below. They also love trading with outsiders. There are few within the city who do not speak the common tongue, traditional elvish as well, as fluently as you and I. However, they do oftentimes speak in their gruff language around visitors to lobby insults, but they know me in these parts, and they know I understand what they say, so they will only speak in the tongue we both understand as long as you are with me. Ah! There he is."

Aegnor leaned down and grabbed a fist-sized rock on the road's edge. Ryker watched, puzzled by the odd behavior, as Aegnor cocked his arm back, took a sharp step forward, and hurled the stone at a small ridge covered in shrubbery on the right side of the rock wall, nearly forty feet up. Ryker watched the stone sail into the bushes, expecting to hear a clang of stone against stone as the rock sank into the shrubs toward the wall; instead, he heard a muffled *thunk* and a surprised shout followed by a voice calling out what seemed like curses. The silver-haired elf called up in the same gruff language he heard, but there seemed to be laughter in the tone he spoke with, then switching to the common tongue.

"Let us in, my friend! My apprentice and I have traveled hard and are looking forward to your King's hospitality."

Ryker heard a deep voice call out in response, though he was still unable to make out the other man, or woman perhaps, that was speaking to Aegnor.

"You have arrived at the Great Marbled Cavern of the dwarven kingdom. We keep to our own and implore you to do the same. Turn back. Our King does not wish to offer hospitality to strange men knocking at his door. We have heard news of growing turmoil around the lands. Our doors are closed. You are not welcome."

"We are not welcome? Look again, dwarf. Would you turn away Aegnor of house Turena? We have had our differences, yes, but I have fought alongside your King Thondor on more than one occasion. He may wish to see a familiar face."

A scoff echoed from above in disbelief that this man was who he claimed, and if he were, surely the King Thondor would not be pleased to see him. "You are a bold man coming here, Sir Aegnor. I will permit your entry, but do not expect a gracious welcome. King Thondor will likely throw you out himself if he does not wish to take your head. Wait while I open the gate."

Ryker furrowed his brow and looked at the elf, puzzled. "What happened between you and Thondor? You've teased this once, but... It seems it might help to know before I am face-to-face with the man."

Aegnor did not look like he would answer his apprentice at first as he worked his jaw searching for words. It was almost as if the older elf was embarrassed by something. "Well, there are a handful of reasons we have butted heads in the past... Two reasons, really. As you know, elves can live for thousands of years. Few creatures in these lands can match our longevity. Anyway, I am over seven hundred years old, and there are far older of my kind. Second, in longevity to the elves are the dwarves, who can live well past five hundred easily. They, unlike elves, age rapidly in their youth, and then ageing grinds nearly to a halt in their

172

older years. This is likely odd for you, being human, as your lives wink in and out of existence in what can be just a blink of an eye to some. Anyway, I remind you of this because I knew King Thondor in my youth when I was still only around three, maybe four hundred years old."

A distant look took hold as Aegnor thought back to his youth. "I still served in the Queen's Army at that time, leading ten battalions of Elites while also serving as her champion in single combat challenges issued. Back then, Celestra and Thondor's father, the King at the time, had a dispute over some of the border lines between the foothills north of the Perampla Mountains. There were a few minor battles over the area, but Celestra did not have the heart for full-blown war against the dwarves, not so soon after the death of Kei-Tel and our victory over a divine entity. Though centuries had passed, the pain of all the deaths that occurred during that time had not been alleviated and still hasn't been for many, for that matter. But I digress. These lands were highly rich in the purest steel mines in Western Divinoros. Resources at the time were key for building our defense at Ice Bridge Hold. So still needing a victory but not liking the prospects of war, she suggested a contest of champions to settle these lands."

Aegnor paused his story as the massive Greystone cracked, a sound so loud Ryker thought the mountain itself had split as two Greystone doors seemed to form from the basalt-framed gate and began slowly folding outward. A rush of air caused dust to kick up through the small gap that was forming.

"Now, the champion on the side of the dwarves was none other than the now King Thondor, at the time Prince Thondor. He was well-known and built a reputation as a great fighter and feared brawler. He must have been no more than forty or so at the time. It was unprecedented for a dwarf to have such prominence, such success so young. So going into the combat, I was... not nervous, but intrigued." The door continued creaking open. Now, a few inches parted the doors.

"The terms of the bout were set, and this is when the Celestra told me that Thondor's father insisted that this contest would be a battle to the death. No leave for surrender. One of us would die. The battle would then be decided. I remind you, I was young at the time, but the news enraged me! That this dwarf king, this pathetic ruler of what I thought to be a feeble people, thought his son could contend with me? I was known throughout the lands, even then, as the best duelist to have set foot in this world. Never lost in single combat and was rarely ever truly tested. And so, I had my mind set to embarrass Prince Thondor."

"On the day of the duel, I made no spectacle about my business there. I burst into action at the start of the bout with furious intent. I set out to tear Thondor apart. Instantly. Embarrassingly. But to my shock, my initial onslaught was withstood. I was a hurricane battering a rocky

173

shoreline that refused to be moved. Still, just as a rock will erode over time, giving way to the will of the water and winds, Thondor eventually fell. The fight lasted nearly a quarter-hour, and in that time, I gained respect for the prince. So worse than killing him and giving him a prompt, honorable death, I spared his life." The door was now open enough for the pair to walk through, and they started forward now leading their mounts by hand. "It was a blow to his pride that he has never fully forgiven me for."

Ryker frowned, unable to imagine a desire to die over being spared in a duel. That said, he had never been the pride of a kingdom with the hopes of an entire people resting on his back.

As they entered, they were greeted by a short man no more than four and a half feet tall, but he had a heaviness about him. He was not fat, not in the slightest. He was built like a wild boar, more thickly muscled than any human Ryker had seen, and it looked as if his bones were twice as thick and twice as dense as a human or elf based on the heavy footfalls. His forearm was a knot of muscle as large as Ryker's leg, and each of the dwarves' legs was as thick as tree trunks. The man was wrapped in a deer pelt cloak with a chainmail shirt lying over a stone-colored tunic. A dark orange beard was braided down, hanging to the center of his chest. He walked up with a massive two-handed ax serving as his walking stick. Ryker and Aegnor could hear the thud, thud, and click of the man's walking pattern grow louder till he stopped in front of the master and apprentice.

"Alright, so you're Aegnor," the dwarf said, looking the silver-haired elf up and down before turning his focus on Ryker. "And who're you?"

The apprentice responded with a slight bow. "I am Ryker. It is a pleasure to meet you, master dwarf. I am, Aegnor's apprentice."

"Okay," the dwarf said with a shrug, not seeming to care much. He continued his nonchalant chatter, "And don't call me dwarf. Do people go 'round calling you human, boy?" As he turned and waved the pair in through the doors of Greystone, he said, "My name is Algir. I'll show you the way to his majesty's throne room. It's a bit of a walk."

As the pair led their steeds deeper into the cavern, Aegnor leaned in close. "The second reason that Thondor doesn't like me is I used to court his sister. She would always say that she liked fine elven silks."

Ryker's mouth fell open, and he laughed, sending sounds echoing off the walls.

Ryker - Chapter 24 - Great Marbled Caverns

The trio—elf, dwarf, and human—strode along a massive hallway. The floor was completely smooth and polished stone. Veins of vibrant quartzite and marble ran along the floors, walls, and a ceiling that rose fifty feet above Ryker's head. Ryker thought it slightly puzzling that such small people would need such grand sizes in their halls, but he appreciated the illusion of spaciousness the tall ceilings afforded. As did Xantharyia, who had yet to act perturbed about entering the underground.

Ryker patted her side appreciatively.

It is wonderful owning such a horse that understands we are safe here and she isn't trapped beneath the earth. The old mules at the farm would be in a terror encased in stone like this.

The hallway was lit by a series of massive oil lamps resting in great iron sconces. The sconces were bolted into walls with giant bolts made of shining precious metals—silver or platinum perhaps—clearly boasting the wealth of the dwarfish race. Each oil lamp seemed to burn different colors and shades of white, yellow, and gold. Ryker glanced around the hallway in amazement.

"Excuse me, Algir, how do you change the color of these lamps?"

The dwarf half-turned his head. "Well, I don't focus on the finer arts of stone and metal, so my understanding is a tad limited, but I am told that these lamps change color by inducing rare mineral powders into the oil to cause the flame to burn differently. Power mages can have similar effects, but we find the powders, if mixed properly, provide a more consistent coloring through the caverns. These different colors are used to mark different tunnels, parts of our city, and even types of shops. Living in such a vast underground and significant darkness, we have come up with unique ways of communicating and marking our locations. These help our people to be able to operate businesses, traffic, and townships efficiently. When you are traveling back to the caverns, you will find gold flames along your right. The white and yellow flames will be on your right if you are heading away towards an exit. Simple. Nearly foolproof."

Ryker was awestruck and fascinated by such a unique lifestyle and again blurted out a question, "Wow, well, how are we not dying of fumes in here? How do you get fresh air underground?"

The dwarf pointed up to the ceiling, and Ryker could now see large shafts incredibly wide and equally tall bolted into the ceiling. "Those are air shafts we have carved throughout the entire mountain city. At various points along the range and in some other locations, these shafts break

175

the surface of the mountains, and massive fans push fresh air in while other shafts pull out the old, stale air. And since the heat from the lantern and the smoke it produces rises, it is harmlessly pulled from our city, and we breathe fresh air within these halls."

"This is amazing," said Ryker in a hushed voice, his mouth agape as he took in the hall.

"This is nothing yet. Just wait until we enter the heart of the mountain," said Algir.

From that point, the travel persisted mostly in silence. The only sounds that accompanied the party were the echoing clack of horse hooves and the clink of the battle axe that Algir carried rather than resting in the sling at his back.

After nearly an hour of walking, Ryker started to wonder how deep into the mountain they would be traveling. His question was soon answered as the party broke from the wide-walled tunnel onto a massive stone bridge. Ryker's jaw hung open in amazement at the vast dwarfish city laid before him.

The city stretched out far larger than Stone Guard from one side of the cavern to the next. Portions of the city were carved into the outer edges of the hollowed-out mountain while others hung suspended, like scattered islands, by thick metal cables bolted into the walls surrounding the opening.

The group strode out onto a bridge that stretched toward the middle of the cavern. This was when the true size of the city was revealed. The Great Marbled Caverns stretched a mile overhead and at least the same distance below. In the expansive opening, massive stone towns displayed their grandeur. Some town centers were even jutting out over the open space, looking like a peninsula surrounded by a sea of open cavern air. All were connected to other points about the cavern by interlocking bridges.

The wealth of the dwarves was more apparent than ever here. Ryker took into account the fact that every bolt and bracket on the suspension bridges was plated in precious metal just as the torch sconces had been. Even some buildings in the hanging town centers had roofs plated in precious metal. The shining surfaces refracted the thousands of brilliantly colored lamps, making the cavern shine like a miniature galaxy in the cavernous space. Ryker wagered that just one of the precious metal bolts would be worth more than his family farm had earned since it had been in operation.

People scampered along every bridge and visible town center, evidence that the Great Marbled Caverns was every bit the bustling city that Stone Guard was. Each building and bridge Ryker had seen seemed to be carved and crafted out of pure white marble segments that helped to reflect the lamp light, illuminating the city to a point where navigation was easy. It was not as bright as being above ground in the day, but it was still much brighter than a cloudy night. A metal rail system wound about among the bridges and buildings, picking dwarves up from various platforms and bridges before depositing them in different areas in strange wagon-like constructions Ryker had never seen.

Ryker felt uneasy looking over the edge of the bridge the small party now strode upon, giving him the feeling his balance may fail him from such great heights, but his curiosity outweighed his nerves. As he glanced over the side, he realized he could not see the bottom of the city. More buildings protruded into the open air in the depths below.

"How in God's name did you build this place?" Ryker blurted out.

Algir chuckled at the apprentice's agog expression. "Over the course of many, many millennia. Our race possesses some of the finest craftsmen in the world. Our stone working is unmatched, and the metalwork of our youngest smiths stands apart even from the best of the elves."

Aegnor nodded his unwilling ascent at the comment, surprising Ryker. The dwarf continued, "Our people may be reclusive and distrustful of outsiders, but within our walls," the dwarf said, raising his arms to gesture at the city above them, "we are innovators. There are rail shuttles, air shafts, and fans, and all this machinery is a blending of magical power and mechanical ingenuity. For example, using magnetic metals allowed us to build heavy shuttles that float above their rails, making propulsion easier for the tram's power mages to move the tram cars with a force of air channeled into a compression funnel. Massive efficiencies are gained when we weave the arcane arts with the science of stone and metal. Truly a brilliant thing." Ryker now strode side by side with the dwarf as he opened up more to the conversation, explaining the intricate engineering that went into building the great dwarfish city.

The party soon crossed the bridge to a large city complex suspended in the center of the mountain. The party, now surrounded by the dwarfish people, was beginning to garner attention. The people were not hostile, but Ryker became cognizant of the number of eyes on him and his mentor. Aegnor leaned close to his apprentice, "Do not worry over their stares. They hardly see many people of the other races, typically only merchants. Not only that, but we walked in here with two Ravanians. They hold a presence anywhere, and especially within the burrows beneath a mountain."

Ryker nodded as he gazed over the crowds. They were now forming to the party's side as they marched through the polished marble city.

Most of the male dwarves held appearances and statures similar to those of their guide, Algir—all sporting large beards and carrying heavy weapons in thick study arms. But Ryker was shocked to notice the women were often taller than their male counterparts. Most of the

177

females Ryker saw were nearly five feet tall and lithe when compared to the men. This is not to say they were frail-looking. Most held a very muscular stature, looking as though they could hold their own with Ryker and his brothers in hard labor on the farm. But many of the women were quite pretty. Ryker was beginning to understand how someone like Aegnor and a dwarfish girl could have a romantic interest in one another.

Aegnor seemed to sense his thoughts and raised an eyebrow at his apprentice. "Knowing two species can procreate doesn't explain the desire to, but from some of the looks you've been giving and where they have lingered, I take it you now understand now, ay?"

Ryker let out a small chuckle as he shook his head, though he could feel the heat rising to his cheeks once again. He was slightly surprised by the fact that he and Aegnor had grown close enough to divulge information on past relationships in their time together. Never in his wildest dreams would he have thought to have had such kinship with an elf, much less an elf of such renown.

The group came to a halt before a massive marble building. While the dimensions of the building were fairly simplistic—a large square building with a slanted stone roof—the craftsmanship was opulent. The base of the building material appeared to be large blocks of marble stone. Amongst the large white blocks were smaller stones carved of black granite, silver, and gold pieces in various shapes. These smaller pieces were laid into the walls, forming mesmerizing geometric patterns along the massive structure. There were no elaborate carvings or statues placed about. The design itself was simple and, in that simplicity, beautiful. The building was a blatant statement that perfecting the plain was a path toward revealing the innate beauty of the material used; a statement by the dwarf's master craftsmen that there is no skill in forcing material into a shape that people would recognize or require some elaborate interpretation to understand and to deem it "art."

Algir waved over two guards from the group of ten standing at the entrance of the building. He then turned to Ryker and Aegnor and gestured toward the building with his thumb. "King Thondor will be within the palace, but you cannot bring your steeds in there. We have a stable around the back of the building. Our guards can take them for you while we head in." As if understanding the dwarf, Xantharyia whinnied and scampered about. As the guards drew closer, she reared up on her hind legs, lashing out with the front hooves.

"I think we better take them ourselves," Ryker said. "Xantharyia won't allow anyone else to lead her in most cases." It caused a little inconvenience to be unable to leave the horses in the care of capable hands, but a feeling of pride welled up in his chest as he realized the closeness of the bond his beautiful mare felt to him. He scratched the horse under her chin, then pulled her face toward his own, kissing her on the nose.

"Let's go, girl." He set off after the two guards who were now leading them to the stables. Ryker followed at a distance, giving the Ravanian steed plenty of space between herself and her would-be handlers. As Aegnor strode by Algir, he called out to the dwarf, "Let Thondor know who has come to see him. It may be best not to surprise his majesty with news of my arrival." Algir nodded in agreement and strode into the palace.

After settling Xantharyia and Maximus into their stalls and warning the stall hand of their ferocious tempers, the master and apprentice strode back to the palace entrance alongside the two heavily outfitted guards. Ryker was impressed the men were able to move under all the mail and heavy plate they donned but shrugged off the thought as he recalled the sturdiness of Algir's form. These people possessed a raw strength far greater than his own.

The pair strode into the palace in accompaniment of the guards, passing through the atrium toward a set of closed, heavy-looking iron doors that lead into the throne room. Ryker would have been taken aback by the immaculate decor lining the atrium halls, but he was distracted by the enraged, muffled shouts that sounded from the other side of the doors.

"I fear our friend Algir may be getting an earful for allowing us into Thondor's city... Better for us if he lets the King vent off some of his displeasure now. When we get in there, do not speak unless spoken to, and allow me to start the talking. It sounds as though I have not been forgiven these past centuries. Dwarves can be a stubborn people, holding grudges longer than the years that pass in your human lifetimes."

Ryker nodded his acknowledgment as they stopped in front of the doors that led to the throne room.

A trio of dwarfish guards stood on either side of the doors. After they looked over the pair with expressions that seemed to say *good luck, fools*, the guardsmen temporarily seized any weaponry Ryker and Aegnor carried. After being relieved of their weaponry, and once the shouts from behind the doors had begun to settle, a guardsman asked if they were ready to see the King.

Aegnor nodded at the dwarf amongst the trio who was garbed in gold plate. With that nod, the golden-clad dwarf slammed the butt of his two-headed battle axe into the marble floor three times in quick succession, generating a loud bang that resounded through the halls. Silence from the other side of the doors followed, and then the doors swung slowly inward.

Ryker watched the narrow crack of light flowing through the doors as the room beyond began to reveal itself. Algir knelt, head bowed in

179

the center of a pure white marbled floor. In front of him was a massive throne of black granite with veins of gold running through the black rock. Two smaller golden thrones winged the massive high-backed seat of the King, though those remained empty. Only King Thondor sat upon his throne now, and Ryker figured the two others must be for his Queen and heir.

As Ryker and Aegnor strode in, the King stared daggers at the silver-haired elf and barely seemed to notice that Ryker accompanied him. King Thondor's very presence demanded attention. He sat in what Ryker thought must be ceremonious garb. His trousers were dark leather, and a golden tunic hung about his torso loosely, revealing much of a hairy, muscled chest beneath. Across the back of his shoulders, a black wolf pelt was draped, connected around his neck with a gold chain. His tunic sleeves were cuffed with granite links, and his black leather boots seemed to be laced with a silver cable. A sturdy, simple golden crown sat upon his head, pressing down onto a crop of neat, short, trimmed black hair peppered with gray. The black in the hair washed out along his temples and faded into a solid gray beard. His beard was well kept, braided into a precise shape, and still reaching nearly the center of his chest. His graying hair framed a face beet-red with rage. Veins pulse along the man's forehead, a visage made all the more terrifying by his storm-gray eyes locked on to Aegnor with extreme dislike.

Next to the throne was a massive war hammer resting on its head, so the handle was ready for the King to grasp at a moment's notice. While the weapon was a thing of beauty, an iron head framed with gold circlets on the flat end that fed into a twisted silver handle, Ryker got the sense this man knew how to use the hammer as more than just a decorative piece to accent the throne he sat upon, a fact he could feel in this man's presence.

A menacing voice with the weight of a rockslide rang through the hall through slightly parted lips. "Aegnor. I did not expect to have you as a visitor when I stepped out of my bedchambers this morning."

The silver-haired elf bowed slightly, acknowledging the King, and, in a slightly mocking tone, responded, "My dear King Thondor! It is a pleasure to see you again after all these years. What has it been, two, maybe three, centuries?"

Thondor grumbled, "Not long enough, I say. After the continued public embarrassment you wish to inflict on my family, I thought you might have the decency to leave us be. At the least, after all you've done here, I'd have thought you'd have the good sense to stay away for fear of retribution within these halls. It seems I was wrong. You were arrogant in your youth and have yet to do away with that trait, it would appear."

The King made a show of looking Aegnor up and down once again, his mouth furling in a scowl. "And you also haven't rid yourself of your... shall we say flamboyant tastes either," Thondor thundered, gesturing at Aegnor's attire, seeming to take offense at his form-fitting elven silk clothes. He caught sight of the tear in the garb. "Though how interesting, the great Aegnor Turena must have fallen on hard times. The elf I knew would never have worn such clothes if they possessed even the slightest wrinkle, much less a tear."

"Ahhh, a keen eye, Thondor. Normally, I wouldn't, but alas, I was on the road and only had this on hand. I was rather hoping Zondra might be present; she enjoyed my elvish finery in all our previous encounters."

Thondor's face grew a deeper shade of red, and the fire behind his eyes now seemed a torrent. Based on the reaction, Ryker guessed that Zondra must have been King Thondor's sister. Aegnor continued, "And the rip in the sleeve is courtesy of my apprentice here. He has grown in his dueling ability. Landed a lucky blow in this morning's training session before we arrived at your southern gate."

The fire in Thondor's eyes was replaced by surprise, then curiosity as he shifted his storm-filled gaze onto the human that accompanied the enemy of his youth. "And you are?" the King rumbled, pushing himself from his chair and hefting his war hammer before striding toward the pair.

Ryker bowed slightly and responded, "My name is Ryker. I am but a simple farm hand from Stone Guard who was able to impress Aegnor during this past year's Selection and now trains as his apprentice. It is an honor to make your acquaintance, King Thondor."

The dwarf king now stood before Ryker, his discerning gaze sweeping up and down Ryker's frame. Now standing face to face with the King, Ryker was impressed by the man's size. He seemed old, maybe around fifty years, had he been human. His frame was sturdy and powerful, thicker than their guide Algir was. The way he casually swung his war hammer between his hands told of surprising agility and speed, not to mention the absurd strength to toss around such a clearly heavy weapon without any strain.

Ryker was not at all skeptical of the fact that Thondor was a fearsome warrior in his own right and the second most dangerous man in this room. Finally breaking the silence, Thondor grumbled again, "The pleasure is mine, young Ryker. Few in the world could have come close to cutting your master during a duel. In fact, I believe the only warrior who ever had a chance to kill him in single combat was me, many years ago, when I was far stronger and far faster than I am now. Unfortunately, a couple of unlucky twists of footing while I was pressing an advantage meant I lost the only time I crossed weapons with the *great Aegnor*," he said mockingly.

181

Turning to Aegnor, the King carried on, "Now tell me, you old fool. What are you doing in my kingdom?"

Aegnor smiled at the insult, seemingly pleased to have caused the King to break his calm demeanor.

He responded without resentment. "I need to see Baelin. I am hoping he has made progress in his studies. I also bring you word of uncertain times above the crust of the earth. Celesta believes Omnes's power seeps into this world once more. There have been disturbances and brutal killings in the villages and townships north of Turenian. The deaths are... let's summarize and say violent in nature, reminiscent of what Celestra saw long ago. The body fragments found... those people were not killed by any creature local to the region, of that much she is certain. I am also hoping that you do not have similar news north of the Marbled Caverns."

King Thondor sighed. The rage seemed to flow from him. He turned on his heel, strode back toward the throne he got up from, and sat down heavily. "Still gallivanting the country playing hero then. That was never a good enough reason for you to leave Zondra. She had eyes to marry you then before you broke her heart. I would have thundered down all the might of the Marbled Caverns on you then had she not stayed my hand. But alas, she seems to have forgiven you, forgotten you even. And moved on with her life, no less. Found a new man who treats her like the princess she is. Has a beautiful little family of her own running around this place now."

The King's glare returned. "I won't allow you to meddle with her heart again. You leave her out of any business while you are back in the Caverns. If I find out you've dabbled in her affairs, I'll skin you alive and feed you to the moles."

Aegnor nodded, his face showing genuine regret. "She was too good a woman for me then, and it sounds like she remains far more than I have ever deserved. You have my word, King Thondor. I did not come to tangle up her life."

"Good," the King bellowed as he slammed his war hammer onto the ground. "I couldn't be sure since you came in parading your Ravanians like some stupid godling half-breed seeking the awe of all my citizens."

Aegnor chuckled again. "I thought they would annoy you, the traditional living fossil you are."

The King smiled at the offhanded insult, breaking his last vestige of rageful demeanor as Aegnor carried on. "But it's more than that. Where we plan to go and for the trials I fear may be ahead of us, we will need horses brave enough to face the dark power of Omnes. No other breed would suffice."

The corner of Thondor's lips twitched, and Ryker looked in shock between the two men, two of the most powerful men in all of Divinoros.

182

He did not expect the grievances between the pair to fall away over a few bouts of insulting one another. It seemed that time maybe did heal old wounds and that the two, despite their differences, respected one another.

"Go about your business then. And to the point of your visit, we have had no news of murders or killings north of the mountains that I am aware of. There have been rumors that the Shroud has been active, pulsating, and occasionally shrieking. My most recent message last month declared that everything was under control. High Lord Niall of Ice Bridge Hold seems confident they can repel anything that may emerge and have seen nothing physical emerge yet," rumbled Thondor. "I will have Algir act as your guide while you are in the city. How long do you anticipate spending in the caverns?"

"We wish to depart within the next week, weather permitting, and depending on the news from Baelin," Aegnor responded.

Thondor grunted his agreement, then spoke, "That is fine. Algir will show you to StoneHouse. Wonderful inn. Even has plumbing for hot water and a faucet for mead is available in most rooms. Wonderful place, I'll say. All I require for my hospitality is this. You allow me to throw you a feast in three days."

Aegnor furrowed his brow, but a wicked smile crossed Thondor's face, "For entertainment at this feast, I wish young Ryker here to duel my eldest son. A contest of champions, shall we say. A repeat of what occurred so long ago. Your pupil versus mine. Though this time, we will call the victor before a death blow is struck."

Ryker grew pale; the only contest he ever fought in was against Aegnor, and that was just to showcase his skill set. But before he could refuse, Aegnor responded, "A fair proposition. What does your son fight with? I will need to prepare Ryker against either axe or hammer, I presume?"

"Axe," the King responded.

Ryker & Baelin - Chapter 25 - The Archives

Aegnor and Ryker walked from the King's palace, and the apprentice looked to his master and raised an eyebrow.

"What?" Aegnor intoned. "I think that went better than expected. I was worried he would try to cave my head in with that ridiculous hammer. To think Thondor has the gall to say the Ravanians are excessively attention-grabbing while carrying that totem…"

They chuckled subtly as they continued to the stable to retrieve their steeds before rejoining Algir in the open square in front of the palace. Ryker was still nervous regarding the duel, and Aegnor seemed to sense the apprentice's apprehension. "And don't worry about the duel. We will train hard for the next few days. Axes are clumsy weapons. Dangerous, most definitely, especially in the hands of a well-trained wielder, but you'll be fine. Probably."

"Ready?" Algir's gruff voice sounded, and before the men could reply, their dwarven guide strode through the square, passing by a stone government building and at least four ale houses within a quarter mile of one another.

"Do you really have enough citizens to fill all the alehouses?" Ryker commented.

Algir laughed, "Oh yes, oh yes. You arrived early in the day, so they have yet to fill up. But here in the Great Marbled Caverns, we like to say our people's true passion and gift is brewing mead and brewing ales. Stone and metalwork are just our pastimes."

Ryker smiled at this. "Well, the ingenuity of your metal and stonework on display is astonishingly impressive. I look forward to tasting the ale."

Aegnor chimed in, "Yes, it has been some time since I've been under the mountains… been some time since I've had freshly tapped barrel dwarven ale… Since you have never visited this great kingdom, I suppose we can make a couple of appearances at some ale houses near the inn, but we still have work to do today before we imbibe."

The kingdom became no more ordinary as the party walked through it. It was as if the party walked through an alien world brought forth in a fevered dream. If anything, Ryker only grew more impressed with every block and invention they had passed. On the trail to StoneHouse, they crossed two additional bridges. These were shorter than the initial bridge they came to the city on, but they were linked between granite city blocks held suspended in mid-air by vast steel cables thicker than Ryker's childhood home. It was astounding how the dwarves made use of the space in the hollowed-out mountain. He peppered Algir with questions and finally said, "Algir, thank you for your patience. I don't believe I have quit blabbering since we departed the palace."

The dwarf simply smiled. "Do not apologize for your questions, young Ryker. I appreciate the curiosity you have for my people and our way of life. I am glad to have shared our culture with you and glad you will experience more of it during your stay. And now, we have arrived." The dwarf gestured to the end of a short block to a building equivalent to the size of the King's palace but crafted entirely by marble plates. The building did not have the attention to detail the palace held, but it was still beautiful and clearly crafted by master stoneworkers.

It seems the dwarves take pride in all their work, inn or palace. Each building and each piece of work is crafted with intention. I suppose if you're going to do something, you may as well do it right.

Aegnor and Ryker spoke with the innkeeper and checked into a large room with two separate cots. Unfortunately, separate rooms were not available for the men, the inn being rather popular. Still, they were glad to sleep elevated above the ground after so many weeks, months for that matter, sleeping outside on the hard, cold ground.

The room was simple but large and elegant. Large enough to fit all the bedrooms of Ryker's farmhouse, he thought. The floors, walls, and ceilings were designed with polished marble tiles held together with golden seams as if the precious metal had been blended into some form of grout between the slabs. The dwarf king lived up to his word. There was a large sink crafted of black granite with thick veins of gold and just to the side of the water spigot, a simple tap was fixed to the wall.

Two beer tankards sat next to the tap, ready for use. Ryker, of course, tested it immediately and smiled in satisfaction, froth clinging to his upper lip, as cool ale bubbled down his throat. He answered Aegnor's unamused expression with a simple shrug and said, "We talked about it on the way here... figured I should make sure it works! I've never seen anything like this." The luxury was unlike any he had experienced, yet the cold stone walls seemed to be lacking something...

Warmth. Laughter. Familiarity. Suddenly, Ryker was hit with an overwhelming longing for home. He missed the laughter of Ayden and verbal sparring matches with Declan. He missed Jeb's calming presence that permeated the house after the disappearance of their parents.

Before he was able to dwell on his sorrows, Aegnor called out, "Leave your things. We are headed to the Archives."

No rest for the weary. Better to push forward. No good ever comes from lamenting your fate and dwelling on your problems.

...

Baelin sat in a silent section of the Archives that was rarely visited, rubbing his palms against his temples in slow, tight circles. The frustration had been building in his research over the past couple of months. After learning that this Durenthi had stolen the cloak of Omnes, the only further entries regarded the man's plans to get back to his family and find a remote section of the world to live in peace for the remainder of their lives. After this revelation, the journal simply ended abruptly.

In all great tales, the malefactor of the story reveals their great plans with their damned source of stolen power, some profession of intent. It's irksome, frankly, that this Durenthi seemed content to disappear, happy to live his life in mystery. Smart, I must admit if one's wish is to live in peace, but damn! Where do I go from here?

Baelin dedicated himself to thoroughly scouring the Archives' records of death certificates, determined to uncover any information regarding the life of the man in question. It was a dead end.

He found no record of death for any man named Durenthi. Not at least that were likely to have been the man he sought. And this, unfortunately, meant the trail in his most recent breakthrough had run cold.

He even tried to change up his tactics. He dug back through books and historical text from the period just after Omnes had fallen, now looking for any indications of significant cloaks or daggers that may be tied to anomalous activities. He found nothing.

And so, the old dwarf, frustrated, leaned back into his chair and muttered to himself, "Guess that's it. Dead end, after dead end, after dead end. Gods, I'm tired of my search and these dusty damned books! Don't think my back can take another day hunching over them. I need to spend my final decades with some company that speaks out loud, not aging before pages of stories that were scribed centuries before I was young."

A silky voice echoed through the hall as two tall figures strode down the dark hallway toward him, "Well, if it is company you seek, I think you will find yourself in luck, old friend."

Baelin started before assuming a deep frown. The face that spoke hadn't entered the light of Baelin's lamp, but he knew that voice anywhere. The dwarf bolted upright, "Aegnor? Is that you?"

The smooth response came back, "Indeed. It has been far too long."

Baelin shot out of his chair in such a hurry he banged his knobbed knees on the small table, sending the books he had spent all morning scouring over, flying to the floor. He continued his momentum, storming toward Aegnor, where he clasped the elf's forearm. "You don't look like you have aged a day my friend. It's been what? Only a hundred years or so, is it?"

"Far, far too long indeed," Aegnor said with a grin across his face. "You know, I would love to say the same to you, but last I saw you; you still could have made me break a sweat on the dueling grounds. Now, I think my apprentice could handle you!"

"Ahhhh, you damn elves never age," the old dwarf scoffed, waving his hands away as if it were a ridiculous statement. "Apprentice, you say?"

Baelin watched as a formidably built human stepped forward. "Yes, sir, my name is Ryker. I'm from Stone Guard City. It is a pleasure to make your acquaintance."

"The pleasure is mine, young man. I must say I am surprised to see Aegnor take on another apprentice, much less a human apprentice... Never thought I'd see the day. There must be something special in you, I dare say. He's only ever trained one other person you know. Never met her myself, but I have heard tales of her deeds. She must have been born a few hundred years before you... If you accomplish half as much as her... Well, I dare say your name will be passed down through history. I hope to live long enough to know of your story"

"Well, let us hope I can muster up some semblance of success," Ryker said. "Though it's interesting that you mention he had an apprentice before me. I was not aware he'd had one."

Baelin watched the man look to Aegnor with a questioning brow, but the elf refused to relinquish any detail, maintaining an impassive expression. The dwarf almost laughed as the move did little to deter the apprentice. Ryker turned back to the dwarf. "You must tell me more! What was her name?"

Baelin smiled but shook his head. "Oh, it is not my place to reveal her identity even if I could. I only know of her as the Ghost. If I knew her true name and she traced that back to me, well, I fear my life would be cut short. She's the only person I reckon that I would be as scared to cross as Aegnor here." He gave Aegnor an appraising look. "Maybe more so."

A look of shock crossed the apprentice's face. Tales of a "Ghost" that stalked Divinoros, a wraith of a long-dead elf intent on carrying out the subtle elimination of many nobles and high born that were causing turmoil throughout Divinoros were well known amongst all races.

Aegnor cut in before more questions bubbled from his apprentice. Baelin liked the boy, not many of his kind were so keen and eager to learn.

"I hate to get straight to business, Baelin, but I fear things are urgent in Eastern Divinoros. Celestra has reason to believe Omnes's power is returning in the north. She believes his beasts are responsible for killing sites recently found around some of the towns north of Turenian. I need

187

to know if you have found anything to cast out the Shroud once and for all."

Baelin stroked his white beard and gestured to Aegnor and Ryker to be seated at the table. Once sitting, Baelin looked both elf and human in the eye. "I've recently had a breakthrough. But it seems I've hit a new wall." Baelin then went on to summarize the accounts he found in the diary from the elf Durenthi. "It's been impossible to corroborate the story, but the Queen of Elves would be able to. According to this man's tale, she was there when Kei-Tel fell, not just on the battlefield but in the immediate aftermath of his death. And if Durenthi is to be believed, she would have seen the cloak and dagger with her own eyes. Ordered their transfer south. It is my belief, Aegnor, that Omnes never truly left this world, but rather laid dormant in its shadows. I think these items may tether him here in some fashion."

Baelin noticed Aegnor's mood darken as he finished his tale.

The elf remained speechless for a moment. "If he never left, that means he's had a millennium to plan his return, to plan a vengeful ascent as the sole authority in these lands. If that's the case... we need to eradicate the remnant of his power before he can return to full form. And if we can't, Celestra needs to consolidate her forces."

The weight of that simple statement seemed to hang over the small party. In the ensuing silence, the dark shadowy recesses of the nook they occupied suddenly seemed malevolent, haunting Baelin's mind.

Ryker was the first to break the silence. Baelin was unsurprised. After just minutes into meeting the boy, he knew he would need answers amongst all the uncertainty being introduced to his world. *This is the same reason I bury myself in these books I suppose. The more I know, the less I believe can surprise me. Funny how the revers of that seems to be true.*

"So, what are we going to do? *Is* there anything we can do?"

Aegnor exhaled deeply and stood. "For now, and in the immediate days to come... There is nothing to do. We need more information. Thondor would not agree to ready his army before this information is confirmed by Celestra. Even then, he would need hard proof that his kingdom was at risk before he would commit any forces to the cause. The dwarves haven't left this mountain in force since the Second War, and even then, it was after most of the fighting had ceased. Not to mention we have nowhere yet to ask him to march. Maybe north to reinforce Ice Bridge Hold, but he said there was yet to be any activity there."

Baelin looked ready to cut in, in defense of his people. "I mean no offense, my friend. You are a cautious people, and it has clearly served your kind well. Despite this, we will warn him that Omnes is readying

188

himself, so Thondor can move quickly once we have validated the threat and identified the location we need to fight."

Aegnor's finger thrummed as he tapped against the table he leaned into. "In the meantime, Baelin, can you continue your search for any secondary texts that might have reference to these items, their powers, and their resting places? Ryker and I will be in the Marbled Caverns until the day after Thondor throws his feast. Hopefully, we will have proof of these items' existence by then. If we do not, I will travel to Turenian to confirm the details of this diary with the Queen."

Agenor focused on the dwarf with an appraising look. "Baelin, I would like you to travel with us. Celestra told me she was looking to acquire more information and texts from the old religion last we spoke. This is part of what brought me here. Based on the unrest I've seen on my journey west... I think war is coming. It's as if the very land is holding its breath in anticipation." Baelin nodded, and Aegnor continued.

"The issue is I have no way of pinpointing where and when the enemy is going to make himself known. I assume the Shroud, given the fact we are seeing attacks in the north. But in the Year of Darkness, the beasts only came in force on the Western continent... These attacks have been in the east."

Aegnor paused, and Baelin believed he was trying to gauge what this meant. No answers came as the elf just shook his head in frustration. "If possible, we need to end this war before it even begins. Dissipate any remnants of Omnes's power still on Divinoros and sever any ties that may hold him here to our world. Celestra has told me of the carnage wrought during the Dark God's first campaign. I fear the violence in a second. For that, Baelin, you may just be the key to cracking the code of victory against a God."

Baelin shrugged. "I'll keep looking for now. I do not have an answer for you yet on travel. It has been over a hundred years since I have stood aboard a vessel. I do not know that my body can take the rigors. This isn't a no, but I need to think about it first."

Aegnor nodded, knowing better than to argue with a stubborn dwarf. "We will leave you to it then, old friend. Ryker here is dueling Thondor's son in three days, during the feast. I am assuming he is looking to have me humiliated as payback for besting him so long ago. I think he underestimates Ryker here. You should join, Baelin. I could use your keen eye to help correct some missteps and poor habits he shows during their bout."

Baelin smiled. "I will do my best to be in attendance."

...

Aegnor and Ryker strode to the nearest rail shuttle platform, heading back toward the blockade where StoneHouse Inn was built. The rail system they were on traversed multiple miles in only a matter of minutes. The shuttle seemed to glide on thin air as a short dwarf in colorful green robes performed some sort of magical chant that propelled the shuttle forward at a blistering speed.

The pair soon arrived on the street that ran into the Stonehouse Inn, and Aegnor nodded to a tavern they were close by. "Come," Aegnor called to his apprentice. "It's been a long road; the night is upon us, and our world seems to be heading into a war of immense magnitude. I think we have earned a couple of pints."

Ryker nodded and put on a tired smile. "I think you're right, Master. I feel like I'm drowning in a mess of such scale, such proportion, that I fail to see how I belong in it. I mean, my family is respectable, but we aren't nobles. We're farmers. Even though I was successful in the Selection, if you hadn't taken me as an apprentice, I would be standing watch over some gate in some small city asking merchants about their business before they entered... Not in my wildest of dreams was I gallivanting about the world to speak with Monarchs and help to cultivate battle strategies against divine forces."

Aegnor looked to his apprentice with those discerning silver eyes. "You have done well, Ryker. And you have come a long way from the day I first met you. I would dare say you are close to equal to any human soldier I know. Your talents would be wasted guarding a wall or plowing fields." At these words, Ryker felt immense pride.

Aegnor sat at a stool with a sigh, leaning forward to rest his elbows against a barrel that was currently serving as a small drinking table. He flagged down a waitress for two pints of strong ale and the daily meal, then continued.

"Many people grow comfortable with their lot in life; they possess a potential for something greater, but they settle for peace, settle for quiet. Enjoy complacency rather than subjecting themselves to the discomfort that forces growth. This robs the world of their true potential and very possibly impacts all of Divinoros. Those people... Those people are weak, selfish even. Not only are they afraid to push the limits of what they can accomplish, but they are also serving a moral obligation to better themselves. In doing so, they rob society, rob their loved ones, of the true gifts they can provide. Your story has just begun, and I daresay there are many pages still to come, but your fingerprints will be felt on this world before you leave it. And I believe the world, and any you meet, will be better off for it."

The waitress returned with the pints as Aegnor finished his statement. Ryker responded by simply raising his mug, and the pair clinked their wooden tankards together and drank deeply.

190

The pressures Ryker felt faded as the first mug disappeared. The ale was every bit as good as described, better than he'd hoped. The second round of frothing ale was ordered before any food was delivered and promptly consumed. Despite the agreement on a couple of pints, Aegnor and Ryker soon were lost in the carefree joys of intoxication, content to delay their responsibilities to the morning as the pints continued flowing. They were simply enjoying the simple pleasures that ordinary life held, a brief reprieve from the weighty tasks that had been laid out before them.

Soon, the worries of Omnes, the worries of pending war, and the worries of how the pair fit into the tumultuous events that approached faded into the back of their minds. Algir's promise rang true; the tavern continually filled with dwarven folks as the night carried on. Once Ryker was certain the establishment was full, a small group of musicians entered and soon began playing songs. It wasn't long before the merry dwarven people started pulling barrels and chairs in the center of the ale house aside to form a makeshift dancing space. People sang along with the music and young women pulled hesitant men to dance with them on the floor. Spectators were laughing and cheering, and Aegnor and Ryker joined in the clapping and merriment.

The waitress who had been serving Aegnor and Ryker even convinced the apprentice to take her out on the dance floor. "'ave'nt seen to many humans 'n the Caverns. I'd like to see if you'd be able to keep up with the likes of us. Plus, you ain't too bad on the eyes, boy. What'd you say to a dance?" she had said with a wink.

He had adamantly shook his head at first, feeling his face turn bright red, "No, no, no, I couldn't. I don't know the dances!"

Aegnor chuckled at his apprentice's embarrassment and lack of smooth seduction. The cute waitress replied, "Oh, don't you worry, darling, I can be a very good teacher." Ultimately, the woman's persistence and the ale's strength convinced Ryker to dance with a pretty woman. She was a lovely girl with dark brown hair and emerald green eyes. She only came up to Ryker's chest, which was taller than most dwarven men and average amongst the women, and it made for tricky hand placement as they partook in the joyful jig. Ryker was a quick study, easily catching on with the movements and, after doing so, rather enjoying himself.

After the pair had multiple dances and Ryker was near to excusing himself, the woman pulled her body close and, with a smile on her lips, whispered into his ear, "I will be off in just over an hour. Maybe I can show you around a couple of my favorite late-night spots?"

Ryker smiled and mulled over the offer.

It would be nice to see more of the city, even nicer to do so in the company of a pretty woman.

191

Not to mention, he had a longing to extend this night and continue to forget the struggles of his everyday life. But alas, reason won out in the end; despite his impaired judgment, he felt a responsibility for his duties and knew he would need to retire shortly. Aegnor was not one to skip over early morning training, no matter how much the pair drank the night before. He looked at the young woman and replied, "I would truly like nothing more. Unfortunately, I have a demanding mentor, and I really should be retiring shortly. But I thank you for the dance instructions and lovely evening."

She gave a mocking pout before saying, "Oh, you aren't so bad... the pleasure was all mine." Then, with a smile, she leaned into him and pressed her soft lips to his cheek, pulling herself into him briefly before moving back. The people around cheered and jeered at the young man, and he caught Aegnor laughing at the table. She looked at him slyly, "Just a little taste of what you could be missing out on, plus who knows the next chance I'll have to kiss a human," she teased. Ryker was smiling as she spun on her heel and headed back behind the bar to tend to her other customers.

As the apprentice returned to the table, Aegnor still sat drinking, his lips curled in amusement, "Seems you have grown well acquainted with the bar hand, eh?"

Ryker laughed and shook his head. "I must say, the dwarves are a truly delightful people..." Aegnor raised an eyebrow at him, and Ryker simply shrugged a dumb smile plain on his face. The pair laughed before polishing off their pints and getting up to stumble back toward the inn.

Once the two were settled in the cots, Ryker asked, "Aegnor, do you mind if I ask you something?" The liquor had given him courage.

"Go ahead," the elf replied.

"Well, after today's events, it seems unlikely I'll ever have a truly, well, an ordinary life. You surely haven't. I don't want to miss out on the little things like... have you ever been in love? I know the King talked about Zondra. Why didn't you marry her?"

The room fell silent. Ryker could almost feel the instant tension in Aegnor. A palpable hesitation could be felt in the quiet.

"It's not an easy life I have led so far. Maybe one day, I will unburden myself from the workings of the world. I have only ever truly been in love, the kind you speak of, once. And I made the decision to leave her. I made it for her. To keep her from the dangers I continually threw myself into. The path you've chosen with me... You will miss out on nearly all the simple pleasures in life. Family, friends, love. These are things we protect but are excluded from enjoying ourselves."

Aegnor hesitated again. "But as the King said, it seems that my decision was rewarded, and Zondra has the life we talked about creating together... I was young then, though, and what she wanted was a life I

192

was not yet ready to live, for there was still so much for me to do. It is still something I could never have. That fact doesn't ease even the pain I feel now, though I am happy for her.

Ryker felt he should offer a consoling word, but Aegnor continued. "And now, at this point in my life. Well, now I am a tool perfected for death and destruction, for tearing apart threats to Divinoros. But building something, building a family, fostering relationships of that magnitude… I do not think I would even know where to begin. So, in my youth, I broke Zondra's heart. Tore mine apart right along with it. And…" Aegnor tapered off, and for a while, neither spoke. Then Aegnor broke the silence and said, "Go to sleep. Tomorrow, I will be swinging an ax in your direction."

Captain Malfius - Chapter 26 - Cursed Isles

Captain Malfius stood at the stern of the Grim Siren. She was a well-seasoned vessel, as clearly seen by the worn wood. However, the love of her captain is shown through her obvious and meticulous maintenance. There wasn't a ship in the Queen's own fleet that was better kept or better proven than she was. Malfius had obtained her after raiding a pirate fleet that had been terrorizing merchant ships around Reef Ridge Port nearly half a century ago. Despite her looks, she had gotten the captain out of more than one sticky situation.

The Grim Siren wasn't the biggest barge, the best armed, or the fastest, though she could move in a hurry when the need arose. No, what made the ole Siren the best vessel in the ocean was the maneuverability of the ship paired with a captain possessing unprecedented genius on the open sea. Malfius was a maestro of the ocean, the Grim Siren and her sailors his orchestra. She could turn on a dime and avoid the heavy fire from others or dodge incoming vessels that could travel faster, and with the mind of Malfius guiding her... they had yet to meet their match.

Captain Malfius was born in a small fishing village northwest of Reef Ridge Port. His parents moved to the town before he was born. His mother and father fought for Queen Celestra for centuries, and after retiring from their duty, they wished to settle down somewhere nice and quiet to raise their family. They chose Oceanfjord, and soon after settling down, they had their first child. Malfius.

Now, Oceanfjord was not an ordinary environment for an elf to grow up in. The town was entirely human outside of his family and their High Lord. Starting at a young age, all residents of their village worked in the volatile waters of the surrounding seas. Farming kelp, fishing, clam diving, it was as if the people there had been born for the ocean, as if the Vitala had mistakenly forgotten to give these people gills and fins.

Malfius was no different from the other people of Oceanfjord, despite his race, and since his earliest memory, he held a deeply seeded love for the water.

His father purchased a fishing vessel when he was still a boy and staffed the boat with hardened sea-faring humans of Oceanfjord. He taught his firstborn son everything he knew about the seas. Malfius took to the lessons with enthusiasm, and he could soon read the waters and skies better than his father or any other Captain in the town. He showed a natural knack for predicting the temperament of Mother Nature and how to command a vessel for proper navigation to avoid her wrath and harness her power in a ship's sails.

Before Malfius stood taller than his father's midsection, he could command the entire crew himself. It didn't take long for his talents to be recognized, and on his twenty-fifth birthday, he was recruited by the High Lord of Reef Ridge Port to serve as her youngest naval Captain in recorded history. He accepted but demanded he pick his own crew. The first of which were many who sailed the seas with him in Oceanfjord, much to the chagrin of his elvish contingents. He and his crew of rough humans never looked back, quickly rising through the ranks in Reef Ridge and gaining notice from the more influential political figures who commanded fleets of their own.

Malfius caught a lot of flack from traditional navy men and women who would only employ elves to ensure the cohesion of the crew as they continued to work together for hundreds of years. Still, Malfius preferred the company of his human crew. Despite the inconvenience of finding new men and women with far greater frequency, he found the humans who worked for him were quick to adapt to uncertain circumstances. And uncertain circumstances were the norm at sea. With each variation of crew he commanded, the newbies were quickly integrated into the crew he kept. He found humans innately possessed a courage that elves had to work years to get, and they always spoke their minds, being less concerned with the haughty mannerisms elves clung to with fervor.

Malfius often wondered why this was the case. Perhaps it was because they thought life was too short to keep their mouths shut. Whatever the reason, Malfius had avoided disaster on more than one occasion by listening to his crew's concerns.

Now, as the heavy mist marking the border of the Cursed Isles came into view, his first mate, a woman called Blackbraid, strode next to him to scan the seas as the Grim Siren cut silently over glass-like water into the most dangerous stretch of seas this world had to offer.

"I don't like this mission one bit Cap'n. Crew's scared. In truth, been pissin' themselves since you told 'em we're headed through the Isles." Blackbraid said. "Damn those that pompous Sandivarian High Lord, sir, feels like we're on a suicide run. Won't do much for no one if we break on rocks and demons feed on our souls."

Not turning, Captain Malfius replied, "Ay, men 'r right to feel that way. 'Ve sailed these waters. They're as dangerous as the stories make them out to be. Orders are orders, though. Once we pass into the mist… Things get worse in the mist. Get the crew to come to deck Blackbraid. Don't believe none of 'em, but myself and 'ol Farsen 've made this journey. His brain's still scrambled from it, too. Need to tell 'em what we'll be seeing along the way."

Blackbraid nodded and turned to the crew, shouting from the stern, "Form up, you ragtag bastards! Captains got announcements 'fore we enter the Isles! Listen up if ya value yer miserable lives and hope to keep 'em."

The crew formed up in uneven columns, looking up toward Captain Malfius. The red-haired elf strode down the stairs from the stern to the main deck, walking back and forth along his crewmen's front line, hands clasped behind his back. "Blackbraid tells me ye been pissing yerselves. Frought with worry over sailing these godsforsaken waters." He paused as the men laughed nervously. "Well, yer right to be. This ain't no place for the living to go, but circumstances take us there regardless! I've sailed through these islands once before. Nearly lost my mind. 'Ol Farsen did lose his." More laughter was quickly quieted with his next statement.

"Nearly lost my life too. Did lose half my sanity. Worse still, nearly beached me damn vessel on one of the islands as fear ripped into my mind, fear telling me I would never make it through! Voices, vestiges of evil piercing my mental...Demons haunt these waters. Tales are true. Whispering evil to ya, the worst things ya ever heard. Break into your mind, show you visions. Visions of contorted futures."

The crew looked between one another, worry clear on their faces. "Ahhh, but don' fret. No demon spawn is 'nough to stop the crew manning ol Grim Siren!"

A few "Hear! Hear!" cries emanated from the crew.

"We'll be prepared best we can. When we enter this mist yer minds *will* be attacked. Ain't no question 'bout it. Ancient forces, forces that belonged to this land far before we elves and we humans had our run on it, will look to drive ya mad. Daemaron, King of demons, was defeated here, right where the central island sits, and his essence still taints the air. We will stay far, far from its shores, but lessers of his kind stalk these seas with fervor. Mus' live within the mists, and they will call to you. Terrible things they say... 'Nough to make you want to pull yer ear off, claw out yer eyes. 'Nough to make you slit yer own throat."

Malfius rubbed at his neck, remembering the seductive voice from his previous venture through these waters. "You can plug your ears with wax, but it won't do a damn thing. They penetrate yer soul and permeate directly into yer thoughts. Musn't give in to their calls. Listen to but one voice once we enter. Mine! I will say when to row forward and when to reverse. Any questions?"

The hardened, typically unflappable crew was silent. Each person nodded. Then ol' man Farsen shouted, "Quit your scared whimpering, you soft scared sons of whores. I've been through here before. Listen to Cap'n. You'll be fine." They laughed at the senile old man, and each man took their place on a row seat. Malfius strode back up to the stern of Grim Siren and tied himself to the banister behind his steering wheel. Blackbraid followed and did the same. He shouted for his crew to tie themselves in as well. He wasn't worried about choppy or violent waters, but he had watched brave men break and throw themselves overboard to drown and escape the voices that would soon be scratching along the insides of their skulls.

Before long, they plunged into a wall of mist so dense that Malfius could hardly see a few paces before the prow of the ship. And as they pressed in, heavy silence enveloped the vessel. The normal sound of a breeze biting at furled sails and the consistent sloshing of small waves against the ship's prow faded into nothing. It was as if the fog had swallowed all sound, determined to envelop the Grim Siren in an eerie stillness, a silence fitting to the haunted stretch of sea. It was almost as if they had sailed into a different world. A land of perpetual gray, where fear hung in the air as if it were as tangible as the air they breathed in.

Malfius was already beginning to regret accepting Lord Sennin's mission as flashbacks of his previous passage entered his mind. But he cast the thought aside as soon as it crossed his mind and yelled to his crew, "Forward paddle." He felt the ship lurch forward as his crew rowed with a practiced cadence, but he couldn't hear the paddle strokes. Another sound the mist seemed to swallow.

Malfius diligently scanned around the front of his ship. He knew the waters were shallow, and some passages of this stretch of ocean wound through narrow openings of stone formations jutting up through the water's surface between the islands of the archipelago.

He saw two large shadows of darker gray pass by the starboard side of his ship, and as they passed by a large stone formation, an alluring, suave voice with an unabashed air of power began to mutter in his head.

Oh my, my, my. Captain Malfius, if I am not mistaken.

Malfius heard a deep inhale as if someone was drinking in his scent, and a cold hand of fear squeezed at his heart.

I am so, so glad you decided to come back to me. I had such fun trying to claim you the last time you wandered into my domain. And now I get another pass at you... Plus! Look here! You have brought some tasty-looking parcels of human meat sacks with you.

Malfius shook his head and shouted, "Slower now! Slow portside turn." he waited as the ship shifted. "Straight and be ready for the reverse."

Captain, Captain Captain, prepare for a reverse? Afraid you're going to ram into some rock, are we? Down your ship, watch your crew drown. And this first mate of yours... Wouldn't mind prancing about in her skin for a while. I wager you crack your hull against a rock formation any minute now. It'd be a shame to happen so soon, though. I haven't got to have my fun.

Malfius shook his head, trying to shake the voice.

Let's play a game, dear Captain since you refuse to speak with me. Oh, I know! Let's make a bet, shall we deary? I think I can get one of your boys here to crack open their skull against that beautiful side rail before you travel another hundred yards. Which... might not matter since you are too distracted to see the rock formation in front of you.

A massive dark form hidden in the mist raced toward the ship directly ahead of the Grim Siren. Malfius shouted, "Reverse row! Reverse row!" as he cranked the wheel of the vessel to its port side. He was nearly thrown from his feet as the ship lurched to the side and clipped the massive stone pillar that sped by their starboard.

Close call, but we're still afloat, thought Malfius. "Continue forward row!"

Tck, tck, tck. Don't lose your focus so soon, Captain. Already so close to sinking your boat and killing your crew. Would you like to know what my kind do with the dead that wash up on our shores? It's not so bad for the dead, really... the unfortunate ones are the ones who wash up ashore living... But ahhh, it is so. Much. Fun. See?

Visions were thrust into Malfius' brain. He saw his crew wash ashore onto some rocky, barren island. Most of the crew was dead except himself and ol' man Farson, who were dragging themselves ashore exhausted and choking up seawater. Then, manifesting from nowhere, a chaotic, red-tinged energy began piercing him and Farsen, animating their limbs against their control as maniacal laughter swirled in the air. The pair were forced to dance about, ragdolls used for play by malevolent forces.

Malfius shook his head, trying to clear the visions from his mind as he guided the vessel past another formation of stone and the wreckage of a navy ship.

I wasn't done showing you what was going to happen to your precious little crew captain. Very rude not to listen to a guest aboard your vessel...

Malfius folded over and clutched at his head as visions pierced his brain once again. He saw his dead crew scattered and broken along the rough-hewn shore. Battered bodies were now rising from the rocky shoreline. Their bodies were twisted and broken, but the bones snapped back into place as they stood. Those who drowned were violently throwing up water, laughing uncontrollably as they vomited up salt water and blood, red-tinged foam forming at the corners of their smiling mouths.

They turned on Malfius and Farson's dancing form, moving to encircle the pair, lips pulled back in unnatural smiles as if they were all in on some cruel joke. He screamed at them, calling out their names, begging them to help him, to help Farson, but their swirling red eyes were not their own. The crew's bodies were claimed by the demons that haunted the area. With stretched-out arms, the crew seized the pair, clawing and pulling at limbs, their nails sinking, raking skin. Malfius could feel the pain as his crew clawed into him, crazed smiles on their faces. And then...

Malfius heard a distant call of a familiar voice and whipped his hands over his face, remembering he was still on his ship, still captaining the vessel. As his vision cleared, he saw Blackbraid standing next to him. She was shouting his name and pointing ahead. Malfius's eyes went wide as he saw a graveyard of vessels floating in the water before them.

"Reverse paddle!" the Captain called to his crew, and he felt the ship slow. It continued to slow until they were traveling in reverse. "There'd be a reason all those ships have crashed there. We'll go 'round," Malfius said to Blackbraid, his voice ragged and breathless. "You call the order." He was barely avoiding panicking, but Blackbraid standing beside him gave him strength.

Ahhh... So, she is the spine of this ship. I see Malfius. Have it your way. It will be she who suffers. I haven't been able to break a mind in so long. I am glad you brought me so many... chances to do so. So many weak points to play on. Now, since she is so formidable, this human woman you employ. Let us see how she will fare.

The vision swallowed Malfius once more. The demon crew still held them in place, but now it was Blackbraid alive next to him. The demons forced Captain Malfius to his knees. He cried out, "I shouldn't have come here. Please let her go! Just take me." The hoard surrounding Malfius and Blackbraid laughed.

A red-eyed Farson stepped in front of Malfius and spoke in a chilling voice eerily similar to the one that rang in Malfius's conscious mind.

Let her go, Captain? Oh no, I couldn't do that! We are just starting to have our fun.

The flock of demons snickered and laughed around them. Farson produced a blade from his belt, an old dagger Malfius had seen flay countless snapper, mackerel, and other fish.

I think it would be much more fun to kill Blackbraid slowly. And the best part is we can make you watch.

The smile vanished from Farson's face as it contorted into a demented scowl with deranged intent. He jolted forward toward Malfius.

To make sure you see, I'm going to peel off your eyelids. Make sure you don't miss a thing.

The blade cut into the thin film of the lids covering his eyes. He strained to pull his head free from the knife's edge, but he had no control over his movement and was resigned to howl in pain as the demon Farson tossed the flaps of skin to the beach before turning his glee-filled gaze on Blackbraid.

Now, I hope you enjoy seeing your first mate flayed captain. I think I'll start with the skin before carving the meat beneath.

A hard slap to his cheek pulled him from his vision and left him savoring the slightly stinging cheek.

Blackbraid stood next to him. "Captain, you alright?"

Malfius shook his head, taking in his surroundings. "I'm fine Blackbraid. Stay close, though, ya hear? The forces here are coming for me. Hoping to crash the ship, I imagine."

The first mate nodded her ascent, but fear showed in her eyes now, and her vision seemed to grow distant. Malfius imagined the assault on her mind had just begun in earnest, and Malfius tried to hold back the fear at the thought. More of the demons must have descended on the crew.

The ship jolted toward the starboard side as they collided with a rock that was hidden beneath the ocean surface.

Close, close, close, Captain. A few more bumps and the hull might just give way, then how easy it will be to claim you all.

He could hear the excitement in the voice.

I have been so bored locked away here. A couple more meat suites to play with sounds wonderful.

The voice pauses for just a moment. *Until you rot away, that is. Let me show you the games we'll play!*

"Get. Out. O. Me. Head. You. Arse," Captain Malfius grumbled.

The voice in his head sighed. *Fine... let's see which of your men I can break then.*

Seconds later, he heard screaming from the deck below. He looked down and saw one of his rowers crying and thrashing about. The man stood up suddenly, shouting, "Not me. Not me. Get out of my head. Please, get out of my head." The rest of the crew was shouting at the crewman to sit back on his rowing bench, but none dared to move in his direction. They would have had to untie themselves from the boat. That rope around their waists was their only sense of security. But the panicked sailor was pulling against his restraint and scrabbling as the knot that held him to the boat. He was muttering, "I don't want to end up like them. I will not end up like them." He was soon free of his harness. He rushed to the Grim Siren's side and leaped overboard head-first into the shallow waters. The crew was horrified, and some quit rowing until Malfius's voice rang out clearly. "Keep rowing forward! Don't give in to the voices!"

The man who jumped overboard didn't make another sound. His body now belonged to this place, and Malfius knew there could be no rescue. Another crew member stood frantic and panicked. He unsheathed the dagger at his belt with fumbling fingers and, without warning, viciously, and repeatedly sunk the blade into his chest, screaming, "You won't take me alive!" until only a burble escaped his lips, and he crumbled off his seat.

"Steady men!" Malfius shouted. "Blackbraid, get down there. Knock these fools out if you must. Keep them in their seats."

Blackbraid nodded, returning to herself, though a new fear showed in her eyes. She quickly un-tied herself and began heading in the direction of the panicked men. Malfius knew her mind and thought her strong enough to resist the demon's urgings. As soon as one man fell, another would begin shrieking in fear. They needed to get through the Cursed Isles before the crew overwhelmed Blackbraid, who was now restraining the newest crazed crew member, their newest female recruit. He called to the crew, who was still sane, "Forward row! Double time!"

It was reckless to row so hard in such dense fog, but Malfius thought this was likely the lesser of two dangers. He would take his chance wrecking his ship over losing more men to mental attacks in the Isles.

Captain, I am so disappointed you are running. I rather enjoy your company... But alas, you have nearly passed through our domain, and my master wishes me to leave you in peace for now. He seems to think you will be frequenting these waters in the months to come.

I look forward to seeing you then, Captain Malfius.

With that, the eerie silence returned. No sound of waves, no sound of birds, no sounds of frantic paddling from the crew below. Not until they broke from the mist.

The sun returned to the skies, greeting the vessel. It was like being reunited with a long-lost friend who you believed to be long dead. Hope that was extinguished in the mist was instantly revived in the warm rays. The familiar scents of being on the open water returned to Malfius's sanity, however shaky his grasp was on it after the encounter with a demon.

He looked over his crew, and the joy the sun brought was stamped out. He had no idea how long they were in the mist, but it felt like days. Most of the men below had streams of tears running down their faces. Some embraced those around while others huddled into themselves, knees tucked under their chins, rocking back and forth, muttering incoherently to themselves. No one moved toward the pool of red, slowly growing from beneath the man who stabbed himself to death. Malfius knew he would need to be the one to dispose of the corpse. To send him off to the sea to rest.

"We are through now! We are safe now! Back on the open waters, we know best," Malfius called down to the crew. He was met with nothing but weary nods. It was just a day now until they reached the ports of Turenian. He could only hope the demon was wrong and that he would leave this place behind him for good.

201

Nienna - Chapter 27 - Mysterious Friends

Nienna's head pounded. It felt as though someone had chiseled at her temple with a pickaxe. She awoke disoriented and was confused by the fact that stars hung in a night sky visible between the dark underside of leaves and limbs of the trees high above.

How could it still be nighttime?

She slowly pushed herself off the ground with one arm, and an involuntary groan escaped her lips. Whatever pain she felt in her head was a nice breeze compared to the deep wound in her side set alight with the twisting motion.

A small hill to her left shifted at the sound of her movement, a large lump of darkness rising from the earth into the formation of Zarou's silhouette. The large beast reached out his claws to stretch before plodding over to Nienna to run his scaly head into her shoulder. Despite the pain, she welcomed the gesture, glad to know Zarou stood guard over her.

Memories of the krakenshi and of Kimo's transformation flared in her mind as the fog of deep slumber resulting from blood loss faded. *I don't understand how this could have happened. They must have been infected by the Knife's Gifted. The Knife must have harnessed and twisted Omnes's power to his own purpose, and he can corrupt anyone who is wounded by his dark power.*

Panic filled Nienna's mind as she shoved herself to her feet despite the pain and yanked up her tattered shirt to reveal her wound.

She recalled the abhorrent state of Kimo and Joralf's wounds. She pulled up her bloodied tunic to reveal a neatly placed bandage that was wrapped around her midsection with the skill level of a professional healer. No dark tendril ran along the site of the wound. Confusion racked her brain. Then she remembered the two figures she had seen strolling up to her before the loss of blood overwhelmed her.

She was about to pull the bandage back to inspect the wound further when a gentle but stern voice sounded from the woods behind her, undoubtedly female, "I wouldn't do that if I were you." Nienna spun to see a shape approaching her from the woods, a small child in tow. "Don't want to pull away any scabbing that's formed. I already changed it while you slept. This bandage will last for a long while. And do not worry, it does not look infected."

Thank the Gods it's not infected. That must mean only the Gifted can leave behind the cursed touch. Not the beasts of darkness born from the Gifteds' soiled touch.

Soon, Nienna could make out the features of the woman in her fifties and the small exotic-looking child following the woman in jagged, skittish movement, hiding behind trees, shrubby, and the like.

Memories flashed back to her of the moments before her world went dark. She recalled the cape the woman had previously donned that seemed to fall in and out of the shadows with every step she took. The material had the same visage as she approached now. The cloak seemed to be blowing and wisping in wild patterns despite the perfectly still night. Strangely, it seemed to cling to the deepest shadows, reluctant to let go of those dark recesses as the woman continued forward.

How odd; her and the cloak. Not to mention the child thing in tow.

The child-like creature was hard to make out as it showed no more than half her face at once while observing Nienna. It approached tentatively, using trees and shrubs for cover to peek out from behind.

The woman spoke again, "How are you feeling, Nienna, the Ghost of Divinoros?" Nienna furrowed her brows and reached to rest one of her hands on the daggers still sheathed behind her back.

"How do you know who I am?" she asked. Her eyes locked on the older woman. She wasn't sure why, but she didn't feel confident that she and Zarou would be able to overpower the woman and humanoid creature should things turn ugly. And she did *not* like that this woman seemed to know who she was.

"I didn't know you, but my friend Princess Kassandra went into your mind when she healed your side. A name is a small price to pay for the lifesaving service she provided. Would you not agree?" The kindly woman asked.

Nienna's brow furrowed. "*Princess* Kassandra?" She took in the small creature again, and recognition rushed over her. They were in the Feyrenthia Forest. The Queen of the Faye folk resided and protected these woods. Not Celestra, Kei-Tel, nor any monarch before them ever dared to try to expand their influence into the deeper recesses of the Feyrenthia Forest. It was common knowledge that strange powers resided in the woods. Powers better left alone. From what she recalled, not even Daemaron or Drakkonian waged their war here.

The small child-sized creature was now peering out at Nienna from behind a tree no more than ten feet away. The purpose of the vine circle resting on her head was now abundantly clear. Nienna found herself in the presence of one of the most powerful creatures in all Divinoros.

Nienna painfully bowed to the small girl. Only slightly, as she gave no one, no man, elf, God, or creature, a bow low enough to indicate subordination, but Princess Kassandra deserved respect. Straightening pained Nienna, but she took a steadying breath and then said, "Thank you, princess. You have done me a great service. An evil force comes to destroy the land, and I have a very important message to deliver in hopes of saving the world from that fate. I fear if I had died, the world, even yours, may have suffered. You should be wary of the threat these monsters' presence poses your people, Princess."

The woman strode closer to Nienna and began scratching under Zarou's chin. The great lion purred, and any tenseness Nienna felt with the situation faded away. Zarou seemed to have a sixth sense of danger. If he accepted her company, she would follow his lead. The human woman spoke, "She doesn't often speak, you know. She knows our common tongue, though. And she is aware of the krakenshi that dealt you your wound. She is older than any of even your species. I haven't seen her ever show interest in contacting or conversing with any of your kind passing through Feyrenthia before."

"Then why did you help me?" Nienna asked, directing her question at the small child-like creature.

"Simple, she sensed a dark power in the forest, and her mother sent her to resolve the issue. In my time with the Faye, I have not been able to dissociate completely their diminutive size from how fearsome they can be and how powerful they are. I asked to accompany her. I suppose that is just the mother in me." Nienna didn't respond but prodded around her midsection.

The woman continued, "Anyway, by the time we arrived, you and your sand lion were already dealing with the situation. I prefer not to use my magic unless I must; the strain of the power is just exhausting these days, and well, Kassandra was content to see how an elf might fare against a krakenshi. It's been ages since she had seen one. Sorry, I can't help but to ramble on. Guess it's been a while since I've spoken words with someone. It just feels nice!"

Nienna looked at the woman. "While I appreciate the healing, I would have preferred you jump in sooner… Guess that wasn't your call to make, though." Nienna looked over to where Princess Kassandra had been, but she was no longer behind the tree. She was now much closer. Hanging on the back of Zarou's neck, her green hair and pale blue skin were just visible as she peaked around his head to observe Nienna. "And did you say you use magic?"

The woman smiled. "Why yes, I did! Used to be known fairly well known throughout the kingdom. That was until I let a handsome man sweep me off my feet long ago. Convinced me to give up the adventuring life of a power mage." Her eyes went distant as she let her memories swarm over her for a moment. "The name is Avanya. Pleased to make your acquaintance, Nienna."

"And yours as well. Frankly, I am glad the Feyrenthians sensed this darkness. You said Kassandra has seen krakenshi before?"

A force of sharp ice slammed into Nienna's consciousness, and a cold, rasping voice whispered in her mind.

*"Do not address me as if I was not standing here amongst you, elf.
I may not choose to speak, but my presence will not be ignored."*

Kassandra's small pale blue form hung from Zarou's neck before
dropping to the ground and joining the two women speaking. She sat
cross-legged in amongst the decomposing leaves and dirt and twirled
her long fingers through the decomposing earthly matter.

"I am sorry, Princess Kassandra. I meant no offense. I have never
had the honor of meeting your kind. Please take any slight of etiquette
as a lack of knowledge, not an intention of disrespect. Would you tell
me about your previous encounters?"

Kassandra's large emerald eyes looked into Nienna and bore
through her consciousness; her entire mind was on display for the girl-
sized Faye. She knew why Nienna asked such questions and decided to
answer.

*"It was long ago when your old King Kei-Tel, walked these lands.
No krakenshi army ever ventured into the Feyrenthia forest, but his evil
permeated this world to the core. Fayen folk have a deep connection to
the earth, and we could sense his force swarming from the gate open in
the Arctic.*

*"We saw the monster's savagery through the eyes of scouts on the
Western continent... I... I did not like the beasts. I have no special love
in my heart for humans or for elves, but the hunger for power
permeating off of these creatures was insatiable. They would kill every
living thing they could sink their claws into. Simple wildlife slain and
left to rot with no purpose. And so, when the same force began to leak
back into our world once more, my mother was prepared. We have been
on the lookout within our forest. For should the beasts of Omnes return
to this world and threaten Feyrenthia, we will stop at nothing to kill
them all."*

Kassandra's small mouth did not so much as twitch when she spoke
to Nienna, but her head tilted unnervingly as she continued to stare with
her lidless eyes, hands ceaselessly fidgeting in the ground below.

"I had no idea you were alive at the time. I am bringing news of
recent events to Queen Celestra. I would hope she could see the value in
allying herself with your Queen. I could..."

"No!" Kassandra's mental shout surprised Nienna. *"Our people
would never ally with any elf, man, or dwarf. Your kind has hunted our
kin since the dawn of time, telling horrific stories to your children to
fear our people. From a young age, your kind treats us as outcasts,
monsters to be lumped in with the likes of Omnes's beasts or lesser
demons. There will be no alliance with your Queen."*

The girl shifted her position close to Nienna, rising from all fours to
stand directly in front of her. Her head tilted up as she stared at Nienna.

"Our kind will continue to care for our own. Feyrenthia forest will forever be a haven to those who protect it and those who mean no harm. I thank you for killing the foul beasts that have come here. For that, I will offer you two gifts. One was your life. You will be fully healed by the morning.

Secondly, remember the things that cling to the shadows. You have seen more here than you yet realize. And remember that one's will may conquer the greatest evils, but the touch of corruption stains deep, and souls are lost with no guiding lights to lead them back."

Nienna was confused, not understanding what Kassandra meant. Nienna wanted to ask more, but without hesitation or another word, Princess Kassandra snapped her fingers and disappeared from sight only the gouges in the soil left by her trailing fingers showing signs she was ever present.

Avanya sighed. "Great… She keeps doing that… Anyway, I should go as well. I'm surprised she talked to you… You were only out for a couple of hours. Her magic heals quickly. You can still make it to Turenian by week's end if you make haste. Until next time, Ghost."

With that, she turned away. Nienna watched her form fade as she spun, drowned out by a deep darkness cast behind her shadowy cloak. In a matter of seconds, she could no longer make out where the woman was. She seemed to melt into the night right after the Feyean princess.

Nienna rubbed her temples, wondering if she had been hit over the head too hard in the Narrows and was now just dreaming. But no, the pain was too real for this to be fiction. She grabbed onto Zarou's reins, and the pair continued on their journey to Turenian.

Nienna - Chapter 28 - Her Majesty

The guards were just changing shifts in the early morning when they noticed two silhouetted figures emerging from the blazing orange horizon. The sky was set alight by the rising sun in the east. They saw a pair approaching Turenian's city gate. It was early, far earlier than the guards typically saw folk streaming toward the capital city. Typically, one small party of travelers wouldn't concern the guards much, but there was a hulking form, far larger than a horse, loping alongside the elvish figure.

Unable to discern if the approaching pair was a threat, one of the guardsmen shouted to his comrades positioned at the top of the wall, "Heyo! Incoming parties. Hundred paces out! Ready bows. Fire if they appear to be a threat."

The city guards of Turenian were as skilled in combat as the elves making up the Elite battalions, and they were trained to take no risks when it came to guarding Her Majesty's capital.

A response from above reached the guardsman's ears: "We see her. She looks like a bloody ridgeback with her, but I thought those were wiped out over a hundred years back... Maybe a sand lion?"

The guard on the ground shouted back, "Ain't native to this region. But arm the ballistae. Bows wouldn't do much against either."

"I haven't even had my morning coffee yet. If it's a sand lion... let's hope it's friendly," the guard on the ground muttered.

...

Nienna walked head down in a mindless trance toward the southern Turenian gate. Zarou grumbled beside her, upset by her distress. She put her hand on the great cat's shoulder. "I'm okay Z. Just a little lost in my thoughts. My side is better."

She paused. "But I don't... I don't know how we fight an enemy with powers like this. And no one can truly help our people stand against them. Not if they continue to spread elsewhere like they have in the desert and not if the fey people refuse to come to the Queen's aid. Maybe we should settle in the forest. Try our luck at integrating with the fey folk. I've heard tales of their power. They've managed to maintain independence even in the time of the dragons and demons. There, we could at least try to live our lives out in peace. I don't think the fey could stand alone should the rest of the world fall, though, so death would eventually come to knock on our door even there."

The great lion raised a lip and snarled.

A smile crossed Nienna's face, and she felt her heart grow warm at her giant beast's love for her, at the knowledge they'd face this mysterious enemy together. "I know, I know. You could tear this world apart should it anger you so. And I suppose you are not one to sit out of a fight, and you being mine, I suppose I'm along for the ride with you, ay?" She mustered a brief smile before a sigh escaped her lips. "But what was that thing that attacked me? How did it even come to be? These powers come from a God... If you hadn't been there, I would be dead twice over. What happens when some larger creature emerges?" Zarou had no answer here.

"What happens when more people are turned into those... those things. There's no way Sennin can stand against them. The whole city will fall if they aren't warned. The Knife won't spare the civilians, not the elves, at the very least. The krakenshi... They will tear the city apart." Tears trickled down her cheeks until they dropped from the point of her chin to form mud on the dirt-covered road they walked. Helplessness settled over her. Zarou was clearly agitated that he couldn't comfort her, and a low protective growl rumbled through his maw once again as he tasted fresh salt in the air.

She reached out and put a hand on his giant-scaled shoulder as they continued to walk, calming herself with the knowledge of his stable presence. Breathing deeply, she rubbed her eyes and said, "Ugh, it's okay. There is one person we will need to find after we deliver this package to the Queen. He can help us determine how to contest such a foe." Nienna scowled and muttered, "The *Queen* may even know his whereabouts."

Despite her foul mood, Nienna couldn't help but admire the elf's capital city as she approached the towers dominating the distant horizon. She had spent a large portion of her life in Turenian, being born in a town just north. As a young girl, she would travel there often to help her mother and father carry various goods back to their homestead or to come to the city for the various festivals Celestra regularly hosted.

It was a good time in her life. A peaceful time. She still couldn't believe her mother and father were killed when she was just turning the corner from being a young girl to a naive woman. The loss nearly broke her, and the gaping hole in her heart left empty by their departure from life, had never been filled again. She had no aunts and no uncles to care for her. Of course, some members of her community offered to take her in. Many did so out of the kindness of their hearts, but she had been pretty as a younger woman, and some men seemed too eager for a young woman like her to come live in their home.

So she left, being old enough to recognize a predator playing the part of a sheep. She sought to earn a living with the skills her father had taught her—bowmanship and hunting. She was quite skilled in both, and she could skin a buck faster than her father when she reached the young age of twelve. So, she was quickly picked up to work in a local butchery. As she got older, her work took a dark turn. But a lucrative offer can be irresistible, depending on how it is presented.

A man came into the shop and noticed how handily she could wield a knife at stupefying speed as she flayed a hog with perfection, peeling skin away from the meat that she quickly parted into cutlets, roast, trimmings, and waste. She broke the beast down in a matter of minutes. Each morsel wrapped perfectly.

The man later told her he knew her skill was beyond any other butcher he had met because her hands lacked a single scar. He felt the skill with the blade and her good looks might be beneficial in a job he had accepted, a job he needed a partner on. A job he was willing to split the proceeds of evenly should she help him.

That was the first day she met Sajien. A short, well-muscled elf with a devious mind, light brown skin, dark swirling eyes she could fall into, and thick black hair. He was older than she was and alluring. She agreed to help instantly, and the pair worked together for years after that. She completed many contracts within the city, some lone jobs, some with Sajien. Nienna forced her mind to other things, not wishing to think of how she and Sajien parted, his betrayal, his setup.

Despite the turmoil of her youth and her mixed experience within the city, nothing could diminish the grandeur of the walls and spires splayed out before her. The wall she approached eclipsed in size any other city she had seen. It was crafted of giant smooth granite blocks procured from the Dwarvish kingdom and ferried across the Aeronian Straights.

Rumor was the wall enhancements were the first major order Queen Celestra enacted once she ascended to the throne following Kei-Tel's death. The design was intended to make it difficult for any creature to scale quickly—a notion that Nienna thought ridiculous until her recent encounters with the Gifted and krakenshi. The walls always seemed excessive, but now Nienna could only hope they would be enough for what was to come pounding at the doors of Celestra. To make the climb more difficult, the entire granite wall was polished to the point that it gleamed. At present, it reflected the early morning sun and appeared like a great fiery moat surrounded by tall green-brown grass. Looking it over now, she doubted even Zarou could scale it.

Behind the massive wall, she could make out two domineering basalt towers doing their best to touch the heavens. Each roof was plated with gold, like two burning suns set over the city. The larger of the two towers was dedicated to medicine and housed the most powerful life mages in the world.

209

If only Joralf and Kimo held out a little longer... One of the healers there surely could have saved them.

The second tower was the center of merchant and builder guilds. These spires were always bustling with activity as deals were struck and innovations were discussed with fervor fueled by copious amounts of caffeinated tea and coffees the merchants were more than happy to sell. The only city that invented like the Turenians was the Marbled Caverns, and only maybe. Nienna doubted the people who feared fresh air could have the necessary imagination to match her elven brethren in the second tower, a tower dedicated to the Goddess Sapiena.

Most impressive in the skyline in front was a massive castle constructed of pure white marble. The castle sat on a large plateau in the center of the city and had three spires that reached heights great enough that if one were to scale it, one could look down upon the basalt buildings. The sheer size of the structure was an architectural feat, but the building was immaculately decorated inside and out. And while she knew it was there, from the distance she was standing, Nienna could not make out the golden trim that lined every window, door, and corner of the building. It was designed as a symbol of light in a world that had a history of darkness. Comporian's Castle, it was called, had finished its construction two hundred years ago despite Celestra ordering the building to be constructed to commemorate their great fallen king Kei-Tel, just fifty years after his death.

To build something like this... Perhaps the Queen can stand against this new dark force, Nienna mused as the faces of the stationed guards at the southern gate came into view. She could sense their trepidation, and she understood why. Dawn had just broken, and as she looked down, she saw she was covered in blood, dirt, and remnants of black fluid that had splattered from a monster. Not to mention, she traveled with an indomitable force of nature that was capable of killing nearly anything that fell in sight, should Zarou wish it.

She staggered up to the guards, who looked at her with wary expressions. She knew she looked like something from a nightmare. She felt as though she had just emerged from one after all. "Ehhh ma'am... you don't look well, if you don't mind me saying so... Are you injured?" one of the guards asked a tall, dark-haired elf. Nienna shook her head. "Okay, well, I need to ask, what's your business here in Turenian? Also, I should warn you there are two archers above watching your entry, not to mention an armed ballista, so no sudden movements." His eyes were fixed on Zarou as he spoke.

Nienna slowly looked up, spotted the archers, and then slowly fixed her gaze back on the dark-haired guard and sighed in annoyance despite the man doing his job. "Do you really think they could stop him killing you," she gestured with her arm to Zarou, "even if they wanted to?" She

210

shook her head before the guard could answer, "They could not. And my business here is with the Queen. I carry precious cargo from Sennin in Sandivar."

"You mean High Lord Sennin... High Lord of the desert?" The guard looked shocked. For no one so disheveled could possibly be an emissary for a noble High Lord.

Nienna was not feeling overly patient, and the questions from the guards were testing it mightily. "Yes, you fool. How many Sennins from Sandivar are you aware of? It has not been an easy journey, as you can see. Three Elites accompanied me when I set off. They were killed on our travels. It was not an easy path, and Celestra..." Nienna paused, "*Queen* Celestra will want to hear my story in addition to what High Lord Sennin sends." She looked at the guard flatly, but he seemed unconvinced.

Nienna presented the seal High Lord Sennin had given her. "Now you have two options: let me pass peacefully, and the Queen will thank you for your service. The other option is I have my lion bite off your God's damned head and walk through regardless." She didn't raise her voice; she didn't need to. She could see the words struck home. The guards chose to let her pass rather than question the legitimacy of her writ.

The guard looked toward his partner, standing closer to the gate. Then he glanced nervously at the imposing sand lion that stood towering over the guards. The beast's scales rippled as he lowered his shoulders as if ready to spring at the man. "Please pass through, ma'am. I am sorry to cause you the inconvenience. But my colleague must escort you, you understand."

The walk within the city's walls to Comporian Castle was easy so early in the morning. The streets were clear, apart from a small handful of servants scurrying about to secure required assortments for their employer's morning meals and clergy of religious institutions steeped in morning prayer. They all stopped to gawk at the odd pair walking past them with a member of the esteemed city guard in tow. Had they been passing in the middle of the day, they may have caused a spectacle, and the crowds would have slowed their progress. But, with conditions as they were, they arrived at the central castle after a short stroll.

Guards stood out front and reacted with reservations similar to those of the guards at the southern gate, but after a similar conversation, the party of twelve soldiers finally agreed to allow Nienna to pass.

"You're not taking that monster in with you," the head of the Queen's guard spoke. The man was a hardened burley soldier frustratingly immune to Nienna's intimidation tactics. The two debated back and forth for a couple of minutes until Zarou apparently grew tired of the bickering. He stood, walked toward the head of the guard, and

211

lowered his body until eyes came level with the elves. A low rumble flowed through the displayed teeth on the lion's face. Then, in a rush of movement, Zarou lashed forward, snapping his teeth around the guard's glaive. He yanked it free from the man's hands and tossed the weapon to the side. Equally startled, the remainder of the guards scrambled for an instant until their training kicked in, and they directed their weapons at the lion.

Zarou gave them no notice and stalked at the head of the guard, slowly backing the man toward the entry to the castle while he shouted in a panicked voice, "Get your beast off me! I order you back now!"

Nienna suppressed a chuckle and shouted to the other guardsmen and women, "Do not attack him, or he will kill you."

Reluctantly, they stayed their weapons and watched as Zarou prowled forward toward the head of the Queen's Guard, who now was pale, scrambling backward, eyes terrified. He tripped, and Zarou placed a massive paw on the man's chest and elongated his claws so that one point dug uncomfortably into the man's collar. Zarou then went still apart from a quick twitch at the end of his tail. "Any more demands for him to stay outside? And I would choose your next words carefully. He doesn't seem to like it much when you call him names."

A scent of ammonia became thick in the air as a small puddle formed around the man. He seemingly forgot to clench his bladder, and Nienna spoke again, "Now, now, Captain, I wouldn't have thought a man such as you would piss themselves in the face of death. As you can see, both my and my companions' patience has been exhausted. Now, why don't you pick one of your guards to present me to your Queen."

At that moment, a silver-haired woman strode out from the castle, taking in the scene. "Ahem, I would expect someone sent as Sennin's ambassador to conduct herself with much more dignity," she berated Nienna.

Nienna glared at the woman, who quickly readjusted her glasses before glaring directly back at Nienna and continuing in short, quipped speech. "Get. Your. Cat. *Off* the captain of the Queen's guard. *Now!* If you do not, neither of you will be granted an audience, and you will have wasted your time and your companions' lives to get here."

Nienna was fuming at being spoken to like a child, but a large retinue of guardsmen followed the old-timer from the castle, and she was clearly accustomed to having people abide by her direction.

So, Nienna waved her hand, and Zarou picked up his paw. The old silver-haired elf huffed and then spun on her heel. "Follow me. Now." she led Nienna and Zarou into the castle, through massive halls of opulent white marble and gold trim, toward a pair of heavy-set doors with massive iron hinges. "This here leads to the throne room. The

Queen will be with you shortly. *Try* to comport yourselves with a modicum of manner."

Nienna and Zarou strode into the center of the room, where Zarou sat. Following his lead, Nienna sat on the white marble floor instead of a plain wooden chair placed before the throne. Nienna leaned back against the front leg of her sand lion and closed her eyes, utterly exhausted from her travels.

When she opened them, she let her eyes wander to take in the throne room fully for the first time and was awed by the massive space of polished white marble. A dark red carpet laid in contrast against the white floor. It ran from the door she had entered to a spot in front of a slightly raised marble stage, so pure in color the raised ledge was barely discernable from the surrounding floor, where the Queen's throne sat. The stage and throne were carved from one monstrous stone, and the throne chair rose seamlessly from the platform into a grand marble throne. The chair was blindingly bright, reflecting sunlight over the room that entered from four large windows set into the ceiling, angled at the throne. It cast the seat in angelic radiance. Thick veins of gold were running down the backside of the throne, curving down over the right armrest. A statement of her Majesty's wealth.

The left side of the carpet was lined with four statues about the size of a large elvish man but with slightly bulkier, muscled builds than was common among her race. They were evenly spaced from the open door to the throne.

The first statue, closest to the door, was a clearly feminine figure. Reminiscent of the rest of the hall, she was carved of marble with heavy gold veins, holding a book in one hand while resting the other on the hilt of a sword fastened to her waist, a golden helm held in the crook of the same arm.

Following was a statue shaped from an enormous solid ruby. Another female figure, frozen in a pose where she stood on the tips of her toes, reaching with an outstretched hand that gently revealed a rock struggling from a lifeless lump into a human form. It appeared as though the woman stood in the wind, her billowing ruby dress swung frozen in form about her, pressed tightly against her front side, revealing a masterfully carved physique beneath the layer of stone fabric. The woman seemed to hold the gentleness and indomitable strength that only a mother possesses.

Next to the ruby Goddess was a man carved of brilliant topaz. He was permanently garbed in an elegant tunic with a breastplate secured over the garb, encapsulating his muscled chest. In his left hand, a large silver war hammer was suspended, clasped in a veined stone fist. In the right hand, he held a tall walking staff of knobbed petrified wood. Most interesting was the emblem of balance, hanging in perfect harmony

213

between the left and right scales, carved into the breastplate at the center of his chest.

And finally, there was a statue carved of black obsidian. The facial details of the statues were wildly life-like, and embedded in the face of this statue was an uncanny, almost cruel smile. The face held eyes that seemed to follow whoever gazed upon it. Two massive swords were sheathed to the man's hips. For some reason, the statue seemed to call toward her, and she stood and walked a little closer to the base of the statue's pedestal. Bright beams gleamed like iridescent stars blinking in and out as light reflected off the precise edges of the otherwise smooth obsidian as she approached the figure. She noticed some odd details in the statue as she stood in front of Omnes' replication. His cloak seemed to be carved into separate humanoid beings trying to pull themselves free of the fabric; it was shown as if each portion of fabric pulled in a different direction, giving it the impression of billowing in the wind. She also noticed the dagger clutched tightly in a powerful, gauntleted fist. A strange sense of familiarity washed over Nienna, but she couldn't place her finger on what struck that chord in her mind.

Nienna thought hard for a moment but was jolted back to the present as the doors at the back of the throne room burst open. A female elf strode into the hall.

She was a tall woman with dark red hair, apart from the subtle streaks of gray strands that ran through it. She was beautiful, but her looks held the strength of hardships earned from enduring trial after trial for many years, culminating in slight crow's feet, subtle wrinkles, and small scars peppering her face.

She looked at Nienna; her emerald-green eyes were radiant pools of knowledge and wisdom. She was garbed in an emerald dress that seemed to make her eyes shine even brighter. The dress was suspended with a golden chain that was sewn to the fabric near her right collarbone and looped over the opposite shoulder. The billowing fabric was held tight to her waist with a polished leather belt also supporting a long sword ending in an elegant hilt. Her shoulders were completely exposed, showing a lithe form and strong muscular definition that could only be formed by familiarity with weapons training. A strength was visible that age appeared to have done little to diminish. She carried herself straight-backed and regal, though she did not seem overbearing and pretentious. This was a woman who had experienced trials of her own, overcame them, and was better off for having done so. While never working with the Queen directly, usually taking contracts through various agents, she appeared to be everything she had heard through rumor, and that was rare indeed.

"It seems you have taken interest in the Manifestation of the Gods. Are you familiar with Aristocres? He created them just after Kei-Tel's death ceremony." She strode toward Nienna and Zarou. "This is Sapiena," she said, pausing by the first marbled figure. "I do my best to live life in her mold. A God of wisdom, thoughtfulness, and strategy. I have done well in that sense, but oftentimes, I fear our people wished me to be more like her," said the Queen, gesturing to the ruby figure.

"Vitala is the mother of this world, of what this world is today at least. I have tried to be nurturing in my time, but alas, no mortal, even elves, can accomplish everything they set their minds to. I fear the past, and I fear of what may come. I let these thoughts haunting me lead to a harsher, stricter, and more controlling rule than I once envisioned when I was young. I like to think I have improved in this area over my rule. But, I am still far from being loved in the way Kei-Tel had managed."

The Queen shifted her cutting gaze to Nienna. "I still believe it necessary. The threats imposed onto Divinoros fall on me to eradicate. Doing so requires a strong hand." Tiredness seemed to fringe the edges of her otherwise authoritative voice. "Trying to maintain control of this land often feels as though I'm grasping at straws… And there is more than one of the High Lords who resent the control and restriction I place upon them. Perhaps I do need to loosen my grip? Love them and respect them as Vitalia would. Allow them to rule in their own ways, independently of a central elven rule. God's… Lord Frenir might drop dead of excitement to hear me say that…"

She paused in her speech as she strode closer to Nienna, who had yet to speak up but slowed again before the topaz figure. "And here we have the great Comporian, the only God who could have possibly withstood the wrath of Omnes on his own so many years ago. I often wonder how he would judge my reign. He stood as the God of judgment, balance incarnate, his word being the difference between right and wrong. The true definition of morality is defined by his word, by his honor. I fear his lack of involvement in the face of Omnes's wrath is as clear a verdict as there ever has been on our people… He cares not for our fate for we have failed him in some way? But perhaps… perhaps his nature of discipline, his belief in free will, kept him from interfering in our war so long ago. He embodies neutrality, after all, judging actions one takes rather than imposing his own will to force them to act according to his will, but… Well, we could have used a divine power then."

"And finally," now standing directly in front of Nienna, the assassin felt the full weight of the Queen's gaze until its weight slid from her and fell on the statue of Omnes, "The God of power. His hunger for it exterminated most of the life on this planet. Of all the Gods I would hope to meet in person, he is the last I would choose. And unfortunately, he is the only one I believe I have ever walked on the lands of Divinoros with. And he, I fear, is the one I will most likely face again." Nienna saw a pained expression rack the Queen's visage.

She finally fixed her oppressive gaze on Nienna, and she could feel those stunning emerald eyes boring down on her, scrutinizing every movement she made, noticing every small scar along her delicate face, arms, and hands. She could feel the Queen analyzing each piece of torn and tattered clothing, the fresh cuts and scratches earned on her travel north from the desert, and most of all, the weariness, fear, and trepidation in her eyes.

"My guards tell me you forced your way into this audience," she looked toward Zarou, whose scaled body was still curled up in a sunbeam, eyes closed in a light nap. "No doubt your lion here helped with your persuasion." A small smile cracked the Queen's stone façade as she stepped over to Zarou. Without the hesitation of fear, Celestra reached up and scratched behind his ears. His eye, as large as the woman's head, shot open to gaze at her. The Queen was unperturbed and continued her scratching. Seeing his partner was not in immediate danger, Zarou closed his eyes and vibrated happily as the Queen scratched, the slight smile now growing to a full grin on her majesty's painted red lips.

"I have not seen a Sand lion in some time, not since I was just a century and thirty years of age. They are one of the most beautiful creatures I have laid my eyes on. I am sure it is a most intriguing story how you came across such a companion. Equally interesting, I would guess, is how you earned his trust. It's a very difficult thing to do. They say, you know, that a sand lion can see into the hearts of all creatures. They only ever imprint on those with pure hearts and intentions… Perhaps you can tell me another time. For now, though, what is his name?"

Nienna was surprised, most people didn't care to ask for Zarou's name, thinking him nothing more than a mindless beast she had tamed. How wrong they were. "His name is Zarou," Nienna said, waiting for the Queen to ask her name, but the question did not come.

The Queen ceased scratching Zarou, walked up to her throne, sat down gracefully, again bringing her attention to Nienna, and spoke. "Now then, Nienna, you have demanded my attention, so how may I help you?"

Though she tried, Nienna was unable to keep the surprise, the shock, from her face. Only one man knew her true name, and the fey now, of course. Anyone else who caught wind of her name she had dealt with, or so she thought.

The Queen noticed her surprise. "Oh, don't look so shocked, girl. You think I would not know the identity of one of the most powerful agents operating within my Kingdom? Your secret is safe with me. Your work has never interfered with my own, and until a time comes that our interests don't align, I see no reason we cannot coexist amicably... For now, at least... Now, please, spare me the suspense and tell me why you are here."

Nienna felt the strength of the Queen now. She was no fool, no aged monarch who had grown complacent on her throne of power. She was diligent, she was thorough, and she kept up with the happenings within her kingdom. *I wonder how much my news will change her outlook on the world, how much surprise it will bring.* Nienna retrieved a large book from the saddleback on Zarou's harness and turned back to face the Queen, jumping right into a straightforward answer. The Queen might be the only one who could even hope to oppose the Bankhofts. Nienna had already decided she needed to know everything."Your Majesty, I was asked by Lord Sennin to bring you this text. But on my travels north from Sandivar, I ran into very serious trouble, an awakening of a divine power... A power strong enough to destroy your kingdom if left unattended, I fear."

Queen Celestra stiffened slightly at the sight of the book and tilted her head quizzically as she looked over Nienna. "You didn't pass through the Narrow, did you? I haven't received any merchants from Lady Elba or Lord Sennin in months. I assumed bandits, but I would imagine that both would have quelled any of that quickly. They each have large groups of Elites stationed. I even sent a fleet around the peninsula just last week to bring me news."

Nienna nodded, "Yes. I did pass through the city. There is a reason you have not received any merchants from the Narrows and beyond. I fear the city has fallen under the control of a human criminal organization that operates out of the Badlands. I understand you have feuded with them for centuries, that you tried to uproot them before. The Bankhofts. After meeting them... I'm not surprised that you sent thousands to annihilate them. I am equally unsurprised that your entire force was slaughtered." Nienna was sure the news would bring worry to Celestra, but the Queen continued sitting calmly, the only distress she felt shown by a tapping of her finger on the arm of her throne.

Celestra was silent for some time before speaking. "Finally making his move, I see... Tell me your story. Now. And start from the beginning."

And so, Nienna did. She started with the tale of her and Zarou traveling deep into the Badlands and confronting the Knife head-on. She hinted at the power the man possessed here. She told the tale of her travel north, she spoke of the Elites, she spoke of a city under the oppression of a new ruler, she spoke of the Gifted, the Knife's ability to cut into the fabric of reality and disappear into a void before her very eyes. She told of her companions' wounds festering, burying Joralf, and witnessing the

217

twisted transfiguration of Kimo's corpse. She spoke of the wounds she suffered and the healing performed by Princess Kassandra of the fey people. And finally ended with, "And now I am here before you, exhausted, hungry, and recounting a miserable tale."

The Queen remained expressionless throughout the story. Giving Nienna every bit of her attention. Her Majesty held off with any questions, knowing that they could always be asked upon the completion of Nienna's retelling of her journey north. Now, quiet persisted for a few moments, and the Queen absorbed the story before rising to speak.

"I am so sorry for the loss of your companions, Nienna." She spoke softly as she placed a reassuring hand upon her shoulder, "I know better than most the sting of loss at the hands of such horror. What you tell me is highly troubling."

Celestra ran her hands along the side of her face before pacing back and forth along the stage supporting her throne, deep in thought. "If we are to believe that the Knife has held the Narrows for the past month, not only is he well ahead in his planning, but I have been supplying his forces with food and weapons shipments intended for Sennin. And anything he has sent our way has surely been intercepted as well. Not to mention, there is no way the Bankhoft family would make this move if they were not fully prepared to march on Sandivar." She paused as if contemplating how much she should tell an assassin. "I know of this dagger you spoke of. I believe its power is documented in the book you brought me. And it is replicated here in this throne room clenched in the fist of Omnes." Nienna nodded, now realizing the familiarity in the blade the statue gripped.

The Queen stood and seemed as though she would dismiss Nienna. Nienna nearly sighed in relief, knowing she deserved as much after her trials. And with Nienna's information, she knew Celestra now needed to plan how to get a supporting force through the Narrows to Sennin quickly. As if the fates themselves heard her musings, one of the Queen's attendants burst into the room. "Your majesty. You have another visitor here. He said he just arrived from Sandivar to our ports with news of the city."

News from Sandivar... How could someone have gotten around the peninsula so fast to bring news from the city? It must be more outdated than mine.

"Send him in. Now," the Queen ordered, turning to Nienna. "I wish for you to stay here. How quickly could you be ready to travel? I am beginning to feel I may need to ask more of you before this day is over."

Nienna was about to respond with laughter. *This woman thinks to ask for favors from me! I have no intention of dying in this fight with the divine at her behest. Maybe I should flee north with Zarou. No need to be sacrificed with the rest of the Queen's army. This is her issue, her kingdom, her fight to deal with. I've been close enough to death too many times in this war already, and it's only beginning. If I fight, I decide how to do so with Zarou.*

Before she could respond, the doors at the back of the room slammed open once again, and a tall, bedraggled elf with short-cropped red hair strode through. His eyes were wild, haunted, erratically looking about the hall as if the shadows from the statues were going to jump at him. But they were determined as well.

"Yer Majesty. M'name is Malfius. Captain of the Grim Siren. 'S truly an honor to be in yer presence." He then turned to Nienna and bowed, eyeing the lion beside her cautiously. "M'lady."

Nienna did laugh at that, "Oh, I am no lady, captain, just your everyday espionage and assassination specialist."

The man stared at her for just a second, which seemed like a miracle as the man's eyes were rapidly jittering all about the room they stood in, rarely resting in one place for more than a handful of seconds. Still scanning the room, he continued, "Yer Majesty, I bring news from Sandivar."

Before he could continue, the Queen cut in. "How recent is your information, Captain?"

"I... I can't be certain. Not down to exact days, but I know it is no later than a week. Couldn't be older than a week," he trailed off, mumbling to himself. "How long was I in the mist? Days... days... a week, no, no, couldn't be a week. No more than days... Maybe just hours..." He seemed to remember he stood amongst others and cleared his throat, "Sorry, yer Majesty. See, me.. Well, me and me crew," the Captain shuddered visibly, "we sailed through the Cursed Isles to get here. Urgent. Very Urgent. The news, I mean, things are most urgent, it would seem."

Passed through the Cursed Isles. No wonder the man looked slightly crazed in the eyes like he might flee the room at the sound of a pin dropping unsuspectingly.

The Queen nodded her head, clearly impressed. "Very well then. Traveling through the Isles is no small feat, Captain. Few have dared the journey and survived to tell their tale. Tell me why you were sent."

The captain continued. "Yes, ma'am. A, uh, it's a, well, a frightening place to sail. Some might say I've been making a habit of passing through them waters though, ma'am. Sailed through 'em twice now. Just, just twice. Twice now, and lived both times, it seems... At least most of me made it through... Think my soul gets cut to ribbons on each pass. Never complete 'gain after a journey like that. Better off than some on me ship lost good men. Lost 'em violently..." Malfius's eyes went distant, recalling the horror before refocusing.

"Me and me crew, as I mentioned, were sent to carry a top priority letter from Lord Sennin to yerself," he said, holding the letter out to the Queen, who seized the parchment and cracked Sennin's seal. "The city was surrounded by a human enemy the day we departed. But these humans got some strange power, it seems." Celestra waved her hand at the man to quiet down as she read the letter.

Suddenly, when she had finished reading, she stopped pacing and looked squarely at Nienna. "The Bankhofts have surrounded Sandivar. I fear the city must already be under siege. At least three days ago, Sennin penned a letter detailing a human army surrounding him. He had not received supplemental merchandise in many months, and the stores of food in Sandivar were running low. Not enough to withstand a large-scale siege for more than a couple of months at most. He is asking me to send an army south with reinforcements and supplies. But he does not know the Narrows have already fallen. This Knife character has hamstrung our strongest city in the south, cutting them off from reinforcements and attacking before we can help. My army won't make it through the tight passageway without a massive, time-consuming struggle among the forces in place to defend the city. They could hold it with a fraction of the force we send. It's time we don't have. Nor can we supply help by sailing around the peninsula."

Nienna grasped the gravity of the situation. It was all but certain to her that Sandivar would fall if it hadn't already. No fresh supplies would make it to Sennin in time to make any sort of a difference. The desert lands were lost to the elves. Not to mention, Lord Sennin had limited intel on the power the Gifted had, much less that those injured by a Gifted would turn into what Celestra confirmed as some strange breed of krakenshi.

"Celestra," Nienna called out. "Sandivar is lost. You must fortify your southern border. The Bankhoft army will only grow as more people fall to his soldiers."

Malfius now looked confused, "What that s'posed to mean? Already lost. No, no, yer majesty. Sandivar is our southern stronghold. Can't give that up. Sennin is already planning the d'fense of the city."

"Malfius. Before you arrived, I was debriefed on the power of our enemy in the south. A portion of Omnes's power remains in this world, and the Bankhoft crime family has harnessed and weaponized it. It allows him to create soldiers of immense strength who, in turn, can transform our dead into beasts that resemble krakenshi. Once the Bankhofts attack, Sandivar will not stand long, I fear."

The Queen paused, thinking on her decision, and for the first time, Nienna respected the gravity of her station. Her order would impact the lives of an entire city with the utmost directness. "We are not afforded the luxury to plan at length, it would seem. The situation demands immediate action. Vilde!"

The Queen's attendant sprang into the room from the doorway at the sound of her name. "Fetch Avel and the others in the high council at once. Send them to the war room. Tell them it's crucial." The woman nodded and strode from the hall, the small patter of her feet fading slowly away.

The Queen turned to Malfius. "Captain. I need to ask the impossible of you; I wish I did not, but war is upon us. I need you to sail back to Sandivar carrying a letter to Sennin. The letter will detail orders to the High Lord to gather every able-bodied man, woman, and child in Sandivar and sail to take refuge at Reef Ridge Port. I will also send you a letter for Lady Estora in Reef Ridge describing the situation at hand and how she should act. Time is of the essence. I fear you need to solidify that habit of traversing the realm of the demons."

"But... But... You mean us t'go back into the Cursed Isles...," Captain Malfius started looking a tad paler than he had before he walked in, if that was possible, "Me Majesty... the crew may not stay with me if I issue this order. Fear some, most maybe, will desert. Can I give them till the morning before we depart? There are evils in those waters, unspeakable horrors. We watched our friends lose their minds, bludgeon, stab, and drown themselves to death. The whispers. All because of the whispers. They need time to recover." His mumbled rambling seemed almost to be more to himself than the Queen, but it was clear that rest would be required if this Malfius was to have any hope of delivering the Queen's orders to the southern cities. But she didn't have till morning to delay.

The monarch nodded. "Take the afternoon, but you will leave this evening. I am sorry, Captain. Let your men know that tens of thousands of lives, innocent civilian lives, rely on you."

Then she turned to Nienna. "I know you do not recognize me as your Queen, and I understand you feel no loyalty to the monarchy... I do not have time to rectify whatever misperceptions you have about me or to address any misconceptions regarding my life and rule, so instead of an order, I would like to offer you a contract."

Nienna raised a brow at this. "I'll consider any offer that comes my way, but it better be a damned good one. I have half a mind to refuse you outright now before you get into it," said Nienna. She wasn't keen on getting back on a job so soon after the disaster of a trip north to Turenian. She wanted nothing more than to take a bath and sleep for a week before finding somewhere quiet to spend a few months with Zarou.

Celestra nodded her understanding before saying, "I need you to travel across the Aeronian Straights to the dwarf Kingdom under the

221

Perampla Mountains. I will send you with two tasks. You'll carry a letter to King Thondor, informing him of the insurrection in the desert and the potential of a greater power at play. You must make him understand the true nature of the power that the Knife wields. Make him understand that this is a direct power from the Dark God and that Kei-Tel failed to sever the influence of Omnes in Divinoros completely. I fear the coming war could be more costly than the first against the divine. I have heard of stirrings in the north and think that some of the activity in northern Gradishar could somehow be related to what is happening in the southern deserts."

Celestra paced as she spoke. "Elves, dwarves, and humans will need to strike against this enemy in a united front to succeed against them. Your second task will be to find a man, a researcher, a historian by the name of Baelin. You will give him a second letter from me describing our conversation and the book you brought here," she held the book for Nienna to take, "and describe what you have seen related to the dagger's powers. Confirm to him this *is* the dagger taken from the Obsidian Knight. He may be able to discern some way to stop the Knife from using it."

Nienna sighed and then took the text from the Queen.

I can't get rid of this damn book for the life of me. Nothing good has happened since this came into my life.

"And what payment will I receive for these services, Celestra?" Nienna asked.

The Queen finished her proposal. "Your reward will be half your weight in gold, sole ownership of a two-thousand-acre plot of land just south of Gradishar fully exempt from Turenian's influence or taxation. Plus, more than the pay or land, this would be a favor you are doing for me, and in turn, I will be in your debt."

Nienna raised her eyebrows at the Queen and looked back toward Zarou. The lion's head was raised from the ground, staring directly into her own as if to say *I am with you whatever your decision*. Scenes from the horror of her travels north flashed through her mind. Joralf injured in the tunnels, and Kimo being struck with a Gifted's javelin. She saw flashes of the wounds festering black. She pictured the last breath from each man... the last breath before a new creature from within their bodies was ready to tear itself free of the fleshy exoskeleton. This horror could not be permitted to permeate through the world.

She was a part of this fight now. Like it or not, she would be unable to shrug off this responsibility.

I may as well be paid for my efforts. With that amount of gold, I'll build a castle for her and Zarou to settle in once this war is over. Assuming we still live.

"We will do it," Nienna stated to the Queen, "Can you charter us a ship?"

Celestra nodded. "One more thing Ghost. Your old mentor is on the shores of Western Divinoros. His movements are shadowed to me, but if you find him there... Tell him of our plight."

Nienna could see Celestra wanted to tell the Ghost to tell him more if she found him, but she held her tongue.

And like that, Nienna and Zarou were headed to the docks of Turenian to ferry across the Aeronian Straights—three straight days aboard a vessel. To be honest, she was looking forward to the trip. She and ships had good days and bad. She preferred her feet on solid ground, but it would give her three days' rest, albeit contained to a small vessel. What she was nervous about was how Zarou would fare being cooped up.

She reached up and patted his shoulders, seeing his downtrodden ears slanted down and back as they walked down the docks. Zarou was clearly not looking forward to the next part of their journey. Nienna smiled at that. Zarou, so bold and dangerous even when faced with horrendous beasts from an ancient war, was scared of the water. She forgot just how young her Zarou was. How much of this world she had yet to show him.

Lord Sennin - Chapter 29 - Planted Seeds

Hot, dry air flowed through his nose, filling his lungs. The air didn't flow smoothly, finding repeated restrictions in its drawn-in path, repeatedly re-routed from countless breaks marking the nasal passageway. It didn't bother the Knife. He hungered only for power. Weakness, even his own, was simply ignored and disregarded.

His fist clenched around his cherished obsidian blade. His dark eyes were focused in the distance. Just like his mind, power clouded his vision. He was no longer seeing as a human. The darkness that coursed from blade to body blotted out the brilliant colors sparkling from the dunes and cityscape of the hellish stronghold before him.

Now, the daylight was drowned, and in the distance, Sandivar gleamed as a radiant sun of power waiting for consumption. Waiting for the power of the Omnes, waiting for him, to seize that strength for his own. He breathed heavily, not much longer now.

Once Sandivar falls, the time of humans ruling this world under a true God, a God of pure, unsurmountable force, will blanket Divinoros. Not much longer before the elves of this world squirm beneath my thumb.

He turned to face his force; smaller radiant points spread on the dunes behind him. He smiled, seeing their power. While in numbers, they were smaller than he would have liked, he knew they would be enough. And once Sandivar was his, his army would grow.

...

Just a week after sending Malfius through the Cursed Isles, Lord Sennin stood along Sandivar's battlements. He was brandished in his pristine polished armor, looking down at the great sand ocean splayed out before him. He stood nearly motionless, calmly awaiting the approach of the human scourge that marched on his city. His gaze passed over the golden dunes as a large swarm of black crested and crawled down the face of the great dunes, like so many ants pouring down their hill. The buzz of distant figures continued toward the city until a clean-cut military formation materialized at the base of the ever-changing grainy mountains that dominated the desert landscape.

Orders were being shouted down below, and neat lines of armored crossbowmen trotted through the front gates beneath where Lord Sennin stood. As they poured from the gate, his men formed a large two-column line stretched out to either side of the main gates. The two armies were oriented like pieces on a chess board, and now Sennin awaited his opponent's first move. The High Lord was in the advantageous position of knowing the Knife would be forced to press an attack. After all, they were the besieging army. Seeing as how the largest strength against the invading force—the formidable fortifications—rested beneath the elf lord's feet, there was really no point in losing soldiers trying to press an attack of his own.

This force is not nearly large enough to take Sandivar. They would likely need triple the soldiers they had brought. Despite the rationalization, something gnawed at him. *He wouldn't attack unless he was confident he could take the city. Would he? Is the man so mad?*

He was inclined to wait here upon his walls long enough for the Queen to send supporting troops and fresh rations. The populace was informed of the food shortage. Of course, they had exaggerated how long they could sustain themselves to avoid panic amongst the people, but it was clear that each resident would need to do their part as the city faced an invasion force.

In reality, they would need support within a two-month time period, being highly optimistic if they wished to avoid starvation and making hard choices of cutting certain portions of the people off from food reserves. Of course, riots would ensue at that point, and the war with the Bankhofts would be over then. If this battle persisted, they may have been forced into open combat to avoid that fate, but time was their friend at the moment.

In the past, Sennin remembered the choice, given that circumstance, would have been an easy one to make: simply cut off feeding the humans to save as many elves as possible. Kill the humans if necessary. But it had been centuries since this was accepted practice, and the humans that now graced his city had successfully clawed their way out of the deep oppression levied on them as a result of their ancestors having opened a path for Omnes to step into this world.

Hopefully, there will be no delay in the Queen's response. Assuming Malfius made the journey, I expect a full army to march through the Narrows within the next two weeks. We can watch Celestra cut this force down from our walls, thought Sennin, smiling grimly as he waited for this day's bloody affair.

And wait, he did. The opposing army stood in the distance throughout the day until the sun touched the horizon. Despite the winter month finally bringing slightly fresher air, the desert remained unbearably hot when the sun stood in the sky. Sennin reasoned that the enemy likely preferred to fight in the cool of the night rather than the heat of the day. Not to mention, the sun on the horizon would be blinding for his archers and could skew their aim significantly. He felt confident regardless.

The crossbowmen below were positioned to maximize the stopping force of their heavy bolts against any beast of burden used to move siege machinery and to break through any heavily armored men or women who couldn't be taken down by the rows of archers positioned on the battlements. They also had the ballista armed and ready to fire, awesome weapons capable of crippling any war machines brought into the plane of fighting.

As the sun kissed the sands in the distant sky, a faraway horn sounded, and Sennin could make out the battalions in the sand respond as they began marching toward their position. The force wasn't small by any means, but they could hold out easily against a much larger force, Sennin thought. And he saw only six siege towers.

He knew that there was more than meets the eye with these human soldiers. After all, he and Celestra had sent thousands of men, small armies, to their deaths, violent deaths, against the Bankhofts near the fallen Oasis. Those men were reduced to blood and bits in the Badlands at the hands of these villains who now marched in their direction. He did not know how that had happened, but he was not keen to find out and intended to ensure these monsters stayed behind the impregnable wall of his city.

The enemy force was now only a quarter mile from the wall, just beyond bowshot, and the opposing army's main body stopped marching. They paused for a moment, but only a moment.

On another signal, the front three rows from each battalion sprinted toward the wall. While that rendered the crossbowmen less effective, they would have plenty of time to reload before the army's main body arrived.

They and the archers would be able to cut down this first line of dark-shrouded soldiers with ease.

Sennin remained silent, almost in a trance, as he watched the group grow larger and larger in his view as they grew closer to the wall. His generals started issuing orders from his left and right.

As the enemy grew closer, Sennin noticed a few particularities amongst them... "Hand me the looking glass," Sennin said, motioning hurriedly to one of his runners. He looked through the glass and felt his heart sink through his stomach at the sight. Each man and woman that was running toward them had void black eyes staring dead ahead. Their forms varied wildly from a normal human or elf in eerie ways.

One woman had thick, dark shadows coalescing into massive plated scales and claws that replaced her arms, and another man had a cloak of shadowed tentacles that flowed behind him, but the arms would snap forward with suddenness to strike obstacles from his path or, when the obstacle was too large to smash away, to propel him up and over it. He looked back to the runner, his face now ghostly pale. "Get to General Earion now! Tell him to retreat behind the walls and position themselves

226

for any breaches on the gates. We will do what we can from above as they approach!"

The boy nodded and ran down the stone stairs, descending the back side of the battlement. All Sennin could do was watch and hope the boy reached Earion in time. He turned to face the men lined up on the battlements behind the rows of archers, his Elites. They stood in small mobile groups, ready to deploy quickly to any vulnerable points along the wall, three rows of six men and women each, many supported with power magi. The sight assured the High Lord that Sandivar would not be an easy city for anyone to take, not even these demented forms that descended upon them.

Then, as if to jolt him back to attention, he heard a series of tight "twangs" as hundreds of archers fired their arrows into the flaming orange and purple-painted sky. The arrows formed the silhouette of a wave, blotting out the colored sky. Sennin followed the trajectory until the wave of shafts seemed to halt at their crest before arching to crash down into the enemy's forces. He smiled as pockets of the mysterious forms faltered. But as he continued to watch, he noticed the bodies of what had seemed to be slain forms rise to resume their rabid rush. Only a handful remained unmoving.

He looked down at the rows of soldiers holding crossbows. None had moved from their post yet. *Come on now. Get in the doors, you fools! Get in the doors!* But the soldiers continued to hold their ground, unaware that the rushing force was composed of strange aberrations far faster and more resilient than an army of humans would be.

As the precious moments continued to tick by, it became clear his order of retreat would not come soon enough. The front of the enemy's formation was now only a hundred meters away. *Twang!* Seventy-five… *Twang!* Fifty. Then, a shout and a series of loud *"Twacks!"* sounded through the air as crossbow bolts ravaged the enemy's front lines. Optimism stirred in Sennin as the bolts appeared to be far more effective than the volleys of arrows being lobbed by the archers. Still, despite the improved effectiveness, there were simply not enough men firing bolts into the rushing hoard to stop the enemy's momentum. And so, the wild raiding party advanced on the front lines too quickly for them to retreat with any order.

Lord Sennin watched in horror from a hundred feet above as the clash of forces unfurled. Most of the crossbowmen's second line immediately retreated toward the gate as soon as their first projectile was shot. Seconds later, the front row of crossbowmen fired their bolts to cover the retreating Sandivarian soldiers. The second volley was intended to defend the retreating soldiers while dealing enough damage to allow the first line of crossbowmen to retreat safely under the cover of the archers from above.

The second wave of bolts was sent flying at the mass of approaching bodies, and another group of the sprinting enemy forms toppled to the ground. The holes left by the fallen men were filled by a number of aberrations that had recovered from the first wave of bolts. Still, over half the number of men stood. Many with bolts and arrows stuck in the flesh that oozed blackened blood. The crossbowman screamed as they hastily retreated, their escape impeded by the monsters that descended upon them.

Sennin's forces scrambled over one another, attempting to flee to the safety of the wall. But the rush of black-eyed men tore into their backs with maniacal enthusiasm. Screams of dying men inflicted with vicious wounds filled the night alongside the softer sounds of ripping flesh. With horror, Sennin watched as the Sandivarian soldiers manning the gate had no other option than to slam the doors closed, sealing their comrades to a cruel fate.

Panic engulfed the scene below as over a hundred elves outside the walls abandoned all civility, scrambling over one another, clawing at the gates in a desperate bid to escape their enemy's wrath. It wasn't long before the screams of Sandivarians were replaced by the sound of the enemy ripping at the reinforced gate with frenzied ferocity.

A poor start indeed... Still, they did not breach our walls.

Lord Sennin shouted orders to the archers along the battlement, and arrows rained down from above at the tightly packed enemy group. For all their power, they did not have the sense to space out their formation. After seven more volleys, the archers finally quelled the uproar below and submerged the night into a brief silent reprieve from the violence.

Darkness soon accompanied the silence, casting the city wall into an eerie glow, the stone reflecting the moon's pale light in the absence of any sun. The dull scent of iron was thick in the air, wafting high from the corpses below. It triggered a nervous chatter amongst the defending force. Sennin remained in place, straining to see into the distance, attempting to make out if any more of the opposing force had marched on Sandivar. He saw no movement just yet but believed the Knife would continue to press his advantage. The battle had just begun, and in little time, hundreds of his men had died. Sennin rubbed at his temples and took a deep breath to steady himself before breaking the silence.

"Ready your weapons for close combat!" he shouted toward the rows of Elites behind him. "Their siege towers are few, but they make up for numbers with aggression and some form of magic is bolstering their resistance to death. But death we will give! We will tear the will from their cursed souls." He shouted to the soldiers gathered around him, "The enemy comes for us now. But they are criminals, outlaws, evil men, and evil women who have tapped into some unnatural power they wield for death. But no matter the strength they possess, for with all their

228

power, they will discover themselves crashing against an unyielding mountain." The soldiers banged their weapons against their shields as their defiant shouts filled the air.

A few groans sounded from the darkness below.

There must be survivors!

As if in response to his thought, a small group of soldiers ran from the gates, sifted through mangled corpses, and carried the injured Sandivarians behind the walls, where they would be delivered to the triage tents set up in the city's main square. As the doors closed, the brief reprieve from combat ended. Drums sounded, and the remaining force of three thousand men marched on his city.

Through the looking glass, Sennin did his best to assess the oncoming enemy formations, hoping to discern where the ballistae needed to be aimed to shred any siege towers that approached. The view through the glass was... disheartening. Each man and woman's eyes were as dark as the night, and their shadowed extremities were difficult to make out in the camouflage of night. He watched as the army moved in unison, each of the massive siege towers in tow behind long-haired, lumped-back camels. Each camel was the size of Sennin's juvenile sun dragons.

If only they were mature enough to join this fight and burn this demented army to crisps... but alas, they won't be flying for another year at least, much less breathing fire.

The harmony of snapping bows sprung to life around him. The Bankhoft army came within firing range, but the shafts still seemed to have little effect. Sennin couldn't understand why these men were so damn hard to kill. He thought to imbue the bolts of the archers around him with fire from his magic, but the effort would soon exhaust him. He couldn't pick individual arrows either, as there was no telling whose bolt would find its home in the body of the enemy's force.

For now, I keep my power to myself. I imagine I will need it before the night is complete.

This should have been an easy defense, a swift victory against an adversary lacking the numbers of a legitimate threat. They held the advantage in numbers and the advantage of the defensive walls. But despite proven military strategy saying his side would handily win, he was beginning to feel as though his city was at a disadvantage against this mysterious foe, that a miracle was needed to save them from the same fate as the crossbowmen.

As if the Gods could hear his thoughts and wished to prove him right, a whistling filled the air before coming to an abrupt halt as a long black spear burst through the back of the neck of the archer just to his left, casting flecks of scarlet spray over Sennin's face. The shaft was thrown with such force the spear broke the man's jaw open and tore halfway

229

through his skull before the weapon began wisping away into nothing, allowing the elf's blood to flow out in rampant spurts as he collapsed to the cobbled battlements, twitching.

That's impossible. No one could make a throw with such force at such a distance, and why the hell did the spear evaporate?

A scream sounded further down the battlement, and another black javelin thudded into an archer's shoulder, sending him stumbling over the backside of the wall to open air. He was carried to the triage tent at the base of the wall, but he doubted the man could have survived the impact of such a high fall.

"Archers! Target the bastards throwing these spears!" A general screamed into the air. But the enemy benefited from attacking in the night. Each one of the enemy numbers was outfitted in black and carried weapons that seemed to swallow light itself, which made it nearly impossible to make out who or what was throwing spears through his archers. Lord Sennin watched helplessly as archers continued to die because of it.

After four more archers dropped just strides from where Sennin stood himself, he ordered the bowmen to pull back from the front of the battlements. Not enough enemy soldiers were dying for their efforts, and the High Lord feared the archers would receive the bulk of punishment should they continue to trade volleys of projectiles with the enemy.

The triage tents and hospital buildings will be full by night's end.

On his order, the remaining archers retreated down the backside of the wall to the courtyard where they could provide cover fire should the gates be breached or the wall be taken. The rows of Elites stepped up to the edge of the battlements, shields raised to protect themselves until the enemy presented a clear target.

Once the elves were in position, Sennin scanned the battlefield once again. With no archers to impede their progress, the enemy was now within a quarter mile of their walls, the massive siege towers moving slowly and steadily through the night.

Sennin turned to face another runner. "Get to General Earion and tell him the enemy siege towers are within range of the ballistae. Open fire at once." The young boy scurried along the battlement quicker than any soldier likely could have, dodging around bodies, weapons and soldiers at a full sprint.

The next moments could only be described as helpless as Sennin turned his attention back toward the doom marching through the desert. A sense of foreboding clamped down on his chest, forcing his breath to come in shallow, rapid succession as the looming black siege towers continued to advance.

They will be easy to target and cripple with the mounted ballistae, at least, and there are so few.

Relief passed through his mind as a loud snap sounded, and a ten-foot steel bolt hurtled in the direction of the slowly approaching siege towers. Four more cracks split the air, and Sennin smiled with grim satisfaction as two bolts found their mark on the lead siege tower, splitting the wheels it was pulled upon and rendering it useless. A horrid squealing emanated from two camels pulling a second tower, each skewered with steel, but the other four continued their slow convergence on the city's walls. The High Lord's keen ears picked up on the gears being cranked back as the ballistae were rearmed. The process was slow. Too slow.

Sennin turned the looking glass on his enemy once again and saw a figure in the back of the center battalion performing some sort of ritual. He held a blade high in the air before bringing it to the crook of his arm and pulling hard on the dagger's hilt. As his blood touched the sand, a subtle whisper, like cloth being rubbed together, filled the air, growing louder and louder. The sand burbled around the marching enemy formation. Small figures in the shape of long tentacles could be seen breaking the surface in various areas, breaching the sandy surface before diving back below.

Sennin couldn't be sure if whatever moved was a part of one massive body or an abundance of individual bodies like a swarm of man-sized leeches. The creatures continued to thrash about the surface of the sand, kicking up dust into the air that rose slowly, engulfing the army before them. First, the soldiers disappeared behind a wall of dust, then the camels, and then the siege towers. *Shit!* Finally, when his visibility had disintegrated, the soft sounds of rubbing fabric faded.

His only effective weapon was just made useless, as he could no longer target the slowly approaching towers under the cover of night and sandstorms. "Ready yourselves for a siege!" Sennin shouted. "They will be on us in minutes! Protect your brothers and sisters in arms beside you. Protect your homes behind you. We are the Queen's strength in the south. Let us remind them of why."

It wasn't long before the heavy sound of metal breaking stone broke the army's silence. The heavy doors of the siege engines fell onto the battlement walls, depositing darkness on the doorstep of Sandivar. One was positioned just strides from the High Lord. The crunching sound of falling doors elicited screams from the Elites crushed beneath their weight. Quiet rage filled him. Reacting with lightning speed, Sennin raised his left arm and blasted a ball of fire into the opening of the door. He smiled as the smell of burning flesh and the sounds of screams of those burning alive reached him.

The quick response from the High Lord allowed his forces time to fill the gaps created by the siege tower door and contend with the rain of abnormalities that soon emerged with one cruel intention. Kill, and kill quickly.

Sennin, heart thudding, unsheathed his sword and joined the fight with the small team of Elites nearest him. They sprinted toward the closest tower and the truth of what they were fighting filled Sennin with a dreadful pause. It was something to see from a distance but entirely different to cross blades with. A flood of bodies streamed from the siege tower. Each of the Bankhoft soldiers was covered in ragged black leather armor over black tunics and pants paired to match their black beady eyes. The army had the visage of reapers coming to sow their harvest, the souls of his citizens, his soldiers, and him.

The first man out of the tower leapt at the front line of Elites with reckless abandon. He held just two daggers, one in each hand, but moved with incredible speed, wisping shadows of darkness trailing every movement he made. The defender was able to raise her sword to stop the downward strike, but as she did so, two limbs of black substance erupted from the sides of the man, just below the armpit, and stabbed into the Elite's chest cavity, one taking her through the heart, the other undoubtedly pierced her lung. A gurgle flowed from her parted bloody lips as she collapsed to her knees.

Before Sennin could use his power magic, another highly trained warrior instantly stepped into her place to engage with the manic, black-eyed human. He dodged one of the shadow arms and hacked one of the fleshy black limbs off at the elbow. The monster of a man shrieked and roared, spittle flying. His black eyes, wild with hatred, stared death at the soldier in front of him. Sennin's blood ran cold at the animal-like sound. He was glad to hear it silenced as one of the Elites cut off the man's head and kicked the body over the ramparts.

More filled his place, though. The next man that approached was stalking toward the front line of defenders empty-handed until he was just beyond sword reach. Then, a massive shield swirled into form from the shadows of the night, fitting onto his left arm, and a nasty-looking axe materialized in his open right hand. The weapon was as long as a man, with a head so large, no human, or elf for that matter, should have been able to carry it with one hand. This abomination had no issues with the oversized weapon, and with great rapid sweeps from the axe, he bludgeoned back the front lines easily, clearing space for more of the invading army to flow out of the tower. Sennin did his best to hold the rush of enemies at bay with a breathtaking display of magic. He loosed bolts of refined flame at the exposed flesh of Bankhoft soldiers, curving the lighting-quick flame around the ever-moving Elite soldiers to pierce the flesh of the attackers.

Each lance of flame felled an enemy. He ensured they stayed dead by sending the flame coursing through the fallen's veins until their

232

insides boiled and steamed. He felt he could kill them all if left unimpeded.

This was not to be. A scream erupted from two of the front-line defenders as the hulking form with an axe cleaved off an Elite's leg at the knee and continued in an upward angle until the head of his bulky weapon was buried in the chest of the next Elite. The man's body went limp over the shadow axe lodged in his side. After a few vicious shakes, the dead elf languidly slid from the end of the axe head like butter falling off a hot knife.

The invader lifted his shield in defense as three new Sandivarian soldiers struck at him to avenge their wounded and dead. The raised enemy shield splintered at the first deflection, and on the second impact, a concussive force fragmented the shield, and the wave of energy sent the three elves attacking the man flying backward. Long slivers of black material riddled the bodies of the soldiers closest to the man. The axe-wielding giant had just sacrificed himself to wound a large contingent of the defending force, allowing his brethren to surge forward. He had succeeded.

The Elites were given no reprieve before the next pair of invaders rushed against them. Without hesitation, High Lord Sennin stepped to the front lines. Still relatively fresh despite the energy lost in magical attacks, Sennin was confident he could contend with the dark army. He would force them back as long as needed.

War was horror and violence and long ago lost its appeal to Sennin. But the lack of desire to claim others' lives did nothing to diminish his competency in the task. As ruler of this city, it was his duty to defend and protect his people. He preferred the days where this meant determining trade needs, coordinating city logistics, and even deciding upon rationing plans, but tonight called for a bloody affair, and he intended to spill his enemy's in abundance.

He was immediately required to parry a spear hurled in his direction from a second-line invader. The black-eyed force had been able to push back the defending elvish forces, creating enough room for the invaders to form a front and back line as they pushed against the defending Elites. Sennin knew they could not allow a substantial force to form, as it seemed one enemy was worth three of his Elites. This was a shocking realization when he considered his soldiers were considered some of the fiercest in Divinoros. Sennin shouted to the men behind him, "We hold this line! Not another inch in retreat." He emphasized the statement by sending a flame down his arm until the orange tongues licked along the length of his blade. The sword appeared now to be waiting eagerly to bite into the flesh of their master's enemy.

The minutes passed slowly, and High Lord Sennin fought with vigor through them all. He killed two of the monstrous invaders, though three more men were injured during the fighting. One took a thrusting spear through his mouth, tearing out one cheek and leaving his shattered jaw gaping open as he was carried, barely conscious, to healing mages. Another lost an arm at the shoulder to a dark sword of black matter shortly before the same blade cut fatally deep into the side of a third soldier, puncturing key internal organs. Sennin struck the monster down in swift retribution. But again, he was replaced by another. The black river of contorted humans flowed unabated from the siege towers, clinging to the wall like hungry parasites. And Sennin was beginning to tire. He had cut the flow of flame to his blade to conserve energy, a sign the enemy took as weakness.

The newest combatant emerged confidently from the siege engine and strode directly toward Sennin's line of defenders. The man was enormous. In fact, Sennin had never seen a human so large. The barrel-chested human towered a foot taller than Sennin, making him at least eight feet tall, with forearms as thick as the Ice Backs native in the north and hands that looked as if they could crush rocks with limited effort. Sennin thought the man might even give one of the giant Ice Backs pause in a territorial dispute.

His body was covered with a black metal plate that seemed to grow from the skin beneath, and in his hand, he carried a domineering mace made out of the same mysterious solidified darkness that formed the weapons possessed by the other invaders.

Sennin tested the armor, sending a hive of flaming spikes at what he believed to be weak points in the armor's hinges. As the needles struck, the flame bolts fizzled out, only succeeding in enraging the hulking form.

His eyes locked on the High Lords, and without hesitation, the behemoth ran at Sennin. A soldier attempted to intercept the charging bull, but his form was crumpled over the mace before he was flung over the front side of the tower walls screaming.

When the soldier was no more than five paces away, the man jumped toward Sennin and swung his mace horizontally at neck height. The two Elites flanking Sennin tried to step back from the swinging arc of the mace, but the reach was too long. Sennin knew to duck beneath the blow, allowing the brute to pass by him. He heard loud crunching behind him as the two Elites were crushed with the weight of the mace's head, snapping their necks in quick succession. They collapsed instantly, their broken bodies unmoving beneath their fractured helms.

As Sennin rose from the low spin, he brought his blade around at the hamstring of the beast. He felt the hilt of his sword catch in his hand with the familiar satisfying drag of his blade's edge sinking into flesh, severing muscles and veins before bouncing hard against bone.

The wound was a crippling one. But Sennin watched in horror as the savages' flesh knit back together through dripping tendrils of black tar-like blood. The giant roared loudly, as loud as any desert dragon, and turned his back on the reinforcement of Elites to face Sennin. With shocking speed, the man stomped down at the elf. Sennin barely avoided the leather boot coming toward his knee. He nimbly rolled to one side and stabbed with his sword again at the man's midsection. The elf was rewarded as he again found flesh, the point of his sword sinking into the man's hip.

But it was no more effective than a viper striking a sand lion. The blow had no effect other than the colossal man sporting a somehow angrier snarl than before. He swung his mace again and again, no more perturbed by the stinging blade than a bear might be by a lone bee fighting to protect his hive.

Sennin was undeterred. He refused to allow this man to batter against his reinforcement team, who were busy repelling other combatants able to sneak past the wild duel of masterful killers. The battle was breathtaking, every bit a show of grace and beauty, an elf spiraling through the air like dust dancing through the wind, flame lighting the ground and sky as bits of power magic were used in the contest; the other side, a tidal wave of brute force attempting to swallow up and break everything with its awesome might.

Unfortunately for High Lord Sennin, tidal waves cannot be dodged forever, and this man was no different. After pirouetting around the man, the High Lord found the back of the black-eyed monster exposed and sunk his blade at an upward angle into the small of the man's back between two ridges in his dark carapace armor. He drove forward until his hilt was pressed against the man's ghostly white skin visible in the armor's seam.

He heard the point erupt through the man's rib cage at the front side of his chest. Once lodged in place, Sennin channeled all the magic he had left in his body down his arms and into the sword. There was no question that this was a mortal wound, but monsters do not die easily, and rarely, after defeating such a foe, do you walk away with only shortness of breath.

The man let out a rasping gasp, air no longer filling his pierced lungs. In his last dying moments, he turned to face the elf lord once again, the movement pulling the sword free of Sennin's grasp. He loomed over the elf, black eyes gouging into Sennin's soul with hatred so palpable the elf could feel the brute's rage. The man staggered back, blade still skewering his body, but quickly regained his balance, refusing to lose his feet.

A haunting, joyless, humorless smile split the dead man's face as black tar blood dripped from the grinning mouth, pooling between rotted teeth. He stepped unsteadily at the High Lord. Sennin watched the monster move, but he was exhausted and in disbelief. He had carved away chunks of flesh, cut, sliced, and stabbed this man enough times to kill hundreds, and now he watched in a trance as his enemy slowly stepped forward at him, skewered back to front. "JUST DIE!" he screamed at the evil spawn.

The only reply he got was a withering, blubbering chuckle. Air wheezing from blood-filled lungs. He tried to scramble away but stumbled over a fallen comrade. As he moved to stand up, the beast of a man fell forward, swinging his mace in a last-ditch effort to kill the elf that brought death unto him.

Sennin saw the head of the mace arc down on him but didn't have his feet under him to move away. All he could do was watch as the head of the heavy weapon landed on his armored shoulder. His vision flashed white before exploding in colorful light. The immense pain that accompanied his metal armor breaking, the sound of a tree's limbs cracking in as his shoulder was obliterated, and his ribs beneath fractured caused his world to flash bright once more before going dark. His mind mercifully put him to sleep to spare him the pain that accompanied the grizzly reality of snapped and shattered bones.

Lord Sennin - Chapter 30 - Trojan Horse

Sennin woke up, staring up toward a blinding white light. He sighed deeply; his first thought was that he must have passed back into the realm of his creator. The light must be Vitala reaching out, with all her warmth, to recall his soul to its final resting place with her. But the blinding white slowly to fade to a washed-out tan as his pupils adjusted. Then he heard people scurrying about, voices calling for bandages and water. He heard men and women moaning in agony, incoherent murmuring, and steady whimpers. He was in a triage tent.

Confusion struck him.

Why am I here?

Then, the reminder of intense pain brought back the memories of the previous night's battle in throbbing waves. He resisted as long as he could, but it wasn't long before he joined those muttering in roiling agony. He looked to his right shoulder and found a stained bandage covering what appeared to be a stump of a shoulder.

His brain moved as if stuck in molasses. Comprehension was slow, but as realization crept in, his heart thundered. Panic. Fear. Loss.

No, no, no! Where is my arm? I can feel it. I swear I can feel it there. Why can't I see it? Why can't... Where is my arm? Please, Gods! Please... Gods no...

No words came from his mouth. He stared blankly as his mind was spinning and his body trembled.

A sweet, calming voice pulled him from his stupor. "High Lord Sennin. I am so glad you're awake." She set a cup down on the table beside him. "Water, take it once you are ready. Now, I want you to look at me. I need to check your pupils. Make sure you are not showing any signs of head trauma, okay?"

Sennin turned numbly to stare at the healer, still in deep shock. Her white dress and apron were covered with dried brown gore and chunks of flesh. "My name is Olivi. Can you tell me your place of birth?"

He stared at her momentarily and looked down again at his missing appendage. He replied in a quiet voice. A shallow voice. "Where is my... What happened to my... my arm?" A tear slid down his face. It wasn't because of the pain, despite its pulsating agony. He felt as though he had lost a friend, a lover. He would never be whole again. A hard emotion, as he knew he was luckier than many who had died in the previous night's conflict.

A man near him had just quit kicking after minutes of holding spilled guts; not even the power of healing antidotes and multiple mages could stave off the reaper's grasp of that one's soul.

237

He looked back up at the nurse. "I am High Lord Sennin, ruler of this region, and my thoughts are clear enough. Though I appreciate your concern, Olivi." He stirred, trying to push himself into a seated position with his remaining arm. Before the healing mage could protest, he continued in a flat voice void of emotion. "And I should think I have a great many matters to attend to. Send me a runner. I need to call counsel while the sun still remains in the sky."

Olivi furrowed her brow and then nodded, but as she was beginning to turn in pursuit of a runner, he grabbed her arm and said, "After you fetch a runner, please return here, and tell me everything you know of the night after I was brought to you. And... Thank you... for saving my life."

He was proud of his steady voice and calm outward demeanor, for every fiber of his being urged him to rage at this woman for not saving the arm. He wanted to lay back. To cry and sob at the pain gripping his body, to give into the cold dread that crept into his mind, but instead, he allowed a soft smile to fall over his face, and he nodded appreciatively at the woman.

...

High Lord Sennin was being helped by General Earion, his one remaining arm slung over the shoulders of his most senior general for support on his weak legs. *I need to eat,* Sennin thought, though there was no time at the moment. It had been a very painful afternoon for Sennin. He learned from Olivi he had several compound fractures in the ribs beneath the shoulder that the heavy mace had obliterated. He learned that his leg opposite of the missing arm had been broken in three places where the enemy had trampled him before the Elites were able to push them back and rush him to the triage tent.

Thankfully, the healing mages had mended the leg fractures, but his brain had yet to register the mending and warned his body against placing excessive weight on the appendage. Most unsettling, he learned that the Bankhofts had nearly passed over the Elite's defenses on the wall's battlements when they suddenly pulled back and retreated down the wall just an hour before dawn broke.

They had regrouped their units, of which it appeared they didn't lose anywhere close to a crippling number, at the base of the massive sand dune in the distance once again. Apparently, they were content to have accomplished a strong show of force. To show they possessed overwhelming prowess over one of the strongest armies in all Divinoros.

Most of Sennin's army lived, but the fighting was brutal, and based on the body language and downtrodden looks of the soldiers he passed, it was clear they did not relish the opportunity to foray into battle with

238

the demented humans again. Even though the elves remained in control of Sandivar, the soldiers knew they lost the battle the previous evening. Had it not been for the enemy's tactical mistake of pulling back, Sennin's army would have likely been broken on the first night of the siege. Successfully sacking Sandivar in a single night... This was unheard of and Sennin struggled to grasp the reality of that fact.

Why didn't they push for a decisive victory?

Sennin was perturbed by the thought.

He wished to lay in ruin a majority of the day following his injury, but the sun moving slowly across the sky was a reminder, the ever-present ticking away the daylight. A countdown to unavoidable conflict. While breath passed in his chest, he remained High Lord, and he would defend his city and his subjects however he could.

General Earion informed Lord Sennin that a council of generals had already assembled in the war hall. They had been discussing their next move and how they needed to bolster defenses since dawn broke. Little in the way of effective decisions had been made. As he was half carried into the council chambers, Sennin heard a heated argument unfolding.

"General Straven," came a jeering, high-pitched voice belonging to General Quinn, "you mean to tell me you're scared of this human enemy? We should, what, surrender ourselves to the mercy of this Bankhoft thug? We need to attack! Press our advantage. Those cowards retreated after they breached the wall! They fear the full force of an elvish army! An army headed by Elites."

"You dare accuse me of cowardice?" roared back the deep voice of Straven. "I merely suggest that we were successful once already! We forced them back before they could take the walls. We need to bolster where we were weakest, rely on heavy artillery rather than bowmen, and stand. Our. Ground. Why risk more lives on the sands when we have proven successful staying here? We can hold out until reinforcements arrive."

Two other generals began to talk over one another, split on who they felt was correct between the angry Straven and Quinn. A number of junior captains were shouting in defense of their superiors, and the volume in the chamber rose to uncomfortable heights, setting Sennin's painful head ringing.

It was a scene of chaos and disorderly conduct, which was uncharacteristic of his carefully selected military leaders. Chaos is driven by fear of one's enemy. The enemy that was currently knocking at his gate had clearly succeeded in seeding fear. One junior officer, a human man, saw Sennin hobble in. Sennin freed himself of General Earion's support as he entered and before he could command his units to resume order, the young man turned smartly on one heel and smashed a gauntleted fist against his breastplate in a salute. The movement was

239

sharp and abrupt, and others took notice of the sound of metal clinging. Slowly, the rolling boil of argument stilled, and all members of the room saluted their leader in a similar fashion. Looks of amazement graced their faces, all clearly in disbelief as Sennin stood before them.

High Lord Sennin nodded to the room. He went to move his arm in a salute before he remembered the appendage was taken from him. "It is good to see you all care so much about our city, though I must warn you, your arguments are flawed. Both of you, General Quinn and Straven. We lost the battle yesterday. We were lucky the enemy seemed to fear significant loss to their number, for should they have wished to do so, they could have surely overrun us on the first night of this siege."

The room was quiet. "We have lost the first battle. Nearly lost our great city in a single night. We cannot afford to be divided amongst our own now. No, now is a time where unity must prevail lest we cease to exist in the nights to come."

All who now looked over the wreaked form of a once great warrior in High Lord Sennin nodded their subservience at his word, unwilling to issue a challenge to a man so wounded but finding the courage to still stand before them. Without a word, all parties who once shouted at one another retreated to their seats to rest.

Funny how a grueling and devastating injury could silence a room and garner respect. This lot has never been so swift to adhere to my desire for an orderly assemblage.

"Now, General Quinn brings up a fine point in my eyes. These miscreants, these warped visages of wicked power, have already succeeded once in scaling our walls, and I have no wish to watch them do so again." He saw the hulking elvish woman smile daggers at Straven. "However, the Queen and I had attacked these foes before when the Bankhoft family sacked The Oasis centuries ago. We lost thousands in the deserts outside the Badlands. I do not know how this man has obtained such power, but I do not wish to march our fine soldiers to the same fate as those we marched on the Badlands so many years ago… we will not be an army reduced to bits of flesh, to bits of bone, suspended in pools of blood in sands too saturated to drink anymore."

Looks of horror crossed the faces of those gathered. "I will not send any of you to die violently in the sands beyond these walls. Instead, we will fortify our defensive position. As General Straven noted, our arrows were useless. I do not know how, but these men seem to live through wounds enough to kill ten men. That said, our heavy ballistae bolts seemed to do some damage. Order your soldiers to line the tops of the battlements with our small catapults in between the mounted ballista as well. And I want every heavy artillery catapult to be set by sunset with teams ready to reload at each station. General Earion and General Quinn will take my place, manning the defenses at the top of the walls with their own Elites. Quinn, I want you to organize defensive formations along the battlements and formulate retreat points. General Straven, you will set up a defensive position inside the walls. Coordinate with General Quinn." The generals nodded their ascent.

"We may not prevail. We do not know the power this enemy possesses. So, as for the rest of you, I want the citizens evacuated. Assign your captains to assist the Naval Commander Isco and inform the populous. General Fronsei, you will travel with the citizens and a company of two hundred Elites. You will sail to Reef Ridge Port, seeking refuge. I will send word once this insurrection has been properly dealt with, with summons to return our citizens to their rightful homes. For now, you have till an hour before sunset to be out of the port. Tell citizens to take essentials only."

Sennin looked around at the sullen faces in the room. Some were wrought with fear, others hard with defiance, and some with a gleeful eagerness that Sennin found disturbing. "We edge toward a decisive moment in Sandivarian history. Let us go forth and write a tale of victory."

The assembled group stood, saluted, and set to busily fulfilling their tasks. Sennin requested that one of his servants take the place of Earion to help him move about, allowing Earion to oversee that his orders were carried out swiftly. But, in his current state, there was not much to do, so he hobbled out of the council room, through his grand palace, to the courtyard where his two sun dragons lay in the late afternoon beams.

As he approached, the dragons stood excitedly and shook their massive forms, scales clinking and refracting the sunlight into a brilliant array of colors. Sand sprayed from the crevasses of their scales, and the two bounded over towards the elf, toppling over one another as a couple of puppies might run toward their mother.

The High Lord smiled at their youthful exuberance as the female tackled the male from behind, causing the two powerful creatures to slide up to Sennin's feet in a tangled heap. Their fist-sized eyes stared up at him lovingly. Sennin laughed and scratched at the underside of the dragon's chin, who snorted in delight.

The two had grown significantly in the past months. They had been smaller than the Ghost's sand lion just months ago, but now were his equivalent in size, maybe larger, with far more bulk than the sand lion carried. Soon, they would be able to fly, then fire would follow, and if they were able to live long enough, they would one day possess far more wisdom than even he hoped to obtain in his extended lifetime.

It was sad that few escaped cruel hunting practices to live that long, but he hoped these two might be the exception. With a sigh, he settled himself in the sand beside the two and sat there for some time. There was nothing he could do by forcing himself into the middle of the preparations, weak as he was. He was now a crippled form and in his depressed state, believed he would only be a hindrance to those around him. *Better to remove myself*, he thought.

So, Sennin allowed himself a moment of solitude in the company of two creatures who had no more care in the world than a strong urge to please Sennin in hopes of winning more scratches than the other. Life was funny, thought the one-armed elf as he sat in the sand. He felt as if he could weep in sorrow, at his pain, at his limbless shoulder, at the death of his soldier, at the unimaginable force of the enemy now descending on him. But for a few short moments, the only thing that filled his heart was the knowledge that he had the unconditional love and affection of these two massive dragon younglings wriggling their bodies, attempting to lay their heads near him while their tails swished contentedly behind them.

Finally distracted from his wartime duties, Sennin drifted briefly to sleep only to fall into a horrific nightmare of his city under siege, the citizens being raped and slaughtered as the monsters under the Knifes' control pillaged and looted Sandivar, striping her of her former glory and civility.

The elf jolted upright. His servant was nowhere to be seen. The city was quiet, apart from where the fighting would take place, and shouts of orders echoed through the city emptied of its citizens. But Sennin smiled at the haunting silence, pleased his people were safe, off in the open sea.

The High Lord struggled to his feet, using the slumbering dragons for support as he pushed himself to an upright position. The sky was beginning to darken, and the High Lord assumed the attack from the Bankhofts would likely begin soon. He strode toward the city gates at a leisurely pace till a blood-curdling screech emanated from within the walls of Sandivar. The sound seemed to cause the air to reverberate around Sennin's ears. It was a powerful sound, powerful enough to wake the two slumbering dragons, who stood rapidly and immediately became warry. Their white scales, gleaming in the light of the rising moon and fading sun, stood on end, ruffling in anticipation of danger.

The sound was no scream a human could elicit, though those soon followed. Sennin furrowed his brow. He could hear no activity on the wall, and he couldn't understand why screams would rise from within the walls. "I must hurry. Ignore the pain. Help your people," Sennin told himself as he jogged toward the disturbance. The sun dragons who followed him comforted Sennin.

As they grew closer, Sennin realized they were approaching the triage tents. *There shouldn't be screams like that coming from here.* By the time they had reached the scene of chaos, things seemed to have settled slightly.

There was a massive crowd of soldiers and nurses surrounding a collapsed mound of black that was slowly wisping away into the dusk. The mound of darkness was a dead beast with three red eyes on each side of a massive triangular head. It had six legs, three to each side of its long torso, with a nasty-looking claw at the end of each powerful limb. At the end of its sleek black body, reminiscent of the material that made up the dark weapons the human army carried, a long, powerful tail twitched as the monster's final death throws rattled its body.

"What happened here?" Sennin demanded as he took in the site of the giant collapsed beast. The monster still had the top half of a human nurse in its vicious saw-like jaws. Torn pieces of flesh and armor stuck to its long claws.

General Straven stepped forward, "High Lord, this… well, whatever this is, just pulled itself from behind the triage tent where we've put our dead till we can bury them. We don't... We don't know where it came from."

Sennin took in the monster's appearance, and his skin went pale. "I think I have seen this beast before. Celestra showed me pictures of the creatures they slaughtered in the thousands during Omnes's assault. This is a krakenshi. This is one of the most feared creatures ever to walk our land. An agent of the Dark God. How the hell is this thing in our walls?" Sennin looked around for an answer. The fact that no one seemed to notice the two gleaming white sun dragons, now as tall at the shoulder as any elf present, was proof of the terror these monsters could seed in the minds of mortals.

General Earion's voice sounded from atop the battlements, "Ready the heavy artillery! Crossbows load and aim! I want these bastards slaughtered before they reach the godsdamn wall!" Soldiers began to bustle about, and General Straven moved his men into position. Sennin nodded to a number of soldiers nearby, indicating they would need to see to the disposal of the humans and elves killed by the krakenshi. Luckily, the black monstrosity started to dissipate as a black smoking liquid flowed from the wounds hacked into its hide.

One less thing to clean up.

Giant balls of flames began launching through the ever-darkening sky from atop the ramparts. Sharp twangs sounded as crossbowmen and ballistae loosed bolts at the general's orders. Sennin heard screams of burning men filling the sky from beyond the wall.

But before a smile crossed his face at the thought of the Bankhoft men burning under heavy artillery, another deafening shriek filled the night sky near the tirage center. Sennin turned to the source of the sound and felt bile rising in his throat at the sight. A man, or what was once a man, was attempting to crawl from the tent. His arms and legs scrabbled and went limp as his torso erupted to reveal a krakenshi pulling itself

243

free from his insides. Four more men fell to the floor of the triage tent behind him, violently seizing as long black limbs carved bloody paths to freedom through the sides of the squirming human and elvish bodies. It was the sight of horror, and the army nearby shrunk away from the site of these horrible creatures' gory birth. More than one soldier lost the contents of their stomach at the sight. Some even fled to the port, not remembering that it now stood void of ships.

Among them, only the sun dragons seemed not to fear the monsters. Both his dragons roared defiantly at the divine abominations, drowning out the high-pitched shrieks with a thundering roar. The male, Krino, didn't wait for any orders, and he sprang at the first krakenshi, now fully freed of its husk. The male dragon streaked across the open expanse in one bound, cratering into the monster with his ivory talons sinking deep into the side of the krakenshi, tearing the flesh of its form in great chunks.

The monster was not easily subdued, and it managed to roll with the pouncing dragon, somehow shaking itself free of him. Krino rolled in the midst of the seizing humans. More dead soldiers who passed from injuries suffered during the previous night's battle were now joining in the strange transformation.

Sennin feared that even the sun dragons would be unable to repel the number of krakenshi that were beginning to shake free their fleshy husks. Krino leaped back at the injured krakenshi, and the pair of giants rolled again, causing the very earth to shake around them as they tumbled between the city's buildings, collapsing walls and shattering carts with the fury of their fighting.

More than one bystander was crushed as the two giants wrestled. The dragon had managed to pin the six-legged fiend on its back, his front claw holding down four legs. Krino used his back claws to rake over and over again at the belly of the krakenshi, ripping chunks of dissipating flesh from the creature until an oozing black hole replaced the once-powerful abdomen. The struggling monster was rendered still. But by the time one was dead, six more had arisen. High Lord Sennin tried to call to the nearest soldiers hoping to organize the panicked soldiers into a unified front, but no one could hear him over the roar of dragons and shrill cries of the beasts they battled.

Both dragons fought against the rising swarm of krakenshi, and they were able to dispatch two more of the monsters quickly. Krino had bit through the neck of another dark form that rushed him while the female, Kiara, tore the arms off another with her own powerful claws. Three more krakenshi pulled free of their human shells.

Four monsters now rushed the dragons. Sennin couldn't take his eyes off the scene as dread filled him. There were simply too many. "My Lord, we must flee!" he heard his servant shouting from somewhere that sounded far away. As the servant grabbed and pulled on Sennin's arm,

244

begging him to flee, the High Lord shrugged him off. Sennin couldn't peel his eyes from the fray, from the fear that gripped his heart, seeing his beloved dragons fighting an insurmountable enemy. He was far too weak to be of any help in his crippled state.

Kiara slashed at one monster, scoring a deep wound along its side, but as she did, one of its brethren jumped on her back and used its six legs to cut and scratch at her tan leathery wings. She roared in anger and shook violently, attempting to break free. It held tight until the male tackled the beast from her back. Trails of scarlet blood flowed down Kiara's sides as she drew her lips back in a snarl. Krino held the tackled monster to the ground and tore out the beast's throat with his dagger-like teeth until the wriggling beast ceased his movements.

However, the bold move to save his sister left him vulnerable, and three krakenshi swarmed Krino, biting, clawing, and tearing at the dragon too fast for him to fend off the attackers. Kiara roared in frustration as two different beasts held her at bay, keeping her from springing to Krino's aid. At this point, soldiers had regained their composure and were forming a defensive line, but they were not fast enough to help the dragons.

Sennin fell to his knees, unable to breathe as Krino succumbed to the rabid onslaught. Sennin cried out in anguish as he tried to stand, to run to his dragon's aid despite his condition. But as he reached for his weapon with an arm that no longer existed, he knew he could make no difference in this fight. And so, he watched in horror, helpless, with tears streaming down his cheeks, as a sharp black claws slipped between the scales in Krino's shoulder. The male whimpered and collapsed beneath a tangle of dark limbs. The swarm of monsters did not relent, stabbing, biting, and clawing. A vicious frenzy as unnatural monsters tore into the hide of scales. Light whimpers and cries of pain carried clearly past the sounds of combat as the Krino struggled to break free from the hoard of monsters, bright blood painted over his white scaled frame.

Helplessness gripped Sennin's heart. He knew at this moment that the physical pain of a lost limb was a minor inconvenience when compared to the pain of witnessing his beloved dragon fall. "No! Get up, Krino! Run!" The dragon gave one last effort at the sound of his master's voice, striving with all his tremendous might to heed Sennin's words, but the muscles of the dragon gave out from under the hoard that attacked him. Small whimpers escaped the fray as the noble beast fell still. Dead at the hands of Omnes' minions.

Sennin felt breathless at the sight but managed another plea. "Kiara flea! Get out of here! Kiara, please! Run!" The words were filled with all the hurt and begging that he could muster. He had lost Krino, and he couldn't bear to lose another of his beloved companions, but fate seemed set on cruel intent that night.

Sennin started to tremble as four more krakenshi swarmed her. She tried to jump over the hoard, but a group of legs stretched out and grasped her hindquarters, pulling her back to the ground in a heavy thump. She screamed and struck out at the monsters ferociously, desperately. Her wondrous eyes locked with Sennin's, filled with fear and panic. A plea for help. As her eyes locked on Sennin's own, he felt his heart break. Sennin heard her cries slowly fade as she joined her brother in the heavens beyond.

All is lost. I have failed Sandivar. Failed Celestra. May the Gods see her through what is to come.

Looking away, he saw distorted human forms pushing back the guard on the battlements far above. He saw panic in the ranks of his army behind the great wall.

How could a power like this ever be defeated? The age of elf is over. We cannot contend with this, the High Lord thought hollowly. He watched countless elves being cut down atop the wall, pain and dread freezing him in place. He saw his men and women sheared into pieces by the krakenshi birthed within their walls. He saw his army fall, his city fall.

Then, a monstrous krakenshi approached him, six red eyes locked on his broken form, jaws oscillating with displays of power. White scales were stuck in its teeth. He closed his eyes. He was numb inside. Everything he loved had crumpled in minutes before his very eyes. Death now would be a mercy to him. And it was a mercy the power of Omens was happy to grant.

The last sensation in High Lord Sennin's decorated life was that of piercing teeth sinking into his skull. But before the bone gave way, Sennin exacted a feeble retribution for his lost companions. For his dead comrades. He harnessed the innate power within himself and released all the magic bound to his form in one concussive pulse that tore his body apart. A powerful explosion eviscerated everything near him, ripping through the krakenshi that gripped his skull and all that still picked at the corpses of Krino and Kiara.

Ryker - Chapter 31 - Lingering Flames

The next couple of days passed in a blur for Ryker. The morning started with physical training, beginning with a warm-up run of five miles at the first morning bell. Ryker now kept pace with the elf, though his exertion to maintain that pace seemed far greater than that which Aegnor was required to exert. The pair garnered plenty of curious eyes as they bounded down the streets of suspended village centers.

The run was followed by brutal combat training. Ryker was used to deflecting swords with his own longsword and lengthy dagger, but defending against an axe was a completely different style of combat. The heavy head of the weapon would gather far more momentum and force with each arching blow that Aegnor sent his way than a traditional sword strike. Each blow from the axe carried a massive impact that would jar his body to the core.

He lost the first few sparring sessions quickly, but by the end of the second day, Ryker fared as well against Agenor with an axe as he did against Aegnor with a blade. Which is to say, he could hold his ground for a respectable amount of time, making Aegnor defend or parry a few attacks of his own before the bout was ultimately lost to the elf by some new maneuver he had yet to demonstrate to the apprentice. In his training against a new weapon, he was pleased with how quickly he was able to adapt his fighting style. He found the advantage of weight and power behind the axe was also its greatest weakness. His faster movements and greater agility with a lighter weapon allowed Ryker a nimble fluidity to the fighting style he and Aegnor believed could allow him to prevail in the duel to come.

"The key," Aegnor would tell him, "is not to disrupt your opponent's momentum in full, or he will batter you to a pulp. Those who fight with axes try to flow one movement into the next. It is such a heavy weapon that quick changes in direction or restarting motion from a standstill causes your opponent to exert more energy; thus, they will tire out more quickly. You need to focus on impacting a series of strikes through careful deflection and avoidance."

Ryker was pleased with his performance against his master on the morning of the feast. He landed a couple of near blows that would have surely struck home on any opponent other than the great Aegnor while also avoiding nearly all of the potentially devastating impacts from the elf's powerful swings.

So, feeling confident in his ability and pleased with Ryker's proficiency, the pair went to wash up and dress for the evening's events. After cleaning up, they visited the stable to run Xantharyia and Maximus. If they thought the pair of them running was cause for attention, they were not prepared for the crowds a Ravanian could draw, much less two Ravanians as imposing as the palomino mare and all-black stallion.

The run for the horses ended up turning into a long walk as the streets clogged with dwarves pointing at the massive beasts rarely seen beneath the mountain. It didn't matter much to Ryker. He was only glad to spend more time with Xantharyia, petting her main as they patrolled through the streets. While they couldn't communicate directly, Ryker knew she was agitated at the lack of attention and limited exercise she had gotten the previous two days, evident in her tossing her mane at his patting and sideways glance given to her chosen rider. He vowed to be more attentive to the majestic steed during the remainder of their stay in the caverns.

The pair came to a stop when Aegnor suddenly pulled up his reins in a near panic. When Ryker glanced at the elf, he noticed that Aegnor had gone ghostly white. He looked terrified, though Ryker couldn't begin to guess at what he saw. He loosened his sword in its scabbard in response. Standing before the two horses, a small woman strode out from the crowd with a little girl and boy. She held one of the children's hands in each of her own. Behind her was a younger woman who looked to be attending the trio. None of the figures appeared to be a threat, and so Ryker re-sheathed his sword up to the hilt.

The beauty of both dwarven maidens took Ryker aback. The older of the two, clasping the children's hands, was tall for a dwarf and could nearly be mistaken for a human woman had it not been for the clear strength she possessed in her thick, muscled limbs. Despite the muscular figure, she still maintained a definite and striking feminine figure. The curves of her breast and hips were hugged by a tight-fitting black dress with a slit running partially up the right leg. A white wolf's cloak was draped over her shoulders, held on by a silver chain that clasped around her neck, reminiscent of King Thondor's garb. She had wavy ombre hair, just showing signs of grey streaks, that hung down to rest below her shoulders on the left side of her face, while the right side was pulled in a braid that wound along the side of her head before falling down her back to reveal a jawline that balanced strength and femininity beneath her flawless golden-brown skin. Ryker thought she must have been one of the most beautiful women he had ever seen, even amongst the elves.

The two children held a resemblance to the woman, undoubtedly her own. The younger of the two women, who trailed slightly behind the mother and children, looked vaguely familiar to Ryker as well. Her stature was slightly shorter than the older woman, more consistent with what he had come to expect from dwarven females, and lacked some of the built-up muscle of the black-dressed dwarf. Despite that, she was equally striking. A golden dress hugged her well-endowed body, and her

248

hips swung in mesmerizing rhythm from side to side as she stopped to stand beside the small boy in front of the horses.

Ryker found it difficult to take his eyes off her, and he felt his face beginning to blush once she noticed his gaze. She had a black wolf's pelt held in place by a golden chain partially covering the nape of her neck. Her face was slender, housing a pair of storm-gray eyes that contrasted beautifully against her jet-black hair. Her hair was wound into an intricate bun apart from two strands hanging down the sides of her face, framing her features.

A hush seemed to descend upon the gathered dwarves as Aegnor stiffly, slowly let himself down from the great black Ravanian. Not knowing what else to do, Ryker followed suit quickly dismounting Xantharyia. He did not know why he felt so nervous, but his stomach was tight with anticipation.

I wish Aegnor were not so wary. I seem to be feeding off his energy.

Aegnor strode to stand before the woman and bowed more deeply than Ryker had ever seen his master bow. He hadn't paid monarchs or High Lords this much respect.

As he stood, he spoke, and Ryker immediately understood his deference.

"Princess Zondra, I was not sure I would see you on this visit to the Caverns. Though I am glad our paths crossed. It… It is good to ahhh... That is to say, I am glad… I am glad to see you once again."

Ryker watched his master fumbling to get out a smooth sentence. He fought back the urge to chuckle as all the suave grace of the almighty Aegnor was washed away by the presence of this woman he had loved long ago.

Zondra smiled graciously, and in a voice smoother than the silk Aegnor donned, she responded, "It is good to see you as well, Aegnor. It has been centuries, has it not? Let me introduce you to my daughter Liara and my son Geron."

Aegnor gave a slight bow to each of the children, who giggled at the towering elf's gesture. "And this here is Princess Alreyia, my niece and Thondor's daughter. Alreyia, this is the only man who ever bested your father in a duel. As though I'm sure you've heard the tale from Thondor, I feel that the story may have been biased. I must correct the tale and let you know that the loss did not only come because of our King's bad footing. Aegnor just happens to be that good," she said with a slight smile on her face.

Aegnor bowed once more to Princess Alreyia, who stepped forth and spoke a sound that fell sweetly on Ryker's ears. "It is a pleasure to meet you, Aegnor. My father has told me much about your adventures, the feats you have managed, and the legendary duel between you both." She turned to face Ryker and spoke again. "And you must be someone

249

of great significance to be traveling with one such as this. Though I do not recognize you."

Ryker could discern her lack of affection for the human race from the contemptuous tone and sharp gaze she cast in his direction. Like elves, the dwarves believed themselves to be a superior species, though they never, as a people, held the same level of hostility toward humans as the elves did after the Year of Darkness. Strangely, though, her obvious dislike for him was now something that he subconsciously wanted to change, though he didn't know why.

Ryker now stepped forward, coming in line with his teacher and following his mentor's example by bowing deeply to both Princess Zondra and Alreyia. "My name is Ryker. I am not one of great importance. I come from a farm on the southern side of Stone Guard. It was lovely but not grand. I now travel with Aegnor, training as his apprentice."

Then he knelt in front of the children with a wave and smile. "And it is great to meet you as well, Liara and Geron. You must tell me the meaning of your names! I've never heard them before in Stone Guard." The little girl and boy smiled and giggled before starting to talk over one another, "My name comes from an old hero!", "And mine was passed down from grandmother! Some say it means", "Hey, I wasn't done telling him about mine!" the boy cut in.

Ryker laughed as the two struggled to get a word in and said, "Well, those sound like very strong names! I have a younger brother named Ayden back home. He must be turning eleven this year. Not much older than you two, I would imagine."

The little girl shouted, "I'm eight, and my little brother just turned six last week!"

Sensing that Aegnor wanted to speak to Zondra, Ryker tried to help his mentor get a little privacy. "Well, if it's okay with your mother, I would love to introduce you to my horse, Xantharyia. Aegnor's steed is called Maximus. I can even tell you the story of how I won Xantharyia's favor by fending off a pack of wolves in the plains of Ravenford!" The pair immediately began jumping up and down, shouting, "Yes! I want to pet her!" "Can I sit on her saddle?"

Princess Zondra smiled at Ryker and nodded, "Please and thank you Ryker." Then she said to her children, "Go on but listen to Ryker. I will be right here."

Ryker led the children away, leaving Aegnor in the presence of the two princesses. As he walked, he turned to find Alreyia eyeing him with a curious expression, though it seemed less hostile than before.

So, to pass the time for the next few minutes, Ryker played babysitter, showing the children the fittings on the saddle, where he would keep his sword and let them pet the mane and nose of the patient steeds, who seemed to understand they were in the presence of children and treated them gently.

He didn't mind the task. It was a nice moment of normalcy in a life that spiraled so far from his life on the farm that he wasn't sure if that part of him still existed. He had an apple he had intended to save for later, but he cut in two so the children could feed the horses for their good manners. Both Liara and Geron squealed with laughter and excitement when he placed the pair on Xantharyia's saddle. To the small dwarven children, Ryker imagined it must have felt as though they were flying through the air.

Taking the reins for Xantharyia and Maximus, he walked past the Princesses and Aegnor, saying he would take them on a short walk and return, with Zondra's permission. As he passed, Princess Alreyia grabbed Maximus's reins and offered to join him, allowing the former lovers a brief period of privacy before they would continue their separate ways.

Alreyia spoke first. "You seem good with the children."

Ryker shrugged, "I haven't seen Ayden, my youngest brother, or any of my family for well over half a year now, though it feels longer. These two remind me of him, still so joyous and carefree. There's something wonderful about the wealth of naivety that the young possess. I sometimes miss the ignorant bliss of youth. Allowing those older and wiser to deal with the world. It's sad that as you grow, the only payment accepted for knowledge seems to be the stores of naivety we are born with."

She nodded, and Ryker continued. "I miss being around Ayden for that reason. He had no fears or pressures weighing him down. Just unabated enthusiasm in everything we did together," he said, smiling at the princess.

She returned the smile before asking, "So you were close with your brother then?"

Ryker nodded. "With all of them, really. Jeb, the oldest, got sent up north a few years back to serve at the Hold, which was hard on the family. My mother and father got sent away soon after that, and we haven't had any communication with them for over a year—some errand or mission for High Lord Frenir. Those two departures really forced Declan, my second oldest brother, to take over the family farming operations and me... Well, I tried to keep what remained of the family acting like a family. We were inseparable until I left. I'm sure Dec and Ayden still are that way, but I can't wait till our travels take us back to Stone Guard. They won't believe how I've changed." Ryker was shocked to find himself telling her everything about himself. It was nice to talk to someone who at least seemed his age, though it was hard to tell when in the company of semi-mortal races.

251

The next five minutes passed in a blur as the pair chatted about small things, family, home cities, and how Ryker came to train with Aegnor. Soon enough, they were back where Princess Zondra and Aegnor stood, and he was sad to see his time with the princess ending.

Zondra smiled thanks to Ryker as he helped Laila and Geron from Xantharyia's saddle, returning the giddy pair back to their mother. Aegnor bowed once more, less grandiose than his first, to the princesses and bound back up upon the back of Maximus, turning the horse and walking away from the party with little of a farewell.

Ryker furrowed his brow at the sudden departure and said before following, "It was a pleasure to meet you both. I suppose I will be seeing you at the feast tonight. Princess Alreyia, I would be forever in your debt if you told your brother to go easy on me in the duel."

Alreyia laughed, "Oh, it won't matter what I say. He will come for your blood. But here's a tip. Protect your knees. He always seems to like going for those first."

Nienna - Chapter 32 - Old Wise Men

Nienna saw the coast come into view. The land mass was growing larger each time she was able to raise her head up and peer over the bow of the ship. Nienna had a love-hate relationship with the sea, and unfortunately for her, this trip was comprised of the latter. She had spent the better part of the last three days being sick or attempting to be sick as she hung over the ship's banister. Once nothing was left in her stomach, she hoped the nausea would abate, but her hope was to no avail as she dry-heaved nothing for hours on end.

A cruel trick the body plays at... Allowing one to be sick beyond the point of being empty.

Zarou, on the other hand... Well, she felt slightly foolish for worrying over how he would fare. Despite being born in the driest lands the eastern continent had to offer, despite Nienna's concern at having the large lion on a confined vessel, Zarou loved the sea. He spent every moment laying out in the sun or pouncing over the side of the ship into the cold ocean water to chase down fish that were too mobile in the clear blue channel for him to ever catch.

The sailors were wary of the lion at the beginning of their journey, but no longer. After days of Zarou watching them with fascinated eyes as they pulled in fish and crab traps, often trying to sneak a few of the sailors' catch for his own, they gradually grew fond of the great-scaled beast. By the third day, Nienna caught them tossing a fish or two toward the lion, only to cheer as Zarou snapped them from the air.

Currently, Nienna saw two men playing their new favorite game of keep away. They stood tossing a flailing sea bass back and forth over Zarou's head to taunt him. He let the game go on for a minute as he watched the bass sail overhead. His pupils expanded as his eyes tracked the fish with hungry intent. He wriggled back on his haunches, waiting to lunge for the delicious air-bound morsel. Then, with no warning, he jolted up quick as lightning, spearing the bass through with a razor-sharp claw. Before he even touched back down on the ship, he had pulled the fish into his mouth with enough time to contort his body to land silently on all four paws. The sailors roared with delight at the spectacle. Two of the men scratched behind his ear as they passed by, and Zarou rumbled, satisfied to be receiving so much attention. Nienna, despite her angry stomach, smiled at the scene, happy to be away from danger, away from death, even if just for a few days.

He deserves this... Can't help but think I'm dragging him into a war he needn't play any part in.

The boat soon docked at Veilenthia—a quaint fishing village nestled into a bay surrounded by the jagged peaks in the southwest portion of

253

the Perampla Mountains. The steep slopes met the ocean at a harsh angle, creating a beautiful fjord that protected the village from the harsh winds that could rage in the Aeronian Straights. The air was chilled, but the sun shone bright overhead. Its rays were working hard to break the cold grasp of winter and pull the region forward into a season of growth. The winter, in turn, struggled, unwilling to fully relent its hold just yet. A light morning frost still covered the town, reflecting the morning's rays off its surface to highlight the wide array of rainbow-colored houses of Veilenthia. Bright pinks, oranges, and yellows set against a white backdrop. Scattered splotches of dark green foliage poked through the frosty layer at random, adding bursts of life to the scenic village.

It's beautiful.

Due to the steep mountains, the primarily human city was required to be creative in its construction.

Amazing to see the ingenuity resulting in these people.

They seemed to be simple in many ways, small fish markets, shops, and people leisurely strolling between, but the stairs and harshly sloped paths carving their way from the small port and bustling markets to the peaks beyond the highest homes told a different story. At the top of the nearest peak, a distinct cathedral stood proud.

Incredible… How did they carry the stone to the top?

Nienna stood alongside Zarou, admiring the scene as they approached over the foamy sea crests. "Maybe one day we can find a nice place like this to settle in and relax. Live out our days in a quiet peace." She reached up and scratched behind the lion's ear, and he purred affectionately, reverberating the air around the fair elf, sending a tickle along her body with the vibration. "Well, you seem to like the idea." Zarou licked Nienna's arm as if agreeing to her terms, then nuzzled his head into her side, nearly toppling her over.

And just like that, the few days of relative peace were over. Nienna would have liked to explore the quaint town, but the Queen had been clear in her message, and more than that, Nienna knew she carried vital information that could swing the tides of imminent war that would soon crash with devastating effects on all mortal beings. So, after quickly refreshing in a small shop that sold tasty pastries and a fine dark caffeinated beverage, the pair were off. Nienna rode on the back of her great lion as he sprinted through the city toward a large mountain ravine at a blistering speed.

According to the Queen, the eastern gate of the tunnels that lead to the Great Marbled Caverns was only a quarter day's trip from the docks of Veilenthia, and once inside, their underground transit system could deposit her at the city's center in just a handful of hours. The information proved true. After finding the well-hidden gate, thanks to the help of Zarou's keen smell and her sharp eyes, the two were able to find a long

254

access tunnel that burrowed underground at a sharp angle for nearly a mile.

The large tunnel grew as it deepened, eventually reaching a height of nearly thirty feet. The path hit a dead end at what appeared to be a flat, polished basalt wall. But there was a pair of dwarves in rugged uniforms standing guard just before the impasse. After showing them Queen Celestra's seal, the guards slammed their fists on the thick stone wall in unison. The walls rose into the ceiling in response, allowing for her and Zarou to pass.

There must be powerful magic here. No living creature could lift such a wall.

The guards were short-tongued but helpful enough. She got directions to the transit system and was pleased to find the next tram would arrive shortly to give her direct passage to the center of the caverns. It had been some time since the elf had visited the grand dwarven kingdom and time had done little to dull the thrill that came with seeing the immense cavern city carved beneath a mountain. Entire townships suspended over vast darkness by great jeweled cables was astounding. The place gleamed brilliantly, being lit by a variety of colors of oil lamp torches. The unique colors reflected from the riches displayed everywhere caused the whole city to shine. She would need to present herself to King Thondor soon but finding Baelin and delivering this scripture and the Queen's letter was her priority.

She strode the city admiring its fine craftsmanship, and it turned out the dwarven people were equally impressed by her and her lion. The people's eyes went wide at the sight of the pair casually strolling through the city streets, boarding rail shuttles, and talking to passersby. She heard the people whispering. "Another guest on a beast of legend." "Can you believe our luck... Ravanians and Sand lions... I'll be damned." Nienna didn't think anything of the comments other than to note the oddity.

It didn't take too much effort to get an answer on the whereabouts of a dwarf named Baelin. People were keen to answer her, afraid that a failure to do so might result in them landing on the menu of the lion's afternoon snack. That, and the fact that Baelin was a quite famous dwarf.

He was known for his knowledge and mastery over all topics of history, from the time of the creation onward, and his grand contributions to philosophy and socioeconomic policy, not to mention the fact that many thought the old dwarf had gone mad in his old age. Mad and obsessed with the vanished Gods and their origins. Utterly consumed by a quest for knowledge that no longer existed in this world. Fame had long since passed Baelin by, and the people now laughed at the old dwarf for locking himself away in the city's Archive, toiling about the same text year after year, and getting no further in his studies.

One helpful young man, no older than twenty, shared a little gossip when she asked about directions to the Archives and where she would likely find this Baelin. Despite many thinking him mad for decades, a pair of visitors were also looking for the old dwarf just a couple of days back. Apparently, they were quite the odd pair: one human and one elf, each with massive horses as grand as Ravanians of legend. *That explains the whispers... I must ask Baelin who his visitors were.*

The young dwarf didn't know their names, but they must have been esteemed guests as there was a feast in their honor tonight. But the important thing, the boy told her, was they were believed to be seeking out Baelin in hopes of learning more about Omnes and the mysterious people who once sought to use his power for their own. Nienna shivered as her mind flashed back to the Knife standing just in front of her, grinning with black eyes. She knew exactly what people did with power like that. They murdered, destroyed, and tormented any who stood in their way. She was keen to seek these two out and understand their purpose for being here. But, alas, that would need to wait till the festivities later in the evening, and Baelin may be willing to part with his knowledge of who the guests were if he was familiar with her legend.

Nienna soon walked into the entryway of the Archives and instantly understood how someone could spend a lifetime within these walls. Books were held floor to ceiling in the grand expanse. It was impressive. Nienna sighed and said, "Well Z. How do you suppose we're going to find one dusty old dwarf amongst this hedge maze?" Zarou eyed her with one massive yellow eye, then turned his head and worked his way down the aisles laid out before them.

Dwarves scurried past; none were keen to speak to the intruders of their silent sanctuary. Nienna tried to catch a couple as they squirmed by the narrow passage to get around her lion, "Excuse me! Please could you..." but no one stopped to speak with her. All were too engaged in whatever manuscript, novel, or scroll they carried to bother with polite conversation, though they were happy enough to cast a meaningful glare as they passed.

Perturbed by the noise I am making, I presume. If someone would just talk to me I would be quiet!

Nienna and Zarou were beginning to cause quite the distraction, her shouting at dwarves for help and Zarou's scales scratching deep gouges into the sides of wooden bookshelves lining the narrow passages. "Ma'am! Excuse me! Ma'am!" came a shrill, upset voice from behind Nienna. She turned and found herself face to face with a small dwarven woman. She had long white hair that was braided neatly down her back and a pair of half-moon wire spectacles were hanging from the point of her nose.

256

Her head tilted down as she stared daggers into Nienna, her eyes just above the top of the wireframes. "This is a library, miss! These are the most famous archives in Divinoros! You *cannot* go around molesting our guests and shouting through the halls! I am afraid I am going to have to ask you to leave." The stubborn old woman emphasized her gesture by placing her hands on her hips and staring hard into Nienna's eyes.

Nienna nearly smiled at the scolding. It had been quite some time since anyone, even monarchs, dared talk to her in such a chastising tone. But in the Archives, it appeared as though this elderly woman was the master of her domain. "I am sorry to have caused such a disturbance. I am here on the order of Queen Celestra, who asked me to find a man named Baelin; she wanted me to deliver something. Once I have, I will leave, and I will do so quietly without causing another fuss. Could you help me?"

The old dwarf gave her a long look, weighing the options of helping them or attempting to beat them back to the entrance with a rolled scroll in her grip. Finally, and only after a long moment of consideration, she strode past Nienna at a brisk pace and said, "Very well, follow me." She wound them through the massive Archives, dodging in and out of the rows and rows of books. Nienna pondered how much knowledge was stored in this place and wondered how wise the people who spent their lives here must be.

But does knowing things make you wise? Or does knowing the right things at the right time and understanding how to use that knowledge make you wise? Do you need experience to truly understand something, or does reading accounts of an event give you the same insight? After all, it is easy to sit in a dark room and dream up fantasies of how societies should be and operate and how you should respond in certain situations, but it's another thing entirely to put those concepts into action.

The aged librarian suddenly stopped, tearing Nienna from her thoughts, and pointed down a long, dark hallway. "He is down that hallway in a small cove just past the line of books on the right." She then turned the wrinkled, shaking finger on Nienna. "No more disturbances out of you down here, you hear? If I catch wind of another complaint, I'll throw you out myself." She surprised Nienna then by giving not only the elf a knowing look of disapproval but also Zarou.

I like her, Nienna decided at that moment.

Nienna nodded her gratitude to the elderly woman. "Yes, Ma'am. We thank you for your help." Then she and Zarou strode down the narrow section to find an old man scratching notes into a journal as he read through a beaten book. He looked up in surprise to see her, and then his eyes darted to her lion, and they grew very wide. "Ummm, hello there. Is there something that I can help you with?"

Nienna sat down across the table from the old man, weary after her long day of travel. "You are Baelin. Yes?" The old dwarf nodded slowly. Nienna continued, "Great. Well, I hope I am not interrupting anything. I am here on request from Queen Celestra. You can relax; I am not here to harm you in any way. I am here to tell you a story. My story, the story of the Queen's battle on the frozen plains, and once we are done with that," she pulled out and waved the cursed manuscript at the dwarf. "I have a gift that I believe you will find intriguing given your recent, well maybe recent isn't the right word, let's call it your *current* field of study."

The dwarf raised a bushy eyebrow, clearly intrigued. He held up a finger indicating for her to pause, made a final note in his notepad, marked his page in the worn journal he had been reading, and sat back in his chair, folding his arms to give her his full attention. "How rare to have so many guests looking for me in such a short time. Well, my lady, you have captured my attention. Please go on."

And so, Nienna did. She told him of her experiences in the Sandivar, her encounter with the Bankhoft family in the ruins of the Badlands. She told him of her travels north, her passage through the Narrows. The strange "Gifted" that had assaulted her and her team of Elites. She told him of her mortally wounded companions and how their lives faded slowly, agonizingly, to death and darkness. How this death did not allow them to fade peacefully; instead, it enabled darkness to rip itself from their insides into the form of Omnes's hideous and cruel beasts of war. This was the story of the return, the rebirth, of the krakenshi into the land of Divinoros. She told him of her encounter with Celestra, how the Queen had written and confirmed the divine power of the dagger of Omnes's Obsidian Knight, and how that dagger must now be in the hands of a dangerous human.

Throughout the tale, Nienna was impressed by the old man's reticence. She could see the questions and excitement burning in his eyes. But he did not interrupt her tale, not even once. He listened, intent on understanding all she had to say, and waited until she finished before speaking. Finally, once Nienna had recanted her personal tale in full and recounted what Celestra had told her of the Second War, she pulled the linen covering off the text she carried. "And finally, Master Baelin, I have this text. The manuscript recovered from the heart of the Badlands, offered to me by the Knife himself. I have no idea what it says. I have looked through it countless times, but its contents refuse to be forthcoming with me. Celestra seems to think you will be the one to crack its code and reveal its secrets."

Baelin took the book but held Nienna's eye. His question knocked her off kilter for a moment. "What is your name?" the old man asked.

"I go by many. Most call me the Ghost. Though that is not the name my mother gave me," Nienna responded.

258

A knowing smile crossed the old dwarf's face. "Ahhhh yes, I figured as much. Not many would survive the trials you detailed today. You know I was visited by another elf just a couple of days back. Aegnor, who I believe you know quite well, based on the tales he has told me of you. He and I go way back, hundreds of years. I believe he and I became old friends before the pair of you ever met. He used to go on and on about his apprentice. I am glad I had lived long enough to finally meet her." The old elf opened the cover of the old text but continued his mutterings. "I am curious to see what his new apprentice goes on to do. It would be hard for him to match the talents you possess. Especially being a human."

Nienna stared blankly at the man, stunned. "Aegnor... Aegnor is here, and he has a new apprentice. I thought he would never teach another... So, he is the other visitor in the Marbled Caverns, then?"

Baelin smiled warmly back to the young woman. "Yes, he is here. You should attend the King's feast tonight. You will find them both there. King Thondor has not yet relinquished his grudge against your former teacher. He is setting up a contest of arms between his eldest son and the young apprentice Ryker. I assume his intent is to embarrass the boy, and Aegnor through him. I was planning to attend, but," he held up the text Nienna handed him and ran a hand over its cover, "I likely won't make it now. I need to spend some time with your gift here."

I need to talk to Aegnor, I don't really care to be in his company, but he might have insight on how to thwart the dark uprising.

Not only that, but Nienna still needed to see the Dwarven King. It was part of Celestra's request that she was to report what she knew in hopes of persuading Thondor to take up arms in alliance with the Queen. To send her men to help defend the southern border of Turenian and men to reinforce the Hold to the north. Plus, if Nienna was honest with herself, she was interested in seeing this new apprentice Aegnor took. It had been over a hundred years since she last spoke with the elf, and things had ended poorly between the two. On top of the shock of being in the same city as Aegnor, she was also slightly jealous that the silver-haired man had a new apprentice, a new block of clay to mold into a weapon of his own design.

"Perhaps I will attend," Nienna said with a grin.

Ryker - Chapter 33 - Golden Son

The banquet hall in King Thondor's castle was lined with tables along the perimeter, leaving a large open space in the center of the room. A throne was set up with a long table lined in front and smaller chairs placed to either side of the throne where the guests of honor and the King's family would be seated during the feast. The tables formed a vast space in the center of the room that would serve as the dance floor at traditional feasts, but tonight, the space would be used first for a duel.

The space was now bustling with the Elite class of the Marbled Caverns and important politicians. Men and women bobbed between groups of finely dressed aristocrats to exchange pleasantries. The men were garbed in extravagant dress mail, male dwarves rarely went anywhere without functional armor, and the ladies were in ornate dresses. Amongst the well-tailored gentry, the kitchen and serving staff buzzed through the crowd, filling tankards with fine ale as the night's guests enjoyed copious refreshments before the event. As the crowd grew more intoxicated, so did the frenzied energy and anticipation in the room grow until it reached a point where the excitement was nearly palpable.

An invite from King Thondor to join him in a feast was a great honor indeed, but to witness his first-born son, and heir to the throne, a position traditionally called the Golden Son in the caverns, duel the apprentice of the mythical Aegnor. That was something of a different magnitude.

Aegnor wore a fine silk tunic common to the elves, while Ryker was wearing armor that Aegnor had procured from a smithy he knew in the city. "Best metal worker Divinoros has to offer," Aegnor had told him after a tale of how the man had once repaired his armor after a run-in with an Ice Dragon. Ryker felt the part of an honored guest in his beautifully crafted but simple, lightweight breastplate set over a dark tunic. The plate was fitted tight to his form, inclusive of vambraces, grieves, and his helm currently tucked in the crux of his arm. Aegnor had told his apprentice that no human armor would be its equal. His shining greaves were placed over dark trousers, and his plated gloves were tucked into the sword belt that was secured around his waist.

Ryker recalled his visage in the StoneHouse's mirror before leaving. He looked formidable, dignified, and dangerous, resembling a young prince from fairy tales his mother used to tell. He was far different from the eighteen-year-old boy who had been a farm hand not long ago. Now, Aegnor steered Ryker through the hall, introducing the apprentice to the who's who of dwarven politics and decision-makers. All treated the elf with great respect, and most did the same to Ryker, wishing him luck in the upcoming contest.

The boisterous conversation, nearing a boiling frenzy, died down to a hushed whisper as the doors nearest the throne burst open. A jester walked out and called out, "King Thondor and his family grace you with their presence. Kneel before your King!"

The hall dropped to a knee, each man and woman bowing their heads in respect as King Thondor breached the doorway. Ryker was about to follow suit when he felt Aegnor's arm reach out and suspend his apprentice by the upper arm. In a low voice, he stated, "I remind you. You bow to no man. No woman. Not any longer, Ryker. Not since you decided to study under me." Ryker did not respond but straightened up and stood in a stiff parade rest, hands clasped behind his back, as he watched the group of dwarves approach.

King Thondor walked at the head of the party. He wore an elegant golden tunic trimmed in vibrant emerald green. His shoulders donned the black wolf's pelt, which was the symbol of the Thondor family. On his arm, a short, rather masculine, dwarven woman walked. She was handsome but not traditionally beautiful. A smaller black wolf pelt was draped over the broad shoulders her emerald dress failed to cover, and a simple, elegant golden crown rested upon her head. They were followed by Princess Alreyia, who held the hands of Leila and Geron. She looked ravishing in a thinly strapped emerald dress that hugged her body in tasteful fashion. The slit in her dress revealed a toned leg with every other step she took. Ryker smiled at her and was elated to see her gaze linger on him before she winked and looked away, a small smile touching her lips.

Next in line was Princess Zondra looking as stunning as she had in their previous run-in. The man next to her was a brute of a dwarf. He was larger than King Thondor, and each step he took sent a violent noise through the chamber. His wavy black hair fell to his shoulders, and his unruly beard was forced into a braid that hung to his belly. His furious gaze, filled with known resentment, bore down on Aegnor, who returned the stare, his expression remaining unconcerned. Ryker could see the man growing red with rage as Aegnor refused to be intimidated by the boar of a dwarf. The dwarf finally broke his gaze when Princess Zondra caught his midsection with her elbow and muttered something in his ear before steering the burly man toward the table stretched to the sides of the throne.

The party was seated, and the guests stumbled to follow suit. Once the hall had settled, King Thondor stood and strode out to the center of the banquet hall.

His voice boomed through the silent hall. "Good men and women of the Caverns, it is a joy to be in your company this eve." Thondor lifted his arms as he addressed the crowd. "We have esteemed guests amongst us tonight. The legendary Aegnor, the elf who spared my life so long ago in the war between elves and dwarves, and with him a human apprentice, a young man by the name of Ryker... A simple farm hand, I am told." King Thondor turned slowly as he spoke, but now his gaze fell upon Ryker, "I do not believe this. There is something more to the boy, I believe."

He lowered his voice to speak directly to the human apprentice. "Aegnor wouldn't waste his time with you if you had no potential." Thondor then resumed his speech, "And so, tonight, we shall see what makes this human so special. Aegnor has agreed that his apprentice will duel for us tonight." Small claps came from the audience. "And the man Ryker is to face is none other than your Golden Son!"

The crowd broke into a chant at the words, "Thonir!", "Thonir!", "Thonir!"

Aegnor leaned into his apprentice, "When Prince Thonir enters, do not shy from his gaze. When the fight begins, remember your training and fight without mercy. Play into their assumption of you. You're a simple man with a simple background, still unschooled in the way of the sword. The less he thinks of your ability the easier it will be to slip within his guard."

"Prince Thonir!" boomed the Dwarven King, swinging one outstretched arm back to the door he had previously marched through. A bear-like dwarf, standing as high as Ryker's chest and as wide as a horse, burst through the doorway. The man was covered in a gleaming gold plate sitting over silver mail. His golden greaves and golden boots set off a barrage of thunder with each step, drowning out the applause from the spectators who now stood and cheered.

The man's dark eyes were fixed on Ryker, filled with a fire of a singular purpose, a purpose of pulverizing a foe that stained his family's esteemed reputation. He finally came to stand two paces in front of Ryker after circling the room to bask in the applause of his kinsman. The apprentice refused to break Thonir's gaze, though he started to question Aegnor's judgment. The dwarf prince that stood before him looked like a hardened man who had seen combat. His dark hair, already dampened with sweat, was matted to his forehead. His rageful eyes sat above a large, flat nose, clearly having suffered more than one break from being smashed repeatedly. A large scar ran up his neck to the back of his left ear, and another thin pale line broke the hairline above his left eye continuing to beneath his eye socket, where a blade must have nearly claimed his eye, and on the right side of his head, his ear was swollen like cauliflower with unnatural knobs of cartilage pressing tension against the skin, signs of frequent grappling.

This Prince Thonir was clearly no stranger to battle, conflict, or fighting. Given he was the firstborn son of a dwarf who was hundreds of years old, he was likely practicing with an axe before Ryker's parents had even been born. He doubted there was any likelihood of succeeding in this contest. Despite that fact, he didn't want to let Aegnor down.

I was raised in the palms of hard physical labor and had grown under the tutelage of the most famous living being on Divinoros. Maybe... Who am I kidding... I stand no chance here.

"Now," the King roared, walking around the trio of elf, human, and dwarf who stood at the center of the cleared space, "tonight's contest will take place with dulled blades. The victor will be decided in a best of three bouts, ending each round with either a killing blow, as ruled by the judges, or severe injury."

As he spoke, four black-robed figures took place in the corners of the staged arena. "Our life mages here will be working to disable struck limbs during each bout and to repair any fatal wounds. Should they have adequate time to treat the combatant, of course. Now, men, bring out your chosen weapons."

The Golden Son reached behind his head and pulled loose a massive two-handed battle axe. The weapon's handle was a twisted wooden limb polished to a shine. The shaft alone reached nearly twice as long as Ryker's blade. Strange runes of silver were implanted along the shaft, no doubt reinforcing the wooden handle with magic. Ryker doubted that he would be able to cut through the handle, and, as such, he discarded the idea, knowing it would not be a viable strategy.

The head of the axe was single-sided and shaped like the curve of a crescent moon. The blade was a superbly designed silver piece with the edge lined in gold to match the man's armor. Just like the haft, the head of the weapon was inlaid with runes to ensure no damage would befall the blade while it was wielded.

Ryker was suitably impressed as he unsheathed his rather dull-looking longsword. Despite its simple appearance, Ryker knew the craftsmanship that went into his blade made it the equal of any weapon the dwarven royalty would carry. The master who designed his weapon simply preferred to maintain anonymity in his work, so it was absent of signature markings or elaborate embellishments. In Ryker's left hand, he unsheathed a dagger nearly a foot and a half in length. He had determined that in a fight like this, the force from a blow of the axe from someone like Thonir would shatter most shields instantly, maybe even his arm beneath, and so he opted to hold weapons in each hand.

His only chance at winning the day would be to use speed and sudden movement to get within the dwarves' guard.

Once the weapons were unveiled, one of the mages stepped forward and cast a spell as he ran his fingers along the sharp edges of each presented weapon. The air around the edges of the weapons seemed to condense into a slim, slightly visible, but transparent barrier that ran along the blade's length. Puzzled, he drew his dagger across his left

263

forearm, amazed to see that the blade felt dull. It dragged over his skin harmlessly, not leaving so much as a mark. Then his hand below the cut went numb, and his sword clattered to the stone floor.

The audience laughed as a mage waved a hand toward Ryker. He felt the feeling in his hand return instantly. He flexed his fingers into a fist, testing there were no further restrictions, then led to grab a sword. "So, that's what you meant by struck limbs would be *disabled*. Strange feeling… This is going to be fun." Ryker said as he flashed a grin toward the Dwarf King.

King Thondor nodded with a smile toward Ryker and then called to Aegnor, "Come almighty Aegnor, let us be seated to watch what should be a grand contest."

Aegnor walked past Ryker toward the seats near the King's throne and muttered a last piece of advice to his apprentice, "Remember the blades are dulled, but a heavy weapon like that could still club your brains in. Keep your guard up. Move with intention and move with speed."

The pair retired to their seats, the King's place in the center of the room supplanted by a jester who would be calling the match and scoring points. Ryker whipped his longsword in circular motions, allowing his wrist and forearm tendons to stretch and loosen. He was surprised by how excited he felt. Nervous undoubtedly, but he looked forward to testing his skill against an opponent at least partially less deadly than his master.

"Contestants take your places," the court jester called. Ryker and the Golden Son circled one another till the dwarf faced the King and Aegnor, and Ryker faced the main doors leading into the massive room. The jester looked toward the dwarf. "Are you ready?" the golden man nodded in affirmation and snarled in rage, swinging the massive axe about his body with surprising velocity and grace. As the jester turned to Ryker, he noticed a cloaked figure, a little taller than himself, slipping in the double doors at the back of the hall unnoticed by most of the feast's patrons.

The figure wore a black cloak, and despite having the hood pulled up to mask her face, it was evident to Ryker that the grace and fluidity that the stranger moved with marked her as a woman. Before the doors shut behind her, a slight hand caught the edge of the hood, pulling the garment back to reveal the figure beneath, which proved Ryker's assumption.

Blonde hair tumbled down the woman's back and over her shoulder, reaching the deep violet tunic she wore beneath. Oddly, Ryker thought he saw she wore pants, which is not customary for any woman at a social event such as this. Ryker was awestruck by the woman's beauty despite little attempt to show it off. Her eyes were as blue as a clear summer sky, larger than ordinary, and just as pleasant to behold as it was to sit outside on a cloudless day.

The swirling pools of color seemed almost feline in nature, sitting above sharp cheekbones and an angular face. Her brows were thinner than most humans, giving her the visage of an elf, though she was far fairer than even his traveling companion was. Her gaze quickly shifted across the room before falling on him. He didn't know why, but he felt his mouth go instantly dry, and the nerves he was already feeling from the upcoming duel seemed to strengthen tenfold.

Why is it that a beautiful woman's gaze on me sends me into more of a panic than squaring off against the most dangerous elf in the world for daily sparring sessions, being hunted by wolves, or even charging down bandits?

Ryker didn't realize he was lost in his own thoughts until the jester clapped in front of his face.

"Human. Are you listening?" the jester's voice rang in the apprentice's ear, drawing him from his own mind and pulling his gaze back to his present task. "Are you ready, apprentice Ryker?" the jester repeated. Ryker bounced up and down on his toes a couple of times before nodding his head. "Then begin!"

The crowd burst into an instant uproar as Thonir took one step toward the apprentice before quickly closing on Ryker with his axe held high above his head. He moved with a suddenness and speed Ryker wouldn't have thought the compact dwarf to be capable of. But he was, of course, anticipating a furious offensive onslaught from the dwarf early on if his battle rage was anything to gauge by.

Ryker cleanly pirouetted to the side as the blade of the axe whistled just inches from his ear. As he spun, he brought his sword around in a long arching backhanded swing. He aimed where he thought the dwarf's neck would be, hoping to bring a quick end to the initial round of the duel. But Thonir was too fast and unpredictable in his movements.

Instead of standing in place as his axe clanged into the stone floor, a blow that gouged a large chunk of rock from it, the dwarf continued his forward momentum. Thonir rolled away from the apprentice's rebuttal strike, managing to stay below the backhanded sword swipe. Once he regained his feet, he let no time pass before he launched back into a full offensive.

The Golden Son displayed his decades of training with his complex fighting style and the ability to use the momentum of his weapons to propel his subsequent attacks. The axe head swung horizontally, and Ryker jumped back, narrowly avoiding a collision between a fast-moving blade head and his ribs.

That would have surely broken my armor and shattered my ribs.

Thonir allowed the momentum of the blade to whip himself closer to Ryker. As his bear-like body bore down on the apprentice, the Golden Son choked up on the shaft of his axe and slammed the butt of the weapon into Ryker's gut, just beneath the chest plate. The blow landed solidly, and a grunt escaped Ryker as the air rushed from his lungs in a hurry. He stumbled backward, now fighting desperately to avoid the onslaught of attacks. Thonir continued to hurtle his way. He gave the human no quarter, no reprieve, no mercy.

Ryker knew this first round was favoring the dwarf. He had spent the entire bout defending and dodging. He needed to press an offensive, but he was struggling to get within the reach of the mighty axe that continually swung at him from different angles. The weapon's length was effective at keeping Ryker too far to truly threaten the dwarf in any way with his longsword or dagger.

Think, Ryker. I need to break his guard.

The apprentice saw the dwarf readying himself for another powerful overhead swing. In anticipation, Ryker reversed his retreat and stepped forward, crossing his dagger behind the longsword. As Thonir brought the axe down, the apprentice caught the blow against his sword, cutting all of the Golden Son's momentum. With a massive effort, he threw the axe to the side but, in doing so, lost his left-handed grip on the dagger. The smaller blade clattered to the floor. Ryker didn't attempt to recover the dropped blade, knowing he could not waste the opportunity of curbing the dwarf's momentum, and instead let the clanging metal serve as an effective distraction.

Your entire being is a weapon. Fight voraciously. Unpredictably.

He balled his now freed-up gauntleted hand into a fist and furiously smashed the dwarf in the face with his left hand. He saw the surprise in the dwarf's eyes with the first punch; he felt the bone of his opponent's nose crack with the second blow of his bloodied grieve, and after the third, the dwarf finally stumbled backward, dazed.

Blood streamed down the Golden Son's face, dark red pouring like a faucet from the man's nose. Ryker shuddered as a crazed expression overtook the man, and a red smile formed beneath the crooked nose and bloodied mustache. "Alright, boy," the dwarf spat bloody spray into the air with each word, "looks like this will be more fun than I thought!"

Ryker nodded, "Come on, you oaf, I've got some more for you."

He was underestimating me. That advantage is fading now.

The dwarf came at Ryker once again, but this time, he wielded his axe more like a staff, using each end to rain blows down on the apprentice. Ryker parried with his longsword, but not having a weapon in his left hand was a severe disadvantage against the powerful strikes of a heavy axe. Soon, the head of the axe cracked into Ryker's knee, and he collapsed as the lower portion of his leg ceased to function, and pain flooded his mind from his crushed kneecap. The loss of function startled him nearly as much as the pain, leaving him defenseless to the next powerful blow that caught him in the ribs.

He heard a sickening crunch as at least three ribs broke on impact beneath the plate. Ryker's eyes welled with tears as he gasped. *Shit. Aegnor didn't lie. A dulled blade can still hurt.*

The crowd was in an uproar at the electric first round of the contest, taking up chants of the dwarven prince's name. Most, it seemed, thought Ryker would be defeated quickly and easily, seeing as he was just a young human. They were glad to be proven wrong and get some true entertainment before their meal.

One of the mages approached Ryker. "Allow me," was all the shrouded dwarf said as he placed the tips of his fingers, one hand against Ryker's damaged ribs and one against his knee. He muttered something resembling gibberish to Ryker, and then a strange feeling of something crawling under his skin tickled his nerves as his bones wove back together. The apprentice did his best not to squirm and shriek out at the odd, uncomfortable sensation. Soon, the feeling faded, and Ryker stood up, still panting.

He could see that Prince Thonir was already standing in his starting place. Another of the mages present had healed his nose, though nothing was done to wipe the blood that still stained the bottom half of his face. Ryker looked to his master as he stood to resume the fight, hoping for instruction, but Aegnor was engaged in conversation with the mysterious woman who had snuck in just before the duel had begun. The she-elf had her arms crossed and her lips pressed in a thin line. It seemed almost as if the pair knew one another; there were no introductions, and it was clear there was no love between them. He made a mental note to check into this stranger once he had finished his role in the night's entertainment.

"Round one will go to the Golden Son," the jester yelled, and the crowd of dwarves cheered louder.

"You fight well for a human, boy," the Prince called as Ryker began toward his place. Despite the words, there was no smile on his face.

"Well, I've had good teachers, your highness. I can't help that I wasn't born into an immortal race. And you should be careful now. You don't want this room to remember a *boy* wiping the floor with you after this next round." Ryker said this last piece, grinning.

Prince Thonir laughed at Ryker's insult. Princess Alreyia also seemed to have heard, covering her face to hide her chuckle as her eyes looked over the human she had met just days ago.

The court jester confirmed the combatants were once again ready before shouting, "Begin!" It was now Ryker's turn to jump into attack and see how the Golden Son handled a full offensive. Before Thonir had a chance to build momentum in his weapon, Ryker jumped forward with three quick stabs of his longsword that forced the Golden Son into a defensive stance.

He was able to successfully perry each of the blows with the haft of his axe, but Ryker followed that up with a slash intended to cleave a man from collarbone to hip. Thonir was forced to raise his axe overhead to intercept the blow. As the sword was blocked, Ryker stepped in close and jammed his knife up into the now-exposed armpit of the dwarf in what would surely be a killing move. The Prince reacted surprisingly quickly. He rotated his body away from the dagger strike, causing the blade to miss the apprentice's targeted area.

Still, the point of the dagger caught the back of Thonir's tricep, and the prince emitted a grunting sound as the mage's magic went to work, inflicting pain and immobility at the sight of the would-be wound.

Ryker was fueled by the minor success, and energy welled up inside him. He continued his attack in earnest, wielding the dagger and the sword with breathtaking speed.

He dropped in and out of different fighting styles with fluidly and without thought. He struck out at the dwarf with every part of his body, from weapons to feet, knees, and fists. The coordinated randomness kept the Prince guessing where and how he would strike next. It was as if each limb operated independently but in harmony. Prince Thonir was a formidable fighter, though, and he managed to evade most of Ryker's attacks, even finding small openings of his own to press against his challenger despite his wounded tricep.

Every member of the crowd was riotous, cheering in shocked awe at the prowess of the dancing human moving with feline grace and the bearish Prince more than equal to his challenge. Gasps and sharp intakes of air resounded through the hall, evidencing the audience's delight. Ryker caught a glimpse of his master watching from the corner of his eye. Aegnor's head nodded his approval of his young protégé.

The strange woman sat between Aegnor and the King, with her arms crossed and eyes fixed on the pair dueling. Ryker thought she might be the only person in the audience who seemed disinterested in the outcome of the bout, a look of boredom plain on her face. He again wondered what brought her here.

His momentary distraction allowed Thonir's heavy axe head to slip under Ryker's sword. The blade crunched heavily into Ryker's shin. The bone didn't break, but the mage's magic was instantaneous. His left leg went numb and useless below the impact while a searing pain at the point of contact dropped Ryker to one knee. The dwarf's face contorted into a vicious smile.

Knowing he had secured his second and final point, he leveled the axe at the apprentice's head, but before the weapon reached him, Ryker let go of his sword and used his one good leg to spring at the dwarf. He caught the Golden Son by surprise, and Prince Thonir fell back hard to the marble floor. His armor rang loudly throughout the banquet hall. Ryker landed on top of the disgruntled dwarf and quickly dragged his dulled dagger blade across Thonir's throat. The dwarf went limp as magic disabled his body.

"Round two goes to the challenger. Apprentice Ryker," the jester called.

Silence throughout the hall. But only for a moment. Loud boos and shouts of surprise and anger rang from the dwarven crowd. "Cheap tactics...Tackling! In a duel!" "That passed for a clean point?" "This isn't a grappling exercise. Take the point away."

Ryker paid them no mind, however. Aegnor had schooled two lessons deep into the apprentice's mind. One, avoid fighting whenever you can, for a single unintended misstep or malfunctioning of equipment can mean death at the hands of even the most novice of foes. Secondly, if you are in a fight, use every method in your arsenal to win. There is no consolation prize in a contest of blades. All the loser receives is death. Not only that, but as a human, Ryker was at a physical disadvantage against nearly every other race on Divinoros. He didn't have the luxury of always fighting clean.

As the mages tended to Thonir and himself, Ryker caught Princess Alreyia's gaze. She quirked an eyebrow at him, a small smile on her face as she clapped. She mouthed, *Well done. I am impressed.* Ryker smiled before his gaze passed over the mysterious elf woman who stared at him with a scowl of slight disappointment. No, it wasn't a look of disappointment, just dislike.

Aegnor waved him over for a quick word. As he approached, Ryker did his best to avoid returning the stare of the woman directly to his side. Aegnor offered no introductions. "Well done. You seem close to entering the state of mind we've been working on. Do not allow distractions. I saw you gazing this way during that round. In the third, do not let your concentration falter. See if you can end him quickly. Remember, constant vigilance to what lies before you can allow you to turn the situation to your advantage. The Golden Son appears to be ready now."

Ryker turned back to the main portion of the square. His breathing was heavy, and he saw the massive chest of the Prince's plate moving up and down as he sucked down air as well. "The third round begins now!" the jester called. As soon as the words left his lips, Thonir charged. Ryker watched the man rush him and felt his mind quickly distinguish how he would attack based on the previous rounds.

Thonir is rage personified in battle. He will attempt to cut you shoulder to hip.

Sure enough, Ryker watched the axe blade move up through the charge as the Prince readied himself to bring the full weight of the massive weapon on an opponent who would struggle to perry. Ryker's mind raced through his body, held still.

Don't fight directly against a far stronger foe. Flow around, be untouchable, flexible, like air.

Ryker knew his next move would be to spin to his left around the swipe of the axe head. The move would place him behind the raging dwarf. But he'd done that before and the Golden Son easily recovered.

He moves too quickly for his weight. Drag your leg behind the spin. Entangle him with your own.

Prince Thonir was nearly on him now, the blade gleaming toward his left shoulder.

Ryker rotated around the blade at the last minute but allowed his leg to drag behind him.

He will fall. But don't let him hit the floor before he's cut down or he'll roll to a standing position. Bring your sword around to the back of his neck.

Ryker heard the axe head cut into the stone floor, followed by a surprised grunt as the dwarves' greaves caught against Ryker's leg that had been kicked out.

Ryker's sword was already in motion. The blade missed its intended target; he was used to attacking a much taller opponent. Ryker watched in annoyance as the blade rang the top of the dwarf's helm. The blow clearly dazed the Prince, who spun wildly around, bringing his weapon level at Ryker's head.

Do not relent. Press your advantage. He is dazed. Feint a parry, then duck the blow. Bring your dagger against the knee as you pivot behind him.

The axe sailed overhead as Ryker tucked his sword and struck with the dagger again, shifting his positioning to come up behind the dwarf.

Drop the dagger and grab his collar.

Ryker moved with perfect timing, claiming a fist full of mail at the back of Thonir's sweaty neck.

Pull him on his back. Look out for a flailing axe swing.

Ryker yanked the Prince hard, and with one leg ruined, he toppled backward, lashing out wildly toward Ryker as he fell. Ryker was ready for this, though, having seen the move play out in his mind.

Ryker calmly evaded the strike before hacking his own steel into the golden vambraces on Prince Thonir's arms. His axe rang loudly as it clattered across the stone floor.

Finally, claim victory. Sword to neck.

Ryker saw the point of his sword resting lightly against the small area of the exposed neck just above Prince Thonir's collarbone.

"I submit," the dwarf growled. After hearing the admitted defeat, Ryker stepped back away from the dwarf.

The hall was silent. No boos or shouts of defiance at the result of the third and final round. Victory was swift. Calculated. In Ryker's mind, he had seen multiple scenarios but picked out the most likely as the fight began, following his intuition. It felt as though he had spent hours thinking through each step of the fight and how best to handle his adversary.

The final round was over in less than three full seconds. Ryker, an apprentice to Aegnor for under a year and a human to boot, had just defeated in a best-of-three contest one of the world's most skilled combatants. One who had been practicing with the axe decades before Ryker's mother bore him into this world.

This was a great victory for me despite the fact that he underestimated my ability. In a true battle, only the first round matters.

Prince Thonir slowly got to his feet. As he turned to face Ryker, a massive grin broke out across his face as he rushed toward the man again. Ryker almost flinched away, but Prince Thonir merely held out his gauntleted arm and clasped Ryker's forearm in a vice-like grip.

"What a duel! My boy, what a duel! You're far quicker than I expected you to be. You fight like one of those damned elves." Gesturing to Aegnor and the female. "Just have some of that human cleverness to you that keeps an enemy surprised by your tactics! Do not leave this kingdom without telling me where you head. We must duel again. Train together even!"

The silence of the spectators was shattered as Aegnor stood in applause, spurring a rolling cheer that built up in the hall till the noise was louder than a raging hurricane. "I would enjoy that, Prince Thonir. I believe I was lucky today, and I'd like the chance to beat you again. And don't be too disheartened by the loss... Remember, I am young and spry compared to you. Never had much of a chance, did you?" Ryker gave the man a smile at the ribbing.

Thonir merely laughed and slammed his meaty paw on Ryker's back, shaking his head. He walked from the center of the ring, cursing, "Damn fleet-footed fighters."

Ryker dared a glance at King Thondor and was surprised to see a lack of malevolence in his gaze, an emotion, he supposed, the enthusiasm of the King's son dissuaded. Instead, curiosity and intrigue were clear on his face.

Ryker - Chapter 34 - Living Legends

Following the contest, Ryker was approached by many who congratulated him on a riveting victory. He simply nodded and smiled as he waded through the crowd toward Aegnor.

His path was intercepted by the dwarven Princess Alreyia, who managed to capture his full attention. She had a teasing smile on her face as she curtsied and then playfully held out her hand. "My Lord, may I, after such a thrilling contest, present you to the almighty Aegnor of the elves and Thondor the great King of dwarves."

Ryker chuckled but played into her bit and bowed low. "Why yes, my Lady, that would be most exquisite." He bowed and kissed the back of her hand. "I do hope you enjoyed the entertainment this eve." Ryker held out his arm to the Princess, who reached out with her own, resting her hand within the crux of his elbow as the two strode toward the King's throne chair.

He enjoyed the Princess's company. He did not know how old she was; she could be decades older than him, but she seemed to act and think more like he did when compared to the likes of his traveling partner, Aegnor, and the other nearly immortal company he'd kept on his travels.

As they approached the King and infamous elf, Alreyia leaned in close to Ryker. "Any idea who that woman with them is?"

Ryker shook his head. "No. I expect we are both about to find out."

"I wonder if those two ever, well, you know?" Princess Alreyia commented. Ryker raised an eyebrow as he glanced at the princess, a look of surprise on his face. "What are you looking at me like that for?! Come now, you can see it, can't you!? There is a tangible tension between the pair."

"Princess! I am afraid this gossip isn't very ladylike of you," Ryker teased.

"Well," Alreyia said, shrugging her shoulders coyly. "She is breathtakingly beautiful... and I mean Aegnor... Who would mind if that man tried to court them? I couldn't say I would be offended by his advances."

The apprentice laughed at that. "Aegnor? Really? You know he is a bit of an old man... coming up on a thousand years soon enough. Won't be long until he is as gray and wrinkled as a sixty-year-old human." The princess laughed at that as they neared the trio before presenting Ryker in grand fashion.

"My Lord, m'Lady, and my King, behold! This evening's champion, and dare I say, the champion of all our hearts. Humble apprentice Ryker, once a simple farmer, has soared far above his station, despite all odds, and bested one of the mightiest warriors in the Marbled Caverns. I now present him to you." The princess voiced in courtly tones before an exaggerated curtsy.

King Thondor's brow furrowed at the speech and mocking lavish display from his daughter, but he managed to choke out a brief congratulations. Ryker nearly started laughing as he saw his mentor struggling to contain a grin that graced his face at the expense of the dwarven King's pride.

Aegnor stepped forward and placed a hand on his apprentice's shoulder. "The final round was adequate, Ryker. However, there are areas in which you must improve immensely. We must fine-tune your battle state. We need to make it easier, more natural, for you to access your cognitive haven."

The strange elf woman never took her eyes off Ryker during the congratulations. Finally, close enough to see her clearly, Ryker was able to confirm his suspicion. She was, simply put, the most beautiful woman he had laid his eyes upon. Her astute gaze on him made him nervous. It was piercing, as if she was gazing into his soul, weighing his worth to be in such esteemed company. Ryker returned the gaze, unwilling to allow her presence to intimidate him despite the fact she was clearly of importance. *Aegnor said we bow to no man. No woman.*

Aegnor noticed the two staring at one another and cleared his throat to draw his apprentice's gaze from her. "Ryker. This is my former apprentice. Perhaps the only individual in Divinoros who could threaten me without trickery. Her name is not mine to share, but you likely have heard stories of the Ghost that stalks our land. *She* is that vengeful wraith. Normally, her visage is a harbinger of death, but today, it is the harbinger of grave news. We have much to discuss, but we can do so with full stomachs after the feast unwinds."

Ryker bowed to the woman. "It is a great honor to make your acquaintance Ghost. I have not heard much about you other than the legends that are told of your deeds. I look forward to getting to know you better over the evening."

She nodded. "You are more skilled than I expected to see from a human. I was curious to meet Aegnor's new apprentice. I look forward to dining together."

Princess Alreyia seemed to squeeze his arm a little tighter after the interaction as she steered Ryker over to the seat where he would be feasting beside her. A place of great honor amongst King Thondor's family.

As they were seated, the King roared, his voice instantly silencing the spectators in the massive hall. "Honored guests! We have just witnessed some of the greatest talents in the art of death that humans and

273

dwarves can offer. I hope you enjoyed the duel, but now," Thondor raised his arms, "We feast, and we drink!"

At that, the doors at the end of the hall burst open. Four massive kegs were wheeled into the hall to replenish the already depleted stock that had been initially provided. Behind the barrels, four dwarves carried a tray with a massive roast animal on top of it. Instantly, the hall was filled with smells of succulent, savory meat and rich spices that reminded Ryker of the roast hog his mother would make for the entire Marriock farm on each winter solstice eve. However, this creature was much larger than the three-hundred-pound hogs that had been raised on the farm for slaughter. Behind the massive animal came platters and platters of roasted roots and potatoes, steamed vegetables that Ryker thought must be native to the mountain region as he had not seen them before, and mushrooms larger than the apprentice's hand.

Ryker turned to Princess Alreyia. "Okay, what in the name of the Gods is that creature we are eating, and where did you find mushrooms that large?"

She laughed at him as the two went to seat themselves next to Aegnor and the mysterious woman whose name would not be revealed. "Everything we are eating here tonight is native to our lands. That is a Magnoar, a wild boar only found on the northern slope of the Perampla Mountains. The mushrooms we grow here in the caves. They seem to like the dark, damp environment. You will find nothing quite as exquisite as these two dishes throughout all of Divinoros."

Ryker enjoyed the remainder of the night. He had been on the road so long with Aegnor that he hadn't realized how much he missed the company of a joyful group of people sharing food and drink. Aegnor shared a few words, but Ryker spent the majority of the meal laughing with Alreyia about small things and stories of youth; he almost felt as if he were back home.

He longed to be around those he loved again, but he feared that day might not come soon enough. The events of the past four days only led in one direction. Barring unforeseen circumstances, he would be traveling to the elven capital of Turenian to consult with Queen Celestra on the evil stirring in this land.

What news did the Ghost bring?

Captain Marriock - Chapter 35 - Fractured Ice

Captain Marriock scratched at his grizzly beard, squinting against the piercing wind that bit at the exposed skin on his face. Its harsh bite slammed against the fur of his ice bear cloak. He was thankful for his position as captain; the bear pelt signified his status amongst the humans and elves stationed in the north, but more than that, nothing was more effective at combating the sub-zero temperatures that descended upon Ice Bridge Hold as winter continued to strangle the surging spring for a few weeks longer.

He strode down the battlements, nodding at the soldiers who stood watch at regular intervals. They were positioned to face outward, toward the direction of the Shroud. That ever-present looming threat hanging in the distance. The wall was built at a distance where the Rift was just visible on a clear sunny day, meaning it was well obscured by the dark, heavy clouds carried on the winter winds this evening.

Each man and elf manning the wall saluted Jebediah as he passed. He smirked inwardly at every elf that was forced to do so. It was rare indeed for their race to be in an inferior position to a human. Still, none had questioned his ascent in the ranks the past week. At least, most had not. Not after the prowess Jebediah showed with his long war hammer and his recurve bow during the heroics he had displayed to save three of the Northern watchmen from a hidden crevasse on a routine patrol. After the daring rescue, Jebediah escorted the injured trio through multiple Ice Back hunting grounds in the area. He killed two of the Ice Backs, even though it was known in the North that no one killed an Ice Back. If you see one, you run and hope it doesn't give chase. Jebediah would have run, but the men he rescued were injured. Fleeing hadn't been an option. Lord Niall had seen fit to promote him to his current post the following day.

Leading men was nothing new to Jebediah. He had overseen the Marriock boys and farm hands for as long as he could remember. *Leadership isn't an inherent ability given to any man or woman. Great leaders only come into existence by having the courage to stand in the face of responsibility and to learn from those experiences;* his father's words rang in his head when the bear pelt was set upon his shoulders.

The only difference now was that he was placed in charge of hardened soldiers rather than laborers. It was easier work in his mind, leading soldiers rather than children and unruly men on the farm. In those days, the people he oversaw were more interested in leisurely

275

going about their business than the season's harvest. Each of these men in the north had been drilled for years in obedience and the importance of a chain of command. Not to mention, all the army of the northern hold did was watch, wait, and, if necessary, kill. Not nearly as complex as cultivating soil, planning crop rotations, planting correctly at certain depths, and channeling aqueducts to water the fields effectively and appropriately.

Captain Marriock paused near the center of the battlements and turned to face out toward the Shroud. He knew the wall of mist was there, but he hated that the mysterious force would fade into the darkness, disappearing each night. This night would be worse than most. A heavy snowfall and tumultuous winds partnered to create a starless night, restricting his vision further.

He leaned over the battlements and looked toward the ground, satisfied he could at least see the base of the mountain. Lit torches lined the length of the base of their great wall, intending to give the guards a clear line of vision along the ground that met the foundation of the stronghold. His focus on watch nights had grown in intensity recently. The previous few days, the Shroud had been acting in a peculiar fashion, succeeding in unnerving his men.

And me, for that matter.

The normally transparent mist had slowly deepened in density, causing the hanging cloud to darken from a smoggy gray to an opaque tempest of dark gray swirling with pure black ribbons deep within the mist. Lord Niall had called a meeting the day this was first reported with Captain Marriock and the three other captains stationed at Ice Bridge Hold. They were implementing a more stringent monitoring system.

Each Captain would take turns running patrols and standing guard atop the wall in rotating half-day shifts, ensuring full battalion coverage each night rather than a reduced watchmen count that had been in place for decades. This order, which effectively doubled the time his men would spend in the ice plains north of the wall or standing atop it, brought groans from the men who were used to half-battalion patrols and guard duty.

Spring can't come soon enough. At least milder weather will lift the men's spirits.

A sudden gust in the already heavy wind licked at Jebediah. Its harsh tone carried a strange sound to his ears. It was only a whisper, but it sounded like someone yelling. It was hard to tell, with the fresh snowfall dampening the sounds of the world. He looked at a soldier standing to his left. "Did you hear something out there, soldier?"

The man wrapped in a bison cloak looked over, eyes screwed to narrow slits and nodded. "I think I did, sir, but the wind may be playing tricks on me, plus my ears are colder than a penguin's pecker. I mean seriously, Captain, I'm freezing my arse out here."

Jebediah nearly laughed at that. But then the whisper sounded again, a little louder than before.

He turned sharply toward the frozen plains beyond the northern wall. "I can't see anything in this damn blizzard," Jebediah grumbled. He strained his eyes in a useless attempt to peer through the storm. He could barely see a hundred yards, so Captain Marriock sought out an elf in his battalion. He came across Merri first. Jebediah sighed sharply, taking a deep breath before he addressed the infuriating, near-mutinous elf. "Merri!" Jebediah shouted over the building winter storm. The elf turned his face toward Jebediah, and his deep frown somehow dropped lower before he immediately turned back to face away from Jebediah.

"How can I help you, *Captain*?" he spit out the last word with disdain.

Captain Marriock held back the sharp retort that sat at the edge of his tongue.

I can't let this man disrespect me like this. He'll turn every elf in my unit into a swarming mutinous force fighting against any order I give.

So instead of insulting the man, Captain Marriock said with all the authority he could muster, "Soldier. I expect you to salute when approached by your superiors. I will wait."

Reluctantly, Merri turned back toward the Captain and half-heartedly saluted.

Fine enough for today.

"Good. Now, I need your input. Captain Theratae is still on patrol. I thought I heard something out there earlier, almost like a scream. Did you hear that as well?" Captain Marriock shouted over the storm. Merri nodded his confirmation. "Shit, well, you have much better eyes than me. A've you seen anything out there?"

Merri shouted back, "I think I have seen a couple of shadows moving far out in the distance. Probably just Theratae's men out there... Though, I can't tell for sure. It could be anything, really. Human, elf, horse, Ice Back. Can't make out any detail in this weather."

Before Jebediah could respond, another definite shout cut through the air.

He and Merri looked at one another before Jebediah grabbed the bull horn on his belt and blew three loud signals into the air. Immediately after the horns were sounded, massive fires were lit at every fifty paces on the battlements. The fires were set in large mirror-backed chamber towers. The famous elven engineer Lady Lefaye built the encased mirror-like surface, capable of swiveling to reflect fire light brightly in a focused direction. As the torch tower nearest was set alight, a metal door to the front side of the chamber opened to shoot a beam of light out onto the grounds in front of the wall.

Behind him, Jebediah could hear men and women rousing. He dared a glance back down the ramparts, seeing small warm lights spark into existence as slumbering soldiers continued to be roused from the barracks to suit up and join as supporting forces on the top of the wall. Everyone knew the horn signals, and everyone responded in kind. Something stirred north of the wall.

With the defensive fort scrambling to get their soldiers in position for any scenario, Captain Jebediah returned his attention to the front side of the wall. He stared intensely for what seemed like ages, infinitely grateful to the wondrous woman who invented their lanterns, and then he saw it. A small figure on horseback far in the distance. He was moving quickly and waving his arms about despite moving at a full gallop. Jebediah couldn't make out anything the man said but ordered one of the spot lamp beams to be focused on the incoming rider.

As the beam fell on the figure, tracing his movements, Jebediah could make out the dark pelt cloak signifying the figure as a member of the Ice Bridge Guard. "Can you hear what he's saying?" Jebediah asked Merri, knowing his elf ears, along with his eyes, were sharper than his own. But Merri shook his head. The Captain blew a long note on his horn, followed by two short calls. The signal of imminent danger. The men on the front of the battlements knocked arrows in bows at the command, holding the weapon at the ready. Had the conditions been better, Jebediah would have preferred to command by voice, but his men trained diligently every day to master the different horn calls.

The horse continued to thunder toward them. Horse and rider were close enough now to see the snow being kicked up with each stride of the long-haired steed. "Ge... do... the... r... arr..." Jebediah still couldn't make out what was being yelled. But the disjointed, unintelligible sounds continued to reach his ear and now carried a panicked tone.

"Sir, there is something behind him," Merri called over the wind.

In response, Jebediah shouted at the light tower nearest him, "Scan behind the rider. I need to know what in the Gods is after him!" He grabbed a soldier trotting into a supporting position. "Run the wall. Tell the spot lamp to scan the ground behind the rider." The man ran off and soon focused beams of light cut through the darkness to unveil the mysterious foes chasing the man.

Those are no ice backs or bears.

Captain Marriock's' heart dropped as two massive six-legged beasts of pure black sprinted a hundred yards or so behind the rider. No native creatures north of the wall had six legs. That was a trait of the fabled krakenshi. *This can't be...*

278

What they trained for was finally upon them. Another blow on the horn, and men with bows drew their arrows, aiming at the beasts flashing in and out of pockets of darkness between beams of light in the distance. He followed that up with a longer horn blast, and men along the wall dropped torches down the front side of the wall, igniting trenches of oil at its base.

"Get...own... they... r... ar..." The man was yelling frantically. He was not close enough to hear clearly. "Get down ...hey... are in... th...ky..". Merri went pale. "What is it?" Jebediah demanded, "What is he saying?"

Merri responded, "He is yelling, 'Get down! They are in the...'" Merri never finished as a great winged shadow descended from above, peeling its hideous form from the night sky with immense speed. The monster moved too quickly for Jebediah to take in much of its form, other than the long black talons that pierced the elf's shoulders with the sound of a butcher stabbing into a hog. A panicked wail from the elf cut off the words he was about to speak. Jebediah froze as Merri was dragged from the back side of the wall and dropped eighty feet into the courtyard beneath. He landed on another soldier, and neither moved again, both bodies broken. The creature circled back around, looking for its next victim.

Leaders are forged by the experiences they endure.

Captain Marriock was jarred, undoubtedly, but he did not hesitate. He grabbed a bow and began knocking and firing arrows toward the airborne beast as he moved along the battlements, shouting repeatedly, "Look to the skies! Look to the skies! They are coming from above!" He only hoped his voice would carry far enough to warn the others. But screams and dull thudding that could only be produced by bodies falling from great heights were already carrying from along the battlements.

The creature that had slain Merri was now swirling down toward Jebediah. The arrows he had fired missed their mark.

As bloody useless as shooting at an eagle diving.

Fear threatened to paralyze Jebediah as the wraith descended. The creature was unnatural. Its cruel form was vaguely humanoid in its head and torso, but the end of each leg was armed with large talons in the mold of the great eagles that claimed the skies of Stone Guard. Each arm ended in long, slender fingers with pointed claws replacing the fingernails. The beast flew on massive black wings that appeared to be made of shadows, more solid in the main body of the wing but a wisping smoke along the edges.

Jebediah watched the atrocity flap its massive wings twice, propelling itself toward him at an uncanny speed. He had time to fire one more arrow, which was easily evaded with a sideways roll, and then the beast was on him. His training gave him time to loosen his hammer from his sheath before the impact.

He swung the head of his weapon at the creature, breaking its left leg at the knee and rendering one talon unusable with a satisfying crunch. That was not enough to stop the winged nightmare. It sank the other talon into Jebediah's shoulder. He screamed out in agony as the talon pierced his outerwear and crushed his mail into his flesh with uncanny force. But the chain held firm.

The monster strained against Jebediah's additional weight. Each flap of the wings dragged the Captain closer to the front edge of the battlement. He felt his back slam into the short wall and, to his horror, felt himself being dragged out over the long drop. A drop from a fatal height to the unprotected front side of the wall. He tried to cling to the edge of the wall with his heels. He could hear men running to his aid.

If he could only hold out a moment longer... but, alas, the stone was slick from snow, and with another flap of its wings, the wraith pulled Jebediah over the edge of the wall. Before the talon could release, Jebediah swung the pointed edge of the hammer at the beast's chest in wild desperation. A last effort to kill the creature that had surely just ended his life.

The talon released him, and he hung in the sky, weightless for a moment as his hammer arced toward the beast. The wraith could not evade this blow, and with a sickening squelch, the hammer sunk into the wraith's chest. It screeched as it flapped its wings in vain, supporting the pair mid-air, for a moment, before its body convulsed and its wings stilled to allow gravity to plummet the pair to the earth below.

With a fervent desire to survive, the Captain used the hammer embedded in his enemy to pull himself up the dead monster's body. He positioned himself over the monster's chest, allowing for the drag from his wings to slow the fall. He hoped the creature's body would act as a cushion for him.

Foolish, I am dead. What's the point of this last-minute fight against fate?

The collision came stronger than any hammer blow. Jebediah's world jerked as he came to a sudden stop. His positioning over the winged creature and the freshly fallen snow served their purpose. The Captain's weight caved in the creature's abdomen, which ruptured sending rancid black fluid from its innards to stain the surrounding snow and soak Jebediah.

The force of such a fall pushed the air from his lungs, and his vision blurred. Once he did catch his breath, a blinding pain sent his vision spiraling again. Multiple ribs were cracked from the force of the fall and his left shoulder may have been dislocated, but the Captain fared better than the other bodies that now littered the front side of the wall.

Broken forms of his soldiers lay at the base in bent, unmoving forms. Their open eyes glassed over, unmoving stares blank as snowflakes landed on their warm surface. They were, no doubt, dragged from the battlements as he was. He hoped that his men remaining at the top of the hold now fared better.

It took him a moment to stand. He then threw his arm up until the tendons in his shoulder stretched to a point near ripping, and the ball of his arm cracked back into its socket. Once the tears faded from his eyes, the Captain realized how decidedly desperate his situation had become. He had seen the monsters chasing the lone rider through the storm from the battlements above, and he now stood alone, exposed, in the darkness.

He looked to blow a signal from his bullhorn, but the horn had been shattered in the fall. He quickly took in his surroundings and saw he was no more than a hundred yards from the main wall gate. The rider he saw fleeing the six-legged creatures was close to the gate now as well. Four krakenshi close on his heels. Jebediah sprinted, adrenaline and desperation propelling him at a speed he did not realize he was capable of.

Funny how death knocking at the door has a way of motivating a man beyond their known capabilities. I'm going to feel my ribs tomorrow if I make it that far.

Jebediah thought as he held his chest with one hand, his hammer in another.

He reached the gate just before the rider. It was open, and the guards were ready to slam the iron gates shut after he and the rider passed through. But once the horse cantered in, the men were too slow to seal off the hold's northern entrance. The lead krakenshi barreled through the closing gate. Its limbs were outstretched with violent intent. The vermin finally caught its target in the short tunnel leading from the ice plains out to the main fortress courtyard.

The krakenshi sunk its front four legs into the side of the panting animal, skewering its insides. The horse's scream pierced Jebediah's ears. The tangle of flesh hit the ground, and the horse's neck snapped with a sharp crack under its attacker's added weight. As they rolled, the monster's maw engulfed the upper half of the rider, cutting off his shouts of terror as two serrated mandibles separated his upper half from his legs just above the waist. The rolling motion of the monster and its victims sent the soldiers' entrails sailing through the air, blood splattering the walls of the tunnel in viscous horror.

He had no time to see the aftermath of the tumble as the three trailing krakenshi stormed at the gate. Captain Marriock screamed, "Close the gate! Now! There are more coming after these! Get the damn gate closed!"

Still, the gate did not close fast enough.

Two of the remaining three monsters had run past Jebediah and the gate guards were now occupied in a fight to the death. The final trailing monster stalked at Jebediah. It snapped its lower mandibles against the solid upper jaw, making a crackling sound, before it released a terrible screech that Jebediah attributed to excitement at the prospect of tearing apart its next victim. The krakenshi lunged directly at Jebediah, ready for a quick kill.

Captain Marriock, broken and bruised, was not useless in the contest of killing. He had grown familiar with fending off larger, stronger creatures than this krakenshi whenever he came across an ice pack or ice bear; knowing how to handle such a strong opponent, he rolled beneath the creature. As he stood, he saw its thick tail whipping at him too late to avoid the blow. The thick tail slammed into his ribs and fresh tears were brought to his eyes as his already ruined ribcage took yet another blow. He barely felt anything as he collided with the stone wall he was flung into.

Coughing, he forced himself back to his feet.

At least I'm not coughing up blood yet. I must have avoided puncturing a lung. Be glad for the little things.

He looked at the krakenshi, who had already turned and was approaching him again. He over-emphasized his injuries, pretending to be unable to move from his place, hoping to goad the beast into a careless strike. His deception succeeded, and the krakenshi snapped out at his newest prey, razor teeth flashing in the flickering torch light.

At the last second, Jebediah stepped sideways. The skull of the beast slammed into the stone wall, stunning it for just a moment, allowing Jebediah to bring the head of his heavy hammer down in a broad arc on the back of the monster's skull. The head of the ancient foe split, and its body collapsed, but Jeb brought down another blow to ensure it wouldn't stand again. He turned to the gate, which still stood open. Monsters now loomed in the darkness at the end of his vision. He could hear a low rumble through the heavy snow. Hundreds of feet marching with cruel intent.

They've brought an army... He slammed the gate closed, knowing it would need to be reinforced to hold back what now bore down upon them.

He sprinted into the courtyard, which was already littered with soldiers' bodies contorted at odd angles, large pools of scarlet saturating the snow around them. Victims of the night wraiths. Others lay hacked and torn among two dissipating bodies of dead krakenshi. The third beast was still raging at a group of soldiers who had surrounded the monster. With that situation in hand, Captain Marriock scanned for the wench and chain holding the reinforced gate aloft. It was designed to drop in place behind the main gate.

282

He ran over and slammed his hammer against the chain once. Twice. And finally, on the third swing, Jebediah severed a link in the chain and the reinforced metal gate slammed closed just before a powerful collision sounded against the iron. Red eyes and twisted monsters pressed against the gaps in the gate, snarling and clawing in futility at the metal.

Captain Marriock turned to face the soldiers remaining in the courtyard. "Get a battalion down here now. That gate won't hold forever. Find ten archers to fire through the gaps in the gate while they form up. Kill the beasts crowded against it. It will slow the attempts of their breach and hopefully thin their ranks. We need to eliminate any chance of them swarming behind our walls. This is our weakest point." Four men ran off at once to fetch soldiers at Marriock's order.

Sounds of war raged around Jebediah. Screams of the dying filled the snowy night. Occasionally, Jebediah would see a shape plummet over the ramparts above, signaling another man from his battalion had fallen prey to the flying wraiths. He hated seeing his men dying without him amongst them. He prayed a few had heard his warning before he'd been dragged over the front of the wall. He hoped that they managed to kill as much as be killed.

The dull thud of marching boots filled the alleys leading to the front gate entrance. "Marriock!" It was the familiar voice of Lord Neill. The elf looked to be in shambles compared to his usual state, his uniform splattered with dark blood freed from the veins of these heinous creatures. "What is going on out here? Why the hell aren't you on the wall? And what in the God's name are these flying monsters?" Lord Niall asked in rapid fashion as he halted before his newest Captain in arms.

Jebediah ordered the men Niall marched with into place. He then had the archers begin to fire arrows into the krakenshi pressing into the iron gate. Only after he was satisfied with the pained squealing of the krakenshi did the young captain turn to Lord Niall and recount the night's events.

Lord Niall stared back at Jebediah, his face growing grimmer with each passing second, "Get back to your men. We will hold the gate here. Once enough of these horrors gather at our base, trigger the collapse. As soon as the defense has been initiated, get any survivors back here to aid in holding our weak points till we retreat past the inner wall." Not waiting for Jebediah's response, Lord Niall spun and began shouting orders at the men in the courtyard, organizing the defense and retreat points for once the gate had broken.

Captain Marriock nodded and sprinted toward the closest stairs leading to the top of the battlements. He gritted his teeth, sucking air between the gaps, as sharp pangs continued to stab in his side. He was severely hindered in his ability to catch a full breath of air by the pain. But his men, his brothers in arms, were in the firm grasp of chaos and death, and that thought drove him to keep his feet churning regardless of the searing in his side.

He soon arrived at the stairs winding up toward the top of the battlements. When he finally crested the final star, he collapsed to his hands and knees, gasping in rapid, shallow breaths as his ribs would permit. He puked. Then, he shakily pushed himself upright, more to avoid the proximity to his bile rather than being ready to do so.

Jebediah took in his surroundings only to find the fresh snow had been dyed red with blood. Fresh flakes of perfect white descended and melded into the grotesque color as they landed on the exposed innards of dead soldiers.

The air was heavy with the metallic scent of blood. It was too much. He puked a second time. After a couple of seconds to gain composure, he pushed his gloved hand into the snow-covered battlements, forcing himself free. He was right back in the middle of the meat grinder. Shadowed figures hummed through the skies at breakneck speeds, sliding in and out of the dark night, avoiding the beams of the spot lamps that still cut through the darkness as their operators strove to trace the wraith's movements.

Arrows flew in every direction, and occasionally, a winged figure would plummet as the shaft found its mark. Far more common was the sight of a man or elf being dragged into the sky and dropped over the side of the wall.

Marriock assessed his positioning to find he was at the center of the wall. He needed to get to the trigger of the wall's fail-safe. A trap intended to be deployed should they ever be overrun. He wanted to clear the wall of his men before he deployed the collapse, but he didn't have time to backtrack. The initiation mechanism was in a tower carved into the mountainside, where their man-made barrier met nature's own blockade on the far left of the wall. If he took his time to clear the right side… *There is no time. The gate would be overrun…* So Jebediah ran to his left, heart heavy with the knowledge that his men would die from his actions.

His path was relatively quiet. He shouted at men and women to retreat to the courtyard as he went. Around one of the spot lamp towers, he found a group of soldiers. They had formed a tight unit of two archers, a pikeman, and a swordsman. Jebediah was impressed as they killed at least three wraiths and fended off the attack of another as he approached. They had been successful in the night's bloody affair, observed by the dark stains and disintegrating winged creatures around them.

They stared at him in awe, one shouting, "How you ain't dead Cap'? Saw you go over the wall myself!"

He shouted at them, "No time to explain. Move as fast as you can to the right side of the wall and then retreat to the courtyard. Tell all who you find to retreat. Report to Niall for further instruction once you've arrived, he's coordinating the defense there. Spread the order now. You have till I get to the other side to clear out before I spring the collapse." Before they turned to run, Jebediah gave one more command that sickened him to his core, "Leave the wounded. You won't have time to get them to safety."

The men nodded before sprinting in the direction Jebediah had come from, screaming the order of retreat. Nodding in satisfaction, Jebediah turned just in time to catch a wraith darting in his direction. He quickly brought his hammer in an upward strike, landing the head of the heavy blunt instrument under the jaw of the raging creature. The Captain felt the jaw bone break under the force, followed by a sharp crack as the base of the enemy's skull split, discharging foul black blood all over the Captain.

Well, that's just great... Jebediah thought as he wiped the muck from his face and ran again. He ordered each man he passed to retreat. He needed to get everyone off the wall. As he continued running, exhaustion continued creeping in. His vision blurred and darkness crept in at the edges of his sight. He shook his head to clear the fog.

Now is no time to pass out.

Taking a moment, Jebediah leaned to the front battlement and peeked his head over the side to see what had gathered below. Bodies of an overwhelming krakenshi force now filled the base of the wall. The mass of monsters was thickest in front of the iron gate, where they crawled over one another, attempting to be first through the gate as if some insanity drove them forward with reckless abandon, intent on killing whatever these walls protected.

It won't be long before they break through. They look like ants swarming a dropped morsel of food. But these are no ants easily squashed under a boot. These are rabid dogs, crazed wolves, bloodthirsty and angry. There were hundreds, maybe more than a thousand now. And more continued to stream from the darkness beyond with no indication the flow would be cut off.

The sound was horrible; screeching and clawing now drowned out even the wind. Jebediah signed, clenched his ribs with his one free hand, and started running. Again. He was nearly a hundred yards from the side tower nestled up to the side of the mountain face. The main tower room was empty; a flameless torch and a pail of tar were the only objects in the room other than the smooth stone of the tower and the rough mountainside. Without pause, Jebediah dropped his hammer and grabbed the lifeless torch from its iron sconce. Just beneath was the tar pail and hidden behind was a block of flint stone. Soaking the torch,

Jebediah began scratching at the flint stone with his belt knife, frantically struggling to get the torch lit.

His hands were shaking violently as adrenaline surged through his veins, making the effort doubly difficult. He struck his belt knife against the stone; the spark didn't take. He heard a rush of air followed by a thud behind him. He struck the stone a second time, but the sound distracted him, and the sparks sailed past the torch, leaving the tar-soaked end dripping to the ground below. A gurgling, chittering sound came from behind him. He dared a glance up and saw that one of the wraiths had landed and was moving cautiously toward him. He forced himself to look back to the flint stone. On his third attempt, the torch burst alight and the Captain sprung into immediate action. He turned and waved the flame at the wraith causing the dark monster to jump back in fright, snarling. It recovered quickly from the surprise of the flame but not quick enough to avoid the knife that Jebediah plunged into the crook of the beast's neck. It fell limp, swiping its claws weakly at Jebediah as he twisted the knife, ensuring he effectively ruined the anatomy around the blade's entry site.

With the immediate threat dealt with, Jebediah returned to the tower to look for the trigger point along the surface of the rough mountain making up the fourth wall of the tower. He found the small hole leading directly into the mountain. The hole was no bigger than the size of a fist and was marked with elvish runes, indicating the world-shaking that would accompany the Captain setting of the trap. He paused for a moment.

Did everyone get cleared of the wall... Maybe I should wait. I can't... I can't kill my men who've been stranded up here. Jebediah's heart pounded. *No. They cleared out. They're trained for this. They signed on for this. Those stranded here are prepared to die in defense of their world. Do it now before it's too late.*

Jebediah plunged the lit torch into the hole, springing free another inspired invention of Lady Lefaye. A series of insulated, muffled explosions sounded off in rapid succession, beginning near Jebediah before running the length of Ice Bridge Hold's fortifications to the opposite end of the wall.

Captain Jebediah ran for the nearest stairs, hurling himself down the backside of the wall as the night filled with the sound of stone cracking, a mountain of stone shifting. Then, the top twenty feet of the wall began to slide and crumble toward the front side of the where the Blankenship had amassed.

Thousands of tons of tumbling stones plummeted toward the earth in a wave that no living being on Divinoros could survive. He smiled in grim satisfaction, knowing the weight of upper battlements would crush hundreds of beasts below. He coughed violently, spitting blood. Gritting his teeth, Captain Marriock continued his run, now much slower than before, back toward the courtyard where Lord Niall would be directing and ordering his army.

He couldn't help the bloody smile that crossed his face as a thunderous force shook the ground and filled the air with a plume of snow and dust. Hundreds of shrieking cries were cut off as the dark mass hammering at their front gate was obliterated. The smile soon faded. With the battlements gone, so too was the hope of holding back the enemy for any great length of time should they have a reserve force.

The quarter-mile walk back to the central portion of the courtyard seemed to take ages in Jebediah's pained state, but soon he saw the regal Lord Niall, blood-soaked and issuing orders to the haggard men who had survived the continued assault from the wraiths above.

"Lord Niall, we killed hundreds of those krakenshi, but with no targets on the wall, I expect these night wraiths to start attacking us in full force here," Jebediah said as he approached his leader.

Niall simply nodded his agreement. "Yes, they will. Already have been, in fact. I also expect Omnes to release another swarm of krakenshi as well. I don't understand how he is back, but there can be no other purpose for this evening other than overwhelming the wall and catching the southern cities unaware."

"How can we hold him?"

Lord Niall assessed his newest captain with a stern gaze before talking in a quiet tone. "You are no fool. We cannot. The best we can do is delay his forces and ensure the remainder of the world learns of the assault that is about to befall them. Take two of the fastest riders you have. I want you to carry a message south detailing what has happened here. You will need one to go to Reyvothia. Hopefully, Lord Evaino will see reason and evacuate the city. They can sail past the Draconian Isle to Turenian to join forces with the Queen. Another rider will be dispatched to Veilenthia carrying a warning as well. You have the most crucial task. You must find a passage into the Great Marbled Caverns and rouse the sleeping giant that avoided our first war with the Dark God. Tell those lazy, fearful rock lovers of the horror you have seen here. With luck, King Thondor will see reason and assist the elves in the war that is coming. From there, continue south to your home, you are familiar with Lord Frenir and must warn him to prepare for assault. Stone Guard is the greatest strength in the west."

"I wish to stay and fight sir, I signed up for this outfit to protect my family, to protect the people that call Divinoros home. I will not flee while my heart still beats," Jebediah responded.

I cannot flee and leave my brothers here to die while I run.

"You will do as ordered! I chose you for a reason. Dwarves are suspicious of my race. Our people live too long to forget past injustices.

287

While they may not like your kind, they don't outright resent you. If we are to have the support of their proud race it must be a human to convince them." Lord Niall saw the disappointment in Jebediah's eyes and his tone softened. "This will not be the only fight, son. This is merely the first battle in a long war to come, the beginning of a conquest waged on this land by a power that may prove overwhelming. Should our brethren survive in the future, you must not fail in this crucial task. Ride fast, Captain."

"Yessir. I will leave at once." Jebediah turned then and locked eyes with a slender elf who was very small for his race and went by the name of Alfur. He waved the elf over and then saw a human from his company, Garin, who was known for his ability on horseback and skill with a recurve bow.

Both men weaved their way through crowds of armed soldiers scrambling into defensive formations before saluting Jebediah. "Go ready five horses for travel. We ride to warn the southern cities of an impending invasion. I want each horse set up with two weeks of rations. I'll give you the details of our mission once we have departed."

The two saluted and ran ahead of Jebediah to the stables to ready their steeds and collect the supplies that would be needed for their trip. Jebediah wanted the extra horses for himself and Garin, who had a longer journey than Alfur, whom he planned to send to Reyvothia. They would need to switch between the horses on the longer journey as the riding would be hard. Jebediah sighed and winced at the pain in his side.

This will be a damned long ride. I need to find a healer to at least repair my lung.

Ryker - Chapter 36 - Granite Counsel

Ryker had wished Princess Alreyia farewell after the feast. He was summoned to follow Aegnor, the mysterious elven woman, King Thondor, his wife Queen Rundura, Prince Thonir, the angry-looking dwarf who had married Princess Zondra, who went by General Hognar, and a frizzy-haired female dwarven mage called Bylgia.

The party wove their way through the many halls of the dwarven palace to a large room centered around a massive stone table. Ryker nearly yelped in surprise as a massive, scaled lion larger than Xantharyia stalked into the room after the party had entered.

No one moved or spoke for a couple of moments until Aegnor broke the tension by walking up to the beast and scratching its massive maw before the giant feline went to lie behind the mysterious elven woman. "It is good to see you again, Zarou," Aegnor said to the cat. I think you may have doubled in size since our paths last crossed." The great beast purred at the affection, and the entire council was somewhat calmed after that.

"What the hell is that?" Ryker whispered under his breath to Aegnor once his master settled in beside him.

"The perfect killing machine. A sand lion. He travels with the Ghost."

At the center of the table stood a topographical recreation of Divinoros. Ryker was struck by the detail of the carved and painted stones. The Perampla Mountains stood erected above the remainder of the painted green plains north of Ravenford, and the oceans were shallow depressions painted blue till they were intercepted by the lush, green-painted grasslands and forest surrounding the elven capital. The southern portion of the map was dominated by waving dunes indicating the deserts of Sandivar, while the northern part of the continents was largely painted a light icy blue to signify the frozen wastelands.

The northmost tip of the eastern and western land masses were divided by a great crack in the map, almost as if the carver had become drunk and dropped his chisel deep into the surface, breaking the pristine landscape. This blemish, Ryker knew, was the Rift, which was accompanied by painted black tendrils leaking from the fracture in the stone to signify the Shroud that hung above it. Each major city and large town was marked with miniature replicas of the city and figurine markers that were placed to signify the standing army positioned in each area.

Ryker was pulled from his reverence after three more generals to King Thondor entered the room and the Dwarf King called for all to be seated. "You have been summoned to an emergency council to hear the news coming from eastern Divinoros, a message relayed to us from

Queen Celestra herself." Thondor held out his hand and gestured for the Ghost to speak.

Her voice wafted through the air intoxicatingly, her every word landing sweetly on Ryker's ears. He only wished the message matched her pleasant tone. "Lords, Ladies, King and Queen. I bring a dark tiding from the east. A sleeping power has reclaimed a foothold in this land. It was nurtured to health and strengthened in the wastelands beyond elven reach in the deepest recesses of the Sandivar desert. Omnes's power has returned, and once again, it threatens all life in this land. It seems that the power of the Dark God rests in the hands of a human crime lord. A man known as the Knife."

"The Knife?" questioned Bylgia. "That is impossible. I trained in the deserts with the great elven mage Olimis, and we fought against a man called the Knife, but that was over five hundred years ago. No human can survive that long."

"The Knife is merely a title in the Bankhoft family. The Knife serves as a monarch of sorts to their people. The title is claimed by killing the previous ruler of the house. I have met the current man in power, and I assure you, his strength is very real. Had we been forced into a longer encounter with the man, I think he could have killed me and Zarou with ease."

The lion growled a low rumble echoing in the chamber in defiance of the she-elf's claim. The loud sound silenced all others in the room. Once satisfied that the room understood he was not scared of any man, God powers or not, he ceased the growl and continued to lick at a section of scales that was regrowing on his left forepaw to alleviate an insatiable itch. "Zarou may disagree at our easy dispatching, but I assure you his power is very real, a sand lion submits to no one."

Prince Thonir stood. "How is this possible? Omnes was cast into the depths of the Rift a millennia ago. We received a report a month ago that they were experiencing unusual activity along the Shroud, but there hasn't been a report of any materializations. Not to mention the Rift, if Omnes were even stirring there, and the deserts of Sandivar are located on opposite ends of the world. Could this be something else?"

"I am afraid not, Prince Thonir. I have seen this enemy myself. The Knife is in possession of a dagger that he is using to convert and infect men with an ancient power. Me and my companions who came across them have come to learn that these converts are called the Gifted. I have killed three on my travels from Sandivar to Turenian. Out of my party, myself, and three of Lord Sennin's Elites, I was the only one to survive the encounters, in large part because of Zarou. Further, Celestra confirmed this dagger is an artifact that was left behind by the Obsidian Knight we believe Kei-Tel to have killed."

290

Aegnor spoke now. "Three of these Gifted were able to kill three Elites? Despite being in the company of yourself and Zarou… Were they just ordinary humans before they were converted?"

"Let me start from the beginning and you will begin to understand the true gravity of the situation. Late last year my services were requisitioned by Lord Sennin to retrieve an ancient text that was said to be in the Badlands. The Queen had attempted to take back these lands from the humans nearly a millennia ago, but you likely remember her humiliating defeats at the hands of these humans, once believed to be a mere nuisance. Over the centuries, different spies and soldiers were sent to the sacked city of Oasis on behalf of the elven monarch to seek out documents and artifacts she had stored in the southern city after the war on Omnes. Those missions continually failed, eventually leaving Queen Celestra with the hope that we could broker a deal with the Bankhofts. This human family was now in sole possession and control of the Badlands, and Celestra accurately deduced that these men were now in possession of the objects the Queen sought out despite precautions she took to hide them in the fallen city. So, I was sent on behalf of Her Majesty through Lord Sennin to broker a deal for a large manuscript from the head of the family."

"Where is this book now?" King Thondor interrupted.

"Before joining the evening's festivities, I sought out a dwarf called Baelin and left the document with him. He is looking over it now to corroborate the history of Omnes against the application of the power described within its pages. I understand there is no one walking Divinoros better suited to piecing together this information from our histories."

King Thondor nodded his agreement. "Good. Baelin will report his findings. Continue elf."

"The retrieval of the manuscript was my first run-in with these people's strange dark powers. The Knife threatened my life during the exchange. I wouldn't have escaped had I not had Zarou with me." Ryker watched as the elf casually pat the massive feline's paw, big enough to crush the life out of any bipedal in the room. "He had a dagger that seemed to emanate some sort of power. The earth hummed and shook when he revealed the obsidian blade from an ancient-looking scabbard. Not to mention, his eyes ran black as if they were filled with tar once the blade had been freed. I was able to escape, despite the man's attempt to take the negotiated payment and my life while keeping the book. Soon after I returned with the manuscript in hand, Sennin asked that I take the document North to Turenian and deliver it personally to Her Majesty." The she-elf gave Aegnor a piercing glare as the Queen's name came up yet again.

291

"Why would Lord Sennin send a hand for hire over his own men? No offense meant, my lady," the Golden Son commented.

"He planned to send his own, but apparently, traveling north through the Narrows had been increasingly risky. Merchants were frequently reporting being accosted on their travels, often having members of their caravans killed on the main road. It had been weeks since the last successful merchant run had reached the markets of Sandivar from Turenian. So, being a highly important mission, I was sent alongside a small team of Elites. Plenty of strength for a mission like this, or so we thought. We were wrong. By the time we reached the Narrows, the city was already lost. Plucked by the Knife from right underneath the Monarchy's very nose. Queen Celestra believes the Bankhofts look to squeeze and starve Sandivar, forcing their collapse over the coming months and claiming the southern deserts as his own. Based on what we saw, he is well on his way to doing just that. With the monsters he summons, I would not be shocked if Sandivar has already fallen. From there, if they have any naval force, they will spread like wildfire into the western side of Divinoros. Easier to hold back Turenian's forces in the Narrows and take Reef Ridge or Ocean Fjord than take on the Queen's capital city.

"The Narrows is where we first encountered the Gifted. While attempting to pass through, we were arrested by the city guard, two of whom were humans. But they seemed to have an ancient presence about them. They escorted us deep into the walls of the Narrows, looking to execute us quietly without causing an unnecessary scene by attacking us in the plaza amongst the small population of remaining citizens. We were able to get a jump on them, but they each had unique abilities. Their eyes were black, and the shadows around them seemed to coagulate into unpredictable weapons. The four of us were able to kill these two Gifted, but one of my companions was hurt. Pierced by the manifested darkness wielded."

Ryker stared at the woman in fascination. He could hardly believe the cruelty that one person could endure. Nienna saw the pity in his eyes, and her steely gaze fell upon him like a hammer on hot iron, quickly reshaping the sympathy he'd felt.

"Scouting ahead, I saw something I didn't think possible. I saw the Knife addressing a group of guards assembled at the gate where we planned to depart. No more than twenty to thirty men. Nothing I and two healthy Elites couldn't handle. But then I saw that cursed dagger from the desert. I couldn't comprehend how the Knife had gotten to the Narrows as this evil man plunged the blade down into a kneeling guard's neck. The man didn't die, however, merely bled, convulsed, and then stood, allowing blood to pour from his open wound in a steady flow of red that slowly turned black. His eyes went dark, and I knew I had just watched another of the Gifted being born into our world. Then, with the same dagger, the Knife cut what looked to be a hole in reality, stepped into the spatial rift, and was gone."

King Thondor chimed in, "What do you mean, was gone? What are you talking about?"

"I do not know what I saw, only that I saw it. The world split around the blade, and the man stepped in. When the hole was stitched back together, the Knife was gone."

This was the first time Ryker chimed in. "Well, this is a guess, but Aegnor was just teaching me about the Gods coming to this world and how the elves aided them in dispelling the Demon King so long ago. That means they don't reside in this world. Could the blade be this man opening a hole in the plane where the Gods reside, a space beyond our own at least?"

Aegnor nodded in agreement. "That seems to make sense to me, though *what* is happening is of little importance. The fact that he can use this to move around the world... popping into existence where he pleases... That is... Concerning. Please continue your tale, Ghost."

"Knowing the danger of the Gifted did little to sway my team's plans— we had a mission, and there is only one Northern Gate leading from the Narrows to Turenian. So, we fought our way through, but the Gifted had managed to wound another of my traveling companions. Still, we fled north and took shelter in Feyrenthia Forest just south of Turenian. We planned to rest here, lick our wounded, and then continue north. But those forests played the role of the graveyard for the Elites." Ryker noticed the Ghost seemed to shake slightly as she took a moment to compose herself.

"The wounds left by the dark weapons infected the bodies of the wounded elves. An unusual infection... it spread in their veins and ultimately claimed their lives. But the Dark Gods' cruel plot was not yet over. Some evil power from the Gifted somehow festered in my companions' lifeless bodies, the power seemed to incubate inside them until something triggered the power to..." Nienna cleared her throat to keep the word from catching. "To emerge." Tears brimmed the elf's lids as she remembered the krakenshi ripping itself free from Kimo's body.

She continued in a hushed tone. "Creatures tore themselves from the wounded's insides, mangling their corpses as dark monsters, krakenshi in form, pulled themselves free of fleshy husks. Horrible creatures... I witnessed the creatures of Omnes's war being born into Divinoros anew, through the death of an elf. I again would have died had Zarou not been in the forest with me."

Nienna thought to tell the group of her encounter with the princess of the Fey and the strange lady Avanya in Feyrenthia Forest, but for some reason, she opted not to, preferring to leave the pair out of her tale.

She leaned back and rubbed her hands across her face to wipe away the trailing tears, signaling that her tale was nearing its end.

The council stared at the elf with a mixture of empathy and curiousness on their faces. All remained silent, allowing the clearly rattled elf to continue in her story. She told of her escape from the forests and her meeting with Queen Celestra. She told how the Queen had confirmed the legitimacy of the power held in the dagger that was now in the Bankhoft's possessions and emphasized the peril that pressed on Sandivar from the report of the disheveled Captain Malfius that had interrupted her meeting with the Queen.

"The Queen fears the return of Omnes is upon us, King Thondor. She seeks an alliance between our two great races. Together, we may have a chance at repelling the evil that is now descending upon us. They have moved in the shadows, and this is just the beginning. I fear if we are ununited, we will be crushed. Even now, Sandivar is likely under siege, and we do not know if the North can hold against any appearance of power there."

King Thondor scratched at his beard as he took a moment to think through his response. Ryker was impressed the man didn't immediately burst out with his initial thoughts and assumptions on the matter. It seemed his first impressions of the mountain King, being hot-headed and forceful, was not the full story of the dwarf's inner workings. Of course, he was an ancient being, hundreds of years older than Ryker. Despite the fact the dwarves were more akin to humans than elves, in many ways, they still had much more practice in their long lives at avoiding being swayed by their emotions. He would remember that for any future encounters with elders of this long-standing race.

"I would hear the opinions of the counsel," Thondor said, again surprising Ryker with his desire to hear from his subordinates before making a final decision. It seemed he knew that asking this before giving his own thoughts would allow his underlings to provide their unbiased read on the situation, avoiding the influence of what Thondor would say in regard to the matter.

Lady Bylgia was the first to speak up. "If what our fair elven companion says is true, I fear we must lend our support to our fellow races. The might of the Marbled Caverns is enough to crack the world open should we choose to do so. Leaving such a powerful enemy free to conquer territory surrounding us would leave your kingdom vulnerable in the future, should Celestra fail to deal with the situation on her own."

Prince Thonir chimed in now. "Yes, but this isn't our fight. The Queen is struggling with attacks up and down the Eastern continent. We just received reports a month ago from Ice Bridge Hold that there has not been any major activity at the Rift. Unusual movement in the Shroud, sure, but that can hardly be called threatening. Even if it were, is that not why the Hold was built to begin with? To stop any flow south, should another wave of beasts appear. Why throw away dwarven lives in a war that is not our own? We are protected here."

General Hognar slammed his fist into the table. "Here, here. King Thondor, do not waste the lives of dwarves on the likes of these arrogant, delicate, self-proclaimed 'rulers' of Divinoros. They do not get to summon us to their battle as if we are their subjects! They offer allegiance? Humph! The 'Queen' of elves doesn't even have the decency to send a representative from her own counsel to greet you. Instead, she sends an assassin. Let the elves fend for themselves." Hognar glared briefly at Nienna, but his eyes quickly found and settled on Aegnor, hatred for the elf clear on his face.

Aegnor responded. "I understand both the Prince and General's reservations, but the Queen sent you an individual of far greater significance than a representative from her counsel. It was calculated to send the Ghost. She is the only elf more dangerous than myself roaming Divinoros. And with no affiliation to any Kingdom, she has sent a representative with no agenda other than her own interests—that interest being her own survival. Not to mention, the fact she was sent and you remain alive should be a sign this alliance is offered in good faith. If the Ghost is concerned about this threat… I believe that the threat impacts more than just the elven kingdom."

Queen Rundara now spoke. "Regardless of the legitimacy of the elf Queen's intentions and fears, I would not have my children, my kin, sent to their deaths in a war that is not their own! A war that poses no immediate threat to our people. Our walls under the mountains have remained a stronghold for many millennia. Since the time of demons and dragons. Omnes's first assault on the land above failed to break our walls. I see no reason to believe this one will."

Ryker found himself nodding with the Queen's reasoning, but he believed it short-sighted. It was clear to him this conflict was not the same as the assault on Divinoros when Kei-Tel ruled the elves. Before the next person could speak, Ryker stood, and the counsel's eyes fell on him. Ryker froze for a moment under the hardened gazes of people who had lived hundreds of times longer than him, and the apprentice's confidence began to fail him.

Aegnor cleared his throat to his left, "Go ahead, Ryker. I brought you into the fold because you have a sharp mind. Have the nerve to speak it."

Ryker nodded and faced Queen Rundara. "With all due respect your Majesty, I believe you, your son, and General Hognar are overlooking the most important piece of information about the tale we were just told. Omnes was never eradicated from Divinoros; he has been tied to this world, his presence, and consciousness, which have been fixed in one

295

place for a thousand years. We cannot know the mind of a God, but I would imagine a divine being has a capacity for strategy and foresight beyond what even the eternal elven and dwarven races can manage. And so, with a thousand years to plan his return, I think it could be… ill-advised to ignore the threat under the assumption you were left untouched during the first war. Omnes nearly succeeded in the year of darkness. This assault on our world is likely to be far more planned, far more *thorough*, than his last invasion. He will not suffer survivors, regardless of your desire to remain neutral. To remain hidden."

Aegnor nodded at Ryker as he reclaimed his seat, impressed with the young man's reasoning. Ryker thought he caught a glimpse of pride in Aegnor's eyes.

"You impress me, Ryker," King Thondor conceded. "But the fact is, as of now, the fighting is restricted to land across seas. We have many cities throughout Divinoros but no dwarven city exists in the Eastern continent. We will not send troops to die for elves on the Eastern continent."

Ryker watched the expressions of Bylgia, Aegnor, and the Ghost purse their lips in disappointment.

"But," the King held up his hands in a placating gesture, "we must prepare." He looked over the massive map of Divinoros splayed out in the center of the room. "Let us assume that this Bankhoft foe has already taken southern Sandivar. With no support and no knowledge of the power that descends upon them, there is little chance that Sennin will succeed in holding the city forever." Ryker watched as the miniature Sandivar bearing Queen Celestra's banner was swept from the map and replaced with black pieces representing Omnes's southern force.

"Sennin is honorable, wouldn't let the civilians be slaughtered, so he would send as many as he could on the Elvish fleet out of the city. He'd only have two options: send his people around the peninsula, which would be a trip too long to complete with citizens to feed along the way. So that leaves the more likely outcome of moving his main population to Reef Ridge Port." The King dropped a handful of blocks to represent the increase in people flowing from Sandivar to Reef Ridge. "We can assume Lady Davarei will have adequate notice to prepare her city for invasion and send word to Ocean Fjord and Stone Guard to give warning when the time comes."

Rykers stomach tightened at the mention of Stone Guard. His brothers had no idea of what was happening in the world. He wished he could do something to warn them. The King continued, "What worries me is Celestra's reports of attacks near Gradishar. Her Army there is larger than the other northern cities' standing military combined, so they should be able to defend both the northern and southern borders of Western Turenian if the attacks in Gradishar prove to be related to what is happening in Sandivar. But would Omnes spend his entire resource base on Turenian? Would he be willing to make that his only point of siege, braving the full might of the elves?"

Aegnor chimed in at this point. "No, he wouldn't. His goal is not crushing Turenian but taking over all of Divinoros. An all-out attack on the capital would allow the elven armies to amass in one location and push back any headway made in the Southern Peninsula. He'll want to spread out our armies, isolate our cities, and blind our leaders so they cannot act quickly enough to defy him. If he attacks smaller cities successfully, he will force Celestra into sending resources to any city under siege, weakening her defensive power in the event of an outright campaign on the capital. Omnes would want to begin attacking northern cities on Western Divinoros, forcing the elven military to be spread out. Chip away at a mighty force over time."

King Thondor nodded his agreement. "We need more information before we can move or assign our forces to support any of the elves' cities." He scanned the room. "The world is changing, it seems. The land has rested for a thousand years, but war, again, beckons us. As we have in the past, the soul of our people will prevail. But we must be diligent in ensuring its survival. That will mean supporting the fools who live above the soil... But we will not send our kin to war without knowing where our enemy is, how many our enemy is, and how we will crush them. We need more information first."

"Thonir, send for a runner to seek out Baelin. Offer him a room in the palace. I want to know of anything he uncovers as soon as it's uncovered. Rundara, let's get our civilians up to speed about happenings in the East. Should we need to move to our stronghold under the Drakkonian Islands, or further south, I want the populace to understand the urgency and to be prepared. As for you three," King Thondor turned his gaze on Ryker and the elves, "You are not mine to command. My understanding is you will be leaving in another day. All I ask is we remain in communication. Skilled fighters such as yourselves will always be welcome to stand with our armies should the need arise."

Before the meeting could be dismissed a runner burst through the doors. "Your Majesty. We have a visitor from Ice Bridge Hold who was taken into custody at our northern entrance. He wears the grabs of a Captain. Your soldiers have him detained but he claims to have been sent by Lord Niall and seeks an audience. He is not in good shape but is refusing help from our healers until he has a chance to speak with you."

King Thondor nodded. "Bring him in."

Captain Marriock & Ryker - Chapter 37 – Northern Tidings

Jebediah hadn't been able to heal his ribs fully before their party stormed from the south entrance of Ice Bridge Hold. The most the healing mages could spare was patching a lung that had been punctured in his tumble down the stairs to ensure he didn't bleed out on his journey.

Lord Niall had briefly stepped away from his front-line command post to scribble out four sealed letters detailing the situation in the north and the inevitable fall of the stronghold to the north. Jebediah had given one to Gavin, one to Alfur, and kept two for himself, one for the dwarf King Thondor, and one for High Lord Frenir in Stone Guard.

His men did well stocking the rations for their journey, and after just a day and a half, Alfur split from Jebediah and Gavin, cutting toward the coastal city of Reyvothia while he and Gavin continued south. After another two days of hard riding, where the pair alternated horses every twelve hours and took turns sleeping in the saddle, Gavin also broke to the eastern coastal town of Veilentia.

That left Jebediah alone for the remainder of his trip. Another two days of hard riding passed in a delirious blur. He let the horses rest and eat once or twice. But once they were three day's ride from the dwarven kingdom, he did not stop until the mouth of the Northern Granite Channel stood before him. His gray mount collapsed just before the gate, bloody foam thick on the fringes of his nose. He lay on the cool earth awaiting death. Jebediah wished to follow suit, the pain in his ribs was unbearable, but his message was important. And the thought of his brothers living in Stone Guard drove him forward. It was a combination of wishing to protect his family and the desire to be back with loved ones. He slit the horse's neck. A mercy to speed its transition to the afterlife. He was so tired that he didn't feel a thing as he wiped the warm blood from his dripping dagger.

He imagined he was not a welcoming visage to the guards who were stationed at the gate. He stumbled toward them hunched in a bear pelt, covered in blood, stinking of rotten gore, after slitting the neck of one of the horses that brought him here.

His hunch was right. Two armored guards emerged from shrubbery around the gates, weapons drawn and leveled. "State your business, horse killer, before I give this beast justice for his death!" one of the men yelled.

Aghhh... too loud. Jebediah fought the urge to cover his ears as the voices of the guards set his exhausted mind ringing.

I need to see the King. I can't be delayed.

"I... I am here to see the King. Thondor." Jebediah managed to utter through clenched teeth as he held his ribs. The guard laughed mockingly, "Ha! You, here for the King? That's as likely to happen as Algir's mother bumping uglies with his Majesty behind the Queen's back!"

"Ay," came a gruff voice. "Keep my mother's name out of your mouth." It was the other guard who must have gone by the name Algir.

Jebediah's vision was blurry from the hard ride.

"Now, why don't you get on the one horse that's still living and go back to where ya came from," the first guard shouted. He thrust the butt of his ax at Jeb, looking to push him away from the gate.

"I... I can't go back. Ice Bridge Hold has fallen. I need to see your King." Jebediah hunched over in pain. "My name is Jebediah Marriock, Captain under High Lord Niall. I've been sent with a sealed letter. Please, I need to see your King. Now."

The two dwarven guards looked at one another. The one who must have been Algir chimed up. "All these damn visitors. I can't catch a break. Figured the northern entrance would be quieter. He is wearing the cloak of a Captain. And he's covered in more gore than just his poor horse's blood. Maybe he's telling the truth?"

The other guard scratched at his beard. "Suppose you're right. It is the right attire. Let me see your letter."

Jebediah straightened upright groaning in pain and reached into his pocket to reveal the folded parchment seal closed with a pressed wax circlet, the seal of Lord Niall. After looking, the dwarf Algir huffed. "Okay then follow me. And quit groaning, what's wrong with you anyway?"

Jebediah followed after the grumpy dwarf. "Three broken ribs and seven days galloping on horseback. It's a miracle I made it this far," he responded.

"Ah well, let's hope you didn't make the trip in vain. King Thondor doesn't like unexpected company."

...

Ryker burst to his feet.

Someone with news from the north? I wonder if Jebediah's okay. If there's activity along the Shroud...

The remainder of the group looked about the room in silence, awaiting King Thondor's order. "Let him in, boy." At the order, a familiar dwarf walked through the open doorway to the center of the council chamber. It was Algir who had first shown Ryker the Marbled Caverns and presented both he and Aegnor to the King.

He supported the form of a ragged-looking man who was hunched over in pain. He had a strong build but was standing in a pained position, his left arm pressed against his side protectively as if he were injured. Around his shoulder, a great Ice Bear cloak hung, its once regal pelt smeared with dried blood and a black tar-like substance.

A stench filled the air as the man was marched in, the smell of a carcass yet to be cleaned, still being picked at by crows and carrion. His shoulders were broad beneath the cloak and strong. He looked up at the council... And his face... Ryker knew it immediately. Though the unkempt beard, wind-worn skin, and long matted hair obscured some of his features, Ryker knew his older brother was somehow standing in front of him for the first time in years. Ryker locked eyes with Jebediah and a look of confusion flashed across Jeb's face.

Ryker rushed at Jebediah without hesitation. Aegnor and Nienna sprang to their feet as if they were going to stop Ryker from reaching the man, unsure of his intention. But in this, they were too slow. His face was in a scowl, but it wasn't a scowl of anger. It was an attempt to keep the tears from falling down his face.

Ryker grabbed his brother hard, hugging him with force. "What are you doing here? What happened in the north? You'll never believe what I have been doing."

Jebediah gasped. "Ahhh! Ryker! Get off me, you buffoon! My damn ribs are broken, and I can hardly breathe. And who are you to be questioning me? What are you doing here? In the company of Kings? And elves? And," he said, just now taking notice of Zarou, "whatever the hell that thing is?" Jebediah said as he reactively stepped away from the sand lion.

King Thondor stood and slammed the butt of his war hammer into the floor, grabbing the attention of the room. "Bylgia, heal the Northman. Ryker, while she tends to him, tell me what I am missing here."

Bylgia went into action quickly. Mending the ribs was a short process that seemed to change Jebediah's entire demeanor. All the while, Ryker explained this was his older brother, selected in Stone Guard years ago to train and serve along the northern stronghold under Lord Niall's tutelage.

The King grunted. "Humph. Seems the elves are taking a liking to your family. Now, to break up the reunion. Why have you been sent here?"

Now free of physical ailments, Jebediah stood straight and addressed the King with a courtly posture. "Your Majesty. I am Captain Marriock of Ice Bridge Hold. Six days ago, beasts from the Rift attacked us in the night."

The room stayed silent.

"We fought hard. But this time... Omnes has more than krakenshi and beasts to haunt the grounds. He has summoned wraiths. Winged creatures, flying abominations that came at us from the skies. We were overwhelmed. They came silently, masked by a nighttime storm. We were forced to trigger our last-resort defenses, but I fear. I fear that even that was not enough. The monsters kept coming; like some never-ending nightmare, they emerged from the darkness... They were unrelenting," Jebediah paused, gathering himself before continuing.

"We were going to be overrun. Lord Niall sent me and two other messengers to warn the closest cities. I begged to stay, but he wouldn't allow it. My first message was to be delivered here. My second, to Stone Guard." Jebediah presented the letter to the King, who took it and scanned the document.

He stood, his face grim. "Well, we have the information we need. Prince Thonir. The northern hold has fallen. Ready the army. Reinforce the defensive positions around the caverns and triple guard outposts. I want a legion ready to march north. Bylgia, ready the mages. Have the power mages report directly to the Thonir and prepare the healers for war. And my Queen," he took his wife's hands, looked her deep in the eye and said, "Ready the citizens. We do not need to evacuate just yet. But when we sound the alarm, our people will be transported to our safe haven beneath the Darkkonian Island."

He scanned the room. "War is upon us. Let us ensure we win again."

Chapter 38 - Reunions and Goodbyes

Ryker, Aegnor, and Jebediah retired to their quarters at the StoneHouse immediately after departing King Thondor's council chamber. Ryker told Jeb that he could get a room near them at the inn. "But don't think you get to rest before we talk," Ryker said. "I want to know what happened in the north. And there's a lot you still don't know stirring up in the south. These are strange times in Divinoros, brother."

"Good," his elder brother nodded. "I feel like I could collapse at any minute, but I want to know how you've grown so important to keep such company in my absence." Jebediah had expressed his disbelief that Ryker was introducing him to Aegnor the Great, much less studying under him.

Aegnor asked the Ghost to join them as they departed. She agreed, reluctantly, knowing their party needed to discuss where they were heading in greater detail. Ryker was thankful that the streets were mostly barren at this late hour, apart from a couple of parties still stumbling home in a drunk stupor. If not, the group would have caught the eye of most people in the city. Four outsiders, two astride massive Ravanian steeds, one atop an even larger animal that was far more daunting in the assassin's sand lion, and one covered in week-old gore.

The young apprentice was cognizant of a tangible tension in the air around the party once the she-elf had joined them. Few words were spoken since the council had been adjourned apart from minor back-and-forth between brothers who had been separated for years. Attempting to involve the elves, Ryker said, "So I know elves live basically forever. But how old is your lion, Zarou?"

The Ghost glanced at the human sideways. "Elves do not live forever." Ryker awaited an answer about the lion but didn't appreciate the curt response or the blatant disregard for his true question. Almost immediately, the jitters that Ryker felt in the presence of such a stunning woman faded to the back of his mind. He may be a simple human alongside two nearly immortal beings, but he'd be damned if he let anyone he'd just met disrespect him off-hand.

"Hmm… perhaps not forever, but compared to the *feeble* lifespan of humans, it seems like an eternity. At least long enough to forget basic manners and decorum, it would seem." Ryker retorted.

Aegnor glanced over at his scowling apprentice and Ryker could have sworn that his mentor was holding back a laugh at his response.

"Watch your words, *boy*. You have done nothing to warrant decorum nor manners from me. I am only here because I am curious to hear Aegnor's plan in the upcoming war."

"It's just basic decency… and I'm sure you're old enough to have learned that by human standards, I am a man, not a boy." As soon as the words came out of his mouth, he hated how childish they sounded, but he was frustrated that this arrogant woman he had never met seemed to hold something against him.

I think she must just hate my kind… like elves of old, perhaps?

"I do not judge the world by human standards. So, to me, you will remain a boy. You have done nothing to deserve a title greater than that. In fact, I am shocked that Aegnor has even decided to train you." She looked him up and down with seeming disdain. "Not that it's entirely your fault, just the curse of your race. Weak." She raised her chin, knowing she had gotten the better of Ryker, having successfully baited him into unreasoned retorts. Ryker fumed as he continued alongside Aegnor and Jebediah, who chuckled at the interaction between the pair.

Jebediah looked to be holding back a laugh. "Sounds like the arguments back at the farm," he said smugly before simply shaking his head with a smile as he strode next to Xantharyia. Before Ryker could ask what he found so humorous, his mentor joined in the brief verbal spat.

He was surprised that Aegnor would interject on behalf of his current pupil. "Careful Ni… Careful Ghost. This one may surprise you in the months and years to come. He hasn't studied with me for a cycle of seasons yet and has already bested one of the fiercest warriors in the Marbled Caverns this fine evening. Plus, we both know that one's mettle is not determined by years alone, but by the blood on one's hands and the trial endured. He's spilled his share, triumphed over long odds. And he is only just beginning the infancy of his journey."

Ryker was glad that Aegnor had stood up for him. The apprentice felt it was a signal their bond had strengthened from their time on the road. Jebediah decided to chime in now as well, curiosity outweighing his mostly observatory state, at Aegnor's comments. "Wait… Ryker, I knew you took to Dad's training feverishly. Clearly, Aegnor has added his tutelage as well, but… Killed people? What happened, and what have you been getting into?"

Ryker felt the pain of the wolf's claws and teeth sinking into his leg before images of bandits cut down and beheaded flashed before his eyes. A sadness filled his heart remembering the life fading from men in such a callous manner. Snuffed out. And in their final moments, there was no more dignity to it than crushing a fly, slaughtering cattle. Shaking off the memory, Ryker said, "We will talk about it in the tavern once you clean up. Get a room and meet us. I imagine Aegnor, the Ghost, and I have a lot to talk through."

Jebediah gazed over Ryker, taking in the man who had replaced the young boy he had last seen on the Marriock farm. "Very well," Jeb commented and headed to the innkeeper to secure a room for the evening.

With Jebediah departed, Aegnor and Ryker found stalls to tie up Xantharyia and Maximus for the evening before joining the Ghost at a table in the back corner of the tavern on the first floor of the inn.

Ryker broke the silence the group sat in. "So, the world is changing, it seems. Ancient forces at work once again... How are we going to stop this?" The apprentice directed the question at Aegnor, but the she-elf answered.

"Did you listen to nothing I said? I barely escaped Omnes's reincarnated forces, and only two of the beasts attacked. What makes you believe you will have any impact in this war? Is your ego so inflated?"

"I don't know what I can do. But I'm not going to sit on my hands while dark forces push to eradicate life in our world. I'm going to do *something*. My brothers are in Stone Guard as we speak, likely ignorant as to what transpires in the lands around them. I will do what I can to ensure their safety in the coming war," Ryker retorted.

"Foolish human. You should run back to your little farm. Run back and enjoy the brief months you will have there in peace before the dark wave claims that city just like all the others that are bound to crumble before it."

Ryker glared at the woman, who sighed and leaned back in her stool. "I am going south. To Reef Ridge Port. Hopefully, Sennin will make it out of Sandivar City. Even better, he will still hold the city, and I can sail there. After the dangers associated with the most recent delivery, I expect to recuperate some hazard pay when I see him again."

Aegnor eyed his former pupil. "Your skillset is valued, Ghost. I hope you do not waste your talents chasing coin at a time when the world is in dire need of you."

The she-elf's face flashed with anger, but before she could lash out at Aegnor, he flagged down a waitress and ordered four tankards of strong ale. Her expression faded from anger to remorse, and Ryker got the distinct impression she regretted her off-hand remarks. Despite the front, this woman was clearly scared and hoping for guidance on how to stand against such overwhelming odds. She sought guidance from an old master. Aegnor spoke again as the tankards were placed in front of them. "This will help us settle our nerves. And we will be departing in the morning. I want to enjoy a few fine pints before we depart."

After a long pull from his mug, Aegnor continued, "Jebediah will be heading south to Stone Guard. He will need to warn Lord Frenir of the oncoming wave of Omnes's minions flowing south after the fall of Ice Bridge Hold, but that will only be part of the story. He will need to

304

be warned of what is befalling Sandivar City. Should the enemy choose, they could close in on the stronghold from the north, and the south. The dwarves will reinforce the north, but it is no certainty that they will prevail over the Dark God. Even if Thondor does blockade the passage south, Omnes could bypass the dwarves altogether should they choose to."

Ryker took a long drink from his ale. "Not to mention the Queen is unaware of the situation to the north. The news is bound to shock her. It also means no dwarves will be sent to her immediate aid. It opens a threat from north of Turenian if the beasts have a way to cross the Aeronian Straits near the Drakkonian Isles. Given Jebediah's tale of winged wraiths of the Dark God, the traverse to the Eastern continent is certainly possible."

Aegnor nodded once again. "Yes, if they are not already present there. She needs to be warned. I will go to Turenian to deliver the news."

The Ghost snorted. "What a surprise Aegnor the Great is eager to get back to the bed of her Majesty... How long has it been since you've last visited Celestra? I'm surprised she hasn't convinced you to stay with her yet."

Aegnor looked agitated at the barb but didn't lower himself to its level. Instead of anger, he ignored the comment. He looked to Ryker and then glanced back at Nienna. "I know you have been angry with me since we ended your apprenticeship, but you must know I did what I felt was appropriate and never meant to cause you harm or hurt."

Ryker was lost as to what Aegnor was speaking about, but the words seemed to dull the sharpness of the she-elf's gaze.

What could have passed between them?

"And now I have a favor to ask of you," Aegnor said to the Ghost.

She turned up an eyebrow before Aegnor continued. "You are traveling south, and I wish to send Ryker back to Stone Guard to see his brothers and ensure their safety. But I can only do this if he has someone suitable to continue his training. While Jebediah would be willing, Ryker is not destined to be an ordinary soldier. His talent would be wasted as such."

The Ghost stood. "No! No, no, no. I am not your errand girl. I am going to get *my* payment. I don't need some half-wit and his brother slowing me down."

Aegnor smiled. "Oh, come now! You must see the boy is no fool! No meager swordsman, either! You saw the duel, you were in the council meeting. He is *capable.* And you can help to ensure that potential isn't wasted. Not to mention, they won't slow you down. Xantharyia can easily outpace Zarou, and I will lend Jebediah Maximus if the horse agrees."

She grunted but complained no more about Ryker keeping up with her on their travels. No elf, no creature alive in Divinoros for that matter, would question the abilities of a Ravanian. "Still," she said. "I am no tutor and receive nothing from this arrangement. Where is my incentive?"

"If you agree, I will give you the location of every affiliate organization that caught, tortured, and fought Zarou when he was a cub," Aegnor said flatly.

Ryker noticed the red depths of hate alighting behind the Ghost's eyes. For the first time since he had seen the woman, she appeared as dangerous as the stories of her deeds made her out to be.

"Fine," she said through gritted teeth. "I will do it."

Aegnor leaned back and smiled, taking a long drink from his ale tankard. "Great. Ryker, I hope you're ready. You thought I was tough and didn't pull back blows... I promise you this: She will be worse."

He gave Ryker a knowing smile and dread filled the apprentice's thoughts. He cleared his throat and cleared his mind before turning to face the woman. "Well, if we are going to be traveling together, I wish to start over. You are right; I am not as knowledgeable as you, Aegnor, or many of your race, but I am eager to learn and absorb what you can teach me. My name, as you know, is Ryker, and I would love to know yours."

The apprentice extended an arm, and a cat-like smile crossed the face of the woman seated across from him. Beautiful. Dangerous. She extended her hand. "Maybe this will be fun after all... Aegnor may be a more formidable warrior, but he lacks grace in the finer arts of death and stealth. Let's hope you pick those up as fast as you learned to duel. As for my name, you haven't earned it yet, and I don't know if I can trust you. Call me teacher, Ghost, mentor, master, whatever suits you."

"Fair enough, *elf*," Ryker said once again annoyed at this woman's air of superiority, earning a fierce glare from the Ghost. Before she could respond, Jebediah joined the party, dissipating the tension with a dissembling joyfulness wrought on one who had just narrowly escaped death, knowing all too well his brothers in arms were now dead.

"Ahhh ale! It's been too long since I have had a good one. Everything in the North tastes like a dog's ass. Can't wait for the fresh food on the farm. Nothing beats the hut filled up with the smoke of fried bacon." Jebediah collapsed hard into the empty seat and threw an arm around Ryker before cheering the party and slamming the tankard. Ryker laughed, knowing that his playing along with the cheeriness was what Jebediah needed at this moment. And, in truth, he was elated to be in the company of his older brother for the first time in years.

Before anyone could move, Jebediah ordered a fresh round and stated, "Okay now, apprentice to the most famous elf in the world. An elf that I'm now sharing a table with… Start from the beginning, tell me your tale. And leave no minor detail out of it."

So, the party sat while Ryker and Jebediah shared their tales that reunited them in the dwarven stronghold. Aegnor chimed in once or twice adding necessary color here and there, and the Ghost sat silently, not engaging with the others, though Ryker thought she saw her mean posterior fade as the tale of who Ryker was unfolded.

Once that was concluded, Jebediah and Aegnor bonded and laughed over stories of beating Ryker in duels, Ryker struggling to ride a Ravanian, and the embarrassment of not knowing how to talk with a beautiful dwarven maiden who was very keen on knowing him better just a couple of nights prior. Even the Ghost cracked a smile or two at his behest. The party enjoyed one night in good company and good spirits before the preceding day brought the full weight of their missions down on their heads… Ryker did not rest well… nightmares of responsibility and past deeds haunted his dreams.

Epilogue - The Obsidian Knight Returns

In just a matter of hours, after Jebediah and two other riders fled Ice Bridge Hold, the krakenshi swarm had amassed in an unholy congregation of shrieking limbs and raw power looking to claw through the thick stone of their outer walls. They had not yet gained purchase.

The night had not been quiet. Lord Niall and his men had set up makeshift defenses while battling back the wraiths that tore at flesh with unrelenting tenacity from the shadows of the night sky above. The monsters seemed content to kill his men lazily. Rather than slashing throats and engaging in combat, they would regularly pluck a man, carry him to great heights, and allow gravity to do the hard work of killing or, worse, breaking. They left crumpled forms of moaning flesh amidst the onslaught of krakenshi that mauled them till their cries for help were mercifully quiet.

Lord Niall's main concern was the wall's main gate, krakenshi ripped at the ruined iron, trying to find a purchase to push through and get at the assembled force of elves and humans. He was surprised it had held out as long as it did.

Just as the High Lord was about to order his archers to fire on the hordes through the metal grates, a figure emerged that nearly stopped the elf's heart. The krakenshi quit their frantic scratching and screeching, now shying back from the gate to reveal a figure of humanoid stature. The being was outfitted in a cohesive obsidian armor plate. He held two long black obsidian swords, one in each hand. And he moved them with ease despite the appearance of heavy weight. An aura seemed to descend through the northern stronghold. A palpable force snuffed out torches near the mouth of the gate and caused those in the courtyard to dim. And his eyes. Golden eyes, terrible eyes, shone through his helm and bore directly down onto Lord Niall.

It was clear to this dark specter that he was the commander at Ice Bridge Hold, a title this being was eager to relieve him of. Niall readied his glaive and loosened his sore joints, swinging the weapon about him with speed and grace few men or women in Divinoros could match. The figure laughed. It was a sound that carried to Niall's ears with ease, a booming, low laugh that ricocheted through the air, blocking out any other sound in the courtyard where the first line of defense stood.

The Obsidian Knight held out one arm, a gauntleted fist clenched around the hilt of a massive black sword now hung before him. Then, with barbarous fury, he hacked into the gate's six-inch-thick iron bars.

"Fire!" Lord Niall shouted and a wave of arrows was sent hurtling toward the figure. Niall watched with a growing sense of doom as the dark figure raised an arm. He opened his palm and his sword dissipated before a concussive pulse emanated from his hand. The energy splintered the arrows into dust before they touched him. "Archers fall back!" The archers receded to the second line of defense, a second, smaller wall behind the courtyard. The fortress was built in concentric quarter circles, intended to slow down any force capable of breaching the outer wall. And Lord Niall would do anything in his power to slow down these monsters that assaulted them, though fear was now welling in his heart, begging him, pleading with him, to run. For now that the Obsidian Knight had appeared, he feared he could do little to delay the inevitable.

The archers fell back and were replaced by pikemen and swordsmen just as the gate tumbled forward as the Obsidian Knight slashed through one final hinge. For an instant, the world seemed to freeze in anticipation of the rage to come. One last moment of peace was granted to High Lord Niall. The only sound was the breath of men and the beating of Niall's own heart, ringing in his ears.

The Obsidian Knight cut the silence with a dark, gravelly voice that, despite being spoken softly, carried clearly to the ears of all present, "Go... Kill..." and the hoard of krakenshi obeyed.

Made in the USA
Monee, IL
30 August 2024

64162564R00184